Novels by James M. Cain

"Mr. Cain is a real writer who can construct and tell an exciting story with dazzling swiftness—one of our hard-boiled novelists whose work has a fast rhythm that is art."—WILLIAM ROSE BENÉT

*THE POSTMAN
ALWAYS RINGS TWICE*

SERENADE

MILDRED PIERCE

*LOVE'S
LOVELY COUNTERFEIT*

THREE OF A KIND

THREE

OF A KIND

BY

JAMES M. CAIN

NEW YORK: ALFRED · A · KNOPF

PREFACE

THESE NOVELS, though written fairly recently, really belong to the Depression, rather than the War, and make interesting footnotes to an era. They also make, to anybody who finds me interesting, an interesting commentary on my own development as a novelist, and as I am probably the most mis-read, mis-reviewed, and misunderstood novelist now writing, this may be a good place to say a word about myself, my literary ideals, and my method of composition. I have had, since I began writing, the greatest difficulties with technique, or at any rate fictive technique. I first wanted to be a novelist in my early twenties, but didn't try to be until I was nearly thirty. I went down in the West Virginia coal mines, got a job there, and came back to write a story in that setting, I having acquired, in connection with my newspaper work, quite a background about labor. I wrote three novels that winter, all so bad I dumped them in the wastebasket; the last one I wouldn't have written at all if I hadn't squirmed at the idea of facing my reporter friends with the news that my great American novel was a pipe dream. Yet face them I had to, and for ten years resigned myself to the conviction that I couldn't write a novel. I tried plays with no success, and short stories with very little success, but with a curious discovery. What had made the novel so hopeless was that I didn't seem to have the least idea where I was going with it, or even which paragraph should follow which. But my short stories, which were put into the mouth of some character, marched right along, for if I in the third person faltered and stumbled, my characters in the first person knew perfectly well what they had to say. Yet they were very homely characters, and spoke a gnarled and grotesque jargon that didn't seem quite adapted to long fiction; it seemed to me that after fifty pages of ain'ts, brungs, and fittens, the reader would want to throw the book at me. But then I moved to California and heard the Western roughneck: the boy who is just as elemental inside as his Eastern colleague, but who has been to high school, completes his sentences, and uses reasonably good grammar. Once my ear had put this on wax, so that I had it, I began to wonder if *that* wouldn't be the medium I could use to write novels. This is the origin of the style that is usually associated with me, and that will be found, in a somewhat modified form, in this book. No writer would be telling the truth if he said he didn't think about style, for his style is the very pattern and weave and dye of his work. Yet I confess I usually read comments on this style with some surprise, for I make no conscious effort to be tough, or hard-boiled, or grim, or any of the things I am usually called. I merely try to write as the character would write, and I never forget that the average man, from the fields, the streets, the bars, the offices, and even the gutters of his country, has acquired a vividness of speech that goes beyond anything I could invent, and that if I stick to this heritage, this *logos* of the American countryside, I shall attain a maximum of effectiveness with very little effort. In general my style is rural rather than urban; my ear seems to like fields better than streets. I am glad of this, for I think language loses a bit of its bounce the moment its heels touch concrete.

About the time I was having these meditations on style, I fell under the spell of a man named Vincent Lawrence. You probably associate him with the writing credits of a good many movies, and no doubt have seen his plays; but his influence in Hollywood goes considerably beyond the scripts he has written, admirable as some of them have been. He has laid down principles that are pretty generally incorporated into pictures by now, and for that reason, as well as personal idiosyncrasies that are to say the least of it odd, has become something of a legend. I first met him in New York, when a play of mine had died on the road, and the late Philip Goodman, who produced it, had asked him to read it to see if it could be salvaged for Broadway. It couldn't, as it turned out, but I met this tall, gaunt itinerant of Alpine villages, whose banner bore a strange device indeed: *Technique.* Until then I had been somewhat suspicious of technique. Not that I didn't take pains with what I wrote, but I felt that good writing was gestative rather than fabricative, and that technique for its own sake probably anagramed into formula, and perhaps into hoke. Also, I was for some time thoroughly suspicious of him. The charm, the strange viewpoint on life, were impossible to resist, but like most fanatics, he was incredibly ignorant, and I don't usually associate ignorance with profundity. For example, he talked quite a lot about the One, the Two, and the Three, not seeming to know that these were nothing but the Aristotelean Beginning, Middle, and End. His assumption that he had invented them reminded me of a crackpot I ran into once, in Charles County, Md. He had promised the village of Waldorf a great surprise, one he had been working on for years; I happened to be there the day he came down to the store with it, riding it, as a matter of fact. It was what he called a *pedocycle,* a contraption with high wheels that worked something like a tricycle, but with ratchets instead of a bent-axle drive. It was of wood, all hand-whittled, and it did move at a tolerably lively clip, but he didn't seem aware that even in Charles County they had bicycles by then.

Yet it was amusing, if nothing else, to hear Lawrence ask his friend William Harris, Jr., the theatrical producer, with an amiable grin: "Well, General, who the hell *was* Aristotle, and who did he lick?" He had fantastic names for his friends, and spoke a fantastic language of his own, with words in it I am not sure, well as I have come to know him, I really understand, at least in their relation to his cerebration. So when this wight got me by the lapel, and talked technique at me, I was a little hostile. Until then, my ideal of writing, as well as I can recall it, was that the story correspond with life, mirror it, give a picture whose main element was truth. Lawrence had no objection to this, but insisted that truth was not all. He said if truth were the main object of writing, I would have a hard time competing with a $3 camera. He said if truth were what a writer really worshipped, he would write, not a novel, but a case history. Then he recalled for me Dreiser's play, The Hand of the Potter. He pointed out that this play was truthful enough, but utterly pointless, since it made a plea for a degenerate, without ever once attempting to get you interested in that degenerate.

Writing, narrative writing, whether in the theatre, a book, or a picture house, he said, must first make you *care* about the people whose fortunes you follow. Then he expounded to me the principle of the *love-rack,* as he calls it;—I haven't the faintest idea whether this is a rack on which the lovers are tortured, or something with pegs to hold the shining cloak of romance, or how the word figures in it;—and as it is this which has had such an effect on Hollywood picture writing, I shall give in a little detail what he had to say about it: "O. K., Cain, it's Romeo and Juliet, they're out on the balcony, it's the worst love scene in the world, but anyway it's some kind of love scene, and what makes it? The balcony, lad, that piece of wood that's shoved on just before the curtain goes up. If she ever knocks it over some night, and that guy can really climb up there, it'll lay an egg so bad the Department of Health will move in. In this true story you think you want to write, they meet, they have lunch, they talk, they like each other, they fall in love. That's how it does happen. But I don't pay $5.50 for that. It may be love, but it's not a play. I don't *feel* anything, and making me feel it is what you're after. Look, I'm sitting at a window, looking down at the park. There's two benches there, one with a couple on it holding hands. Well there's no news in that is there? I guess they're in love but they can go right down and get married and send me a card from Niagara Falls and I don't care a bit. On the other bench is a girl reading a book. She's got a little dog there, and every now and then she exercises him by throwing the ball out on the grass and making him bring it back. A guy comes along, takes a look at her, and passes by. But when he takes another look at her I know he likes her looks, and right away I wonder what's going to happen. Now if she looks up from the book, and jumps up and runs over to him and kisses him, it's still love, but I'm bored. But if she looks up, and he walks away quick, I know they're strangers. I see him stop at a peanut vendor's, and I wonder what he's up to. He buys peanuts, comes back, sits on the bench, pays no attention to her. But the dog he pats on the head. He starts on the peanuts, but right away he peels one and pitches it up in the air for the dog. The dog catches it, pricks up his ears for another. Turns out the dog likes peanuts. Next thing, the girl is watching it and laughs. The guy raises his hat, moves over. They both play with the dog. He's done it, Cain, he's *pulled* something, he's got me interested. I stay right there watching them. I ought to be writing a scene, but I want to see how this comes out. After a while, when he flags a cab and they all three drive off together, he, she, and the dog, they're my favorite lovers that day. It's the same way with anything you write. Before you can interest me in story, you got to interest me in *them*."

All this, as I write it now, seems obvious enough, but it didn't seem obvious then, either to me or the picture business. We both moved to Hollywood about that time, he to zoom to incredible wealth, I to hit the deck like a watermelon that has rolled off the stevedore's truck, and to become, briefly, almost as squashy. For I, who had found the newspaper business quite suited to my talents, and had usually been the white-headed boy of editors, now found there was one kind of writing I was no good at: I couldn't write pictures. Lawrence, bringing a gospel that made sense to a picture business reeling from the tangle of problems brought on by the talkies, was learning the difficult art of giving $20 tips without being sent to psychopathic. I, faced with a financial problem if I wanted to stay west, was thinking technique in grim earnest. I began talking to him, instead of listening to him talk to me. I wanted to know why the whole thing couldn't be a love-rack. I wanted to know why, if the main situation was pregnant, if it was such as to create an emotional area in which a man and woman lived, there had to be such special attention to an isolated scene in which they fell in love. I wanted to know why every episode in the story couldn't be invented and moulded and written with a view to its effect on the love story. Lawrence saw no particular objection, and then I somewhat hesitantly revealed what was in my mind. Murder, I said, had always been written from its least interesting angle, which was whether the police would catch the murderer. I was considering, I said, a story in which murder was the love-rack, as it must be to any man and woman who conspire to commit it. But, I said, they would commit the perfect murder. It wouldn't go, of course, quite as they planned it. But in the end they would get away with it, and then what? They would find, I said, that the earth is not big enough for two persons who share such a dreadful secret, and eventually turn on each other. He was enthusiastic, and I wrote it as planned, with no love-rack in the

Lawrence sense. He has always quarreled with me for the first scene between the lovers in that novel, insisting it is commonplace. A commonplace scene was just what I wanted. They were that kind of people, and I still proposed to be true to my ideal of truth, something theatrical people are inclined to be a little perfunctory about. But after this scene, as the dreadful venture became more and more inevitable, I strove for a rising coefficient of intensity, and even hoped that somewhere along the line I would graze passion. The whole thing corresponded to a definition of tragedy I found later in some of my father's writings: that it was the "force of circumstances driving the protagonists to the commission of a dreadful act." I didn't, however, know of that definition at this time. Lawrence liked it, and even gave me a title for it. We were talking one day, about the time he had mailed a play, his first, to a producer. Then, he said, "I almost went nuts. I'd sit and watch for the post-man, and then I'd think, 'You got to cut this out,' and then when I left the window I'd be listening for his ring. How I'd know it was the postman was that he'd always ring twice."

He went on with more of the harrowing tale, but I cut in on him suddenly. I said: "Vincent, I think you've given me a title for that book."

"What's that?"

"The Postman Always Rings Twice."

"Say, he rang twice for Chambers, didn't he?"

"That's the idea."

"And on that second ring, Chambers had to answer, didn't he? Couldn't hide out in the backyard any more."

"His number was up, I'd say."

"I like it."

"Then that's it."

Although only one of them is about murder, these three novels embody this theory of story-building, for they all concern some high adventure on which a man and woman embark. In the case of Career in C Major it is a comic adventure, but to them important. I discover certain unexpected similarities between them. All three, for example, have as their leading male character a big, powerful man in his early thirties. This bothers me much less than you might think. I care almost nothing for what my characters look like, being almost exclusively concerned with their insides. Yet, when a number of people complained, after publication of my novel Serenade, that they had to read half the book before they found out what the singer looked like, I decided, in Mr. Harris's language, to "wrap that up in a little package for them so they've got it and will stop worrying about it." My choice of what a character looks like is completely phoney, and it may surprise you to learn that I haven't the faintest idea what he looks like. The movie writer's description of a character's externals, "a Clark Gable type," would do perfectly for me, and if you don't like the appearance of any of the gentlemen in these pages, you are quite free to switch off to Clark Gable, or Warner Baxter, who played Borland in Career in C Major, or whoever you like. All three stories involve women whose figures are more vivid than their faces, but this doesn't bother me either. In women's appearance I take some interest, but I pay much more attention to their figures than I do to their faces—in real life, I mean. Their faces are masks, more or less consciously controlled. But their bodies, the way they walk, sit, hold their heads, gesticulate, and eat, betray them. But here again, on paper, I am more concerned with what goes on inside them than with what they look like. So if you want to put Loretta Young, who played Doris Borland, in her place or Brenda Marshall, who played Sheila Brent, in her place, it will not affect things in the slightest.

Reading these stories over, I get quite a surprise. I would have said, on the basis of how I felt after finishing them, that I liked Double Indemnity best, Career in C Major next, and The Embezzler least. Now my preference is quite the reverse. In the

Embezzler I find writing that is much simpler, much freer from calculated effect, than I find in the other two. And for long stretches I find the story quite free of what Clifton Fadiman, writing about me, once called "the conscious muscle-flexing." The muscle-flexing is often there, all right, and it is real, but it is not, as so many assume, born of a desire to be tough. I had acquired, I suspect as a result of my first fiasco at novel-writing, such a morbid fear of boring a reader that I certainly got the habit of needling a story at the least hint of a letdown. This bothered Edmund Wilson, too, in an article he wrote about me: he attributed these socko twists and surprises to a leaning toward Hollywood, which is not particularly the case. Recently, I have made steady progress at the art of letting a story secrete its own adrenalin, and I have probably written the last of my intense tales of the type that these represent. The trouble with that approach is that you have to have a "natural," as it is called, before you can start, and a natural is not to be had every day. If what you start with is less, if you shoot at passion and miss by ever so little, you hit lust, which isn't pretty, or even interesting. Again, the whole method, if the least touch of feebleness gets into it, lends itself to what is perilously close to an etude in eroticism. Again, love is not all of life, and I confess that lately, having got past the stymie of style that bothered me for so many years, I want to tell tales of a little wider implication than those which deal exclusively with one man's relation to one woman. In the future, what was valid in the technical organization of my first few novels will be synthetized, I hope, into a somewhat larger technique. What was bad will continue to drop off the cart until in the end most of it will be bounced out.

J. M. C.

Aug. 24, 1942

THREE OF A KIND

CONTENTS

❧

CAREER
IN C MAJOR

CAREER IN C MAJOR

ALL THIS, that I'm going to tell you, started several years ago.
You may have forgotten how things were then, but I won't forget
it so soon, and sometimes I think I'll never forget it. I'm a contractor, junior partner in the Craig-Borland Engineering Company,
and in my business there was *nothing* going on. In your business, I
think there was a little going on, anyway enough to pay the office
help provided they would take a ten per cent cut and forget about
the Christmas bonus. But in my business, nothing. We sat for three
years with our feet on our desks reading magazines, and after the
secretaries left we filled in for a while by answering the telephone.
Then we didn't even do that, because the phone didn't ring any
more. We just sat there, and switched from the monthlies to the
weeklies, because they came out oftener.

It got so bad that when Craig, my partner, came into the office one
day with a comical story about a guy that wanted a concrete chicken
coop built, somewhere out in Connecticut, that we looked at each

3

other shifty-eyed for a minute, and then without saying a word we put on our hats and walked over to Grand Central to take the train. We wanted that coop so bad we could hardly wait to talk to him. We built it on a cost-plus basis, and I don't think there's another one like it in the world. It's insulated concrete, with electric heat control, automatic sewage disposal, accommodations for 5,000 birds, and all for $3,000, of which our share was $300, minus expenses. But it was something to do, something to do. After the coop was built, Craig dug in at his farm up-state, and that left me alone. I want you to remember that, because if I made a fool of myself, I was wide open for that, with nothing to do and nobody to do it with. When you get a little fed up with me, just remember those feet, with no spurs to keep them from falling off the desk, because what we had going on wasn't a war, like now, but a depression.

It was about four-thirty on a fall afternoon when I decided to call it a day and go home. The office is in a remodeled loft on East 35th Street, with a two-story studio for drafting on the ground level, the offices off from that, and the third floor for storage. We own the whole building and owned it then. The house is on East 84th Street, and it's a house, not an apartment. I got it on a deal that covered a couple of apartment houses and a store. It's mine, and was mine then, with nothing owing on it. I decided to walk, and marched along, up Park and over, and it was around five-thirty when I got home. But I had forgotten it was Wednesday, Doris's afternoon at home. I could hear them in there as soon as I opened the door, and I let out a damn under my breath, but there was nothing to do but brush my hair back and go in. It was the usual mob: a couple of Doris' cousins, three women from the Social Center, a woman just back from Russia, a couple of women that have boxes at the Metropolitan Opera, and half a dozen husbands and sons. They were all Social Register, all so cultured that even their eyeballs were lavender, all rich, and all 100% nitwits. They were the special kind of nitwits

you meet in New York and nowhere else, and they might fool you
if you didn't know them, but they're nitwits just the same. Me, I'm
Social Register too, but I wasn't until I married Doris, and I'm a
traitor to the kind that took me in. Give me somebody like Craig,
that's a farmer from Reubenville, that never even heard of the Social
Register, that wouldn't know culture if he met it on the street, but
is an A1 engineer just the same, and has designed a couple of bridges
that have plenty of beauty, if that's what they're talking about.
These friends of Doris's, they've been everywhere, they've read
everything, they know everybody, and I guess now and then they
even do a little good, anyway when they shove money back of something that really needs help. But I don't like them, and they don't
like me.

I went around, though, and shook hands, and didn't tumble that
anything unusual was going on until I saw Lorentz. Lorentz had
been her singing teacher before she married me, and he had been in
Europe since then, and this was the first I knew he was back. And
his name, for some reason, didn't seem to get mentioned much
around our house. You see, Doris is opera-struck, and one of the
things that began to make trouble between us within a month of
the wedding was the great career she gave up to marry me. I kept
telling her I didn't want her to give up her career, and that she
should go on studying. She was only nineteen then, and it certainly
looked like she still had her future before her. But she would come
back with a lot of stuff about a woman's first duty being to her
home, and when Randolph came, and after him Evelyn, I began
to say she had probably been right at that. But that only made it
worse. Then *I* was the one that was blocking her career, and had
been all along, and every time we'd get going good, there'd be a
lot of stuff about Lorentz, and the way he had raved about her
voice, and if she had only listened to him instead of to me, until I
got a little sick of it. Then after a while Lorentz wasn't mentioned

any more, and that suited me fine. I had nothing against him, but he always meant trouble, and the less I heard of him the better I liked it.

I went over and shook hands, and noticed he had got pretty gray since I saw him last. He was five or six years older than I was, about forty I would say, born in this country, but a mixture of Austrian and Italian. He was light, with a little clipped moustache, and about medium height, but his shoulders went back square, and there was something about him that said Europe, not America. I asked him how long he had been back, he said a couple of months, and I said swell. I asked him what he had been doing abroad, he said coaching in the Berlin opera, and I said swell. That seemed to be about all. Next thing I knew I was alone, watching Doris where she was at the table pouring drinks, with her eyes big and dark, and two bright red spots on her cheeks.

Of course the big excitement was that she was going to sing. So I just took a back seat and made sure I had a place for my glass, so I could put it down quick and clap when she got through. I don't know what she sang. In those days I didn't know one song from another. She stood facing us, with a little smile on her face and one elbow on the piano, and looked us over as though we were a whole concert hall full of people, and then she started to sing. But there was one thing that made me feel kind of funny. It was the whisper-whisper rehearsal she had with Lorentz just before she began. They were all sitting around, holding their breaths waiting for her, and there she was on the piano bench with Lorentz, listening to him whisper what she was to do. Once he struck two sharp chords, and she nodded her head. That doesn't sound like much to be upset about, does it? She was in dead earnest, and no foolishness about it. The whole seven years I had been married to her, I don't think I ever got one word out of her that wasn't phoney, and yet with this guy she didn't even try to put on an act.

They left about six-thirty, and I mixed another drink so we could have one while we were dressing for a dinner we had to go to. When I got upstairs she was stretched out on the chaise longue in brassieres, pants, stockings, and high-heeled slippers, looking out of the window. That meant trouble. Doris is a Chinese kimono girl, and she always seems to be gathering it around her so you can't see what's underneath, except that you can, just a little. But when she's got the bit in her teeth, the first sign is that she begins to show everything she's got. She's got plenty, because a sculptor could cast her in bronze for a perfect thirty-four, and never have to do anything more about it at all. She's small, but not too small, with dark red hair, green eyes, and a sad, soulful face, with a sad soulful shape to go with it. It's the kind of shape that makes you want to put your arm around it, but if you do put your arm around it, anyway when she's parading it around to get you excited, that's when you made your big mistake. Then she shrinks and shudders, and gets so refined she can't bear to be touched, and you feel like a heel, and she's one up on you.

I didn't touch her. I poured two drinks, and set one beside her, and said here's how. She kept looking out the window, and in a minute or two saw the drink, and stared at it like she couldn't imagine what it was. That was another little sign, because Doris likes a drink as well as you do or I do, and in fact she's got quite a talent at it, in a quiet, refined way. ". . . Oh no. Thanks just the same."

"You better have a couple, just for foundation. They'll be plenty weak tonight, I can promise you that."

"I couldn't."

"You feel bad?"

"Oh no, it's not that."

"No use wasting it then."

I drained mine and started on hers. She watched me spear the olive, got a wan little smile on her face, and pointed at her throat

"Oh? Bad for the voice, hey?"

"Ruinous."

"I guess it would be, at that."

"You have to give up so many things."

She kept looking at me with that sad, orphan look that she always gets on her face when she's getting ready to be her bitchiest, as though I was far, far away, and she could hardly see me through the mist, and then she went back to looking out the window. "I've decided to resume my career, Leonard."

"Well gee that's great."

"It's going to mean giving up—everything. And it's going to mean work, just slaving drudgery from morning to night—I only pray that God will give me strength to do all that I'll have to do."

"I guess singing's no cinch at that."

"But—something has to be done."

"Yeah? Done about what?"

"About everything. We can't go on like this, Leonard. Don't you see? I know you do the best you can, and that you can't get work when there is no work. But something has to be done. If you can't earn a living, then I'll have to."

Now to you, maybe that sounds like a game little wife stepping up beside her husband to help him fight when the fighting was tough. It wasn't that at all. In the first place, Doris had high-hatted me ever since we had been married, on account of my family, on account of my being a low-brow that couldn't understand all this refined stuff she went in for, on account of everything she could think of. But one thing she hadn't been able to take away from me. I was the one that went out and got the dough, and plenty of it, which was what her fine family didn't seem to have so much of any more. And this meant that at last she had found a way to high-hat me, even on that. Why she was going back to singing was that she wanted to go back to singing, but she wasn't satisfied just to do that. She had to harpoon me with it, and harpoon me where it hurt. And in the second place, all we had between us and starvation was the dough I had salted away in a good bank, enough to last at least three more years, and after that the house, and after that my share of the Craig-Borland Building, and after that a couple of other pieces of property the firm had, if things got that bad, and I had never asked Doris to cut down by one cent on the household expenses, or live any different than we had always lived, or give up anything at all. I mean, it was a lot of hooey, and I began to get sore. I tried not to, but I couldn't help myself. The sight of her lying there like the dying swan, with this noble look on her face, and just working at the job of making me look like a heel, kind of got my goat.

"So. We're just starving to death, are we?"

"Well? Aren't we?"

"Just practically in the poorhouse."

"I worry about it so much that sometimes I'm afraid I'll have a breakdown or something. I don't bother you about it, and I don't ever intend to. There's no use of your knowing what I go through. But—something has to be done. If something isn't done, Leonard, what are we going to come to?"

"So you're going out and have a career, all for the husband and the kiddies, so they can eat, and have peppermint sticks on the Christmas tree, and won't have to bunk in Central Park when the big blizzard comes."

"I even think of that."

"Doris, be your age."

"I'm only trying to—"

"You're only trying to make a bum out of me, and I'm not going to buy it."

"You have to thwart me, don't you Leonard? Always."

"There it goes. I knew it. So I thwart you."

"You've thwarted me ever since I've known you, Leonard. I don't know what there is about you that has to make a woman a drudge, that seems incapable of realizing that she might have aspirations too. I suppose I ought to make allowance—"

"For the pig-sty I was raised in, is that it?"

"Well Leonard, there's *something* about you."

"How long have you had this idea?"

"I've been thinking about it quite some time."

"About two months, hey?"

"Two months? Why two months?"

"It seems funny that this egg comes back from Europe and right away you decide to resume your career."

"How wrong you are. Oh, how wrong you are."

"And by the time he gets his forty a week, or whatever he takes, and his commission on the music you buy, and all the rest of his cuts, you'll be taken for a swell ride. There won't be much left for the husband and kiddies."

"I'm not being taken for a ride."

"No?"

"I'm not paying Lorentz anything."

". . . What?"

"I've explained to him. About our—circumstances."

I hit the roof then. I wanted to know what business she had telling him about our circumstances or anything else. I said I wouldn't be under obligations to him, and that if she was going to have him she had to pay him. She lay there shaking her head, like the pity of it was that I couldn't understand, and never could understand. "Leonard, I couldn't pay Hugo, even if I wanted to—not now."

"Why not *now*?"

"When he knows—how hard it is for us. And it's not important."

"It's plenty important—to me."

"Hugo is that strange being that you don't seem to understand, that you even deny exists—but he exists, just the same. Hugo is an artist. He believes in my voice. That's all. The rest is irrelevant.

Money, time, work, everything."

That gave me the colic so bad I had to stop, count ten, and begin all over again. ". . . Listen, Doris. To hell with all this. Nobody's opposing your career. I'm all for your career, and I don't care what it costs, and I don't care whether it ever brings in a dime. But why the big act? Why do you have to go through all this stuff that I'm thwarting you, and we're starving, and all that? Why can't you just study, and shut up about it?"

"Do we have to go back over all that?"

"And if that's how you feel about it, what the hell did you ever marry me for, anyway?"

That slipped out on me. She didn't say anything, and I took it back. Oh yes, I took it back, because down deep inside of me I knew why she had married me, and I had spent seven years with my ears stopped up, so she'd never have the chance to tell the truth about it. She had married me for the dough I brought in, and that was all she had married me for. For the rest, I just bored her, except for that streak in her that had to torture everybody that came within five feet of her. The whole thing was that I was nuts about her and she didn't give a damn about me, and don't ask me why I was nuts about her. I don't know why I was nuts about her. She was a phoney, she had the face of a saint and the soul of a snake, she treated me like a dog, and still I was nuts about her. So I took it back. I apologized for it. I backed down like I always did, and lost the fight, and wished I had whatever it would take to stand up against her, but I didn't.

"Time to dress, Leonard."

When we got home that night, she undressed in the dressing room, and when she came out she had on one of the Chinese kimonos, and went to the door of the nursery, where the kids had slept before they got old enough to have a room. . . . "I've decided to sleep in here for a while, Leonard. I've got exercises to do when

I get up, and—all sorts of things. There's no reason why you should be disturbed."

"Any way you like."

"Or—perhaps you would be more comfortable in there."

Yes, I even did that. I slept that night in the nursery, and took up my abode there from then on. What I ought to do was go in and sock her in the jaw, I knew that. But I just looked at Peter Rabbit, where he was skipping across the wall in the moonlight, and thought to myself: "Yeah, Borland, that's you all right."

2

SO FOR the next three months there was nothing but vocalizing all over the place, and then it turned out she was ready for a recital in Town Hall. For the month after that we got ready for the recital, and the less said about it the better. Never mind what Town Hall cost, and the advertising cost, and that part. What I hated was drumming up the crowd. I don't know if you know how a high-toned Social Registerite like Doris does when she gets ready to give a recital to show off her technique. She calls up all *her* friends, and sandbags them to buy tickets. Not just to come, you understand, on free tickets, though to me that would be bad enough. To *buy* tickets, at $2 a ticket. And not only does she call up *her* friends, but her husband calls up *his* friends, and all her sisters and her cousins and her aunts call up *their* friends, and those friends have to come through, else it's an unfriendly act. I got so I hated to go in the River Club, for fear I'd run into somebody that was on the list, and that I hadn't buttonholed, and if I let him get out of there without buttonholing him, and Doris found out about it, there'd be so much fuss that I'd buttonhole him, just to save trouble. Oh yes, culture has its practical side when you start up Park Avenue with it. It's not just that I'm a roughneck that I hate it. There are other reasons too.

I don't know when it was that I tumbled that Doris was lousy. But some time in the middle of all that excitement, it just came to me one day that she couldn't sing, that she never could sing, that it was all just a pipe dream. I tried to shake it off, to tell myself that I didn't know anything about it, because that was one thing that had always been taken for granted in our house: that she could have a career if she wanted it. And there was plenty of reason to think so, because she did have a voice, anybody could tell that. It was a high soprano, pretty big, with a liquid quality to it that made it easy for her to do the coloratura stuff she seemed to specialize in. I couldn't shake it off. I just knew she was no good, and didn't know how I knew it. So of course that made it swell. Because in the first place I had to keep on taking her nonsense, knowing all the time she was a fake, and not being able to tell her so. And in the second place, I was so in love with her that I couldn't take my eyes off her when she was around and I hated to see her out there making a fool of herself. And in the third place, there was Lorentz. If I knew she was no good, then he knew she was no good, and what was he giving her free lessons for? He was up pretty often, usually just before dinner, to run over songs with her, and once or twice, while we were waiting for her to come home, I tried to get going with him, to find out what was what. I couldn't. And I knew why I couldn't. It was some more of the blindfold stuff. I was afraid I'd find out something I didn't want to know. Not that I expected him to tell me. But I might find it out just the same, and I didn't want to find it out. I might lie awake half the night wondering about it, and gnaw my fingernails half off down at the office, but when it came to the showdown I didn't want to know. So we would just sit there, and have a drink, and talk about how women are always late. Then Doris would come, and start to yodel. And then I would go upstairs.

The recital was in February, at eleven o'clock of a Friday morning. About nine o'clock I was in the nursery, getting into the cutaway coat and gray striped pants that Doris said I had to wear, when the phone rang in the bedroom and I heard Doris answer. In a minute or two she came in. "Stop that for a minute, Leonard, and listen to me. It's something terribly important."

"Yeah? What is it?"

"Louise Bronson just called up. She was talking last night with Rudolph Hertz." Hertz wasn't his name, but I'll call him that. He was a critic on the Herald Tribune. "You know, he's related to her."

"And?"

"She told him he had to come and give me a review, and he promised to do it. But the fool told him it was tomorrow instead of today, and Leonard, you'll have to call him up and tell him, and be sure and tell him there'll be two tickets for him, in his name at the boxoffice—and make sure they're there."

"Why do I have to call him up?"

"Leonard, I simply haven't time to explain all that to you now. He's the most important man in town, it's just a stroke of blind luck that he promised to give me a review, and I can't lose it just because of a silly mistake over the day."

"His paper keeps track of that for him."

"Leonard, you call him up! You call him up right now! You— stop making me scream, it's frightful for my voice. You call him up! Do you hear me?"

"He won't be at his paper. They don't come down that early."

"Then call him up at his home!"

I went in the bedroom and picked up the phone book. He wasn't in it. I called information. They said they would have to have the address. Doris began screaming at me from the dressing room.

"He lives on Central Park West! In the same building as Louise!"

I gave the address. They said they were very sorry but it was a private number and they wouldn't be able to give it to me. Doris was yelling at me before I even hung up. "Then you'll have to go over there! You'll have to see him."

"I can't go over there. Not at this hour."

"You'll have to go over there! You'll have to see him! And be sure and mention Louise, and his promise to her, and tell him there'll be two tickets for him, in his name at the boxoffice!"

So I hustled on the rest of my clothes, and jumped in a cab, and went over there. I found him in bathrobe and slippers, having breakfast with his wife and another lady, in an alcove just off the living room. I mumbled about Louise Bronson, and how anxious we were to have his opinion on my wife's voice, and about the tickets in his name at the boxoffice, and he listened to me as though he couldn't believe his ears. Then he cut me off, and he cut me off sharp. "My dear fellow, I can't go to every recital in Town Hall just at an hour's notice. If notices were sent out, my paper will send somebody over, and there was no need whatever for you to come to me about it."

"Louise Bronson—"

"Yes, Louise said something to me about a recital, but I don't let her run my department either."

"We were very anxious for your opinion—"

"If so, making a personal call at this hour in the morning was a very bad way to get it."

I felt my face get hot. I jumped up, said I was sorry, and got out of there as fast as I could grab my hat. The recital didn't help any. The place was packed with stooges, and they clapped like hell and it didn't mean a thing. I sat with Randolph and Evelyn, and we clapped too, and after it was over, and about a ton of flowers had gone up, and my flowers too, we went backstage with the whole mob to tell Doris how swell she was, and you would have thought

it was just a happy family party. But as soon as my face wasn't
red any more from thinking about the critic, it got red from
something else. About a third of that audience were children.
That was how they had told us to go to hell, those people we had
sandbagged. They bought tickets, but they sent their children—
with nursemaids.

Doris took the children home, and I went out and ate, and then
went over to the office. I sat there looking at my feet, and thinking
about the critic, and the children at the recital, and sleeping in
the nursery, and Lorentz, and all the rest of it, and I felt just great.
About two-thirty the phone rang. "Mr. Borland?"

"Speaking."

"This is Cecil Carver."

She acted like I ought to know who Cecil Carver was, but I had
never heard the name before. "Yes, Miss Carver? What can I do
for you?"

"Perhaps I ought to explain. I'm a singer. I happened to be
visiting up in Central Park this morning when you called, and I
couldn't help hearing what was said."

"I got a cool reception."

"Pay no attention to it. He's a crusty old curmudgeon until he's
had his coffee, and then he's a dear. I wish you could have heard
the way he was treating me."

That was all hooey, but somehow my face didn't feel red any
more, and besides that, I liked the way she laughed. "You make
me feel better."

"Forget it. I judged from what you said that you were anxious
for a competent opinion on your wife's singing."

"Yes, I was."

"Well, I dropped in at that recital. Would you like to know what
I thought?"

"I'd be delighted."

"Then why don't you come over?" She gave the name of a hotel that was about three blocks away, on Lexington Avenue.

"I don't know of any reason why not."

"Have you still got on that cutaway coat?"

"Yes, I have."

"Oh my, I'll have to make myself look pretty."

"You had better hurry up."

". . . Why?"

"Because I'm coming right over."

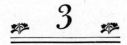

3

SHE HAD a suite up on the tenth floor, with a grand piano in it and music scattered all over the place, and she let me in herself. I took her to be about thirty, but I found out later she was two years younger. Women singers usually look older than they really are. There's something about them that says woman, not girl. She was good-looking all right. She had a pale, ivory skin, but her hair was black, and so were her eyes. I think she had the biggest black eyes I ever saw. She was a little above medium height, and slim, but she was a little heavy in the chest. She had on a blue silk dress, very simple, and it came from a good shop, I could see that. But somehow it didn't look quite right, anyway to somebody that was used to the zip that Doris had in her dresses. She told me afterward she had no talent for dressing at all, that a lot of women on the stage haven't, and that she did what most of them do: go into the best place in town, buy the simplest thing they have, pay plenty for it, and take a chance it will look all right. It looked just about like that, but it didn't make any difference. You didn't think about the dress after you saw those eyes.

She had a drink ready, and asked me if I was a musician. I said no, I was a contractor, and next thing I knew I had had two drinks, and was gabbling about myself like some drummer in a Pullman. She kept smiling and nodding, like concrete railroad bridges were the most fascinating thing she ever heard of in her life, and the big black eyes kept looking at me, and even with the drinks I knew I was making a bit of a fool of myself. I didn't care. It was the first time a woman had taken any interest in me in a blue moon, and I was having a good time, and I had still another drink, and kept right on talking.

After a while, though, I pulled up, and said well, and she switched off to Doris. "Your wife has a remarkable voice."

"Yes?"

". . . It keeps haunting me."

"Is it that good?"

"Yes, it's that good, but that isn't why it haunts me. I keep thinking I've heard it before."

"She used to sing around quite a lot."

"Here? In New York?"

"Yes."

"That couldn't be it. I don't come from New York. I come from Oregon. And I've spent the last five years abroad. Oh well, never mind."

"Then you think she's good?"

"She has a fine voice, a remarkably fine voice, and her tone is well produced. She must have had excellent instruction. Of course . . ."

"Go on. What else?"

". . . I would criticize her style."

"I'm listening."

"Has she been studying long?"

"She studied before we got married. Then for a while she dropped it, and she just started up again recently."

"Oh. Then that accounts for it. Good style, of course, doesn't come in a day. With more work, that ought to come around."

"Then you think she ought to go on?"

"With such looks and such a voice, certainly."

With that we dropped it. In spite of all she said, it added up to faint praise, especially the shifty way she brought up the question of style. She tried to get me going again on concrete, but somehow talking about Doris had taken all the fun out of it. After a few minutes I thanked her for all the trouble she had taken and got up to go. She sat there with a funny look on her face, staring at me. A boy came in with a note, and left, and she read it and said: "Damn."

"Something wrong?"

"I'm singing for the American Legion in Brooklyn tonight, and I promised to do a song they want, and I've forgotten to get the words of it, and the man that was to give them to me has gone out of town, and here's his note saying he'll give me a ring tomorrow—and no words."

"What song?"

"Oh, some song they sing in the Navy. Something about a destroyer. Isn't that annoying?"

"Oh, *that* song."

"You know it?"

"Sure. I had a brother that was a gob."

"Well for heaven's sake sing it."

She sat down to the piano and started to play it. She already knew the tune. I started to sing:

> *You roll and groan and toss and pitch,*
> *You swab the deck, you son-of-a——*

She got up, walked over to the sofa, and sat down, her face perfectly white. I had forgotten about that rhyme, and I began to mumble apologies for it, and explain that there was another way to sing it, so *groan* would rhyme with *moan*. But at that I couldn't see why it would make her sore. She hadn't seemed like the kind that would mind a rhyme, even if it was a little off. But she kept staring at me, and then I got a little sore myself, and said it was a pretty good rhyme, even if she didn't like it. "To hell with the rhyme."

"Oh?"

"Borland, your wife's no good."

"She's not?"

"No, she's not."

"Well—thanks."

"But *you* have a voice."

"I—what?"

"You have a voice such as hasn't been heard since—I don't know when. What a baritone! What a trumpet!"

"I think you're kidding me."

"I'm not kidding you. . . . Want some lessons?"

Her eyes weren't wide open any more. They were half closed to a couple of slits. A creepy feeling began to go up my back. It was time to go, and I knew it. I did *not* go. I went over, sat down, put my arm around her, pushed her down, touched my mouth to her lips. They were hot. We stayed that way a minute, breathing into each other's faces, looking into each other's eyes. Then she mumbled: "Damn you, you'll kiss first."

"I will like hell."

She put her arms around me, tightened. Then she kissed me, and I kissed back.

"You were slow enough."

"I was wondering what you wanted."

"I wanted you, you big gorilla. Ever since you came in there this morning with that foolish song-and-dance about getting Hertz to go to the concert. What made you do that? Didn't you know any better?"

"Yes."

"Then why did you do it?"

"I had to."

". . . You mean she made you?"

"Something like that."

"Couldn't you say no?"

"I guess I couldn't."

She twisted her head around, where it was on my shoulder, and looked at me, and twisted my hair around her fingers. "You're crazy about her, aren't you?"

"More or less."

"I'm sorry I said she was no good. She really has a voice. She might improve, with more work. . . . Maybe I was jealous of her."

"It's all right."

"You see—"

"To hell with it. You said just what I've been thinking all along, so why apologize? She has a voice, and yet she's no good. And yet—"

"You're crazy about her."

"Yes."

She twisted my hair a while, and then started to laugh. "You could have knocked me over with a straw when I saw Hugo Lorentz coming out there to the piano."

"You know him?"

"Known him for years. I hadn't seen him since he played for me in Berlin last winter, and what a night *that* was."

"Yeah?"

"After the concert we walked around to his apartment, and he wept on my shoulder till three o'clock in the morning about some cold-blooded bitch that he's in love with, in New York, and that does nothing but torture him, and every other man she gets into her clutches for that matter. Oh, I got her whole life history. Once a year she'd send Hugo a phonograph record of herself singing some song they had worked on. He thought they were wonderful, and he kept playing them over and over again, till I got so sick of that poop's voice I—" There was a one-beat pause, and then she finished off real quick: "—Well, it was a night, that's all."

"And that was where you heard my wife's voice, wasn't it?"

"What in the world are you talking about?"

"Come on, don't kid me."

". . . I'm sorry, Leonard. I didn't mean to. From what Hugo said, I had pictured some kind of man-eating tigress, and when that dainty, wistful, perfectly beautiful creature came out there today, it never once entered my mind. It didn't anyhow, until just now."

"Then it was?"

"Yes, of course."

"I've had my suspicions about Hugo."

"You needn't have."

"I thought he was taking her for a ride."

"He's not. She's taking him."

"What about these other men she's got her clutches on?"

"For heaven's sake, can't a woman that good-looking have a little bit of a good time? What do you care? You're having a good time, aren't you? Right now? I'll sock you if you say you're not."

"Believe it or not, this is my first offense."

"—And, you've *got* her haven't you?"

"No."

"What?"

"I'm just one other man she's got her clutches on, one more sap to torture. I happen to be married to her, that's all."

"You poor dear. You are crazy about her, aren't you?"

"Come on, what about these other men?"

She thought a long time, and then she said: "Leonard, I'm not going to tell you any more of what Hugo said, except this: That no man gets any favors from her, if that's what you're worried about. And especially Hugo doesn't. She sees that they keep excited, but inside she's as cold as a slab of ice, and thinks of nothing but herself. I think you can take Hugo's word on that. He knows a lot more about women than you do, and he's not kidded about her for one second, even if he is crazy about her. Does that help?"

"Not much. You're not telling me anything I don't know, though. I've kidded myself about it for seven years, but I know. Lorentz, I think, he has the inside track on the rest, but only on account of the music."

"That's what Hugo says."

"What?"

"That she thinks of nothing but her triumphs, feminine, social, and artistic, and especially artistic. She's crazy to be a singer. And that's where he fits in."

"Her triumphs. That's it. Life in our house is nothing but a series of triumphs."

"Leonard, I have an idea."

"Shoot."

"I hate that woman."

"I spend half my time hating her and half my time insane about her. What's she got, anyway?"

"One thing she's got is a face that a man would commit suicide for. Another thing she's got is a figure that if he wasn't quite dead yet, he'd stand up and commit suicide for all over again. And another thing she's got is a healthy professional interest in the male of the species, that enjoys sticking pins into it just to see them wriggle. But if you want her, I'm determined you're going to have her. And really have her. You see, I like you pretty well."

"I like you a little, myself."

"That woman has got to be hurt."

"Oh, hurt hey? And you think you could hurt Doris? Listen,

you'd be going up against something that's forgotten more about
that than you'll ever know. You go and get your head lock on
her and begin twisting her neck. See what happens. She'll be out
in one second flat, in one minute flat she'll have you on the floor,
and in five minutes she'll be pulling your toenails out with red-
hot pliers. Yeah, you hurt her. I'm all sore from trying."

"You didn't hurt her where it hurt."

"And where does it hurt?"

"In that slab of ice she uses for a heart. In the triumph department, baby. You go get yourself a triumph, and see her wriggle out
of that."

"I won the club championship at billiards year before last. It
didn't do a bit of good."

"Wake up. Did you hear what I said about your voice?"

"Oh my God. I thought you had an idea."

"*You're* going to sing in Town Hall."

"I'm not."

"You are. And will that fix her."

"So I'm going to sing in Town Hall? Well in the first place I
can't sing in Town Hall, and in the second place I don't want to
sing in Town Hall, and in the third place it's just plain silly. And
in addition to that, wouldn't that fix her? Just another boughten
recital in Town Hall, with a lot of third-string critics dropping in
for five minutes and another gang of stooges out there laughing
at me. And in addition to that, I don't go out and drum up another
crowd. I've had enough."

"They won't be third-string critics and it won't be a drummed-
up crowd."

"I know that racket, so does she, and—"

"Not if I sing with you."

"What do you want to do, ruin me?"

"I guess that wouldn't do, at that. . . Leonard, you're right. The

Town Hall idea is no good. But—Carnegie, a regular, bona fide appearance with the Philharmonic, that would be different, wouldn't it?"

"Are you crazy?"

"Leonard, if you put yourself in my hands, if you do just what I say, I'll have you singing with the Philharmonic in a year. With that voice, I guarantee it. And let her laugh that off. Just let her laugh that off. Baby, do you want that woman? Do you want her eating out of your hand? Do—"

I opened my eyes to razz it some more, but all of a sudden a picture popped in front of my eyes, of how Doris would look out there, listening to me, and I started to laugh. Yes, it warmed me up.

"What's the matter?"

"It's the most cock-eyed thing I ever heard in my life. But—all right. We'll pretend that's how it's going to come out. Anyway, I'll have an excuse to see you some more."

"You don't need any excuse for that."

"Me, in soup and fish, up there in front of a big orchestra, bellowing at them."

"You'll have to work."

"I'm used to work."

"You'll have to study music, and sight-reading, and harmony, and languages, especially Italian."

..."*Perche devo studiare l'italiano?*"

"You speak Italian?"

"Didn't I tell you I started out as an architect? We all take our two years in Italy, studying the old ruins. Sure, I speak Italian."

"Oh, you *darling*. . . I'll want payment."

"I've got enough money."

"Who's talking about money? I want kisses, and lots of them."

"How about a down payment now? On account?"

"M'm."

It was about six o'clock when I got home, and Ethel Gorman, a cousin of Doris', was still there, and the flowers were all around, and the kids were going from one vase to the other, smelling them, and Doris still had on the recital dress, and the phone was ringing every five minutes, and the reviews from the afternoon papers were all clipped and spread on the piano. They said she revealed an excellent voice and sang acceptably. One of the phone calls kept Doris longer than the others, and when she came back her eyes were shining. "Ethel! Guess who was there!"

"Who?"

"Cecil Carver!"

"No!"

"Alice Hornblow just called up and says she sat next to her, and would have called sooner only she had to make sure who it was from her picture in a magazine, and she was talking to her during the intermission—and Cecil Carver said I was swell!"

"Doris! You don't mean it!"

"Isn't it marvelous! It means—it means more than all those reviews put together. Think of that Ethel—Cecil Carver!"

Now who Cecil Carver was, and what the hell kind of singing she did when she wasn't entertaining contractors in the afternoon, was something we hadn't got around to yet, for some reason. I pasted a dumb look on my face, and kind of droned it out: "And who, may I ask, is Cecil Carver?"

Doris just acted annoyed. "Leonard, don't tell me you don't know who Cecil Carver is. She's the sensation of the season, that's all. She came back from abroad this fall, and after one appearance at the Hippodrome the Philharmonic engaged her, and her recital at Carnegie was the biggest thing this year and she's under contract to the Metropolitan for next season—that's who Cecil Carver is. It would seem to me that you could keep up on things, a little bit."

"Well gee that sounds swell."

She came in that night, to thank me again for the flowers, and to say good night. I thought of my date with Cecil Carver for the next afternoon. What with one thing and another, I was beginning to feel a whole lot better.

4

IT'S ONE thing to start something like that, but it's something else to go through with it. I bought a tuning fork and some exercise books, went up on the third floor of the Craig-Borland Building, locked all the doors and put the windows down, and ha-ha-ha-ed every morning, hoping nobody would hear me. Then in the afternoon I'd go down and take a lesson, and make some payments. I liked paying better than learning, and I felt plenty like a fool. But then Cecil sent me over to Juilliard for a course in sight-reading, and I went in there with a lot of girls wearing thick glasses, and boys that looked like they'd have been better off for a little fresh air. It was taught by a Frenchman named Guizot, and along with the sight-reading he gave us a little harmony. When I found out that music has structure to it, just like a bridge has, right away I began to get interested. I took Guizot on for some private lessons, and began to work. He gave me exercises to do, melodies to harmonize, and chords to unscramble, and I rented a piano, and had that moved in, so I could hear what I was doing. I couldn't play it, but I could hit the chords, and that was the main thing. Then he talked to me about symphonies, and of course I had to dig into them. I bought a little phonograph, and a flock of symphony albums, and got the scores, and began to take them apart, so I could see how they were put together. The scores you don't buy, they cost too much. But I rented them, and first I'd have one for a couple of weeks, and then I'd have another. I

found out there's plenty of difference between one symphony and
another symphony. Beethoven, Mozart, and Brahms were the boys
I liked. All three of them, they took themes that were simple, like
an architectural figure, but they could get cathedrals out of them,
believe me they could.

The sight-reading was tough. It's something you learn easy when
you're young, but to get it at the age of thirty-three isn't so easy.
Do you know what it is? You just stand up there and read it,
without any piano to give you the tune, or anything else. I never
heard of it until Cecil began to talk about it, didn't even know
what it meant. But I took it on, just like the rest of it, and beat
intervals into my head with the piano until I could hear them in
my sleep. After a while I knew I was making progress, but then
when I'd go down to Cecil, and try to read something off while
she played the accompaniment, I'd get all mixed up and have to
stop. She spotted the reason for it. "You're not watching the words.
You can read the exercises because all you have to think about is
the music. But songs have words too, and you have to sing them.
You can't just go la-la-la. Look at the words, don't look at the
notes. Your eye will half see them without your looking at them, but
the main thing is the words. Get them right and the music will
sing itself."

It sounded wrong to me, because what I worried about was the
notes, and it seemed to me I ought to look at them. But I tried
the way she said, and sure enough it came a little better. I kept on
with it, doing harder exercises all the time, and then one day I
knew I wouldn't have to study sight-reading any more. I could
read anything I saw, without even having to stop and think about
keys, or sharps, or flats, or anything else, and that was the end of
it. I could do it.

The ha-ha stuff was the worst. I did what Cecil told me, and
she seemed satisfied, but to me it was just a pain in the neck. But
then one day something happened. It was like a hair parted in my

throat, and a sound came out of it that made me jump. It was like a Caruso record, a big, round high tone that shook the room. I tried it again, and it wouldn't come. I vocalized overtime that day, trying to get it back, and was about to give up when it came again. I opened it up, and stood there listening to it swell. Then I began going still higher with it. It got an edge on it, like a tenor, but at the same time it was big and round and full. I went up with it until I was afraid to go any higher, and then I checked pitch on the piano. It was an A.

That afternoon, Cecil was so excited by it she almost forgot about payment. "It's what I've been waiting for. But I had no idea it was that good."

"Say, it sounds great. How did you know it was there?"

"It's my business to know. What a baritone!"

"To hell with it. Come here."

". . . . . . Sing me one more song."

All right, if you think I'm a sap, falling in love with my own voice so I could hardly wait to work it out every day, and going nuts about music so I just worked at it on a regular schedule, don't say I didn't warn you. And don't be too hard on me. Remember what I told you: there was not one other thing to do, from morning till night. Not one other thing in the world to do.

I had been at it three or four months when I found out how lousy Doris really was, and maybe that wasn't a kick. She couldn't read a note, I had found that out from listening to her work with Lorentz. But the real truth about her I found out by accident. Cecil was so pleased at the way I was coming along that she decided I ought to learn a role, and put me on Germont in Traviata, partly because there wasn't much of it, and partly because it was all lyric, and I'd have to throttle down on my tendency to beef, which seemed to be my main trouble at the time. That was on a Saturday, and I thought I'd surprise her by having the whole

thing learned by Monday. But when I went around to Schirmer's
to get the score, they were closed. It was early summer. I went
home and then I happened to remember that Doris was studying
it too, so I snitched it off the piano and took it up to the nursery
and hid it. Then when she went off to a show that night, I went
to bed with it.

I spent that night on the second act, and was just getting it
pretty well in my head when I heard Doris come in and then go
down again. And what does she do but begin singing Traviata
down there, right in that part I had just been going over. Get how
it was: she downstairs, singing the stuff, and me upstairs, in bed,
holding the book on her. Well, it was murder. In the first place,
she had no rhythm. I guess that was what had bothered me before,
when I knew something was wrong, and didn't know what it was.
To her, the music was just a string of phrases, and that was all.
When she'd get through with one, she'd just go right on to the
next one, without even a stop. I tried to hum my part, under my
breath, in the big duet, and it couldn't be done. Her measures
wouldn't beat. I mean, I'd still have two notes to sing, to fill out
the measure on my part, and she'd already be on to the next
measure on her part. I did nothing but stop and start, trying to
keep up. And then, even within the phrase, she didn't get the notes
right. If she had a string of eighth notes, she'd sing them dotted
eighths and sixteenths, so it set your teeth on edge. And every
time she came to a high note, she'd hold it whether there was a
hold marked over it or not, and regardless of what the other voice
was supposed to be doing. I lay there and listened to it, and got
sorer by the minute. By that time I had a pretty fair idea of how
good you've got to be in music before you're any good at all, and
who gave her the right to high-hat me on her fine artistic soul, and
then sing like that? Who said she had an artistic soul, the way
she butchered a score? But right then I burst out laughing. That
was it. She didn't have any artistic soul. All she had was a thirst

for triumphs. And I, the sap, had fallen for it.

I heard her come in the bedroom, and hid the score under my pillow. She came in after a while, and she was stark naked, except for a scarf around her neck with a spray of orchids pinned to it. I knew then that something was coming. She walked around and then went over and stood looking out the window. "You better watch yourself. Catching cold is no good for the voice."

"It's so hot. I can't bear anything on."

"Don't stand too close to that window."

". . . Remind me to call up Hugo for my Traviata score. I wanted it just now, and couldn't find it. He must have taken it."

"Wasn't that Traviata you were singing?"

"Oh, I know it, so far as that goes. But I hate to lose things. . . I was running over a little of it for Jack Leighton. He thinks he can get me on at the Cathedral. You know he owns some stock."

Jack Leighton was the guy she had gone to the theatre with, and one of her string. I had found out who they all were by watching Lorentz at her parties. He knew her a lot better than I did, Cecil was right about that, and it gave me some kind of a reverse-English kick to check up on her by watching his face while she'd be off in a corner making a date with some guy. Lorentz squirmed, believe me he did. I wasn't the only one.

"That would be swell."

"Of course, it's only a picture house, but it would be a week's work, and they don't pay badly. It would be *something* coming in. And it wouldn't be bad showmanship for them. After all—I am prominent."

"Socialite turns pro, hey?"

"Something like that. Except that by now I hope I can consider myself already a pro."

"That was Jack you went out with?"

"Yes. . . Was it all right to wear his orchids?"

"Sure. Why not?"

She went over and sat down. I was pretty sure the orchids were my cue to get sore, but I didn't. Another night I would have, but Traviata had done something to me. I knew now I was as good as she was, and even better, in the place where she had always high-hatted me, and knew that no matter what she said about the orchids, she couldn't get my goat. I even acted interested in them, the wrong way: "How many did he send?"

"Six. Isn't it a crime?"

"Oh well. He can afford them."

Her foot began to kick. I wasn't marching up to slaughter the way I always marched. She didn't say anything for a minute, and then she did something she never did in a fight with me, because I always saved her the trouble and did it first. I mean, she lost her temper. The regular way was for me to get sore, and the sorer I got, the more angelic, and sad, and persecuted she got. But this time it was different, and I could hear it in her voice when she spoke. "—Even if we can't."

"Why sure we can."

"Oh no we can't. No more, I'm sorry to say."

"If orchids are what it takes to make you happy, we can afford all you want to wear."

"How can we afford orchids, when I've pared our budget to the bone, and—"

"We got a budget?"

"Of course we have."

"First I heard of it."

"There are a lot of things you haven't heard of. I scrimp, and save, and worry, and still I'm so frightened I can hardly sleep at night. I only hope and pray that Jack Leighton can do something for me—even if he's like every other man, and wants his price."

"What price?"

"Don't you know?"

"Well, what the hell. He's human."

"Leonard! You can say that?"

"Sure."

"Suppose he demanded his price—and I paid it?"

"He won't."

"Why not, pray?"

"Because I outweigh him by forty pounds, and can beat hell out of him, and he knows it."

"You can lie there, and look at me, wearing another man's orchids, almost on my knees to him to give me work that we so badly need—you can actually take it that casually—"

She raved on, and her voice went up to a kind of shrieking wail, and I did some fast thinking. When I said what I did about outweighing Jack, it popped into my mind that there was something funny about those orchids, and that it was a funny thing for him to do, send six orchids to Doris, even if I didn't outweigh him.

"And *you* won't."

"Don't be so sure. I'm getting desperate, and—"

"In the first place, you never paid any man his price, because you're not that much on the up-and-up with them. In the second place, if you want to pay it, you just go right ahead and pay. I won't pretend I'll like it, but I'm not going down on my knees to you about it. And in the third place, they're not his orchids."

"They're—what makes you say that?"

"I just happen to remember. When Jack called me up a while ago—"

"He—?"

"Oh yeah, he called me up. During the intermission. To tell me, in case I missed my cigarette case, that he had dropped it in his pocket by mistake."

It wasn't true. Jack hadn't called me up. But I knew Doris never went out during an intermission, and that Jack can't live a half hour without a smoke, so I took a chance. I could feel things breaking my way, and I meant to make the most of it.

"—And just as he hung up, he made a gag about the swell flowers I buy my wife. I had completely forgotten it until just this second."

"Leonard, how can you be so—"

"So you went out and ordered the orchids yourself, didn't you? And rubbed them in his face all night, just to make *him* feel like a bum. And now you come home and tell me he sent them, just to make *me* feel like a bum. . . . And it turns out we *can* afford them, doesn't it?"

"He meant to send some, he told me so—"

"He didn't."

"He did, he did, he *did*! And if I just felt I had to have something to cheer me up—"

"Suppose you go in and go to bed. And shut up. See if that will cheer you up."

She had begun parading around, and now she snapped on the light. "Leonard, you have a perfectly awful look on your face!"

"Yeah, I'm bored. Just plain bored. And to you, I guess a bored man does look pretty awful."

She went out and slammed the door with a terrific bang. It was the first time I had ever taken a decision over her. I pulled out Traviata again. It fell open to the place where Alfredo throws the money in Violetta's face, after she gets him all excited by pretending to be in love with somebody else. It crossed my mind that Alfredo was a bit of a cluck.

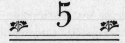

5

IT WAS early in October that I got the wire from Rochester. It had been a lousy summer. In August, Doris took the children up to the Adirondacks, and I wanted to go, but I hated the way she would have asked for separate rooms. So I stayed home, and learned two more roles, and played around with Cecil. I got a letter from Doris, after she had been up there a week, saying Lorentz was there too, because of course she couldn't even write a letter without putting something in it to make you feel rotten. The Lorentz part, it wasn't so good, but I gritted my teeth and hung on. She came home, and around the end of September Cecil went away. She was booked for a fall tour, and wouldn't be back until November. I was surprised how I missed her, and how the music wasn't much fun without her. Then right after that, Doris went away again. She was to sing in Wilkes-Barre. That was a phoney, of course, and all it amounted to was that she had friends there that belonged to some kind of a tony breakfast club, and they had got her invited to sing there.

The day after she left, I got the telegram from Cecil, dated Rochester:

MY TENOR HAS GOT THE PIP STOP IF YOU LOVE ME FOR GOD'S SAKE HOP ON A PLANE QUICK AND COME UP HERE STOP BRING OLD ITALIAN ANTHOLOGIES ALSO OLD ENGLISH ALSO SOME OPERATIC STUFF ESPECIALLY PAGLIACCI TRAVIATA FACTOTUM AND MASKED BALL ALSO CUTAWAY COAT GRAY PANTS FULL EVENING SOUP AND FISH AND PLENTY OF CLEAN SHIRTS STOP LOVE

                                            CECIL

It caught me at the office about ten in the morning, and the messenger waited, and as soon as I read it my heart began to pump, not from excitement, but from fear. Because up to then it had been just a gag, anyway on my end of it. But this brought me face to face with it: Did I mean it enough to get up before people and sing, or not? I stood there looking at it, and then I thought, well what the hell? I called the Newark airport, found they had

a plane leaving around noon, and made a reservation. Then I
wrote a wire to Doris telling her I had been called out of town
on business, and another one to Cecil, telling her I'd be there. Then
I grabbed all the music I might need, went over to the bank and
drew some money, hustled up to the house and packed, and
grabbed a cab.

She met me at the airport, kissed me, and bundled me into a
car she had waiting. "It was sweet of you to come. My but I'm
glad to see you."

"Me too."

"Terribly glad."

"But what happened? I didn't even know you had a tenor."

"Oh, you have to have an assistant artist, to give a little variety.
Sometimes the accompanist fills in with some Liebestraum, but my
man won't play solo. So I let the music bureau sell me a tenor. He
was no good. He was awful in Albany, and he got the bird last night
in Buffalo, so when he turned up this morning with a cold I got
terribly alarmed for his precious throat and sent him home. That's
all."

"What's the bird?"

"Something you'll never forget, if you ever hear it."

"Suppose they give *me* the bird?"

We had been riding along on the back seat, her hand in mine,
just two people that were even gladder to see each other than they
knew they were going to be, and I expected her to laugh and say
something about my wonderful voice, and how they would never
give *me* the bird. She didn't. She took her hand away, and we rode
a little way without saying anything, and then she looked me all
over, like she was measuring everything I had. "Then I'll have to
get somebody else."

"Yeah?"

". . . They *can* give you the bird."

"Hey, let's talk about something pleasant."

"It's a tough racket."

"Maybe I better go home."

"They can give you the bird, and they can give it to anybody. I think you'll win, but you've got to win, don't make any mistake about that. You've got to lam it in their teeth and make them like it."

"So."

"You can go home if you want to, and if that's how you feel about it, you'd better. But if you do, you're licked for good."

"I'm here. I'll give it a fall."

"Look at me now."

"I'm looking."

"Don't let that applause fool you, when you come on. They're a pack of hyenas, they're always a pack of hyenas, just waiting to tear in and pull out your vitals, and the only way you can keep them back is to lick them. It's a battle, and you've got to win."

"When is the concert?"

"Tonight."

"Ouch."

"Did you hear me?"

"I heard you."

When we got to the hotel I took a room and sent up my stuff, and then we went up to her suite. A guy was there, reading a newspaper. "Mr. Wilkins, who plays our accompaniments. Mr. Borland, Ray. Our baritone."

We shook hands, and he fished some papers out of his pocket. "The printer's proofs of the program. It came while you were out, Cecil. He's got to have it back, with corrections, by five o'clock. I don't see anything, but you better take a look at it."

She passed one over to me. It gave me a funny feeling, just to look at it. I've still got that proof, and here it is, in case you're interested:

JOHN FREDERICK JEVONS

PRESENTS

Miss Cecil Carver

SOPRANO

In a Song Recital

AT

THE EASTMAN THEATRE

Thursday Evening, October 5, at 8:30

Leonard Borland, Baritone
Ray Wilkins, Accompanist

Cavatina
>ROSSINI   *Fac Ut Portem Christi Mortem,*
>from the Stabat Mater

>Miss Carver

Three Songs from the 17th Century
>CARISSIMI   *Vittoria, Mio Core*
>SCARLATTI, A.   *O Cessate Di Piagarmi*
>CALDARA   *Come Raggio Di Sol*

>Mr. Borland

Songs
>BRAHMS   *Der Schmied*
>*Von Eviger Liebe*
>*An Die Nachtigall*

>Miss Carver

Songs
  SCHUBERT   *Halt*
                Auf Dem Flusse
                Der Wetterfahne
                Gretchen Am Spinnrade

                Miss Carver

Intermission

Aria
  MOZART   *Batti, Batti*
                From Don Giovanni

                Miss Carver

Aria
  VERDI   *Eri Tu*
                From Un Ballo In Maschera
                (Preceded by the Recitative,
                Alzati! La Tuo Figlio)

                Mr. Borland

Songs from the British Isles
  CAREY   *Sally in Our Alley*
  MOORE   *Oft in the Stilly Night*
  BAYLY   *Gaily the Troubadour*
  MARZIALS   *The Twickenham Ferry*

                Miss Carver

Songs of the Southwest
                Billy the Kid
                Green Grow the Lilacs
                The Trail to Mexico
                Lay Down, Dogies
                Strawberry Roan
                I'd Like to Be in Texas

                Miss Carver

          The piano is a Steinway

"It's all right, pretty nifty. Except that Leonard Borland is gradually on purpose going to turn into Logan Bennett."

"Oh, yes. I meant to ask you about that. Yes, I think that's better. Will you change it, Ray? On the proof that goes to the printer. And make sure it's changed on all his groups."

"I only sing twice?"

"That's all. Did you bring the music I said?"

"Right here in the briefcase."

"Give it to Ray, so he can go over it. He always plays from memory. He never brings music on stage."

"I see."

"You'll attend to the program, Ray?"

"I'm taking it over myself."

Wilkins left, she had me ha-ha for ten minutes, then said my voice was up and stopped me. Some sandwiches and milk came up. "They fed us on the plane. I'm not hungry."

"You better eat. You don't get any dinner."

". . . No dinner?"

"You always sing on an empty stomach. We'll have some supper later."

I tried to eat, and couldn't get much down. Seeing that program made me nervous. When I had eaten what I could, she told me to go in and sleep. "A fat chance I could sleep."

"Lie down, then. Be quiet. No walking around, no vocalizing. That's one thing you can learn. Don't leave your concert in the hotel room."

I went in my room, took off my clothes, and lay down. Somewhere downstairs I could hear Wilkins at the piano, going over the Italian songs. It made me sick to my stomach. None of it was turning out the way I thought it was going to. I had expected a kind of a cock-eyed time, with both of us laughing over what a joke it was that I should be up here, singing with her. Instead of that she was as cold as a woman selling potatoes, and over something I didn't really care about. There didn't seem to be any fun in it.

I must have slept, though, because I had put a call in for seven o'clock, and when it came it woke me up. I went in the bathroom, took a quick shower, and started to dress. My fingers trembled so bad I could hardly get the buttons in my shirt. About a quarter to eight I rang her. She seemed friendly, more like her usual self, and told me to come in.

A hotel maid let me in. Cecil was just finishing dressing, and in a minute or two she came out of the bedroom. She had on a chiffon velvet dress, orange-colored, with salmon-colored belt and salmon-colored shoes. It had a kind of Spanish look to it, and was probably what she had always been told she ought to wear with her eyes, hair, and complexion, and yet it was heavy and stuffy, and made her look exactly like an opera singer all dressed up to give a concert. It startled me, because I had been married for so long to a woman that knew all there was to know about dressing that I had forgotten what frumps they can make of themselves when they really try. She saw my look and glanced in the mirror. "What's the matter?"

"Nothing."

"Don't I look all right?"

"Sure."

She told the maid to go, and then she kept looking at herself in the mirror, and then at me again, but when she lit a cigarette and sat down she wasn't friendly any more. ". . . All right, we'll check over what you're to do."

"I'm listening."

"First, when you come on."

"Yeah, I've been wondering about that. What do I do?"

"At all recitals, the singer comes on from the right, that is, stage right. Left, to the audience. Walk straight out from the wings, past the piano, to the center of the stage. Be quick and brisk about it. Be

aware of them, but don't look at them till you get there. By that
time they'll start to applaud."

"Suppose they don't?"

"If you come on right, they will. That's part of it. I told you, it's
a battle, and it starts the moment you show your face. You've got to
make them applaud, and that means you've got to come on right.
You go right to the center of the stage, stop, face them, and bow.
Bow once, from the hips, as though you meant it."

"O. K., what then?"

"You bow once, but no more. If it's a friendly house, they may
applaud quite a little, but not enough for more than one bow. Besides, it's only a welcome. You haven't done anything yet to war-
rant more than one bow, and if you begin grinning around, you'll
look silly, like some movie star being gracious to his public."

"All right, I got that. What next?"

"Then you start to sing."

"Do I give Wilkins a sign or something?"

"I'll come to that, but I'm not done yet about how you come on.
Look pleasant, but don't paste any deathhouse smile on your face,
don't look sheepish, as though you thought it was a big joke, don't
try to look more confident than you really are. Above all, look as
though you meant business. They came to hear you sing, and as
long as you act as though that's what you're there for, you'll be all
right, and you don't have to kid them with some kind of phoney
act. If you look nervous, that's all right, you're supposed to be
nervous. Have you got that? *Mean* it."

"All right, I got it."

"When you finish your song, stop. If the piano has the actual
finish, hold everything until the last note has been played, no matter
whether they break in with applause or not. Hold everything, then
relax. Don't do any more than that, just in your own mind relax. If
you've done anything with the song at all, they ought to applaud.
When they do, bow. Bow straight to the center. Then take a quarter

turn on your feet, and bow to the left. Then turn again, and bow to the right. Then walk off. As quickly as you can get to the wings without actually running, walk off."

"The way I came on?"

"Right back the way you came on."

"All right, what then?"

"Are you sure you've got that all straight?"

"Wait a minute. Do I do that after every song, or—"

"No, no, no! Not after every song. At the end of your group. You don't leave the stage after every song. There won't be much applause at the end of your first two songs, they only applaud the group. Bow once after the first song, and when the applause has died down, start the second, and then on with the third."

"All right, I got it now."

"If the applause continues, go out, exactly as you went out the first time, and bow three times, first center, then left, then right, then come off."

"Go ahead. What else?"

"Now about the accompanist. Most singers turn and nod to the accompanist when they are ready, but to my mind it's just one more thing that slows it up, that adds to the chill that hangs over a recital anyway. That's why I have Wilkins. He can feel that audience as well as the singer can, and he knows exactly when it's time to start. Another thing about him is that he plays from memory, has no music to fool with, and so he can watch you the whole time you sing. That gives you better support, and it helps you in another way. They don't really notice him, but they feel him there, and when he can't take his eyes off you, they think you must be pretty good. You wait for him. While you're waiting, look them over. Use those five seconds to get acquainted. Look them over in a friendly way, but don't smirk at them. Be sure you look up at the balcony, and all over the house, so they all feel you're singing to them, and not to just a few. Use that time to get the feel of the house, to project yourself out there, even if it's just a little bit."

"Must be a swell five seconds."

"I'm trying to get it through your head that it's a battle, that it's a tough spot at best, and that you have to use every means to win."

"All right. I hear what you say."

"Now go in the bedroom and come out and do it. I want to see you go through it all. The center of the stage is over by the window, and I'm the audience."

I went in the bedroom, then came out and did like she said. "You came on too slow, and your bow is all wrong. Shake the lead out of your feet. And bow from the hips, bow low, as though you meant it. Don't just stand there jerking your head up and down."

I went in and did it over again. "That's better, but you're still much too perfunctory about it. You're not a business man, getting up to give a little talk at the Engineers' Club. You're a singer, getting ready to put on a show, and there's got to be some formality about it."

"Can't I just act natural?"

"If you act natural, you'll look just like what you are, a contractor that thinks he looks like a fool. Can't you understand what I mean? This is a concert, not a meeting to open bids."

I did it all over again, and felt like some kind of a tin soldier on hinges, but she seemed satisfied. "It's a little stiff, but anyway it's how it's done. Now do it three or four more times, so you get used to it."

I did it about ten times, and then she stopped me. "And now one more thing. That first number, *Vittoria Mio Core,* I picked out for you to begin with because it's a good lively tune and you can race through with it without having to worry about fine effects. After that you ought to be all right. But don't forget that it has no introduction. He'll give you one chord, for pitch, and then you start."

"Sure, I know."

"You know, but be ready. One chord, and as soon as you have

the pitch clear in your head, start. Don't let it catch you by surprise."

"I won't."

We had another cigarette, and didn't say much. I looked at the
palms of my hands. They were wet. Wilkins came in. "Taxi's
waiting."

We put on our coats, went down, got in the cab. There was a
little drizzle of rain. "The Eastman Theatre. Stage entrance."

The stage was all set for the recital, with a big piano out there,
and a drop back of it. There was a hole in the drop, so we could look
out. First she would look, and then I would look. Wilkins found a
chair, and read the afternoon paper. She kept looking up. "Balcony's filling. It's a sell-out."

But I wasn't looking at the balcony. All I could see was those
white shirts, marching down into the orchestra. Rochester is a
musical town, and formal, and a lot of those white shirts, they had
those dreamy faces over top of them, with curly moustaches, that
meant musician. They meant musician, and they meant tony musician, and they scared me to death. I don't know what I expected.
Anybody that lives in New York gets to thinking that any town
north of the Harlem River is out in the sticks, and I must have been
looking for a flock of country club boys and their wives, or something, but not this. My mouth began to feel dry. I went over to the
cooler and had a drink, but I kept swallowing.

At 8:25 a stagehand went out and closed the top of the piano. He
came back and another herd of white shirts came down the aisle.
They were hurrying now. Wilkins took out his watch, held it up
to Cecil. "Ready?"

"All right."

We all three went to the wings, stage right. He raised his hand.
"One—two"—then lifted his foot and gave her a little kick in the
tail. She swept out there like she owned the place and the whole
block it was built on. There was a big hand. She bowed once, the

way she had told me to do, and then stood there, looking up, down, and around, a little friendly smile coming on her face every time she warmed up a new bunch, while he was playing the introduction to the Rossini. Then she started to sing. It was the first time I had heard her in public. Well, I didn't need any critic to tell me she was good. She stood there, smiling around, and then, as the introduction stopped, she turned grave, and seemed to get taller, and the first of it came out, low and soft. It was Latin, and she made it sound dramatic. And she made every syllable so distinct that I could even understand what it meant, though it was all of fifteen years since I had had my college Plautus. Then she got to the part where there are a lot of sustained notes, and her voice began to swell and throb so it did things to you. Up to then I hadn't thought she had any knockout of a voice, but I had never heard it when it was really working. Then she came to the fireworks at the end, and you knew there really was a big leaguer in town. She finished, and there was a big hand. Wilkins came off, wiped his hands on his handkerchief. She bowed center, left, and right, and came off. She listened. The applause kept up. She went out and bowed three times again. She came off, stood there and listened, then shook her head. The applause stopped, and she looked at me. "All right, baby. Here's your kick for luck."

She kicked me the way Wilkins had kicked her. He put the handkerchief in his pocket, raised his hand. "One—two—"

I aimed for the center of the stage, got there, and bowed, the way I had practiced. They gave me a hand. Then I looked up, and tried to do what she had told me to do, look them over, top, bottom, and around. But all I could see was faces, faces, faces, all staring at me, all trying to swim down my throat. Then I began to think about that first number, and the one chord I would get, and how I had to be ready. I stood there, and it seemed so long I got a panicky feeling he had forgotten to come out, and that there wouldn't be any opening chord. Then I heard it, and right away started to sing:

Vittoria, vittoria,
Vittoria, vittoria, mio core;
Non lagrimar piu, non lagrimar piu,
E sciolta d'amore la vil servitu!

My voice sounded so big it startled me, and I tried to throttle it down, and couldn't. There's no piano interludes in that song. It goes straight through, for three verses, at a hell of a clip, and the more I tried to pull in, and get myself under some kind of control, the louder it got, and the faster I kept going, until at the finish Wilkins had a hard time keeping up with me. They gave me a little bit of a hand, and I didn't want to bow, I wanted to apologize, and explain that that wasn't the way it was supposed to go. But I bowed, some kind of way.

Then came the *O Cessate*. It's short, and ought to start soft, lead up to a crescendo in the middle, and die away at the end. I was so rung up by then I couldn't sing soft if I tried. I started it, and my voice bellowed all over the place, and it was terrible. There was a bare ripple after that, and Wilkins went into the opening of the *Come Raggio*. That's another that opens soft, and I sang it soft for about two measures, and then I exploded like some radio when you turn it up too quick. After that it was a hog-calling contest. Wilkins saw it was hopeless, and came down on the loud pedal so it would maybe sound as though that was the way it was supposed to go, and a fat chance we could fool that audience. I finished, and on the pianissimo at the end it sounded like a locomotive whistling for a curve. When it was over there was a little scattering of applause, and I bowed. I bowed center, and took the quarter turn to bow to the side. The applause stopped. I kept right on turning and walked off stage.

She was there in the wings, a murderous look on her face. "You've flopped!"

"All right, I've flopped."

"Damn it, you've—"

But Wilkins grabbed her by the arm. "Do you want to lose them for good? Get out there, get out there, get out there!"

She stopped in the middle of a cussword and went on, smiling like nothing had happened at all.

I tried to explain to her in the intermission what had ailed me, but she kept walking away from me, there behind the drop. It wasn't until I saw her blotting her eyes with a handkerchief, to keep the mascara from running down her cheeks, that I knew she was crying. "Well—I'm sorry I ruined your concert."

". . . Oh well. It's a turkey anyhow."

"I didn't do it any good."

"They're as cold as dead fish. There's nothing to do about it. You didn't ruin it."

"Was that the bird?"

"Oh no. You don't know the half of it yet."

"Oh."

"Did you have to blast them out of their seats?"

"I've been telling you. I was nervous."

"After all I've told you about not bellowing. And then you have to—what did you think you were doing, announcing trains?"

"Maybe I'd better go home."

"Maybe you'd better."

"Shall I do this other number?"

"As you like."

She did the Mozart, and took an encore, and came off. Wilkins had heard us rowing, and looked at me, and motioned me on. She went off to her dressing room without looking at me. I went out there. There were one or two handclaps, and I made my bow, and then paid no more attention to them at all. I felt sick and disgusted. He struck the opening chord and I started the recitative. There's a lot of it, and I sang it just mechanically. After two or three phrases I heard a murmur go over the house, and if that was the bird I didn't care. I got to the end of the recitative, and then stepped back a little while he played the introduction to the aria. I heard him mumble, so I could just hear him above the triplets: "You got 'em. Just look noble now, and it's in the bag."

It hit me funny. It relaxed me, and it was just what I needed. I tried to look noble, and I don't know if I did or not, but all the time my voice was coming nice and easy. We got to the end of the first strain, and he really began to go places with the lead into the next. It was the first time all night the piano had really had much to do, and it came over me all of a sudden that the guy was one hell of an accompanist, and that it was a pleasure to sing with him. I went into the next strain, and really made it drip. There was a little break, and I heard him say, "Swell, keep it up." I was nearly to the high G. I took the little leading phrase nice and light, and hit it right on the nose. It felt good, and I began to let it swell. Then I remembered about not yelling, and throttled it back, and finished the phrase under nice control. There wasn't much more, and when I hit the high F at the end, it was just right.

For a second or so after he struck the last chord it was as still as death. Then some guy in the balcony yelled. My heart skipped a beat, but then others began to yell, and what they were yelling was bravo. The applause broke out in a roar then, and I remembered to bow. I bowed center, right, and left, and then I walked off. She was there, and kissed me. Wilkins whipped out his handkerchief, wiped the lipstick off my mouth, and shoved me out there again. I bowed three times again, and hated to leave. When I came back she nodded, told Wilkins to go out with me this time for an encore. "Yeah, but what the hell is his encore?"

"Let him do Traviata."

"O. K."

I went out, and he started Traviata. Now *Di Provenza Il Mar* I guess is the worst sung aria you ever hear, because the boys always think about tone and forget about the music, and that ruins it. I mean they don't sing it smooth, with all the notes even, and that makes it jerky, and takes all the sadness out of it. But it's a cakewalk for me, because I think I told you about all that work I did on music, and it seemed to me that I kind of knew what old man Verdi was trying to do with it when he wrote it. Wilkins started it, and he played it slower than Cecil had been playing it, and I no sooner heard it than I knew that was right too. I took it just the way he had cued me. I just rocked it along, and kept every note even, and didn't beef at all. When I got to the G flat, I held it, then let it swell a little, but only enough to come in right on the forte that follows it, and then on the finish I loaded it with all the tears of the world. You ought to have heard the bravos that time. I went out and took more bows, and it was no trouble to look them in the eye that time. They seemed like the nicest people in the world.

At the end, after she had finished a flock of encores, Cecil took me out for a bow with her, and then my flowers came up, and she pinned one on me, and they clapped some more, and she had me do a duet with her, *"Crudel, Perche, Finora,"* from the Marriage of Figaro. It went so well they wanted more, but she rang down and the three of us went out to eat. Wilkins and I were pretty excited, but she didn't have much to say. When she went out to powder her nose, he started to laugh. "They're all alike, aren't they?"

"How do you mean, all alike?"

"I thought she was a little different, at first. Letting you take that encore, and singing a duet with you, that looked kind of decent. And then I got the idea, somehow, that she liked you. I mean for your sex appeal, or whatever it is that they go for. But you see how she's acting, don't you? They're all alike. Opera singers are the dumbest, pettiest, vainest, cruelest, egotisticalest, jealousest breed of woman you can find on this man's earth, or any man's earth. You did too good, that's all. Two bits that tomorrow morning you're on your way back."

"I think you're wrong."

"I'm not wrong. First the tenor stinks and then the baritone don't stink enough."

"Not Cecil."

"Just Cecil, the ravishing Cecil."

"Something's eating on her, but I don't think it's that."

"You'll see."

"All right, I'll match your two bits."

We got back to the hotel, Wilkins went to his room, and I went up with her for a goodnight cigarette. She snapped on the lights, then went over to the mirror and stood looking at herself. "What's the matter with the dress?"

"Nothing."

"There's something."

". . . It's all wrong."

"I paid enough for it. It came from one of the best shops in New York."

"I guess one of the best shops in New York wouldn't have some lousy Paris copy they would wish off on a singer that didn't know any better. . . . It makes you look like a gold plush sofa. It makes that bozoom look like some dairy, full of Grade A milk for the kiddies. It makes you look about ten years older. It makes you look like an opera singer, all dressed up to screech."

"Isn't the bozoom all right?"

"The bozoom, considered simply as a bozoom, is curviform, exciting, and even distinguished. But for God's sake never dress for anything like that, even if you're secretly stuck on it, which I think you are. That's what a telephone operator does, when she puts on a yoo-hoo blouse. Or a chorus girl, wearing a short skirt to show her legs. Dress the woman, not the shape."

"Did you learn that from her?"

"Anyway I learned it."

She sat down, and kept on looking at the velvet, and fingering it. "All right, I'm a hick."

I went over and sat down beside her and took her hand. "You're not a hick, and you're not to feel that way about it. You asked me, didn't you? You wanted to know. Just to sit there, and keep on saying the dress was all right, when you knew I didn't think so— that wouldn't have been friendly, would it? And what is it? You haven't been yourself tonight."

"I'm a hick. I know I'm a hick, and I don't try to make anybody think any different. You or anybody. . . . I haven't had time to learn how to dress. I've spent my life in studios and hotels and theatres and concert halls and railroad trains, and I've spent most of it broke—until here recently—and all of it working. If you think that teaches you the fine points of dressing, you're mistaken. It doesn't teach you anything, except how tough everything is. And she, she's done nothing all her life but look at herself in a mirror, and—"

"What's she got to do with it?"

"—And study herself, and take all the time she needs to find the exact thing that goes with her, and make some man pay for it, and —all right, she can dress. I know she can dress. I don't have to be told. No woman would have to be told. And—all right, you wanted to know what she's got, I'll tell you what she's got. She's got class, so when she says hop, you—*jump!* And I haven't got it. All right, I know I haven't got it. But was that any reason for you to look at me that way?"

"Is that why you fought with me?"

"Wasn't it enough? As though I was some poor thing that you felt sorry for. That you felt—*ashamed of!* You've never felt ashamed of her, have you?"

"Nor of you."

"Oh, yes. You were ashamed tonight. I could see it in your eye. Why did you have to look at me that way?"

"I wasn't ashamed of you, I was proud of you. Even when you were quarreling with me, back there during the intermission, the back of my head was proud of you. Because it was your work, and there was no fooling around about it, even with me. Because you were a pro at your trade, and were out there to win, no matter whose feelings got hurt. And now you try to tell me I was ashamed of you."

She dropped her head on my shoulder and started to cry. "Oh Leonard, I feel like hell."

"What about? All this is completely imaginary."

"Oh no it isn't. . . . The tenor was all right. He wasn't much good, but I could have done with him, once he got over his cold. I wanted you up here, don't you see? I was so glad to see you, and then I didn't want you to see it, for fear you wouldn't want me to be that glad. And I tried to be businesslike, and I was doing fine— and then you looked at me that way. And then I swallowed that down, because I knew I didn't care how you looked at me, so long as you were here. And then—you flopped. And I knew you weren't just a tenor that would put up with anything for a job. I knew you'd go back, and I was terrified, and furious at you. And then you sang the way *I* wanted you to sing, and I loved you so much I wanted to go out there and hold on to you while you sang the other one. And now you know. Oh no, it's not just imaginary. What have *you* got?"

I held her tight, and patted her cheek, and tried to think of something to say. There wasn't anything to say, not about what she was talking about. I had got so fond of her that I loved every minute I spent with her, and yet there was only one woman that meant to me that she wanted to mean to me, and that was Doris. She could torture me all she wanted to, she could be a phoney and make a fool of me all over town with other men, and yet Cecil had hit it: when she said hop, I jumped.

"*I* know what you've got. You've got big hard shoulders, and shaggy hair, and you're a man, and you build bridges, and to you this is just some kind of foolish tiddle-de-winks game that you play until it's time to go to work. And that's just what it is to me! I don't want to be a singer. I want to be a woman!"

"If I'm a man, you made me one."

"Oh yes, that's the hell of it. It's mostly tiddle-de-winks, but it's partly building yourself up to her level, so you're not afraid of her any more. And that's what I'm helping you at. Making a man out of you, so she can have you . . . I feel like hell. I could go right out that window."

I held her a long time, then, and she stopped crying, and began to play with my hair. "All right, Leonard. I've been rotten, and a poor sport to say anything about it at all, because this isn't how it was supposed to come out—and now I'll stop. I'll be good, and not talk any more about it, and try to give you a pleasant trip. It's a little fun, isn't it, out here playing tiddle-de-winks?"

"It is with you."

"Wouldn't they be surprised, all your friends at the Engineers' Club, if they could see you?"

I wanted to cry, but she wanted me to laugh, so I did, and held her close, and kissed her. "You sang like an angel, and I'm terribly proud of you, and—that's right. Hold me close."

I held her close a long time, and then she started to laugh. It was a real cackle, over something that had struck her funny, I could see that. ". . . What is it?"

"You."

"Tonight? At the hall?"

"Yes."

"?"

But she just kept right on laughing, and didn't tell me what it was about. Later on, though, I found out.

6

WE SANG Syracuse, Cincinnati, and Columbus after that, the same program, and I did all right. She paid my hotel bills, and offered me $50 a night on top of that, but I wouldn't take anything. I was surprised at the reviews I got. Most of them wrote her up, and let me out with a line, but a few of them called me "the surprise of the evening," said I had a voice of "rare power and beauty," and spoke of the "sweep and authority" of my singing. I didn't exactly know what they meant, and it was the first time I knew there was anything like that about me, but I liked them all right and saved them all.

The Columbus concert was on a Thursday, and after we closed with the duet again, and took our bows, and went off, a little wop in gray spats followed her into her dressing room and stayed there quite a while. Then he left and we went out to eat. I was pretty hungry, and I hadn't liked waiting. "Who was your pretty boy friend?"

"That was Mr. Rossi."

"And who is Mr. Rossi?"

"General secretary, business agent, attorney, master of the hounds, bodyguard, scout, and chief cook-and-bottle-washer to Cesare Pagano."

"And who is Cesare Pagano?"

"He's the American Scala Opera Company, the only impresario in the whole history of opera that ever made money out of it."

"And?"

"I'm under contract to them, you know. For four weeks, beginning Monday. After that I go back to New York to get ready for the Metropolitan."

"No, I didn't know."

"I didn't say anything about it."

"Then after tonight I'm fired. Is that it?"

"No. I didn't say anything about it, because I thought I might have a surprise for you. I've been wiring Pagano about you, and wiring him and wiring him—and tonight he sent Rossi over. Rossi thinks you'll do."

"*What?* Me sing in grand opera?"

"Well what did you think you were learning those roles for?"

"I don't know. Just for something to do. Just so I could come down and see you. Just—to see if I could do it. Hell, I never *been* to a grand opera."

"Anyway, I closed with him."

It turned out I was to get $125 a week, which was upped $25 from what he had offered, and that was what they were arguing about. I was to get transportation, pay my own hotel bills, and have a four-week contract, provided I did all right on my first appearance. It sounded so crazy to me I didn't know what to say, and then something else popped in my head. "What about this grand opera, anyway? Do they—dress up or something?"

"Why of course. There's costumes, and scenery—just like any other show."

"*Me*—put on funny clothes and get out there and—do I have to paint up my face?"

"You use make-up, of course."

"It's out."

But then when I asked her what she got, and she said $400 a night, and that she had taken a cut from $500, I knew perfectly well that that was part of what they had been arguing about too, that she had taken that cut to get me in, so I could be with her, and that kind of got me. I thought it was the screwiest thing I had ever heard of, but I finally said yes.

If you think a concert is tough, don't ever try grand opera. I hear it's harder to go out there all alone, with only a piano to play your accompaniments and no scenery to help you out, and I guess it is, when you figure the fine points. But if you've never even heard of the fine points yet, and you're not sure you can even do it at all, you stick to something simple. Remember what I'm telling you: lay off grand opera.

We hit Chicago the next day, just the two of us, because Wilkins went back to New York after the Columbus concert. The first thing we did, after we got hotel rooms, was go around to the costumer's. That's a swell place. There's every kind of costume you ever heard of, hanging on hooks, like people that have just been lynched, from white flannel tenor suits with brass buttons up the front, to suits of armor, to naval uniforms, to cowboy clothes, to evening clothes and silk hats. It's all dark, and dusty, and shabby, and about as romantic as a waxworks.

They were opening in Bohème Monday night, and we were both in it, and that meant the first thing we had to get was the Marcel stuff. She already had her costumes, you understand. This was all on account of me. Marcel was the character I was to sing in the opera, the baritone role. There wasn't any trouble about him. I mean, they didn't have to make any stuff to order, because a pair of plaid pants, a velvet smoking jacket of a coat, and a muffler and floppy hat for the outdoor stuff, were all I had to have. They had that stuff, and I tried it on, and it was all right, and they set it aside. But when it came to the Rigoletto stuff, and they opened a book and showed me a picture of what I would have to have, I almost broke for the station right there. I knew he was supposed to be some kind of a hump-backed jester, but that I would have to come out in a foolish-looking red suit, and actually wear cap and bells, that had never once entered my mind.

"I really got to wear that outfit?"

"Why of course."

"My God."

She paid hardly any attention to me, and went on talking with the costumer. "He has to sing it Wednesday, and he'll have no chance for a fitting Monday. Can you fit Tuesday and deliver Wednesday?"

"Absolutely, Miss. We guarantee it."

"Remember to fit over the hump."

"We'll even measure over the hump. I think he'd better put a hump on right now. By the way, has he got a hump?"

"No, he'll have to get one."

"We have two types of hump. One that goes on with straps, the other with elastic fabric fastenings, adjustable. I recommend the elastic fabric, myself. It's more comfortable, stays in place better, doesn't interfere with breathing—"

"I think that's better."

So I put on a hump, and got measured for the monkey suit. Then it turned out that for two of the acts I would have to have dark stuff, and a cape, and another floppy hat. They argued whether the Bohème hat wouldn't do, and finally decided it would. Then we tried on capes. The one that seemed to be elected hiked up in back, on account of the hump, but the costumer thought I ought to take it, just the same. "We could make you a special one, to hang even all around, but if you take my advice, you'll have this one. That little break in the line won't make much difference, and then, if you have a cape that really fits *you,* without that hump I mean, you can use it in other operas—Lucia, Trovatore, Don Giovanni, you know what I mean? A nice operatic cape comes in handy any time, and—"

"O. K. I'll take that one."

Then it turned out I would have to have a red wig, and we tried

wigs on. When we got around to the Traviata stuff I didn't even
have the heart to look, and ordered blind. Anything short of a hula
skirt, I thought, would be swell. Then it seemed I had to have a
trunk, a special kind, and we got that. I'd hate to tell you what all
that stuff cost. We came out of there with the Marcel stuff, the wig,
the hump, the cape, and a make-up kit done up in two big boxes, the
other stuff to come. When we got back to the hotel we went up and
I dumped the stuff down on the floor. "What's the matter, Mar-
cellino? Don't you feel well?"

"I feel lousy."

There's no rehearsals for principals in the American Scala. You
know your stuff or you don't get hired. But I was a special case, and
Pagano wasn't taking any chances on me. He posted a call for the
whole Bohème cast to take me through it Sunday afternoon, and
maybe you think that wasn't one sore bunch of singers that showed
up at two o'clock. The men were all Italians, and they wanted to go
to a pro football game that was being played that afternoon. The
only other woman in the cast, the one that sang Musetta, was an
American, and she was sore because she was supposed to give a lec-
ture in a Christian Science temple, and had to cancel it. They
couldn't get the theatre, for some reason, so we did it downstairs in
the new cocktail lounge of the hotel, that they didn't use on Sun-
days. Rossi put chairs around to show doors, windows, and other
stuff in the set, took the piano, and started off. The rest of them paid
no attention to him at all, or to me. They knew Bohème frontwards,
backwards, and sidewise, and they sat around with their hats on
the back of their heads, working crossword puzzles in the Sunday
paper. When it came time for them to come in they came in without
even looking up. Cecil acted just like the others. She didn't work
puzzles, but she read a book. Every now and then a tall, disgusted-
looking Italian would walk through and walk out again. I asked
who he was, and they told me Mario, the conductor. He looked like

if he had to listen to me much longer he would get an acute case of the colic. It was all as cheerful as cold gravy with grease caked on the top.

Rossi rehearsed me until I swear blood was running out of my nose, throat, and eyeballs. I never got enough pep in it to suit him. I had always thought grand opera was a slow, solemn, kind of dignified show, but the way he went about it it was a race between some sprinter and a mechanical rabbit. I was surprised how bad the others sounded. It didn't seem to me any of them had enough voice to crush a grape.

Monday I tried to keep quiet and not think about it, but it was one long round of costumes, phone calls, and press releases. I was still singing under the name of Bennett, and when they called me down to give them some stuff about myself to go out to the papers, I was stumped. I wasn't going to say who I really was. I gave them the biography of an uncle that came from Missouri, and went abroad to study medicine. Instead of the medical stuff in Germany, I made it musical stuff in Italy, and it seemed to get by all right. Around six-thirty, when I had just laid down, and thought I could relax a few minutes and get myself a little bit in hand, the phone rang and Cecil said it was time to go. We had to go early, because she had to make me up.

When we went in the stage door of the Auditorium Theatre that night, and I got my first look at that stage, I almost fainted. What I had felt in Rochester was nothing compared to this. In the first place, I had never had any idea that a stage could be that big, and still be a stage and not a blimp hangar. You only see about half of it from out front. The rest of it stretches out through the wings, and back, and up overhead, until you'd think there wasn't any end of it. In the second place, it was all full of men, and monkey wrenches, and scenery going up on pulleys, and noise, so you'd think nobody could possibly sing on it, and be heard more than three feet. And in the third place, there was something about it that felt like big stuff about to happen. I guess that was the worst. Maybe an army head-quarters, the night before a drive, or a convention hall, just before a big political meeting, would affect you that way too, but if you really want to get that feeling, so you really feel it, and it scares you to death, you go in a big opera house about an hour and a half be-fore curtain time.

Cecil didn't waste any time on it. She went right up to No. 7 dressing room, where I was, and I followed her up. She was in No. 1 dressing room, on the other side of the stage. When we got up there, there was nothing in there at all but a long table against the wall, a mirror above that, a couple of chairs, and my trunk, that had been sent around earlier in the day. I opened it, and she took out the make-up kit, and spread it out on the table. "Always watch that you have plenty of cloths and towels. You need them to get the make-up off after you get through."

"All right, I'll watch it."

"Now get out your costume, check every item that goes with it, and hang it on hooks. When you have more than one costume in an opera, hang each one on a separate hook, in the order you'll need them."

"O. K. What else?"

"Now we'll make you up."

She showed me how to put the foundation on, how to apply the color, how to put on the whiskers with gum arabic, and trim them up with a scissors so they looked right. They come in braids, and you ravel them out. She showed me about darkening under the eyes, and made me put on the last touches myself, so I could feel I looked right for the part. Then she had me put on the costume, and inspected me. I looked at myself in the mirror, and thought I looked like the silliest zany that ever came down the pike, but she seemed satisfied, so I shut up about it. "These whiskers tickle."

"They will till the gum dries."

"And they feel like they're falling off."

"Leave them alone. For heaven's sake, get that straight right now. Don't be one of those idiots that go around all night asking everybody if their make-up is in place. Put it on when you dress, and if you put it on right, it'll stay there. Then forget it."

"Don't worry. I'm trying to forget it."

"Around eight o'clock you'll get your first call. Take the hat and muffler with you, and be sure you put them in their proper place on the set. They go on the table near the door, and you put them on for your first exit."

"I know."

"When you've done that, read the curtain calls."

"To hell with curtain calls. If I ever—"

"Read your curtain calls! You're in some and not in others, and God help you if you come bobbing out there on a call that belongs to somebody else."

"Oh."

"Keep quiet. You can vocalize a little, but not much. When you feel your voice is up, stop."

"All right."

"Now I leave you. Good-bye and good luck."

I lit a cigarette, walked around. Then I remembered about the vocalizing. I tried a ha-ha, and it sounded terrible. It was dull, heavy, and lifeless, like a horn in a fog. I looked at my watch. It was twenty to eight. I got panicky that I had only a few minutes, and maybe couldn't get my voice up in time. I began to ha-ha, m'm-m'm, ee-ee, and everything I knew to get a little life into it. There was a knock on the door, and somebody said something in Italian. I took the hat and muffler, and went down.

They were all there, Cecil and the rest, all dressed, all walking around, vocalizing under their breaths. Cecil was in black, with a little shawl, and looked pretty. Just as I got down, the chorus came swarming in from somewhere, in soldier suits, plaid pants like mine, ruffled dresses, and everything you could think of. They weren't in the first act, but Rossi lined them up, and began checking them over. I went on the set and put the hat and muffler where she told me. The tenor came and put his hat beside mine. The basses came and moved both hats, to make more room on the table. There had to be places for their stuff when they came on, later. I went to the bulletin board and read the calls. We were all in the first two of the first act, Cecil, the tenor, the two basses, the comic, and myself, then for the other calls it was only Cecil and the tenor. On the calls for the other acts I was in most of them, but I did what she said, read them over carefully and remembered how they went.

"Places!"

I hurried out on the set and sat down behind the easel. I had already checked that the paint brush was in place. The tenor came on and took his place by the window. His name was Parma. He vocalized a little run, with his mouth closed. I tried to do the same, but nothing happened. I swallowed and tried again. This time it came, but it sounded queer. From the other side of the curtain there came a big burst of handclapping. Parma nodded. "Mario's in. Sound like nice 'ouse."

From where you sat out front, I suppose that twenty seconds between the time Mario got to his stand, and made his bow, and waited till a late couple got down the aisle, and the time he brought down his stick on his strings, was just twenty seconds, and nothing more. To me it was the longest wait I ever had in my life. I looked at the easel, and swallowed, and listened to Parma vocalizing his runs under his breath, and swallowed some more, and I thought nothing would ever happen. And then, all of a sudden, all hell broke loose.

Were you ever birdshooting? If you were, on your first time out, you know what I'm talking about. You were out there, in your new hunting suit, and the dogs were out there, and your friends were out there, and you were all ready for business when the first thing that hit you was the drumming of those wings. Then they were up, and going away from you, and it was time to shoot. But if you could hit anything with that thunder in your ears, you were a better man than I think you are. It was like that with me, when that orchestra sounded off. It was terrific, the most frightening thing I ever heard in my life. And it no sooner started than the curtain went up, except that I never saw it go up. All I saw was that blaze of the footlights in my eyes, so I was so rattled I didn't even know where I was. Cecil had warned me about it a hundred times, but you can't warn anybody about a thing like that. Light was hitting me from everywhere, and then I saw Mario out there, but he looked about a mile away, and my heart just stopped beating.

My heart stopped, but that orchestra didn't. It ripped through that introduction a mile a minute, and I knew then what Rossi had been trying to get through my head about speed. There's a page and a half of it in the score, and that looks like plenty of music, doesn't it? They ate it up in nothing flat, and next thing I knew they were through with it, and it was time for me to sing. Oh yes, I was the lad that had to open the opera. Me, the lousy four-flusher that was so scared he couldn't even breathe.

But they thought about that. Mario found me up there, and that stick came down on me, and it meant get going. I began to sing the phrase that begins *Questo Mar Rosso,* but I swear I had no more to do with it than a rabbit looking at a snake. That stick told my mouth what to do, and it did it, that was all. Oh yes, an operatic conductor knows buck fever when he sees it, and he knows what to do about it.

There was some more stuff in the orchestra, and I sang the next two phrases, where he says that to get even with the picture for looking so cold, he'll drown a Pharaoh. The picture is supposed to be the passage of the Red Sea. But I was to take the brush and actually drown one, and it was a second or two before I remembered about it. When I actually did it, I must have looked funny, because there was a big laugh. I was so rattled I looked around to see what they were laughing at, and in that second I took my eye off Mario. It was the place where I was supposed to shoot a *Che fai?* at the tenor. And while I was off picking daisies, did that conductor wait? He did not. Next thing I knew the orchestra was roaring again, and I had missed the boat. Parma sang the first part of his *Nel cielo bigi* at the window, then as he finished it he crossed in front of me, and it was murderous the way he shot it at me as he went by: "Watch da conductor!"

I watched da conductor. I glued my eyes on him from then on, and didn't miss any more cues, and by the help of hypnotism, prayer, and the rest of them shoving me around, we got through it somehow. What I never got caught up with was the speed. You see, when you learn those roles, and then coach them with a piano, you always think of them as a series of little separate scenes, and you take a little rest after each one, and smoke, and relax. But it's not like that at a performance. It goes right through, and it's cruel the way it sweeps you along.

I remembered the hat and muffler, and when I came off she was back there, smoking a cigarette, ready to go on. "You're doing all right. Sing to them, not to Mario."

She rapped at the door, sang a note or two, put her heel on the cigarette, and went on.

We had a little off-stage stuff coming, I and the two basses, and we stood in the wings listening to them out there, doing their stuff. I found out something about an operatic tenor. He doesn't shoot it in rehearsals, and he doesn't shoot it in the preliminary stuff either. He saves it for the place where it counts. Parma, who at the rehearsal hadn't shown enough even to make me look at him, uncorked a voice that was a beauty. He uncorked a voice, and he uncorked a style that even I knew was good. He took his aria, the *Che Gelida Manina,* slow and easy at first, he just drifted along with it, he made them wait until he was ready to give it to them. But when he did give it to them he had it. That high C near the end was a beauty, and well they knew it. Cecil sang better than I had ever heard her sing. I began to see what they were all talking about, why they paid her the dough.

I went out on the first two calls, like the bulletin said, but when we came in from the second, Parma whispered at me: "You hide, you. You hear me, guy? You keep out a way dat Mario!"

I didn't argue. I got behind some flats out there in the wings and stayed there. Cecil had heard him, and after a few minutes she found me there. "What happened?"

"I missed a cue."

"Well what's he talking about? He missed three."

"I wasn't watching the conductor."

"Oh."

"Is that bad?"

"It's the cardinal sin, the only unforgiveable sin, in all grand opera. Always watch him. Sing to them, try not to let them see you watch him. But—never let him out of your sight. He's the performance, the captain of the ship, the one on whom everything depends. Always watch him."

"I got it now."

The next act I was better. I was getting used to it now. I got a couple of laughs in the first part, and then when it came time for me to take up the waltz song he threw the stick on me and I gave her the gun. It got a hand, but he played through it to the end of the act. The Musetta and I did the carry-off we had practiced, and it went all right. The regular way is for Marcel to pick her up and run off with her, but she was small and I'm big, so instead of that, I threw her up on my shoulder and she kicked and waved, and the curtain came down to cheers. The third act I was all right, and we had another nice curtain. The four of us, Parma, I, Cecil, and the Musetta were in all the calls, and after we took the last one Parma followed me to the hole where I did my hiding. "O.K., boy. Now on a duet."

"Yeah?"

"Make'm *dolce*. Make'm nice, a sweet, no loud at all. No big dramatic. Nice, a sweet, a sad. Yeah?"

"I'll do my best."

"You do like I say, we knock hell out of'm. You watch."

So we went out there, and got through the gingerbread, and he threw down his pen and I threw down my paint brush, and we got out the props, and the orchestra played the introduction to the duet. Then he started to sing, and I woke up. I mean, I got it through my head that when that bird said *dolce* he meant *dolce*. He sang like that bonnet of Mimi's was some little bird he had in his hand, so it made a catch come in your throat to listen to him. When he hit the A he lifted his eyes, with the side of his face to the audience, and held it a little, and then melted off it almost with a sigh. When he did that he looked at me and winked. It was that wink that told me what I had to do. I had to put *dolce* in it. I came in on my beat and tried to do it like he did it. When it came to my little solo, I put tears in it. Maybe they were just imitation tears, but they were tears just the same. When I came to my high F sharp I swelled it a little, then pulled it in and melted off it just like he had melted off the A. When I got through the orchestra had a few bars, and he sat there shaking his head over the bonnet, and out of the side of his mouth he said: "You old son-bitch-bast."

We went into the finish, and laid it right on the end of Mario's stick, and slopped out the tears in buckets. Buckets, hell, we turned the fire hose on them. It stopped the show. They didn't only clap, they cheered, so we had to repeat it. That's dead against the rules, and Mario tried to go on, but they wouldn't let him. We got through the act, and Parma flopped on the bed for the last two *"Mimi's,"* and

the curtain came down to a terrific hand. We took our first two
bows, the whole gang that were in the act, and when we came back
from the second one, Mario was back there. Cecil yelled in my ear,
"Take him out, take him out!" So I took him out. I grabbed him by
one hand, she by the other, and we led him out on the next bow,
and they gave him a big hand, too. That seemed to fix it up about
that missed cue.

It was a half hour before I could start to dress. I went to my dressing room, and had just about got my whiskers pulled off when
about fifty people shoved in from outside, wanting me to autograph
their programs. It was a new one on me, but it's a regular thing at
every performance of grand opera, those people, mostly women,
they come back and tell you how beautifully you sang, and would
you please sign their program for them. So I obliged, and signed
"Logan Bennett." Then I got washed up and met Cecil and we got
a cab and went off to eat. "You hungry, Leonard?"

"As a mule."

"Let's go somewhere."

"All right."

We went to a night club. It had a dance floor, and tables around
that, and booths around the wall. We took a booth. We ordered a
steak for two, and then she ordered some red burgundy to go with
it, and sherry to start. That was unusual with her. She's like most
singers. She'll give you a drink, but she doesn't take much herself.
She saw me look at her. "I want something. I—want to celebrate."

"O.K. with me. Plenty all right."

"Did you enjoy yourself?"

"I enjoyed the final curtain."

"Didn't you enjoy the applause after the *O Mimi* duet? It brought
down the house."

"It was all right."

"Is that all you have to say about it?"

"I liked it fine."

"You mean you really liked it?"

"Yeah, I hate to admit it, but I *really* liked it. That was the prettiest music I heard all night."

The sherry came and we raised our glasses, clinked, and had a sip. "Leonard, I love it."

"You're better at it than in concert."

"You're telling me? I hate concerts. But opera—I just love it, and if you ever hear me saying again that I don't want to be a singer, you'll know I'm temporarily insane. I love it, I love everything about it, the smell, the fights, the high notes, the low notes, the applause, the curtain calls—everything."

"You must feel good tonight."

"I do. Do you?"

"I feel all right."

"Is it—the way you thought it would be?"

"I never thought."

"Not even—just a little bit?"

"You mean, that it's nice, and silly, and cock-eyed, that I should be here with you, and that I should be an opera singer, when all God intended me for was a dumb contractor, and that it's a big joke that came off just the way you hoped it would, and I never believed it would, and—something like that?"

"Yes, that's what I mean."

"Then yes."

"Let's dance."

We danced, and I held her close, and smelled her hair, and she nestled it up against my face. "It's gay, isn't it?"

"Yes."

"I'm almost happy, Leonard."

"Me too."

"Let's go back to our little booth. I want to be kissed."

So we went back to the booth, and she got kissed, and we laughed about the way I had hid from Mario, and drank the wine, and ate steak. I had to cut the steak left-handed, so I wouldn't joggle her head, where it seemed to be parked on my right shoulder.

We stayed a second week in Chicago, and I did my three operas over again, and then we played a week in the Music Hall in Cleveland, and then another week in Murat's Theatre, Indianapolis. Then Cecil's contract was up, and it was time for her to go back and get ready for the Metropolitan.

The Saturday matinee in Indianapolis was Faust. I met Cecil in the main dining room that morning, around ten o'clock, for breakfast, and while we were eating Rossi came over and sat down. He didn't have much to say. He kept asking the waiter if any call had come for him, and bit his fingernails, and pretty soon it came out that the guy that was to sing Wagner that afternoon couldn't come to the theatre, on account of unfortunately being in jail on a traffic charge, and that Rossi was waiting to find out if some singer in Chicago could come down and do it. His call came through, and when he came back he said his man was tied up. That meant somebody from the chorus would have to do it, and that wasn't so good. And then Cecil popped out: "Well what are we talking about, with *him* sitting here. Here, baby. Here's my key, there's a score up in my room; you can just hike yourself up there and learn it."

"*What?* Learn it in one morning and then sing it?"

"There's only a few pages of it. Now. Go."

"Faust is in French, isn't it?"

"Oh damn. He doesn't sing French."

But Rossi fixed that part up. He had a score in Italian, and I was to learn it in that and sing it in that, with the rest of them singing French. So the next thing I knew I was up there in my room with a score, and by one o'clock I had it learned, and by two o'clock Rossi had given me the business, and by three o'clock I was in a costume they dug up, out there doing it. That made more impression on them than anything I had done yet. You see, they don't pay much attention to a guy that knows three roles, all coached up by heart. They know all about them. But a guy that can get a role up quick, and go out there and do it, even if he makes a few mistakes, that guy can really be some use around an opera company. Rossi came to my dressing room after I finished Traviata that night and offered me a contract for the rest of the season. He said Mr. Mario was very pleased with me, especially the way I had gone on in Wagner, and was willing to work with me so I could get up more leading roles, and thought I would fit in all right with their plans. He offered me $150 a week, $25 more than I had been getting. I thanked him, thanked Mr. Mario for the interest he had taken in me, thanked all the others for a pleasant association with them, and said no. He came up to $175. I still said no. He came up to $200. I still said no and asked him not to bid any higher, as it wasn't a question of money. He couldn't figure it out, but after a while we shook hands and that was that.

That night she and I ate in a quiet little place we had found, and at midnight we were practically the only customers. After we ordered she said: "Did Rossi speak to you?"

"Yes, he did."

"Did he offer $150? He said he would."

"He came up to $200, as a matter of fact."

"What did you say?"

"I said no."

". . . Why?"

"What the hell? I'm no singer. What would I be trailing around with this outfit for after you're gone?"

"They play Baltimore, Philadelphia, Boston, and Pittsburgh before they swing West. I could visit you week-ends, maybe oftener than that. I—I might even make a flying trip out to the Coast."

"I'm not the type."

"Who is the type? Leonard, let me ask you something. Is it just because his $200 a week looks like chicken-feed to you? Is it because a big contractor makes a lot more than that?"

"Sometimes he does. Right now he doesn't make a dime."

"If that's what it is, you're making a mistake, no matter what a big contractor makes. Leonard, everything has come out the way I said it would, hasn't it? Now listen to me. With that voice, you can make money that a big contractor never even heard of. After just one season with the American Scala Opera Company, the Metropolitan will grab you sure. It isn't everybody that can sing with the American Scala. Their standards are terribly high, and very well the Metropolitan knows it, and they've raided plenty of Scala singers already. Once you're in the Metropolitan, there's the radio, the phonograph, concert, moving pictures. Leonard, you can be rich. You—you can't help it."

"Contracting's my trade."

"All this—doesn't it mean anything to you?"

"Yeah, for a gag. But not what you mean."

"And in addition to the money, there's fame—"

"Don't want it."

She sat there, and I saw her eyes begin to look wet. "Oh, why don't we both tell the truth? You want to get back to New York—for what's waiting for you in New York. And I—I don't want you ever to go there again."

"No, that's not it."

"Yes it is. I'm doing just exactly the opposite of what I thought I was doing when we started all this. I thought I would be the good fairy, and bring you and her together again. And now, what am I doing? I'm trying to take you away from her. Something I'd hate any other woman for, and now—I might as well tell the truth. I'm just a—home-wrecker."

She looked comic as she said it, and I laughed and she laughed. Then she started to cry. I hadn't heard one word from Doris since I left New York. I had wired her every hotel I had stopped at, and you would think she might have sent me a postcard. There wasn't even that. I sat there, watching Cecil, and trying to let her be a home-wrecker, as she called it. I knew she was swell, I respected everything about her, I didn't have to be told she'd go through hell for me. I tried to feel I was in love with her, so I could say to hell with New York, let's both stay with this outfit and let the rest go hang. I couldn't. And then the next thing I knew I was crying too.

7

WE HIT New York Monday morning, but there was a freight wreck ahead of us, so we were late, and didn't get into Grand Central until ten o'clock. She and I didn't go up the ramp together. I had wired Doris, so I went on ahead, but a fat chance there would be anybody there, so when nobody showed I put Cecil in a cab. We acted like I was just putting her in a cab. I said I'd call her up, she said yes, please do, we waved good-bye, and that was all. I went back and sent the trunk down to the office, then got in a cab with my bag and went on up. On the way, I kept thinking what I was going to say. I had been away six weeks, and what had kept me that long? On the Rochester part, I had it down pat. There had been stuff in the papers about grade-crossing elimination up there, and I went up to see if we could bid on the concrete. But what was I doing in those other places? The best I could think of was that I had taken a swing around to look at "conditions," whatever they were, and it sounded fishy, but I didn't know anything else.

When I got home I let myself in, carried my grip, and called to Doris. There was no answer. I went out in the kitchen, and there was nobody there. I took my grip upstairs, called to Doris again, knocked on the door of the bedroom. Still there was no answer. I went in. The bed was all made up, the room was in order, and no

Doris. The room being in order, though, that didn't prove anything, even at that time of day. Her room was always in order. I took the bag in the nursery, set it down, went out in the hall again, let out a couple more hallo's. Still nothing happened.

I went downstairs, began to get nervous. I wondered if she had walked out on me for good, and taken the children with her, but the house didn't smell like it had been locked up or anything like that. About eleven o'clock Nils came home. He was the houseman. He had been out taking the children to school, he said, and buying some stuff at a market. He said he was glad to see me back, and I shook hands with him, and asked for Christine. Christine is his wife, and does the cooking, and in between acts as maid to Doris and nurse to the children. He said Christine had gone with Mrs. Borland. He acted like I must know all about it, and I hated to show I didn't, so I said oh, of course, and he went on back to the kitchen.

About a quarter to twelve the phone rang. It was Lorentz. "Borland, you'd better come down and get your wife."

". . . What's the matter?"

"I'll tell you."

"Where is she?"

"The Cathedral Theatre. Come to the stage door. I'm at the theatre now. I'll meet you and take you to her."

I had a glimmer, then, of what was going on. I went out, grabbed a cab, and hustled down there. He met me outside, took me in, and showed me a dressing room. I rapped on the door and went in. She was on a couch, and a theatre nurse was with her, and Christine. She was in an awful state. She had on some kind of theatrical looking dress with shiny things on it, and her face was all twisted, and her hands were clenching and unclenching, and I didn't need anybody to tell me she was giving everything she had to fight back hysteria. When she saw me it broke. She cried, and stiffened on the couch, and then kept doubling up in convulsive jerks, where she was fighting for control, and turning away, so I couldn't see her face. The nurse took me by the arm. "It'll be better if you wait outside. Give me a few more minutes with her, and I'll have her in shape to be moved."

I went out in the corridor with Lorentz. "What's this about?"

"She got the bird."

"Oh."

There it was again, this thing that Cecil had said if I ever heard I'd never forget. I still didn't know what it was, but that wasn't what I was thinking about. "She sang here, then?"

"It didn't get that far. She went out there to sing. Then they let her have it. It was murder."

"Just didn't like her, hey?"

"She got too much of a build-up. In the papers."

"I haven't seen the papers. I've been away."

"Yeah, I know. Socialite embraces stage career, that kind of stuff. It was all wrong, and they were ready for her. Just one of those nice morning crowds in a big four-a-day picture house. They didn't even let her open her mouth. By the time I got to the piano the stage manager had to ring down. The curtain dropped in front of her, the orchestra played, and they started the newsreel. I never saw anything like it."

He stood there and smoked, I stood there and smoked, and then I began to get sore. "It would seem to me you would have had more sense than to put her on here."

"I didn't."

"Oh, you did your part."

"I pleaded with her not to do it. Listen, Borland, I'm not kidded about Doris, and I don't think you are either. She can't sing for buttons. She can't even get on the set before they've got her number. I tried my best to head her off. I told her she wasn't ready for it, that she ought to wait, that it wasn't her kind of a show. I even went to Leighton. I scared him, but not enough. You try to stop

Doris when she gets set on something."

"Couldn't you tell her the truth?"

"Could you?"

That stopped me, but I was still sore. "Maybe not. But you started this, just the same. If you knew all this, what did you egg her on for? You're the one that's been giving her lessons, from 'way back, and telling her how good she is, and—"

"All right, Borland, granted. And I think you know all about that too. I'm in love with your wife. And if egging her on is what makes her like me, I'm human. Yeah, I trade on her weakness."

"I've socked guys for less than that."

"Go ahead, if it does you any good. I've about got to the point where a sock, that would be just one more thing. If you think being chief lackey to Doris is a little bit of heaven, you try it—or maybe you have tried it. This finishes me with her, if that interests you. Not because I started it. Not because I egged her on. No—but I *saw* it. I was there, and *saw* them nail her to the cross, and rip her clothes off, and throw rotten eggs at her, and ask her how the vinegar tasted, and all the rest of it. That she'll never forgive me for. But why sock? You're married to her, aren't you? What more do you want?"

He walked off and left me. I found a pay phone, put in a call for a private ambulance. When it came I went in the dressing room again. Doris was up, and Christine was helping her into her fur coat. She was over the hysteria, but she looked like something broken and shrunken. I carried her to the ambulance, put her in it, made her lie down. Christine got in. We started off.

I carried her upstairs, and undressed her, and put her to bed, and called a doctor. Undressing Doris is like pulling the petals off a flower, and a catch kept coming in my throat over how soft she was, and how beautiful she was, and how she wilted into the bed. When the doctor came he said she had to be absolutely quiet, and gave her some pills to make her sleep. He left, and I closed the door, and sat down beside the bed. She put her hand in mine. "Leonard."

"Yes?"

"I'm no good."

"How do you know? From what Lorentz said, they didn't even give you a chance to find out."

"I'm no good."

"A morning show in a picture house—"

"A picture house, a vaudeville house, an opera house, Carnegie Hall—it's all the same. They're out there, and it's up to you. I'm just a punk that's been a headache to everybody she knows, and that's got wise to herself at last. I've got voice, figure, looks—everything but what it takes. Isn't that funny? Everything but what it takes."

"For me, you've got everything it takes."

"You knew, didn't you?"

"How would I know?"

"You knew. You knew all the time. I've been just rotten to you, Leonard. All because you opposed my so-called career."

"I didn't oppose it."

"No, but you didn't believe in it. That was what made me so furious. You were willing to let me do whatever I wanted to do, but you wouldn't believe I could sing. I hated you for it."

"Only for that?"

"Only for that. Oh, you mean Hugo, and Leighton, and all my other official hand-kissers? Don't be silly. I had to tease you a little, didn't I? But that only showed I cared whether you cared."

"Then you do care?"

"What do you think?"

She took my head in her hands, and kissed my eyes, and my brow, and my cheeks, like I was something too holy for her to be worthy to touch, and I was so happy I couldn't even talk. I sat there a long time, my head against hers, while she held my hand

against her cheek, and now and then kissed it. ". . . The pills are
working."

"You want to sleep?"

"No, I don't want to. I could stay this way forever. But I'm
going to. I can't help it."

"I'll leave you."

"Kiss me."

I kissed her, and she put her arms around me, and sighed a
sleepy little sigh. Then she smiled, and I tip-toed out, and I think
she was asleep before I got to the door.

I had a bite to eat, went down to the office, checked on the
trunk, had a look at what mail there was, and raised the windows
to let a little air in the place. Then I sat down at the desk, hooked
my heels on the top, and tried to keep my head from swimming
till it would be time to go back to Doris. I was so excited I wanted
to laugh all the time, but a cold feeling began to creep up my back,
and pretty soon I couldn't fight it off any more. It was about
Cecil. I had to see her, I knew that. I had to put it on the line, how
I felt about Doris, and how she felt about me, and there couldn't
be but one answer to that. Cecil and I, we would have to break. I
tried to tell myself she wouldn't expect to see me for a day or so,
that it would be better to let her get started on her new work, that
if I just let things go along, she would make the move anyway. It
was no good. I had to see her, and I couldn't stall. I walked around
to her hotel. I went past it once, turned around and walked past
it again. Then I came back and went in.

She had the same suite, the same piano, the same piles of music
lying around. She had left the door open when they announced
me from the lobby, and when I went in she was lying on the sofa,
staring at the wall, and didn't even say hello. I sat down and asked
her how she felt after the trip. She said all right. I asked her when
her rehearsals started. She said tomorrow. I said that was swell,

that she'd really be with an outfit where she could do herself justice. ". . . What is it, Leonard?"

Her voice sounded dry, and mine was shaky when I answered.
"Something happened."

"Yes, I heard."

"It—broke her up."

"It generally does."

"It's—made her feel different—about a lot of things. About—
quite a few things."

"Go on, Leonard. What did you come here to tell me? Say it.
I want you to get it over with."

"She wants me back."

"And you?"

"I want her back too."

"All right."

She closed her eyes. There was no more to say and I knew it. I
ought to have walked out of there then. I couldn't do it. I at least
wanted her to know how I felt about her, how much she meant
to me. I went over, sat down beside her, took her hand. ". . . Cecil,
there's a lot of things I'd like to say."

"Yes, I know."

"About how swell you've been, about how much I—"

"Good-bye, Leonard."

". . . I wanted to tell you—"

"There's only one thing a man ever has to tell a woman. You
can't tell me that. I know you can't tell me that, we've been all
over it—don't offer me consolation prizes."

"All right, then. Good-bye."

I bent over and kissed her. She didn't open her eyes, didn't move.
"There's only one thing I ask, Leonard."

"The answer is yes, whatever it is."

"Don't come back."

". . . What?"

80 *Three* OF A KIND

"Don't come back. You're going now. You're going with all my best wishes, and there's no bitterness. I give you my word on that. You've been decent to me, and I've no complaint. You haven't lied to me, and if it hasn't turned out as I thought it would, that's my fault, not yours. But—don't come back. When you go out of that door, you go out of my life. You'll be a memory, nothing more. A sweet, lovely, terrible memory, perhaps—but I'll do my own grieving. Only—don't come back."

"I had sort of hoped—"

"Ah!"

". . . What's the matter?"

"You had sort of hoped that after this little honeymoon blows up, say in another week, you could give me a ring, and come on over, and start up again just as if nothing had happened."

"No. I hoped we could be friends."

"That's what you think you hoped. You know in your heart it was something else. All right, you're going back to her. She's had a bad morning, and been hurt, and you feel sorry for her, and she's whistled at you, and you're running back. But remember what I say, Leonard: you're going back on her terms, not yours. You're still her little whimpering lapdog, and if you think she's not going to dump you down on the floor, or sell you to the gypsies, or put you out in the yard in your little house, or do anything else to you that enters her head, just as soon as this blows over, you're mistaken. That woman is not licked until you've licked her, and if you think this is licking her, it's more than I do, and more than she does."

"No. You're wrong. Doris has had her lesson."

"All right, I'm wrong. For your sake, I hope so. But—don't come back. Don't come running to me again. I'll not be a hot towel—for you or anybody."

"Then friendship's out?"

"It is. I'm sorry."

"All right."

"Come here."

She pulled me down, and kissed me, and turned away quick, and motioned me out. I was on the street before I remembered I had left my coat up there. I went in and sent a bellboy up for it. When he came down I was hoping he would have some kind of a message from her. He didn't. He handed me my coat, I handed him a quarter, and I went out.

When I got back to the house, the kids were home, and came running downstairs, and said did I know we were all going that night to hear Mamma sing. I said there had been a little change in the plans on that, and they were a little down in the mouth, but I said I had brought presents for them, and that fixed it all up, and we went running up to get them. I went in the nursery for my bag. It wasn't there. Then I heard Doris call, and we went in there.

"Were you looking for something?"

"Yes. Are you awake?"

"Been awake. . . . You *might* find it in there."

She gave a funny little smile and pointed to the dressing room. I went in there, and there it was. The kids began jumping up and down when I gave them the candy, and Doris kept smiling and talking over their heads. "I would have had Nils take your things out, but I didn't want him poking around."

"I'll do it."

"Where did you go?"

"Just down to the office to look at my mail."

"No, but I mean—"

"Oh—Rochester, Chicago, Indianapolis, and around. Thought it was about time to look things over."

"Did you have a nice trip?"

"Only fair."

"You certainly took plenty of glad rags."

"Just in case. Didn't really need them, as it turned out."

Christine called the kids, and they went out. I went over to her and took her in my arms. "Why didn't you want Nils poking around?"

"Well—do *you* want him?"

"No."

We both laughed, and she put her head against mine, and let her hair fall over my face, and made a little opening in front of my mouth, and kissed me through that. Oh, don't think Doris couldn't be a sweet armful when she wanted to be. "You glad to be back, Leonard? From Chicago—and the nursery?"

"Yes. Are you?"

"So glad, Leonard, I could—cry."

8

I KEPT letting her hair fall over my face, and holding her a little tighter, and then all of a sudden she jumped up. "Oh my God, the cocktail party!"

"What cocktail party?"

"Gwenny Blair's cocktail party. Her lousy annual stinkaroo that nobody wants to go to and everybody does. I said I'd drop in before the supper show, and I had completely forgotten it. The supper show, think of that. Wasn't I the darling little trouper then? My that seems a long time ago. And it was only this morning."

"Oh, let's skip it."

"What! And have them think I'm dying of grief? I should say not. We're going. And we're going quick, so we can leave before the whole mob gets there. Hurry up. Get dressed."

The last thing I wanted to do was go to Gwenny Blair's cocktail party. I wanted to stay where I was, and inhale hair. There was nothing to it, though, but to get dressed. I began changing my clothes, and she began pulling things out and muttering: ". . . No, not that. . . . It's black, and looks like mourning. . . . And not that. It makes me look too pale. . . . Leonard, I'm going to wear a suit."

"Well, why not?"

"A suit, that's it. Casual, been out all day, just dropped in, got to run in a few minutes, lovely party—it will be, like hell. That's it, a suit."

I always loved Doris when she dropped the act and came out as the calculating little wench that she really was. She heard me laugh, and laughed too. "Right?"

"Quite right."

She was dressed in five minutes flat, and for once she had to wait on me. The suit was dark gray, almost black, and cut so she looked slim as a boy. The blouse was light green, but with a copper tone in it, so it was perfect for her hair. Trust Doris not to put on anything that was just green. When I got downstairs she was pinning on a white camellia that had come on the run from the florist. Another woman would have had a gardenia, but not Doris. She knew the effect of those two shiny green leaves lying flat on the lapel.

"How do I look?"

How she looked was like some nineteen-year-old flapper that spent her first day at the races, cashed $27.50 on a $2 ticket, and was feeling just swell. But she didn't want hooey, she wanted the low-down, so I just nodded, and we started out.

It was only four or five blocks away, in a big penthouse on top of one of those apartment buildings on Park Avenue, so we walked. On the way, she kept damning Gwenny, and all of Gwenny's friends, under her breath, and saying she'd rather take a horse-whipping than go in and face them. But when we got there, she was all smiles. Only twenty or thirty people had shown up by then, and most of them hadn't heard of it. That was the funny thing. I had bought some papers on my way up from Cecil's, and two or three of them had nothing about it at all, and the others let it out with a line. In the theatrical business, bad news is no news. It's only the hits that cause excitement.

So they were all crowding around her with their congratulations, and wanted to know what it felt like to be a big headliner. Of course, that made it swell. But Doris leveled it out without batting an eye. "But I flopped! I'm not a headliner! I'm an *ex*-headliner!"

"You—! Come on, stop being funny!"

"I flopped. I'm out. They gave me my notice."

"*How* could you flop?"

"Oh please, please, don't ask me—it just breaks my heart. And now I can't go to Bermuda! Honestly, it's not the principle of the thing, it's the money! Think of all those lovely, lovely dollars that I'm not going to get!"

She didn't lie about it, or pretend that she had done better than she had done, or pretty it up in any way. She had too much sense for that. But in twenty seconds she had them switched off from the horrible part, and had managed to work it in that she must have been getting a terrific price to go on at all, and had it going her way. Leighton came in while she was talking, and said the publicity was all wrong, and he was going to raise hell about it. They all agreed that was it, and in five minutes they were talking about the Yale game Saturday.

She drifted over to me. "Thank God *that's* over. Was it all right?"

"Perfect."

"Damn them."

"Just a few minutes, and we'll blow. We've still got my bag to unpack."

She nodded, and looked at me, and let her lashes droop over her eyes. It was Eve looking at the apple, and my heart began to pound, and the room swam in front of me.

Lorentz came in. He didn't come over. He waved, and smiled, and Doris waved back, but looked away quick. "I'm a little out of humor with Hugo. He must have known. You did, didn't you? He could have given me some little hint."

I thought of what he had said, but I didn't say anything. I didn't care. I was still groggy from that look.

We got separated then, but pretty soon she had me by the arm, pulling me into a corner. "We've got to go. Make it quick with Gwenny, and then—*out*!"

"Why sure. But what's the matter?"

"The fool."

"Who?"

"Gwenny. I could kill her. She knows how crazy I've been about that woman, and how I've wanted to meet her, and now, today of all days she had to pick out—she's invited her! And she's coming!"

"What woman?"

"Cecil Carver! Haven't you heard me speak of her a hundred times? And now—I can't meet her today. I can't have her—pitying me! . . . Can I?"

"No. We'll blow."

"I'll meet you at the elevator— Oh my, there she is!"

I looked around, and Cecil was just coming in the room. I turned back to Doris, and she wasn't there.

She was with Wilkins, Cecil I mean. That meant she was going to sing. There wasn't much talk while Gwenny was taking her around. They piped down, and waited. They all had money, and position from 'way-back, but all they ever saw was each other. When a real celebrity showed up, they were as excited as a bunch of high school kids meeting some big-league ball player. I was still in the corner, and she didn't see me until Gwenny called me out. She caught her breath. Gwenny introduced me, and I said "How do you do, Miss Carver," and she said "How do you do, Mr. Borland," and went on. But in a minute she came back. "Why didn't you tell me you were coming here?"

"I didn't know it."

"Is she here?"

"Didn't Gwenny tell you?"

"No."

"It was on her account she asked you."

"*Her* account?"

"She's wanted to meet you. So I just found out."

"Gwenny didn't say anything. She called an hour ago and said come on up—and I wanted to go somewhere. I *had* to go somewhere. Why has she wanted to meet me?"

"Admires you. From afar."

"Only that?"

"Yes."

"Where is she?"

"Back there somewhere. In one of the bedrooms, would be the best bet. Hiding."

"From what?"

"You, I think."

"Leonard, what is this? She wants to meet me, she's hiding from me—what are you getting at? She's not a child, to duck behind curtains when teacher comes."

"I should say not."

"Then what is this nonsense?"

"It's no nonsense. Gwenny asked you, as a big favor to her.

But Gwenny hadn't heard about the flop. And on account of the flop, she'd rather not. Just—prefers some other time."

"And that's all?"

"Yeah, but it was an awful flop."

"You're sure you haven't told her about me? Gone and got all full of contrition, and made a clean breast of it, and wiped the slate clean, so you can start all over again—have you? *Have* you?"

"No, not a word."

She stood twisting a handkerchief and thinking, and then she turned and headed back toward the bedrooms. "Cecil—!"

"She had a flop, didn't she? Then I guess I'm the one she wants to talk to."

She went on back. I went over and had a drink. I needed one.

I was on my third when she came back, and I went over to her. "What happened?"

"Nothing."

"What did you say?"

"Told her to forget it. Told her it could happen to anybody— which it can, baby, and don't you forget it."

"What did she say?"

"Asked if it had ever happened to me. I told her it had, and then we talked about Hugo."

"He's here, by the way."

"Is he? She's not bad. I halfway liked her."

She still didn't look at me, but I had the same old feeling about her, of how swell she was, and thought I'd die if I couldn't let her know, anyway a little. "Cecil, can I say something?"

"Leonard, I cut my heart out after you left. I cut it out, and put it in the electric icebox, to freeze into—whatever a heart is made of. Jelly, I guess. Anyway my heart. So if you've got anything to say, you'd better go down there and see if it can still hear you. Me, I've got other things to do. I've got to be gay, and sing tra-la-la-la, and get my talons into the first man that—"

She saw Lorentz then, and went running over to him, and put her arms around him, and kissed him. It was gay, maybe, but it didn't make me feel any better.

Doris came out then, and I hurried to her. I didn't want to let on about Cecil, so I began right where we left off, and asked if she was ready to go. "Oh—the tooth's out now. I think she's going to sing. Let's stay."

"Oh—you saw her then?"

"She came back to powder. I didn't start it. She spoke to me. She remembered me. She came to my recital, you may recall."

"Oh yes, so she did."

"Don't ever meet your gods face to face, and especially not your goddesses. It's a most disillusioning experience. They have clay feet. My, what an awful woman."

"You didn't like her?"

"She knew about it. And she couldn't wait to make me feel better. She was just so tactful and sweet—and mean—that I just hated her. And did she love it. Did she enjoy purring over me."

"Maybe not. Maybe she meant it."

"Of course she meant it—her way."

"And what way is that?"

"Don't be so dense. Perhaps a man doesn't see through those things, but a woman does. Oh yes, she meant it. She meant every word of it—the cat. She was having the time of her life."

I could feel myself getting hot under the collar, and all my romantic humor was gone. After what Cecil had done, and what it had cost her to do it, this kind of talk went against my grain. "And what a frump. Did you ever see such a dress?"

"What's the matter with it?"

"Well—never mind. She did say one thing, though. To forget it. That it can happen to anybody, that it has even happened to her. 'All in a day's work, a thing you expect now and then, so what? Forget it and go on.' Leonard, are you listening?"

"I'm listening."

"That's it. Nothing has happened. How silly I was, to feel that way about it. I don't have to quit. I just go on. Why certainly. Even she had sense enough to know that."

I could hardly believe my eyes, and certainly not my ears. Here it had only been that morning when she was broken on the wheel, when she heard the gong ring for her if ever anybody did. And now, after just a few words from Cecil, she was standing there with her eyes open wide, telling herself that nothing had happened, that it was all just a dream. And all of a sudden, I knew that nothing *had* happened, and that it *was* all just a dream. She was the same old Doris, and it would be about one more day before we'd be right back where we always had been, with me having the fool career rubbed into me morning, noon and night, and everything else just as it was, only worse. I wondered if the way she was acting was what they call pluck. To me, it was not having sense enough to know when you've been hit with a brick.

A whole mob was there by then, and pretty soon Gwenny began to stamp her foot, and got them quiet, and she said Cecil was going to sing. But when Cecil stood up, it wasn't Wilkins that took the piano, it was Lorentz. She made a little speech, and told how he had played for her in Berlin, and how she would do one of the things they had done that night, and how she hoped it would go better this time, and he wouldn't have to yell the words at her from the piano, the way he had then. They all laughed, and she waited till they had found seats and got still, and then she sang the Titania song from Mignon.

She had made her little speech with her arm around Lorentz, and Doris looked like murder, and during the little wait she began to whisper. "That's nice."

"What's nice?"

"She brought her own accompanist, but oh no. She had to have Hugo."

"Well what of it?"

"Don't you see through it?"

"No. They seem to be old friends."

"Oh, *that*'s not it."

"And what *is* it?"

"She knows he's my accompanist, and that he's been attentive to me—"

"And how would she know that?"

"She must know it, from what I said. The first thing she asked me about was Hugo, and—"

"I thought Hugo was out."

"Maybe he is, but *she* doesn't know it. And these people don't know it. My goodness, but you're stupid about some things. Oh no, this I'll not forgive. The other, I pass over. But this is a public matter, and I'll get even with her for it, if I—"

The music started then. About the third bar Doris leaned over to me. "She's flatting."

I wanted to get out of there. I could smell trouble, especially after that crack about getting even. I said something about going, but there was as much chance of getting Doris out of there with that singing going on as there would have been of getting a rat away from a piece of cheese. All I could do was sit there.

After the Mignon, Cecil sang a little cradle song that's been written on Kreisler's Caprice Viennois, and then she came over to Doris. "How was I?"

"Marvelous! I never heard you better."

"I thought I was a little off, myself, but they seem to like it, so I guess it was all right. Do a duet with me?"

Now I ask you, was that being nice to Doris, or wasn't it? Because that was letting her right into the big league park, it was treating her as an equal, and in front of all her friends. Doris looked scared, and stammered something about how she'd love to, if only there was something they could get together on, and Cecil said: "How about *La Dove Prende*?"

"Why—that would be all right, but of course I only know the first part, and—"

"Fine. I'll do the second."

"If you really think I can—"

"Come on, come on, it'll do you good. You've got to ride the horse that threw you, haven't you? We'll knock 'em for a loop, and then good-bye to all that business this morning, and you'll feel fine."

"Well—"

Cecil went back to the piano and Doris put down her handbag. Her face was savage with jealousy, rage, and venom. She whispered to me: "Show me up, hey? We'll see about that!"

Wilkins took the piano, and they started. It was terrible. Mozart has to be sung to beat, and I think I told you Doris' ideas on rhythm. I saw Wilkins look up, but Cecil dead-panned, and they went on with her. She could have sung it backwards and that pair would have carried her through, so it got a hand. They had a little whisper, and then they sang the Barcarolle from the Tales of Hoffman. That was a little more Doris' speed, and a little more that mob's speed too, so they got a big hand on it, and started over to me.

As they left the piano, Doris put her arm around Cecil's waist, and I had a cold feeling that something was about to pop. They got to me, and I started to talk fast, about how fine they had sounded, anything I could think of. They laughed, and Cecil turned to Doris. "Well—how was the support?"

"Oh fine—even if you do try to steal my men."

Doris laughed as she said it, and it wasn't supposed to be such a hell of a dirty crack. It was just a preliminary. I could give you the rest of the talk, almost word for word, the way she intended it to go. First Cecil was supposed to look surprised, and then Doris would apologize, and laugh some more, and say it was only intended as a joke. Then it would come out about Lorentz, and Doris would say please, please, he didn't mean a thing to her—really. And then would come the real dirty crack, something that would mean Lorentz wasn't really worth having, and if Cecil was interested in him she could have him, and welcome.

That was how it was supposed to go, I can guarantee you, knowing Doris. But it never got that far. Cecil winced like she had been hit with a whip. Then she looked me straight in the eye, the first time she had, all day. "Leonard, why did you lie to me?"

"I didn't."

"You did. You let me go to her, and you swore you hadn't told a word—"

She tried to bite it back. It wasn't what I said. It was the look on Doris' face that stopped her. She knew, then, what Doris had really meant, but it was too late. We all three stood there, and Doris looked first at Cecil, and then at me. Then she gave a little rasping laugh, and her eyes were as hard as glass. ". . . Ah—so that was what you were doing in Rochester, and Syracuse, and Columbus, and Chicago, and—"

"I—"

"Don't give me that foolish story again, about looking things over. I've followed her. I've followed her whole career since—I know everything she's done! She sang in all those places, and you—! The fool that I was! I never once thought of it!"

Cecil licked her lips. "Mrs. Borland, I'm sure I've never meant a thing to your husband—"

"Miss Carver, I don't believe you."

Cecil closed her eyes, opened them again, grabbed for the one last thing she could say. "We saw quite a lot of each other, that's true. We could hardly help that. We were singing together. We were singing in the same opera company, and—"

Doris gave a shrieking laugh, and half the room stopped talking and turned around. Gwenny came up, Doris put her head on her shoulder and kept on with that laugh. Then she turned to them all. "Oh my—isn't that funny? If they took a trip together—I don't mind. It means nothing to me—let them enjoy life while they're young. But darlings! Singing together! In the same—I can't stand it! Imagine Leonard—singing—ha-ha-ha-ha-ha-ha!"

Gwenny decided to play it funny. She laughed too. A few others laughed. Then she decided to get witty. "Perhaps he'll sing us something! —From Pagliacci!"

If that was what she said, I think I could have stood it. But that wasn't it. That was only what she thought she said. What she really said was, "From Polly-achy," and at the dumb, ignorant way she pronounced that word, something in me cracked. All the rotten, phoney, mean, cruel stuff I had taken off Doris, and all the stuff I had taken off Gwenny and her kind, came swelling up in my throat, and I knew I was going to kick over the apples or bust. I turned to Gwenny. "Since you ask me, I think I will."

I went in the dining room and found Wilkins. He hadn't heard any of it. "Feeling like playing for me?"

"Sure. What'll it be?"

"How about the Prologue from Pagliacci?"

"The Prologue it is."

We went in and there was a laugh, and they all started to whisper. He started the introduction, and they looked at each other, and looked at me, and looked at Doris. They were her friends, remember, not mine. Cecil came over. "I wouldn't, baby. It was awful, but—I wouldn't. You'll regret it."

"Maybe."

She went away, and I started to sing. At the first *Si puo* Doris sank into a chair. She didn't turn white. She turned gray. I went on. Maybe Tibbett can do it better than I did it that day, but I doubt it. He couldn't take the interest in it, you might say, that I took. I rolled it out and my head felt light and dizzy, because I could see every note of it going like a knife into her heart. When I got to the andante I gave it the gun, and when I reached the high A flat I stepped into it with a smile on my face, and held it, and swelled it, until the room began to shake, then I pulled it in, and cut. I closed it out solemn as I knew, as though a real performance was about to start, and I wanted them to get it all straight.

Wilkins played the finish, and waited. Nothing happened. They sat there like they were frozen, and then they began to talk, as if I wasn't there. He looked up at me, like he was in a madhouse or something. I smiled at him, and bowed three times, the way I was taught, center, left and right. Then I went over and poured myself a drink. When I turned around, Doris was leaving the room. She walked like she had just gone blind.

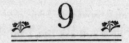

9

I DON'T know how I got out of there. But pretty soon I was down on the twelfth floor, where you change from the private elevator that runs up to the penthouse, to the main cars. Cecil was there, with Wilkins. She was leaning against the wall talking, with her head back against it, and her eyes closed, and he was standing close, listening to her like he thought somebody must be crazy. When they saw me they stopped. We went down, and when we got on the street a cab came up. He offered us a lift, but he had a dinner date uptown instead of down, so I told him to take the cab and I sent the doorman after another one. He went off, and I stood there looking Cecil up and down, and decided she was what

I wanted in the way of a woman, and that I was going to hook up with her for the rest of my life. Maybe the love part wouldn't be so hot, anyway on my part, but I had had all I wanted of that. She was decent, and you could stick to her, and not feel you had a viper on your chest every time you put your arms around her. I hooked my arm in hers, and pressed it, and tried to get over what I felt.

The doorman came, riding the running board of the cab, and I put her in. I fished in my pocket to tip him, but when I tried to get in, the cab was moving away, and all I could see was a gloved hand waving at me from the window. In another second it was gone.

I started down the street. Then I wondered where I was going. Here I had just made a decision that was to change my whole life, and now it seemed to have evaporated into thin air. I crossed Park, and headed for home. My legs felt queer, and I couldn't seem to walk straight. I remembered I had had four drinks. Then I heard myself laugh. It was like hell the four drinks.

I let myself in, and the hall was dark, and upstairs I could hear Evelyn crying. I opened my mouth to call, and nothing came out of it. I groped for the switch. Then I heard a rustle behind me. I half turned, and felt something horrible coming at me. It hit me. She was panting like an animal, and got my face with both hands at once. I went down, and those claws raked me. I must have let out some kind of a yell, because one hand grabbed my mouth, and the other hand raked me again. I tried to throw her off, and couldn't. She held me, and pounded my head against the floor. Then I felt myself being beaten with something. The marks afterward showed it was the heel of her shoe. And all the time she was talking to me, not loud, but in a terrible whisper: ". . . You would do that to me . . . You beast . . . You swine . . . You can have her . . . What do I care who you have . . . But that . . .

But *that* . . . Get out of here . . . Get out of here! *Get out of here!* . . ."

Her voice rose to a scream at that, and upstairs both children began to wail, and I threw her off, and got the door open, and staggered down the steps to the street.

Next thing I knew, I was in Central Park, on a bench. I still had the light topcoat on, that I had worn to the party, but I didn't have my hat. The coat sleeve was down over my hand. I felt the shoulder. It was torn. Something tickled my mouth. I brushed it off, and it was blood. Then I saw blood on the coat. I took out my handkerchief, and my whole face was running blood. I wiped it, and wiped it again, until the whole handkerchief was nothing but a red rag, and it kept on bleeding. I tried to think where I was going to go. I couldn't go to a good hotel. I remembered a dump on Twenty-third Street, where I had once made a speech to a banquet of equipment manufacturers, flagged a cab, and went down there.

I pushed through the revolving door, and hated to cross the lobby. The clerk looked up, with his plastered-on smile, and it stayed plastered on, when he saw me, like in one of those movies where they stop the camera a second, to get a laugh. He swung his turntable around, but slow, like he hated to do it. I registered:

Leonard Borland   City

While I was writing, his hand wandered to the key rack, and then it wandered to a button, and pressed it. In a second a big gimlet-eyed guy was standing beside me, and everything about him said house detective. They looked at each other. The clerk swung the turntable around again, read my card, and spoke mechanically, while he was blotting it, like an announcement on an old-time phonograph record: "Single room, Mr. Borland? We have them at a dollar-and-a-half, two and two-and-a-half. With bath, three, four and five."

"I want a bedroom, bath and sitting room."

I needed a sitting room about as much as an ourang-outang does, but I had to say something to take them off guard. I was in terror they'd give me the bum's rush across that lobby. If they tried that, I didn't know what I would do. I might take the joint apart, and I might do nothing, and just land in the gutter, and that was what I dreaded most of all.

They looked at each other again. "We have a very nice suite on the tenth floor, outside—bedroom, bath, sitting room, and small kitchenette with ice box—seven dollars."

"That'll be all right."

"Ah—have you luggage, Mr. Borland?"

"No."

I took out my bill-fold. I still had a hunk of cash that I'd brought back from the trip, and I laid down a $50 bill. They relaxed, and so did I, and began to talk like myself. "Have you a house doctor?"

"No, but we have one on call."

"Will you get him, and send him up to me as quick as you can? I've—been in an accident."

"Yes, sir. Right away, Mr. Borland."

The house dick took charge of me then. He put his arm around me like I could hardly walk, and called a boy, and took me up to my room, and talked like I had been in a taxi accident, and said it was a crime the way those guys drove. If anybody could get a face like mine in a taxi accident, it would be a miracle, but it was his way of saying everything was O. K., that there would be no questions asked, that he'd take care of me. "You haven't had dinner yet, Mr. Borland?"

"No, I haven't."

"I'll send the waiter up right away."

"Fine."

"Or maybe you'd rather wait till you've seen the doctor? Tell you what I'll do. I'll send the waiter up now, and after the doc gets through, you ring room service and tell them you're ready. I recommend the turkey, sir. They've got nice roast turkey on the bill tonight, fine, young, Vermont turkey, from our farm up there— and the chef has a way with it. He really has, sir."

"Turkey sounds all right."

They sent the coat out to be cleaned and fixed up, and had a boy go down and buy me pajamas on Fourteenth Street, and the doctor came and plastered me up, and I had the turkey and a bottle of wine with it. I kept the waiter while I ate, and we talked and we got along fine. But then he took the table down, and I was alone, and I went in and had a hot bath, and by then it was about half past nine, and there wasn't anything to do but go to bed. I took off my clothes, and put on the Fourteenth Street pajamas, and got in bed, and pulled up their sleazy cotton blankets, and lay there looking at the paper, where it was beginning to peel off the walls. I tried to think what there was funny about that paper. Then I remembered that paper hadn't been used on hotel walls for fifteen years. Only the old ones have paper.

I turned off the light and tried to sleep. I didn't seem to be thinking about anything at all. But every time I'd drop off I'd wake up, dreaming I was standing there, bellowing at the top of my lungs, and nobody would even turn around and look at me. Then one time this horrible thing was coming at me in the dark, and I woke up moaning. I tried to get to sleep again, and couldn't. I told myself it was just a dream, to forget it, but it wasn't just a dream. I must have dropped off, though, because here it was, coming at me again, and this time I wasn't moaning, I was sobbing. I quit kidding myself then. I knew I'd give anything to have it back, what I had pulled at the party that afternoon. It wasn't brave, it wasn't big, it was just plain silly. I had made a jackass of myself, and put something terrible between me and Doris. I began thinking of her, then, and knew it didn't make any difference what she had done to me, or anything else. I wanted her so bad it was just a terrible ache, wanted her worse than ever. And here I was, I had no wife, I had no home, I had no kids, I had no work, I didn't even have Cecil. I was in this lousy dump, and had just made a mess of my life. I think I hit an all-time low that night. I never felt worse. I couldn't feel worse.

❧ 10 ❧

THREE DAYS later, when I could leave, I went up and took a suite at a hotel in the fifties. I took it by the month. I didn't hear anything from Doris. I began reading the society pages after a couple of days, and she was in. Every time I saw her name I saw Leighton's. On the singing, I never opened my trap. One day a guy showed up at the office by the name of Horn. He sat down, and kept looking around kind of puzzled at the drafting room, and in a minute I asked him pretty sharp what he wanted.

"You're Mr. Borland? Mr. Leonard Borland?"

"Yes, I'm Leonard Borland."

"Well—I got the address out of the phone book, but it certainly doesn't look like the right place, and you don't look like the right guy. What are you, in the construction business?"

"That's right."

"I'm looking for the Leonard Borland that sang with the American Scala Opera Company under the name of Logan Bennett. Anyway, I hear he did."

"Where did you hear that?"

"I was in Pittsburgh last week. I heard it from a friend of mine. Giuseppe Rossi."

". . . Well? What of it?"

He knew then he had the right guy, and kept looking me over. "I tell you what of it. I'm connected with this outfit that's giving opera over at the Hippodrome, and—"

"Not interested."

"Rossi said you were pretty good."

"Nice guy, Rossi. Remember me to him if you see him."

"I need a baritone."

"Still not interested."

"If you're as good as he says you are, I could make you a pretty nice proposition. You understand, a singer's no draw until he gets known, but I could offer you $125 a night, say, with three appearances a week guaranteed. That's a little more than Rossi was paying you, isn't it?"

"Yeah, quite a little."

"Well—will you think it over?"

"No, won't think it over."

"Listen, I need a baritone."

"So I judge."

"I got a couple of good tenors, and another one coming. I got a couple of sopranos I think are comers. But in opera, you've got to have one good baritone before you've got a show."

"You certainly have."

"All right then, I'll come up a little. How about a hundred and fifty?"

"Maybe you didn't understand what I said when you came in here. I appreciate what you say, I'm grateful to Rossi,—but I'm just not interested."

The idea of singing made me sick. He went and I put on my hat and engaged in my favorite outdoor sport, about that time. That was walking around the Metropolitan Opera House hoping I'd see Cecil. A couple of days after that I did see her. I raced back to the office as fast as I could get there, and put in a call for her at her hotel. They said she wasn't in. I knew she wouldn't be. That was why I had been watching. I left word that Mr. Borland called. Then for a week I stuck at my desk from nine to six, hoping she would call back. She never did.

All that, what I've just been telling you, was in the last part of November. When the first of December came, it crossed my mind it was funny no bills had been forwarded to me. On the third I found out why. When I came downstairs in the morning and crossed the lobby, the clerk called me and he had my check in his hand, the one I had given him for my next month's room rent. It had bounced. I blinked at it, and I knew then why there hadn't been any bills. Doris was paying her own bills. The money was in a joint account, in her name and mine, and she had drawn every cent of it out, started an account somewhere else, and there I was. I don't know why it never occurred to me that she would do it. It never entered my head.

I said there must be some mistake, and I would see him that afternoon. I went out, and hustled over to Newark, and borrowed $300 from a manufacturer of power shovels we had done some business with. I got back just in time to get in the bank, so I could cover that check before they closed, then went back and told the clerk it was all right, I had drawn on the wrong account, and he could put it through. I went up to my suite and counted my money. I had $75 over what I had deposited in the bank, and $7 over that. My expenses, over the $170 a month I was paying for the suite, were about $50 a week, not counting club dues and other things I couldn't stave off very long. I was just about a week and a half from the boneyard, and I began to feel it again, that thick rage against Doris and the way she treated me. It would suit her fine, I knew, to have me coming on my knees to her, begging for money, and then give me a song and dance about how she had the children to think of, and send me out with the $12 she could spare from the crumbs she was saving for the household. I didn't have to be told how that would go. I walked around the suite, and after a while something in me clicked. I knew I'd never go to her if I starved first. I began to think about Horn and his $150 a night.

Next day he called up. "Mr. Borland?"

"Yes?"

"This is Bert Horn again. Remember?"

"Oh yeah. How are you?"

"All right. Listen, my other tenor got to town last night. Fact of the matter, I stole him off Rossi and that was what I was doing in Pittsburgh. Guy by the name of Parma. You know him?"

"Yeah, I sang with him. Tell him I said hello."

"I will, and he said tell you hello. Listen, if you're as good as *he* says you are, I might raise that offer. I might up the ante to $200."

"Well now you're talking. Come on over."

He came, and looked me over again, and the place over again, and then he laughed and shook his head. "Well, if you're a singer you're the funniest-looking thing in the way of a singer that I ever saw. No offense, but I swear to God you don't look it."

"You play?"

"Some kind of way, yes."

"Come on up."

I took him up on the third floor, where the piano was, and opened the windows, and shoved the Traviata aria in front of him. He played it and I sang it. When I got through he nodded. "I guess they weren't kidding me."

We went down again, and he got down to cases. "All right, how many roles do you know?"

"Three."

". . . Just three."

"Marcel, Germont, and Rigoletto. I sang one other role, but it was a pinch-hitting job, and I wouldn't know it now if I heard it."

"What role was it?"

"Wagner in Faust. I don't sing French, but they let me do it in Italian. They shoved it at me in the morning, I sang it that afternoon, and I had forgotten it by night."

That made the same impression on him it had on the others. An opera impresario, he's a little like a baseball manager. He knows all about smoke. He gets that every day. But a guy that can come out of the bull-pen and finish a ball game, that's different. When he heard that, he quit worrying, and began to lay it out what I'd have to do. The hitch came over the guarantee. With just those three operas, he couldn't make it three times a week, because they weren't giving Traviata on a weekly schedule. He wanted me to get up Trovatore, Lucia, and Aïda, and then later Don Giovanni, and they would revive it if they thought I was right for it. I said I couldn't get up that many roles by the end of the winter if I had to sing three times a week too. So then he had a different idea. "All right, we'll say Lucia and Trovatore, but get Pagliacci up by next week, and then we can put you on three times. You see, ham-and-eggs is once a week too, and—"

". . . What is?"

"Ham and eggs. Cavalleria Rusticana and Pagliacci, the double bill. Pagliacci you can get up quick. After the prologue, which I suppose you know, you have almost nothing to do, just two real scenes, not over ten minutes of actual singing altogether. Then we can—"

"Oh. All right then."

"You'll need a coach. I recommend Lorentz. Hugo Lorentz, I'll give you his address, a good man, works with us, and—"

"You know anybody else?"

". . . Well, there's Siegal. He's more of a voice teacher, but he knows the routines, and—"

"Fine, I'll take him. When do we start?"

"Next week. Get Pagliacci up by then, and then later we can

work you in on the others. But we want to bring you out in Rigoletto. That makes you important."

"Nothing I like so well as to be important."

So by that afternoon I had connected with Siegal, and was back
in the same old groove. I found out then how much Cecil had been
giving me for nothing. Do you know what that bird took? He
charged me $25 an hour, and I had to have him every day. I had
to borrow $200 more in Newark, and it was an awful crimp in my
$600 a week. But at that, $450 was nothing to be sneezed at.

I asked for a rehearsal on Rigoletto, with three or four of the
choristers. In the scene before the courtiers there was some stuff
I wanted to do, and I had to make them slam me down so I really
hit the deck, so when I came crawling back to them I would really
be on my knees. They told me to come over to the theatre. I went
up to the third floor and put on an old suit of corduroys I always
wore around concrete work, and walked over. That was so I
could practice the stage falls. I hadn't remembered about the Hippodrome, while Horn was talking. I mean, it just sounded like a
theatre on Sixth Avenue, and nothing more. So when I went in
the stage door and through, the stage caught me by surprise. I
don't know if you were ever back there to see that stage. It would
have done pretty good for a railroad station if they laid tracks and
put train sheds in, except there would be an awful lot of waste space
up top. But did it feaze me? It did not. I was a pro now. I walked
to the middle of it, let out a couple of big ones, and it felt pretty
good. I stuck out my chest. I thought how I was putting it over on
Doris, and how like hell I would come begging her for anything.

The conductor, Gustav Schultz, was at the piano, and we went
through it. I think he wanted to look me over. I showed them how
I wanted them to heave me, and after a while they got it so it
suited me. When we quit, I saw Parma in the wings, and went

over and shook hands. "Hello boy, hello, how's a old kid?"

"Fine. How's yourself?"

"O. K. Say, is swell, how you do this scene. What da hell? A goddam baritones, run for a bedroom, make little try, audience all a time wonder why he don't get in. Look like he must be weak. Ought to fight like hell, just like you do'm now, and then *pow!*— down he go, just like this!"

He threw his shoulder under my belly, and I went head over heels on to the floor. It was one stage fall I didn't expect. Then he laughed like hell. Singers, they're a funny breed. They've got what you might call a rudimentary sense of humor, in the first place, and they're awful proud of their muscles, in the second place. They spend half their time telling the conductor they're going to knock him back into the customers' laps if he doesn't quit his cussedness, and I'll say for them they could do it if they tried. People think they're a flock of fairies. They're more like wrestlers. Well, singing doesn't come from the spirit. It comes from the belly, and it takes plenty of belly and chest to do it right.

I got up, and laughed, and he and Schultz and I went out and had a drink. He took red wine with seltzer. They don't drink much, but a wop tenor likes red ink.

The afternoon of the performance I put off lunch till three o'clock, then went out and had a good one. I came back to the office and vocalized my voice. I came up quick, and felt good. I was beginning to get nervous. They all get nervous, but this was different from what I had felt before. It had a little tingle to it. I felt I was good. I walked up to the hotel and it was about half past four. I lay down and got a little sleep.

It seemed funny to be putting the make-up on without Cecil bobbing in to give me the double O, but I got it in place, and put on the funny clothes, and tried my voice. It was still up, and was all right. Horn came in, looked me over, and nodded. "The contracts are ready."

"You got them with you?"

"My secretary's bringing them over. I'll be in with them after the show. How do you feel?"

"I feel all right."

There came a knock on the door, and a little wop in a derby hat came in and stood beside me where I was at the table and began to talk about how some of my admirers wanted to hear me sing, but their tickets would cost them a lot, and more stuff like that, and I didn't know what the hell he was talking about, except it seemed to be some kind of a touch. Horn was behind him. He nodded and held up ten fingers. I got my pocketbook, passed out $10 and the guy left. "What was that?"

"The claque."

"What's the claque?"

"A bunch of self-elected noise-makers, that you pay to clap when you sing, and whether they do or not nobody knows. If you don't pay, they're supposed to take some terrible revenge, like blowing whistles at you or something like that. Whether they do or not, nobody knows. I generally go along with them, and so do the singers. They're harmless, just one of those things that opera has like a dog has fleas."

"There was nothing like that in the American Scala."

"Maybe they took care of it for you."

He went, and I wished everything that came up didn't remind me of Cecil. I knew who had taken care of it all right, without being told. And I knew why. Knowing the applause was paid, or any part of it was paid, would have taken all the fun out of it for me. So it was taken care of. I tried my voice again, then remembered she had told me when it was right to leave it alone. There didn't seem to be any help for it. Everywhere I turned, she was standing there beside me.

I went down, then walked over and had a look at the calls. Then my heart skipped a beat. On the first two calls at the end of the second act, we were all in it, me, Parma, the Gilda, and the people in the small parts. Then on the next two it was just the Gilda and me. And then it said:

Mr. Borland (If)

I walked out on the stage to get the feel of the set, and the tingle was clear down to my feet. I made up my mind there wasn't going to be any *if* about it. I was going to get that call or split my throat.

Parma was right in the *Questa o Quella,* so Act I got off to a swell start, and they ripped right along with it. I got a hand when I came on, whether it was the claque or the publicity I don't know, but I don't think it could have all been claque. There had been a lot of stuff in the papers about me. I was singing under my own name now, and it seemed to strike them as a good story that a big contractor should turn into a singer, but anyway it made me feel good, and I hit it right in the scene with the second baritone, and we got a fine curtain. Hippodrome opera wasn't like Metropolitan opera. It was 99-cent opera, and that audience acted the way it felt. The second scene of the act went even better. The bass was a pretty good comic, and I fed to him all I could, so we got away with the duet in swell shape. The Gilda was all right in the *Caro Nome,* not like Cecil, but plenty good. The duets went well, and we got another good curtain, and were on our way.

When it came to the scene before the courtiers, the one I had rehearsed with the choristers, I did it a little different than I had been doing it. I got a break at the start. The Ceprano had one of these small, throaty baritones, and when it came to the place where I was to mock him on *Ch' hai di nuovo, buffon,* I shot it back to him just the way he had given it to me, and it got a big laugh. I had them then, and I chucked tone quality out the window. The first part of the scene I shouted, talked, and whispered, till I got to the place where they slammed me back on my hunkers. Then I remembered Bohême. I came crawling back, and plucked the hem of Marullo's doublet, and gave them tears. I sang it *dolce,* and then some. I opened every spigot there was, and at the end of it I was flat on the floor, hanging on to the high F like my heart would break, and finishing off like I could just barely make myself do it. There wasn't any pause then. The first "bravo" came like a pistol shot before I even got through, and then they came from all over the house, and the applause in a swelling roar. I lay there, the heart bowed down, for quite a time. There were thousands of them, and it took them longer to quiet down than in other places. The Gilda came running on, then, and we did the duet, and the curtain came down.

Did I get that call? I'm telling you I did. I took the Gilda out twice, and then Parma aimed a kick at me, and then there I was, in front of them all alone, trying to remember how to bow. There's nothing like it.

I went to my dressing room, walked around, and was so excited I couldn't even sit down. I wanted to go out there and do it all over again. It didn't seem two minutes before they called me, and I went down for the last act.

The Gilda and I did the stuff that starts it, and then went off, and Parma had it to himself for the *La Donna e Mobile*. I think I've given you the idea by now that that dumb wop is a pretty good tenor. He knocked them over with it, and by the time the Maddalena came on, and the Gilda and I went out again for the quartet, we were in the homestretch of one of those performances you read about. So the quartet started. Well, you've heard the Rigoletto quartet a thousand times, but don't let anybody tell you it's a pushover. The first part goes a mile a minute, the second part slower than hell, and if there's one thing harder to sing than a fast allegro it's a slow andante, and three times out of five something happens, and many times as you've heard it you haven't often heard it right. But we were right. Parma started it like a breeze, and the Maddalena was right on top of him, and the Gilda and I were right on top of her, and we closed out the allegro with all four cylinders clicking and the show doing seventy. Parma laid it down nice on the andante, and we were right with him, and we brought it home just right. We were right on the end of the stick. Well, that stopped the show too. They clapped, and cheered, and clapped some more, and Schultz threw the stick on me to go on, and a fat chance I could. We had to give them some more. So after about a minute, Schultz played the cue for the andante, and Parma started again.

He started, and the Maddalena came in, and the Gilda came in, and I came in. It seemed to me we got in there with it awful quick, but I was so excited by that time I hardly knew where I was, and I didn't pay much attention to it. And then all of a sudden I had this awful feeling that something was wrong.

I want you to get it straight now, what happened. The andante is the same old tune, *Bella figlia dell' amore,* that you've heard all your life and could whistle in your sleep. The tenor sings it through once, then he goes up to a high B flat, holds it, comes down again, and sings it over again. The second time he sings it, the contralto comes in, then the soprano, then the baritone, and they're off into the real quartet. Well, our contralto, the Maddalena, was an old-time operatic hack that had sung it a thousand times, but something got into her, and instead of waiting for Parma to finish that strain once, she came in like she would on the repeat. And she pulled the Gilda in. And the Gilda pulled me in. You remember what I told you about speed? Up there you've got no time to think. You hear your cue, and you come in, and

God help you if you miss the boat. So there was Parma and there
was the orchestra, in one place in the score, and there were the
Maddalena, the Gilda, and me, in another place in the score, and
there was Schultz, trying like a wild man to straighten it out. Not
a whisper from the audience, you understand. So long as you keep
going, and do your best, they'll give you a break, and even if you
crack up and have to start over they'll give you a break—so long
as you do your best. They all want to laugh, but they won't—so
long as you keep your head down and sock.

But I didn't know then what was wrong. All I knew was that
it was getting sourer by the second, and I started looking around
for help. That was all they needed. That one little flash of the
white feather, and they let out a roar.

You can think of a lot of things in one beat of music. It flashed
through my head I had heard the bird at last. It flashed through
my head, in some kind of a dumb way, why I had heard it. I
turned around and faced them. I must have looked sore. They
roared again.

That whole big theatre then was spinning around for me like a
cage with a squirrel in it, and me the squirrel. I had to know where
I was at. I looked over, and tried to see Parma. And then, brother,
and then once more, I committed the cardinal sin of all grand
opera. I forgot to watch the conductor. I didn't know that he had
killed his orchestra, killed his singers, brought the whole thing to
a stop, and was wigwagging Parma to start it over. And here I
came, bellowing out with my part:
Taci e mia sara la cura, la vendetta d'affretar!
They howled. They let out a shriek you could hear in Harlem.
Some egg yelled "Bravo!" A hundred of them yelled "Bravo!" A
million of them yelled "Bravo," and applauded like hell.
I ran.

Next thing I knew, I was by a stairway, holding on to the iron railing, almost twisting it out by the roots trying to keep myself from flying into a million pieces. The Gilda was beside me, yelling at me at the top of her lungs, and don't think a coloratura soprano can't put on a nice job of plain and fancy cussing when she gets sore. The stagehands were standing around, looking at me as though I was some leper that they didn't dare touch. Outside, Schultz was playing the introduction to the stuff between the contralto and the bass. He had had to skip five whole pages. I just stood there, twisting at those iron bars.

Somewhere off, I heard the fire door slam, and next thing I knew, Cecil was there, her eyes big as saucers with horror. She grabbed hold of me. "You go out there and finish this show, or I'll—"

"I can't!"

"You've got to! You've simply got to. You went yellow! You went yellow out there, and you've got to go back and lick them! You've got to!"

"Let me alone!"

"But what are they going to do? You can't let them down like that!"

"I don't *care* what they do!"

"Leonard, listen to me. They're out there. They're all out there, she, and your two kids, and you've got to finish it. You've just go to do it!"

"I won't! I'll *never* go out there—"

They were playing my cue. She took hold of me, tried to pull me away from the stairs, tried to throw me on stage by main force. I hung on. I hung on to that iron like it was a life raft. The bass started singing my part. She looked at me and bit her lip. I saw two tears jump out of her eyes and run down her face. She turned around and left me.

I got to my dressing room, locked the door, and then I cracked. No iron bars there to hold on to. I clenched my teeth, my fists, my toes, and it was no good. Here they came, those awful, hysterical sobs I had heard coming out of Doris that day, and the more I fought them back, the worse they got. I knew the truth then, knew why Cecil had laughed at me that night in Rochester, why Horn had been so doubtful about me, and all the rest of it. I was no trouper, and they knew it. I had smoke, and nothing else. But you can't lick that racket with smoke. You've got to care about it, you can't get by on a little voice and a little music. You've got to dig up the heart to take it when it's tough, and the only way you can find the heart is to love it. I was just another Doris. I had everything but what it takes.

Down on the stage, the bass was doubling for me. He carried the Gilda in, put her on the rock, then picked up a cape, turned around, and did my part. They gave him an ovation. After Parma had taken Schultz out, and they had all taken their bows, they shoved him out there alone, and the audience stood up and gave him a rising vote, in silence, before they started to clap. His name was Woods. Remember it, Woods: the man that had what it takes. But Rigoletto didn't know anything about that, yet. He was up there in his dressing room, blubbering like some kid that saw the boogey man, and looking at himself and his cap and bells. Maybe you think he didn't look sick.

11

BACK IN 1921, when Dempsey fought Carpentier in Jersey, some newspaper hired a lady novelist, I think it was Alice Duer Miller, to do a piece on it. She decided that what she wanted to write up was the loser's dressing room after it was all over. She had been reading all her life about the winner, and thought she would like to know for once what happened to the loser. She found out. What happened to him was nothing. Carpentier was there, and a couple of rubbers were there, working on him, and his manager was there, and that was all. Nobody came in to tell him he had put up a good fight, or that it was a hell of a wallop he hit Dempsey in the second round, or even to borrow a quarter. Outside you could hear them still yelling for Dempsey, but not one in all that crowd had a minute for Gorgeous Georges, the Orchid Man.

That's how it was with me. There were no autograph hunters that night. There were feet, running past the door and voices saying "I'll meet you outside," and tenors showing their friends they knew *"La Donna e Mobile,"* and the whistle brigade, but none of them stopped, none of them had a word for me. It got quiet after a while, and the noise outside died away, and I lit a cigarette and sat there. After a long time there was a tap on the door. I never moved. It came again and still again, and then I heard my first name called. It sounded like Doris, and I went to the door and opened it. She was there, in a little green suit, and a brown felt hat, and brown shoes. She came in without looking at me. "What happened?"

"Weren't you there?"

"I had to take the children home after the second act. I heard some people talking, on my way backstage."

I remembered Lorentz and his real crime at the Cathedral Theatre that day. I was glad there was one person in the world that hadn't seen it. Three, because that meant she had taken the kids out before it happened. ". . . I got the bird."

"Damn them."

She walked around, saying what she thought of them. Cecil never talked like that. She might tell you they were a pack of hyenas, but she never got sore at them, never regarded them as anything but so many people to be licked. But Doris had felt their teeth, and besides she had a gift for polishing them off, you might say, on account of her cobra blood. The cobra strain was what I wanted then. She snarled it out, and I wanted all she could give. Down in my heart, I knew Cecil was right, that it's never anybody's fault but your own. But I was still bleeding. What Doris had to say, it hit the spot.

But it wasn't any consolation scene. That wasn't what she came in there for, I could see that. She seemed to be under some kind of a strain, and kept talking without looking at me. When I started to take the make-up off, she got busy with the towel, and when I was ready for my clothes, she helped me into them. That was funny. Nothing like that had ever happened before. We went out, and got a cab, and I called out the name of my hotel. She didn't say anything. On the way up I kept thinking there was something I had forgotten, something I had intended to do. Then I remembered. I was to sign the contracts. I sat back and watched the El posts go back. That was one thing I didn't have to worry about.

When we got into the lobby, I could see something glaring at me from a chair near the elevators, and I didn't tumble at first to what it was. There had been so many glares coming my way lately that one more didn't make much impression. But then I came out of the fog. It was Craig, my partner, that I hadn't seen since we built the gag chicken coop up in Connecticut, and he had dug in at his place up-state. I blinked, and looked at Doris, and thought maybe that was why she had come around, or anyway had something to do with it. But she seemed as surprised as I was. He still sat there, glaring at us, and then he got up and came over. He didn't shake hands. He started in high, and he was plenty sore. "Where've you been?"

"Why—right here."

"And why here? What's the idea of hiding out in this goddam dump? I've been looking for you all night, and it was just by accident that I found you. Just by accident."

Doris cut in, meeker than I ever heard her. "Why—one of the children was threatened with measles, and Leonard came down here so he wouldn't be quarantined."

"Couldn't he let somebody know?"

"He—it was only to be for a few days."

That seemed to cool him off a little, and I tried to be friendly. "When did you get to town? I thought you were up there milking cows."

"Never mind when I got to town, and never mind the cows. And cut the comedy. Get this."

"I'm listening."

"You've got just forty minutes to make a train, and you pay attention to what I'm telling you."

"Shoot."

"Alabama. You've heard of it?"

"Sounds familiar."

"There's a big government-aid railroad bridge going up down there, and we build bridges, this here Craig-Borland Company that we've got, even if you seem to have forgotten it. You get down there, and you get that contract."

"Where is this bridge?"

"I got no time for that. It's all in here, in this briefcase, the whole thing, and you can read it going down. Here's your tickets for the two of you, and remember, you got thirty-nine minutes. When you get there, I'll wire you our bid. I'll put the whole thing on the wire, it's being figured up now. The main thing now is—get there."

"O. K. Chief."

He turned to Doris. "And you—"

"Yes sir."

"Listen to what I'm telling you. This is a bunch of well-bo'n South'ners dat dey granddaddy had slaves befo' de wa', lo's'n lo's o' slaves, and they've got to be impressed. You hear that? You take a whole floor in that hotel, and you roll out the liquor, and you step on it. You do all the things that your bum, sassiety, high-toned, good-for-nothing upbringing has taught you how to do, and then you do it twice."

"Booh. I know you."

"For once in your life, maybe you can be of some use."

"Just once?"

"If you don't put it across, you needn't come back."

"We'll put it across."

So we put it across. They've got a bird in my business too, that rides the trusses while the scows are taking them out, and flies around and flaps its wings and crows whenever one of them falls in the river. But his wings didn't get much exercise on that job, and neither did his voice. It was my trade. The river got pretty tough once or twice, and we had some close squeaks. But not one of those trusses took a dive.

But I'm ahead of my story. Craig had a paper stuck in his pocket, and after he had laid the law down he began to get sore again and remembered it. He tapped it with his finger. "And you keep in touch with me. If it hadn't been for this, seeing your name in this paper just by accident, I wouldn't have known *where* to look for you."

He took it out and opened it, and pointed to a great big picture of me in the whiskers, and wig and cap, and bells, on the theatrical page. "Is that you?"

Doris let out a cackle that made everybody in the lobby look up. It was just a silvery peal that came from the heart, and did you good to hear it. She wasn't laughing at me. She was laughing at Craig, and when I looked at him I had to laugh too. I had to laugh so hard I folded into one of the lobby chairs, and so did she. The look on that old hard-rock man's face, holding up that picture, was the funniest thing I ever saw in my life, or ever hope to see.

I scrambled up and threw my stuff into a bag, and was so excited over getting back in harness that I kept singing all the time and didn't even feel bad about it, and down in the lobby Doris called the house and we made the train. We had the drawing room, but I was out of cigarettes, and I went in the club car to get some. I would have sent the porter, but he was still making up berths, and I didn't want to bother him. When I got back she was already tucked in, in the upper berth, and all you could see was a tousle of red hair. I undressed, got into the lower. I waited, and she didn't say anything. I turned out my light, and still nothing from her. All you could hear was the wheels, going clickety click. They kind of beat time, and I started to sing the opening of a duet:

La ci darem la mano!
La mi dirai di si
Vedi non e lontano
Partiam ben mio da qui

It was time for her to come in, and I waited. Then: "Did you sing that with her?"

"No, I never did."

"Are you sure?"

"They were going to have me do Don Giovanni. This last outfit, I mean. So I got the score, and found it in there. I had heard you humming it around, so—I learned it."

She came tumbling down the ladder, all floppy in a suit of my pajamas. She slipped in beside me, put her arms around me. "Leonard."

"Yes?"

"I'm glad you flopped. Because I flopped, and—if you could do this one thing I've always wanted to do, and can't—I couldn't stand it. And—"

"Go on. And what?"

"It'll be all mine, now, this that you have in your throat. That's why I came back there. Leonard, when you sang that day it almost killed me. I think you wanted it to. Oh, I've been a terrible wife to you, Leonard. I'm jealous, and spiteful, and mean and nothing will ever change me. But when I get too terrible, just sing to me, and I'll be your slave. I'll come crawling to you, just the way you came crawling to them, in the second act tonight. That woman has given us something that was never there before, and I'm going to thank her, and win her, and make her my friend. Oh, I can, I don't care what has gone before. I can win anybody when I really want them. . . . Now I'll say it. Something you've never heard me say before. I've fallen in love. With my own husband."

I held her tight. She put her mouth against my throat, and began kissing it. "Now sing, and I'll sing."

> *La ci darem la mano!*
> *La mi dirai di si*
> *Vedi non e lontano*
> *Partiam ben mio da qui.*
>
> *Vorrei e non vorrei*
> *Mio trema un poco il cor*
> *Felice e ver sarei*
> *Ma puo burlarmi ancor. . . .*

We sang it together, and it was terrible, and it was the sweetest duet I ever heard. That's all.

THE EMBEZZLER

THE EMBEZZLER

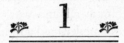
1

I FIRST met her when she came over to the house one night, after calling me on the telephone and asking if she could see me on a matter of business. I had no idea what she wanted, but supposed it was something about the bank. At the time, I was acting cashier at our little Anita Avenue branch, the smallest of the three we've got in Glendale, and the smallest branch we've got, for that matter. In the home office, in Los Angeles, I rate as vice president, but I'd been sent out there to check up on the branch, not on what was wrong with it, but what was right with it. Their ratio of savings deposits to commercial deposits was over twice what we had in any other branch, and the Old Man figured it was time somebody went out there and found out what the trick was, in case they'd invented something the rest of the banking world hadn't heard of.

I found out what the trick was soon enough. It was her husband, a guy named Brent that rated head teller and had charge of the savings department. He'd elected himself little White Father to all those workmen that banked in the branch, and kept after them and made them save until half of them were buying their homes and there wasn't one of them that didn't have a good pile of dough in the bank. It was good for us, and still better for those workmen, but in spite of that I didn't like Brent and I didn't like his way of doing business. I asked him to lunch one day, but he was too busy, and couldn't come. I had to wait till we closed, and then we went to a drugstore while he had a glass of milk, and I tried to get out of him something about how he got those deposits every week, and whether he thought any of his methods could be used by the whole organization. But we got off on the wrong foot, because he thought I really meant to criticize, and it took me half an hour to smooth him down. He was a funny guy, so touchy you could hardly talk to him at all, and with a hymnbook-salesman look to him that made you understand why he regarded his work as a kind of a missionary job among those people that carried their accounts with him. I would say he was around thirty, but he looked older. He was tall and thin, and beginning to get bald, but he walked with a stoop and his face had a gray color that you don't see on a well man. After he drank his milk and ate the two crackers that came with it he took a little tablet out of an envelope he carried in his pocket, dissolved it in his water, and drank it.

But even when he got it through his head I wasn't sharpening an axe for him, he wasn't much help. He kept saying that savings deposits have to be worked up on a personal basis, that the man at the window has to make the depositor feel that he takes an interest in seeing the figures mount up, and more of the same. Once he got a holy look in his eyes, when he said that you can't make the depositor feel that way unless you really feel that way yourself, and for a few seconds he was a little excited, but that died off. It looks all right, as I write it, but it didn't sound good. Of course, a big corporation doesn't like to put things on a personal basis, if it can help it. Institutionalize the bank, but not the man, for the good reason that the man may get an offer somewhere else, and then when he quits he takes all his trade with him. But that wasn't the only reason it didn't sound good. There was something about the guy himself that I just didn't like, and what it was I didn't know, and didn't even have enough interest to find out.

So when his wife called up a couple of weeks later, and asked if she could see me that night, at my home, not at the bank, I guess I wasn't any sweeter about it than I had to be. In the first place, it looked funny she would want to come to my house, instead of the bank, and in the second place it didn't sound like good news, and in the third place, if she stayed late, it was going to cut me out of the fights down at the Legion Stadium, and I kind of look forward to them. Still, there wasn't much I could say except I would see her, so I did. Sam, my Filipino house boy, was going out, so I fixed a highball tray myself, and figured if she was as pious as he was, that would shock her enough that she would leave early.

It didn't shock her a bit. She was quite a lot younger than he was, I would say around twenty-five, with blue eyes, brown hair, and a shape you couldn't take your eyes off of. She was about medium size, but put together so pretty she looked small. Whether she was really good-looking in the face I don't know, but if she wasn't good-looking, there was something about the way she looked at you that had that thing. Her teeth were big and white, and her lips were just the least little bit thick. They gave her a kind of a heavy, sulky look, but one eyebrow had a kind of twitch to it, so she'd say something and no part of her face would move but that, and yet it meant more than most women could put across with everything they had.

All that kind of hit me in the face at once, because it was the last thing I was expecting. I took her coat, and followed her into the living room. She sat down in front of the fire, picked up a cigarette and tapped it on her nail, and began looking around. When her eye lit on the highball tray she was already lighting her cigarette, but she nodded with the smoke curling up in one eye. "Yes, I think I will."

I laughed, and poured her a drink. It was all that had been said, and yet it got us better acquainted than an hour of talk could have done. She asked me a few questions about myself, mainly if I wasn't the same Dave Bennett that used to play halfback for U.S.C., and when I told her I was, she figured out my age. She was one year off. She said thirty-two, and I'm thirty-three. She said she was twelve years old at the time she saw me go down for a touchdown on an intercepted pass, which put her around twenty-five, what I took her for. She sipped her drink. I put a log of wood on the fire. I wasn't quite so hot about the Legion fights.

When she'd finished her drink she put the glass down, motioned me away when I started to fix her another, and said: "Well."

"Yeah, that awful word."

"I'm afraid I have bad news."

"Which is?"

"Charles is sick."

"He certainly doesn't look well."

"He needs an operation."

"What's the matter with him—if it's mentionable?"

"It's mentionable, even if it's pretty annoying. He has a duodenal ulcer, and he's abused himself so much, or at least his stomach, with this intense way he goes about his work, and refusing to go out to lunch, and everything else that he shouldn't do, that it's got to that point. I mean, it's serious. If he had taken better care of himself, it's something that needn't have amounted to much at all. But he's let it go, and now I'm afraid if something isn't done—well, it's going to be very serious. I might as well say it. I got the report today, on the examination he had. It says if he's not operated on at once, he's going to be dead within a month. He's—verging on a perforation."

"And?"

"This part isn't so easy."

". . . How much?"

"Oh, it isn't a question of money. That's all taken care of. He has a policy, one of these clinical hook-ups that entitles him to everything. It's Charles."

"I don't quite follow you."

"I can't seem to get it through his head that this has to be done. I suppose I could, if I showed him what I've just got from the doctors, but I don't want to frighten him any more than I can help. But he's so wrapped up in his work, he's such a fanatic about it, that he positively refuses to leave it. He has some idea that these people, these workers, are all going to ruin if he isn't there to boss them around, and make them save their money, and pay up their installments on their houses, and I don't know what all. I guess it sounds silly to you. It does to me. But—he won't quit."

"You want me to talk to him?"

"Yes, but that's not quite all. I think, if Charles knew that his work was being done the way he wants it done, and that his job would be there waiting for him when he came out of the hospital, that he'd submit without a great deal of fuss. This is what I've been trying to get around to. Will you let me come in and do Charles' work while he's gone?"

". . . Well—it's pretty complicated work."

"Oh no, it's not. At least not to me. You see, I know every detail of it, as well as he does. I not only know the people, from going around with him while he badgered them into being thrifty, but I used to work in the bank. That's where I met him. And—I'll do it beautifully, really. That is, if you don't object to making it a kind of family affair."

I thought it over a few minutes, or tried to. I went over in my mind the reasons against it, and didn't see any that amounted to anything. In fact, it suited me just as well to have her come in, if Brent really had to go to the hospital, because it would peg the job while he was gone, and I wouldn't have to have a general shake-up, with the other three in the branch moving up a notch, and getting all excited about promotions that probably wouldn't last very long anyway. But I may as well tell the truth. All that went through my mind, but another thing that went through my mind was her. It wasn't going to be a bit unpleasant to have her around for the next few weeks. I liked this dame from the start, and for me anyway, she was plenty easy to look at.

"Why—I think that's all right."

"You mean I get the job?"

"Yeah—sure."

"What a relief. I hate to ask for jobs."

"How about another drink?"

"No, thanks. Well—just a little one."

I fixed her another drink, and we talked about her husband a little more, and I told her how his work had attracted the attention of the home office, and it seemed to please her. But then all of a sudden I popped out: "Who are you, anyway?"

"Why—I thought I told you."

"Yeah, but I want to know more."

"Oh, I'm nobody at all, I'm sorry to say. Let's see, who am I? Born, Princeton, N.J., and not named for a while on account of an argument among relatives. Then when they thought my hair was going to be red they named me Sheila, because it had an Irish sound to it. Then—at the age of ten, taken to California. My father got appointed to the history department of U.C.L.A."

"And who is your father?"

"Henry W. Rollinson—"

"Oh, yes, I've heard of him."

"Ph.D. to you, just Hank to me. And—let's see. High school, valedictorian of the class, tagged for college, wouldn't go. Went out and got myself a job instead. In our little bank. Answered an ad in the paper. Said I was eighteen when I was only sixteen, worked there three years, got a $1 raise every year. Then—Charles got interested, and I married him."

"And, would you kindly explain *that*?"

"It happens, doesn't it?"

"Well, it's none of my business. Skip it."

"You mean we're oddly assorted?"

"Slightly."

"It seems so long ago. Did I mention I was nineteen? At that age you're very susceptible to—what would you call it? Idealism?"

". . . Are you still?"

I didn't know I was going to say that, and my voice sounded shaky. She drained her glass and got up.

"Then, let's see. What else is there in my little biography? I have two children, one five, the other three, both girls, and both beautiful. And—I sing alto in the Eurydice Women's Chorus. . . . That's all, and now I have to be going."

"Where'd you put your car?"

"I don't drive. I came by bus."

"Then—may I drive you home?"

"I'd certainly be grateful if you would. . . . By the way, Charles would kill me if he knew I'd come to you. About him, I mean. I'm supposed to be at a picture show. So tomorrow, don't get absent-minded and give me away."

"It's between you and me."

"It sounds underhanded, but he's very peculiar."

I live on Franklin Avenue in Hollywood, and she lived on Mountain Drive, in Glendale. It's about twenty minutes, but when we got in front of her house instead of stopping, I drove on. "I just happened to think; it's awful early for a picture show to let out."

"So it is, isn't it?"

We drove up in the hills. Up to then we had been plenty gabby, but for the rest of the drive we both felt self-conscious and didn't have much to say. When I swung down through Glendale again the Alexander Theatre was just letting out. I set her down on the corner, a little way from her house. She shook hands. "Thanks ever so much."

"Just sell him the idea, and the job's all set."

". . . I feel terribly guilty, but—"

"Yes?"

"I've had a grand time."

2

SHE SOLD me the idea, but she couldn't sell Brent, not that easy, that is. He squawked, and refused to go to the hospital, or do anything about his ailment at all, except take pills for it. She called me up three or four times about it, and those calls seemed to get longer every night. But one day, when he toppled over at the window, and I had to send him home in a private ambulance, there didn't seem to be much more he could say. They hauled him off to the hospital, and she came in next day to take his place, and things went along just about the way she said they would, with her doing the work fine and the depositors plunking down their money just like they had before.

The first night he was in the hospital I went down there with a basket of fruit, more as an official gift from the bank than on my own account, and she was there, and of course after we left him I offered to take her home. So I took her. It turned out she had arranged that the maid should spend her nights at the house, on account of the children, while he was in the hospital, so we took a ride. Next night I took her down, and waited for her outside, and we took another ride. After they got through taking X-rays they operated, and it went off all right, and by that time

she and I had got the habit. I found a newsreel right near the
hospital, and while she was with him I'd go in and look at the
sports, and then we'd go for a little ride.

I didn't make any passes, she didn't tell me I was different from
other guys she'd known, there was nothing like that. We talked
about her kids, and the books we'd read, and sometimes she'd
remember about my old football days, and some of the things
she'd seen me do out there. But mostly we'd just ride along and
say nothing, and I couldn't help feeling glad when she'd say the
doctors wanted Brent to stay there until he was all healed up. He
could have stayed there till Christmas, and I wouldn't have been
sore.

The Anita Avenue Branch, I think I told you, is the smallest
one we've got, just a little bank building on a corner, with an alley
running alongside and a drugstore across the street. It employs
six people, the cashier, the head teller, two other tellers, a girl
bookkeeper, and a guard. George Mason had been cashier, but
they transferred him and sent me out there, so I was acting cashier.
Sheila was taking Brent's place as head teller. Snelling and Helm
were the other two tellers, Miss Church was the bookkeeper, and
Adler the guard. Miss Church went in for a lot of apple-polishing
with me, or anyway what I took to be apple-polishing. They had
to stagger their lunch hours, and she was always insisting that I
go out for a full hour at lunch, that she could relieve at any of
the windows, that there was no need to hurry back, and more of
the same. But I wanted to pull my oar with the rest, so I took a
half hour like the rest of them took, and relieved at whatever
window needed me, and for a couple of hours I wasn't at my desk
at all.

One day Sheila was out, and the others got back a little early,
so I went out. They all ate in a little cafe down the street, so I ate
there too, and when I got there she was alone at a table. I would

have sat down with her, but she didn't look up, and I took a seat a couple of tables away. She was looking out the window, smoking, and pretty soon she doused her cigarette and came over where I was. "You're a little stand-offish today, Mrs. Brent."

"I've been doing a little quiet listening."

"Oh—the two guys in the corner?"

"Do you know who the fat one is?"

"No, I don't."

"That's Bunny Kaiser, the leading furniture man of Glendale. 'She Buys 'Er Stuff from Kaiser'."

"Isn't he putting up a building or something? Seems to me we had a deal on, to handle his bonds."

"He wouldn't sell bonds. It's his building, with his own name chiseled over the door, and he wanted to swing the whole thing himself. But he can't quite make it. The building is up to the first floor now, and he has to make a payment to the contractor. He needs a hundred thousand bucks. Suppose a bright girl got that business for you, would she get a raise?"

"And how would *she* get that business?"

"Sex appeal! Do you think I haven't got it?"

"I didn't say you haven't got it."

"You'd better not."

"Then that's settled."

"And—?"

"When's this payment on the first floor due?"

"Tomorrow."

"Ouch! That doesn't give us much time to work."

"You let *me* work it, and *I'll* put it over."

"All right, you land that loan, it's a two-dollar raise."

"Two-fifty."

"O.K.—two-fifty."

"I'll be late. At the bank, I mean."

"I'll take your window."

So I went back and took her window. About two o'clock a truck driver came in, cashed a pay check with Helm, then came over to me to make a $10 deposit on savings. I took his book, entered the amount, set the $10 so she could put it with her cash when she came in. You understand: they all have cash boxes, and lock them when they go out, and that cash is checked once a month. But when I took out the card in our own file, the total it showed was $150 less than the amount showing in the passbook.

In a bank, you never let the depositor notice anything. You've got that smile on your face, and everything's jake, and that's fair enough, from his end of it, because the bank is responsible, and what his book shows is what he's got, so he can't lose no matter how you play it. Just the same, under that pasted grin, my lips felt a little cold. I picked up his book again, like there was something else I had to do to it, and blobbed a big smear of ink over it. "Well, that's nice, isn't it."

"You sure decorated it."

"I tell you what, I'm a little busy just now—will you leave that with me? Next time you come in, I'll have a new one ready for you."

"Anything you say, Cap."

"This one's kind of shopworn, anyway."

"Yeah, getting greasy."

By that time I had a receipt ready for the book, and copied the amount down in his presence, and passed it out to him. He went and I set the book aside. It had taken a little time, and three more depositors were in line behind him. The first two books corresponded with the cards, but the last one showed a $200 difference, more on his book than we had on our card. I hated to do what he had seen me do with the other guy, but I had to have that book. I started to enter the deposit, and once more a big blob of ink went on the page.

"Say, what you need is a new pen."

"What they need is a new teller. To tell you the truth, I'm a little green on this job, just filling in till Mrs. Brent gets back, and I'm hurrying it. If you'll just leave me this book, now—"

"Sure, that's all right."

I wrote the receipt, and signed it, and he went, and I put that book aside. By that time I had a little breathing spell, with nobody at the window, and I checked those books against the cards. Both accounts, on our records, showed withdrawals, running from $25 to $50, that didn't show on the pass books. Well, brother, it had to show on the pass books. If a depositor wants to withdraw, he can't do it without his book, because that book's his contract, and we're bound by it, and he can't draw any dough unless we write it right down there, what he took out. I began to feel a little sick at my stomach. I began to think of the shifty way Brent had talked when he explained about working the departments up on a personal basis. I began to think about how he refused to go to the hospital, when any sane man would have been begging for the chance. I began to think of that night call Sheila made on me, and all that talk about Brent's taking things so seriously, and that application she made, to take things over while he was gone.

All that went through my head, but I was still thumbing the cards. My head must have been swimming a little, when I first checked them over, but the second time I ran my eye over those two cards, I noticed little light pencil checks beside each one of those withdrawals. It flashed through my mind that maybe that was his code. He had to have a code, if he was trying to get away with anything. If a depositor didn't have his book, and asked for his balance, he had to be able to tell him. I flipped all the cards over. There were light pencil checks on at least half of them, every one against a withdrawal, none of them against a deposit. I wanted to run those checked amounts off on the adding machine, but I didn't. I was afraid Miss Church would start her apple-polishing again, and offer to do it for me. I flipped the cards over one at a time, slow, and added the amounts in my head. If I was accurate I didn't know. I've got an adding machine mind, and I can do some of those vaudeville stunts without much trouble, but I was too excited to be sure. That didn't matter, that day. I wouldn't be far off. And those little pencil checks, by the time I had turned every card, added up to a little more than eighty-five hundred dollars.

Just before closing time, around three o'clock, Sheila came in with the fat guy, Bunny Kaiser. I found out why sex appeal had worked, where all our contact men, trying to make a deal for bonds a few months before, had flopped. It was the first time he had ever borrowed a dollar in his life, and he not only hated it, he was so ashamed of it he couldn't even look at me. Her way of making him feel better was not to argue about it at all, but to pat him on the hand, and it was pathetic the way he ate it up. After a while she gave me the sign to beat it, so I went back and got the vault closed, and chased the rest of them out of there as fast as I could. Then we fixed the thing up, I called the main office for O.K.'s, and around four-thirty he left. She stuck out her hand, pretty excited, and I took it. She began trucking around the floor, snapping her fingers and singing some tune while she danced. All of a sudden she stopped, and made motions like she was brushing herself off.

"Well—is there something *on* me?"

". . . No. Why?"

"You've been *looking* at me—for an *hour*!"

"I was—looking at the dress."

"Is there anything the *matter* with it?"

"It's different from what girls generally wear around a bank. It—doesn't look like an office dress."

"I made it myself."

"Then that accounts for it."

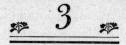

BROTHER, IF you want to find out how much you think of a
woman, just get the idea she's been playing you for a sucker. I
was trembling when I got home, and still trembling when I went
up to my room and lay down. I had a mess on my hands, and I
knew I had to do something about it. But all I could think of was
the way she had taken me for a ride, or I thought she had anyway,
and how I had fallen for it, and what a sap I was. My face would
feel hot when I thought of those automobile rides, and how I had
been too gentlemanly to start anything. Then I would think how
she must be laughing at me, and dig my face into the pillow.
After a while I got to thinking about tonight. I had a date to take
her to the hospital, like I had for the past week, and wondered
what I was going to do about that. What I wanted to do was give
her a stand-up and never set eyes on her again, but I couldn't.
After what she had said at the bank, about me looking at her, she
might tumble I was wise if I didn't show up. I wasn't ready for
that yet. Whatever I had to do, I wanted my hands free till I had
time to think.

So I was waiting, down the street from her house, where we'd
been meeting on account of what the neighbors might think if I
kept coming to the door, and in a few minutes here she came, and
I gave the little tap on the horn and she got in. She didn't say
anything about me looking at her, or what had been said. She kept
talking about Kaiser, and how we had put over a fine deal, and
how there was plenty more business of the same kind that could
be had if I'd only let her go out after it. I went along with it, and
for the first time since I'd known her, she got just the least little
bit flirty. Nothing that meant much, just some stuff about what a

team we could make if we really put our minds to it. But it brought me back to what my face had been red about in the afternoon, and when she went in the hospital I was trembling again.

I didn't go to the newsreel that night. I sat in the car for the whole hour she was in there, paying her visit to him, and the longer I sat the sorer I got. I hated that woman when she came out of the hospital, and then, while she was climbing in beside me, an idea hit me between the eyes. If that was her game, how far would she go with me? I watched her light a cigarette, and then felt my mouth go dry and hot. I'd soon find out. Instead of heading for the hills, or the ocean, or any of the places we'd been driving, I headed home.

We went in, and I lit the fire without turning on the living room light. I mumbled something about a drink, and went out in the kitchen. What I really wanted was to see if Sam was in. He wasn't, and that meant he wouldn't be in till one or two o'clock, so that was all right. I fixed the highball tray, and went in the living room with it. She had taken off her hat, and was sitting in front of the fire, or to one side of it. There are two sofas in my living room, both of them half facing the fire, and she was on one of them swinging her foot at the flames. I made two highballs, put them on the low table between the sofas, and sat down beside her. She looked up, took her drink, and began to sip it. I made a crack about how black her eyes looked in the firelight, she said they were blue, but it sounded like she wouldn't mind hearing more. I put my arm around her.

Well, a whole book could be written about how a woman blocks passes when she doesn't mean to play. If she slaps your face she's just a fool, and you might as well go home. If she hands you a lot of stuff that makes *you* feel like a fool, she doesn't know her stuff yet, and you better leave her alone. But if she plays it so you're stopped, and yet nothing much has happened, and you don't feel like a fool, she knows her stuff, and she's all right, and you can stick around and take it as it comes, and you won't wake up next morning wishing that you hadn't. That was what she did. She didn't pull away, she didn't act surprised, she didn't get off any bum gags. But she didn't come to me either, and in a minute or two she leaned forward to pick up her glass, and when she leaned back she wasn't inside of my arm.

I was too sick in my mind though, and too sure I had her sized up right for a trollop, to pay any attention to that, or even figure out what it meant. It went through my mind, just once, that whatever I had to do, down at the bank, I was putting myself in an awful spot, and playing right into her hands, to start something I couldn't stop. But that only made my mouth feel dryer and hotter.

I put my arm around her again, and pulled her to me. She didn't do anything about it at all, one way or the other. I put my cheek against hers, and began to nose around to her mouth. She didn't do anything about that either, but her mouth seemed kind of hard to reach. I put my hand on her cheek, and then deliberately let it slide down to her neck, and unbuttoned the top button of her dress. She took my hand away, buttoned her dress, and reached for her drink again, so when she sat back I didn't have her.

That sip took a long time, and I just sat there, looking at her. When she put the glass down I had my arm around her before she could even lean back. With my other hand I made a swipe, and brushed her dress up clear to where her garters met her girdle. What she did then I don't know, because something happened that I didn't expect. Those legs were so beautiful, and so soft, and warm, that something caught me in the throat, and for about one second I had no idea what was going on. Next thing I knew she was standing in front of the fireplace, looking down at me with a drawn face. "Will you kindly tell me what's got into you tonight?"

"Why—nothing particular."

"Please. I want to know."

"Why, I find you exciting, that's all."

"Is it something I've done?"

"I didn't notice you doing anything."

"Something's come over you, and I don't know what. Ever since I came in the bank today, with Bunny Kaiser, you've been looking at me in a way that's cold, and hard, and ugly. What is it? Is it what I said at lunch, about my having sex appeal?"

"Well, you've got it. We agreed on that."

"Do you know what I think?"

"No, but I'd like to."

"I think that remark of mine, or something, has suddenly wakened you up to the fact that I'm a married woman, that I've been seeing quite a little of you, and that you think it's now up to you to be loyal to the ancient masculine tradition, and try to make me."

"Anyway, I'm trying."

She reached for her drink, changed her mind, lit a cigarette instead. She stood there for a minute, looking into the fire, inhaling the smoke. Then:

". . . I don't say it couldn't be done. After all, my home life hasn't been such a waltz dream for the last year or so. It's not so pleasant to sit by your husband while he's coming out of ether, and then have him begin mumbling another woman's name, instead of your own. I guess that's why I've taken rides with you every night. They've been a little breath of something pleasant. Something more than that. Something romantic, and if I pretended they haven't meant a lot to me, I wouldn't be telling the truth. They've been—little moments under the moon. And then today, when I landed Kaiser, and was bringing him in, I was all excited about it, not so much for the business it meant to the bank, which I don't give a damn about, or the two-dollar-and-a-half

raise, which I don't give a damn about either, but because it was
something you and I had done together, something we'd talk
about tonight, and it would be—another moment under the moon,
a very bright moon. And then, before I'd been in the bank more
than a minute or two, I saw that look in your eye. And tonight,
you've been—perfectly horrible. It could have been done, I think.
I'm afraid I'm only too human. But not this way. And not any
more. Could I borrow your telephone?"

I thought maybe she really wanted the bath, so I took her to
the extension in my bedroom. I sat down by the fire quite a while,
and waited. It was all swimming around in my head, and it hadn't
come out at all like I expected. Down somewhere inside of me, it
began to gnaw at me that I had to tell her, I had to come out with
the whole thing, when all of a sudden the bell rang. When I
opened the door a taxi driver was standing there.

"You called for a cab?"

"No, nobody called."

He fished out a piece of paper and peered at it, when she came
downstairs. "I guess that's my cab."

"Oh, you ordered it?"

"Yes. Thanks ever so much. It's been so pleasant."

She was as cold as a dead man's foot, and she was down the
walk and gone before I could think of anything to say. I watched
her get in the cab, watched it drive off, then closed the door and
went back in the living room. When I sat down on the sofa I
could still smell her perfume, and her glass was only half drunk.
That catch came in my throat again, and I began to curse at myself
out loud, even while I was pouring myself a drink.

I had started to find out what she was up to, but all I had found
out was that I was nuts about her. I went over and over it till I
was dizzy, and nothing she had done, and nothing she had said,
proved anything. She might be on the up-and-up, and she might

be playing me for a still worse sucker than I had thought she was, a sucker that was going to play her game for her, and not even get anything for it. In the bank, she treated me just like she treated the others, pleasant, polite and pretty. I didn't take her to the hospital any more, and that was how we went along for three or four days.

Then came the day for the monthly check on cash, and I tried to kid myself that was what I had been waiting for, before I did anything about the shortage. So I went around with Helm, and checked them all. They opened their boxes, and Helm counted them up, and I counted his count. She stood there while I was counting hers, with a dead-pan that could mean anything, and of course it checked to the cent. Down in my heart I knew it would. Those false entries had all been made to balance the cash, and as they went back for a couple of years, there wasn't a chance that it would show anything in just one month.

That afternoon when I went home I had it out with myself, and woke up that I wasn't going to do anything about that shortage, that I couldn't do anything about it, until at least I had spoken to her, anyway acted like a white man.

So that night I drove over to Glendale, and parked right on Mountain Drive where I had always parked. I went early, in case she started sooner when she went by bus, and I waited a long time. I waited so long I almost gave up, but then along about half past seven, here she came out of the house, and walking fast. I waited till she was about a hundred feet away, and then I gave that same little tap on the horn I had given before. She started to run, and I had this sick feeling that she was going by without even speaking, so I didn't look. I wouldn't give her that much satisfaction. But before I knew it the door opened and slammed, and there she was on the seat beside me, and she was squeezing my hand, and half whispering:

"I'm so glad you came. So glad."

We didn't say much going in. I went to the newsreel, but what came out on the screen I couldn't tell you. I was going over and over in my mind what I was going to say to her, or at least trying to. But every time when I'd get talking about it, I'd find myself starting off about her home life, and trying to find out if Brent really had taken up with another woman, and more of the same that only meant one thing. It meant I wanted her for myself. And it meant I was trying to make myself believe that she didn't know anything about the shortage, that she had been on the up-and-up all the time, that she really liked me. I went back to the car, and got in, and pretty soon she came out of the hospital, and ran down the steps. Then she stopped, and stood there like she was thinking. Then she started for the car again, but she wasn't running now. She was walking slow. When she got in she leaned back and closed her eyes.

"Dave?"

It was the first time she had ever called me by my first name. I felt my heart jump. "Yes, Sheila?"

"Could we have a fire tonight?"

"I'd love it."

"I've—I've got to talk to you."

So I drove to my house. Sam let us in, but I chased him out. We went in the living room, and once more I didn't turn on the light. She helped me light the fire, and I started into the kitchen to fix something to drink, but she stopped me.

"I don't want anything to drink. Unless you do."

"No. I don't drink much."

"Let's sit down."

She sat on the sofa, where she had been before, and I sat beside her. I didn't try any passes. She looked in the fire a long time, and then she took my arm and pulled it around her. "Am I terrible?"

"No."

"I want it there."

I started to kiss her, but she raised her hand, covered my lips with her fingers, then pushed my face away. She dropped her head on my shoulder, closed her eyes, and didn't speak for a long time. Then: "Dave, there's something I've got to tell you."

"What is it?"

"It's pretty tragic, and it involves the bank, and if you don't want to hear it from me, this way, just say so and I'll go home."

". . . All right. Shoot."

"Charles is short in his accounts."

"How much?"

"A little over nine thousand dollars. Nine one one three point two six, if you want the exact amount. I've been suspecting it. I noticed one or two things. He kept saying I must have made mistakes in my bookkeeping, but tonight I made him admit it."

"Well. That's not so good."

"How bad is it?"

"It's pretty bad."

"Dave, tell me the truth about it. I've got to know. What will they do to him? Will they put him in prison?"

"I'm afraid they will."

"What, actually, does happen?"

"A good bit of what happens is up to the bonding company. If they get tough, he needn't expect much mercy. It's dead open-and-shut. They put him under arrest, have him indicted, and the rest of it's a question of how hard they bear down, and how it hits the court. Sometimes, of course, there are extenuating circumstances—"

"There aren't any. He didn't spend that money on me, or on the children, or on his home. I've kept all expenses within his salary, and I've even managed to save a little for him, every week."

"Yeah, I noticed your account."

"He spent it on another woman."

"I see."

"Does it make any difference if restitution is made?"

"All the difference in the world."

"If so, would he get off completely free?"

"There again, it all depends on the bonding company, and the deal that could be made with them. They might figure they'd make any kind of a deal, to get the money back, but as a rule they're not lenient. They can't be. The way they look at it, every guy that gets away with it means ten guys next year that'll try to get away with it."

"Suppose they never knew it?"

"I don't get you."

"Suppose I could find a way to put the money back, I mean suppose I could get the money, and then found a way to make the records conform, so nobody ever knew there was anything wrong."

"It couldn't be done."

"Oh yes, it could."

"The passbooks would give it away. Sooner or later."

"Not the way I'd do it."

"That—I would have to think about."

"You know what this means to me, don't you?"

"I think so."

"It's not on account of me. Or Charles. I try not to wish ill to anybody, but if he had to pay, it might be what he deserves. It's on account of my two children. Dave, I can't have them spend the rest of their lives knowing their father was a convict, that he'd been in prison. Do you, can you, understand what that means, Dave?"

For the first time since she had begun to talk, I looked at her then. She was still in my arms, but she was turned to me in a strained, tense kind of way, and her eyes looked haunted. I patted her head, and tried to think. But I knew there was one thing I had to do. I had to clear up my end of it. She had come clean with me, and for a while, anyway, I believed in her. I had to come clean with her.

"Sheila?"

"Yes?"

"I've got to tell *you* something."

". . . What is it, Dave?"

"I've known this all along. For at least a week."

"Is that why you were looking at me that day?"

"Yes. It's why I acted that way, that night. I thought you knew it. I thought you had known it, even when you came to me that night, to ask for the job. I thought you were playing me for a sucker, and I wanted to find out how far you'd go, to get me where you wanted me. Well—that clears *that* up."

She was sitting up now, looking at me hard.

"Dave, I *didn't* know it."

"I know you didn't—*now,* I know it."

"I knew about *her*—this woman he's been—going around with. I wondered sometimes where he got the money. But this, I had no idea. Until two or three days ago. Until I began to notice discrepancies in the passbooks."

"Yeah, that's what I noticed."

"And that's why you turned seducer?"

"Yeah. It's not very natural to me, I guess. I didn't fool you any. What I'm trying to say is I don't feel that way about you. I want you every way there is to want somebody, but—I mean it. Do you know what I'm getting at, if anything?"

She nodded, and all of a sudden we were in each other's arms, and I was kissing her, and she was kissing back, and her lips were warm and soft, and once more I had that feeling in my throat, that catch like I wanted to cry or something. We sat there a long time, not saying anything, just holding each other close. We were half-way to her house before we remembered about the shortage and what we were going to do about it. She begged me once more to give her a chance to save her children from the disgrace. I told her I'd have to think it over, but I knew in my heart I was going to do anything she asked me to.

"*WHERE ARE* you going to get this money?"

"There's only one place I can possibly get it."

"Which is?"

"My father."

"Has he got that much dough?"

"I don't know. . . . He owns his house. Out in Westwood. He could get something on that. He has a little money. I don't know how much. But for the last few years his only daughter hasn't been any expense. I guess he can get it."

"How's he going to feel about it?"

"He's going to hate it. And if he lets me have it, it won't be on account of Charles. He bears no goodwill to Charles, I can tell you that. And it won't be on account of me. He was pretty bitter when I even considered marrying Charles, and when I actually went and did it—well, we won't go into that. But for his grandchildren's sake, he might. Oh, what a mess. What an awful thing."

It was the next night, and we were sitting in the car, where I had parked on one of the terraces overlooking the ocean. I suppose it was around eight-thirty, as she hadn't stayed at the hospital very long. She sat looking out at the surf, and then suddenly said I might as well drive her over to her father's. I did, and she didn't have much to say. I parked near the house, and she went in, and she stayed a long time. It must have been eleven o'clock when she came out. She got in the car, and then she broke down and cried, and there wasn't much I could do. When she got a little bit under control, I asked, "Well, what luck?"

"Oh, he'll do it, but it was awful."

"If he got sore, you can't blame him much."

"He didn't get sore. He just sat there, and shook his head, and there was no question about whether he'd let me have the money or not. But—Dave, an old man, he's been paying on that house for fifteen years, and last year he got it clear. If he wants to, he can spend his summers in Canada, he and Mamma both. And now— it's all gone, he'll have to start paying all over again, all because of this. And he never said a word."

"What did your mother say?"

"I didn't tell her. I suppose he will, but I couldn't. I waited till she went to bed. That's what kept me so long. Fifteen years, paying regularly every month, and now it's to go, all because Charles fell for a simpleton that isn't worth the powder and shot to blow her to hell."

I didn't sleep very well that night. I kept thinking of the old history professor, and his house, and Sheila, and Brent lying down there in the hospital with a tube in his belly. Up to then I hadn't thought much about him. I didn't like him, and he was washed up with Sheila, and I had just conveniently not thought of him at all. I thought of him now, though, and wondered who the sim- pleton was that he had fallen for, and whether he was as nuts about her as I was about Sheila. Then I got to wondering whether I thought enough of her to embezzle for her, and that brought me sitting up in bed, staring out the window at the night. I could say I wouldn't, that I had never stolen from anybody, and never would, but here I was already mixed up in it some kind of way. It was a week since I uncovered that shortage, and I hadn't said a word about it to the home office, and I was getting ready to help her cover up.

Something popped in me then, about Brent, I mean, and I quit kidding myself. I did some hard figuring in bed there, and I didn't like it a bit, but I knew what I had to do. Next night, instead of heading for the ocean, I headed for my house again, and pretty soon we were back in front of the fire. I had mixed a drink this time, because at least I felt at peace with myself, and I held her in my arms quite a while before I got to it. Then: "Sheila?"

"Yes?"

"I've had it out with myself."

"Dave, you're not going to turn him in?"

"No, but I've decided there's only one person that can take that rap."

"Who do you mean?"

"Me."

"I don't understand you."

"All right, I drove you over to see your father last night, and he took it pretty hard. Fifteen years, paying on that house, and now it's all got to go, and he don't get anything out of it at all. Why should he pay? I got a house, too, and I do get something out of it."

"What do *you* get out of it?"

"You."

"What are you talking about?"

"I mean I got to cough up that nine thousand bucks."

"You *will* not!"

"Look, let's quit kidding ourselves. All right, Brent stole the dough, he spent it on a cutie, he treated you lousy. He's father of two children that happen also to be your father's grandchildren, and that means your father's got to pay. Well, ain't that great. Here's the only thing that matters about this: Brent's down and out. He's in the shadow of the penitentiary, he's in the hospital recovering from one of the worst operations there is, he's in one hell of a spot. But me—I'm in love with his wife. While he's down,

I'm getting ready to take her away from him, the one thing he's got left. O.K., that's not so pretty, but that's how I feel about it. But the least I can do is kick in with that dough. So, I'm doing it. So, quit bothering your old man. So, that's all."

"I can't let you do it."

"Why not?"

"If you paid that money, then I'd be bought."

She got up and began to walk around the room. "You've practically said so yourself. You're getting ready to take a man's wife away from him, and you're going to salve your conscience by replacing the money he stole. That's all very well for him, since he doesn't seem to want his wife anyway. But can't you see where it puts me? What can I say to you now? Or what could I say, if I let you put up that money? I can't pay you back. Not in ten years could I make enough to pay you nine thousand dollars. I'm just your—creature."

I watched her as she moved around, touching the furniture with her hands, not looking at me, and then all of a sudden a hot, wild feeling went through me, and the blood began to pound in my head. I went over and jerked her around, so she was facing me. "Listen, there's not many guys that feel for a woman nine thousand dollars' worth. What's the matter with that? Don't you want to be bought?"

I took her in my arms, and shoved my lips against hers. "Is that so tough?"

She opened her mouth, so our teeth were clicking, and just breathed it: "It's grand, just grand."

She kissed me then, hard. "So it was just a lot of hooey you were handing me?"

"Just hooey, nothing but hooey. Oh, it's so good to be bought. I feel like something in a veil, and a harem skirt—and I just love it."

"Now—we'll put that money back."

"Yes, together."

"We'll start tomorrow."

"Isn't that funny. I'm completely in your power. I'm your slave, and I feel so safe, and know that nothing's going to happen to me, ever."

"That's right. It's a life sentence for you."

"Dave, I've fallen in love."

"Me, too."

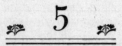

5

IF YOU think it's hard to steal money from a bank, you're right. But it's nothing like as hard as it is to put the money back. Maybe I haven't made it quite clear yet what that bird was doing. In the first place, when there's a shortage in a bank, it's always in the savings, because no statements are rendered on them. The commercial depositor, the guy with a checking account, I mean, gets a statement every month. But no statements are rendered to savings depositors. They show up with their passbooks, and plunk their money down, and the deposit is entered in their books, and their books are their statements. They never see the bank's cards, so naturally the thing can go on a long time before it's found out, and when it's found out, it's most likely to be by accident, like this was, because Brent didn't figure on his trip to the hospital.

Well, what Brent had done was fix up a cover for himself with all this stuff about putting it on a personal basis, so no savings depositor that came in the bank would ever deal with anybody but him. That ought to have made George Mason suspicious, but Brent was getting the business in, and you don't quarrel with a guy that's doing good. When he got that part the way he wanted it, with him the only one that ever touched the savings file, and the depositors dealing only with him, he went about it exactly the way they all go about it. He picked accounts where he knew he wouldn't be likely to run into trouble, and he'd make out a false withdrawal slip, generally for somewhere around fifty bucks. He'd sign the depositor's name to it, just forge it, but he didn't have to be very good at that part, because nobody passed on those signatures but himself. Then he'd put fifty bucks in his pocket, and of course the false withdrawal slip would balance his cash. Our card had to balance too, of course, so he'd enter the withdrawal on that, but beside each false entry he'd make that little light pencil check that I had caught, and that would tell him what the right balance ought to be, in case the depositor made some inquiry.

Well, how were you going to get that money put back, so the daily cash would balance, so the cards would balance, and so the passbooks would balance, and at the same time leave it so nothing would show later, when the auditors came around? It had me stumped, and I don't mind telling you for a while I began to get cold feet. What I wanted to do was report it, as was, let Sheila fork up the dough, without saying where she got it, and let Brent get fired and go look himself up a job. It didn't look like they would do much to him, if the money was put back. But she wouldn't hear of that. She was afraid they might send him up anyway, and then I would be putting up the money all for nothing, her children would have to grow up under the disgrace, and where we would be was nowhere. There wasn't much I could say to that. I figured they would probably let him off, but I couldn't be sure.

It was Sheila that figured out the way. We were riding along one night, just one or two nights after I told her I was going to put up the dough myself, when she began to talk. "The cards, the cash, and the passbooks, is that it?"

"That's all."

"The cards and the cash are easy."

"Oh yeah?"

"That money goes back the same way it came out. Only instead of false withdrawals, I make out false deposits. The cash balances, the posting balances, and the card balances."

"And the passbooks don't balance. Listen. If there's only one passbook—just one—that can tell on us after you're out of there, and I'm out, we're sunk. The only chance we've got is that the thing is never suspected at all—that no question is ever raised. And, what's more, we don't dare make a move till we see every one of the passbooks on those phoney accounts. We think we've got his code, how he ticked his false withdrawals, but we can't be sure, and maybe he didn't tick them all. Unless we can make a clean job of this, I don't touch it. Him going to jail is one thing. All three of us going, and me losing my job and nine thousand bucks—oh no."

"All right then, the passbooks."

"That's it—the passbooks."

"Now when a passbook gets filled up, or there's some mistake on it, what do we do?"

"Give him a new one, don't we?"

"Containing how many entries?"

"One, I suppose. His total as of that date."

"That's right. And that one entry tells no tales. It checks with the card, and there's not one figure to check against all those back entries—withdrawals and deposits and so on, running back for years. All right, then; so far, perfect. Now what do we do with his old book? Regularly, I mean."

"Well—what *do* we do with it?"

"We put it under a punch, the punch that goes through every page and marks it void, and give it back to him."

"And then he's got it—any time an auditor calls for it. Gee, that's a big help."

"But if he doesn't want it?"

"What are you getting at?"

"If he doesn't want it, we destroy it. It's no good to us, is it? And it's not ours, it's his. But he doesn't want it."

"Are you *sure* we destroy it?"

"I've torn up a thousand of them. . . . And that's just what we're going to do now. Between now and the next check on my cash, we're going to get all those books in. First we check totals, to know exactly where we're at. Then the depositor gets a new book that tells no tales."

"Why does he get a new book?"

"He didn't notice it when he brought the old one in, but the stitching is awfully strained, and it's almost falling apart. Or I've accidentally smeared lipstick on it. Or I just think it's time he got one of our nice new books, for luck. So he gets a new book with one entry in it—just his total, that's all. Then I say: 'You don't want this, do you?' And the way I'll say it, that old book seems positively *contaminated*. And then, right in front of his eyes, as though it's the way we do it every day, I'll tear it up, and drop it in the wastebasket."

"Suppose he *does* want it?"

"Then I'll put it under the punch, and give it to him. But somehow that punch is going to make its neat little holes in the exact place where the footings are, and it's going to be impossible for him, or an auditor, or anybody else, to read those figures. I'll punch five or six times, you know, and his book will be like Swiss cheese, more holes than anything else."

"And all the time you're getting those holes in exactly the right place, he's going to be on the other side of the window looking at you, wondering what all the hocus-pocus is about."

"Oh no—it won't take more than a second or two. You see, I've been practicing. I can do it in a jiffy. . . . But he won't want that book back. Trust me. I know how to do it."

There was just a little note of pleading on that, as she said it. I had to think it over. I did think it over, for quite a while, and I began to have the feeling that on her end of it, if that was all, she could put it over all right. But then something else began to bother me. "How many of these doctored accounts are there?"

"Forty-seven."

"And how are you going to get those passbooks in?"

"Well, interest is due on them. I thought I could send out little printed slips,—signed 'per Sheila Brent,' in ink, so they'd be sure to come to me about it,—asking them to bring in their books for interest credits. I never saw anybody that wouldn't bring in his book if it meant a dollar and twenty-two cents. And a printed slip looks perfectly open and above-board, doesn't it?"

"Yeah, a printed slip is about the most harmless, open, and above-board thing there is. But this is what I'm thinking: You send out your printed slips, and within a couple of days all those books come in, and you can't hold them forever. You've got to hand them back—or the new ones they're going to get—or somebody's going to get suspicious. That means the money's got to be put back all at once. That's going to make one awful bulge in your cash. Everybody in the bank is going to wonder at the reason for it, because it's going to show in the posting."

"I've thought of that. I don't have to send out all those slips at once. I can send out four or five a day. And then, even if they do come in bunches—the passbooks I mean—I can issue the new books, right away as the old ones are presented, but make the adjustments on the cards and in my cash little by little—three or four hundred dollars a day. That's not much."

"No, but while that's going on, we're completely defenseless. We've got our chins hanging out and no way in the world of putting up a guard. I mean, while you're holding out those adjustment entries, so you can edge them in gradually, your cash doesn't balance the books. If then something happened—so I had to call for a cash audit on the spot, or if I got called away to the home office for a couple of days, or something happened to you, so you couldn't come to work—then watch that ship go out of water. You may get away with it. But it'll have to be done, everything squared up, before the next check on your cash. That's twenty-one days from now. And at that, a three- or four-hundred dollar bulge in your cash every day is going to look mighty funny. In the bank, I mean."

"I could gag it off. I could say I'm keeping after them, to keep their deposits up, the way Charles always did. I don't think there's any danger. The cash will be there."

So that was how we did it. She had the slips printed, and began mailing them out, three or four at a time. For the first few days' replacement, the cash replacement I mean, I had enough on my own checking account. For the rest, I had to go out and plaster my house. For that I went to the Federal people. It took about a week, and I had to start an outside account, so nobody in the bank would know what I was up to. I took eight thousand bucks, and if you don't think that hurt you never plastered your house. Of course, it would be our luck that when the first of those books came in, she was out to lunch, and I was on the window myself. I took in the book, and receipted for it, but Church was only three or four feet away, running a column on one of the adding machines. She heard what I said to the depositor, and was at my elbow before I even knew how she got there.

"I can do that for you, Mr. Bennett. I'll only be a minute, and there'll be no need for him to leave his book."

"Well—I'd rather Mrs. Brent handled it."

"Oh, *very* well, then."

She switched away then, in a huff, and I could feel the sweat in the palms of my hands. That night I warned Sheila. "That Church can bust it up."

"How?"

"Her damned apple-polishing. She horned in today, wanted to balance that book for me. I had to chase her."

"Leave her to me."

"For God's sake don't let her suspect anything."

"I won't, don't worry."

From then on, we made a kind of a routine out of it. She'd get in three or four books, ask the depositors to leave them with her till next day. She'd make out new cards, and tell me the exact amount she needed, that night. I'd hand her that much in cash. Next day, she'd slip it into her cash box, make out new cards for the depositors, slip them in the file, then make out new passbooks and have them ready when the depositors called. Every day we'd be that much nearer home, both praying that nothing would tip it before we got the whole replacement made. Most days I'd say we plugged about $400 into the cash, one or two days a little more.

One night, maybe a week after we started putting the money back, they had the big dinner dance for the whole organization. I guess about a thousand people were there, in the main ball room of one of the Los Angeles hotels, and it was a pretty nice get-together. They don't make a pep meeting out of it. The Old Man doesn't like that kind of thing. He just has a kind of a family gathering, makes them a little speech, and then the dancing starts, and he stands around watching them enjoy themselves. I guess you've heard of A. R. Ferguson. He's founder of the bank, and the minute you look at him you know he's a big shot. He's not tall, but he's straight and stocky, with a little white moustache that makes him look like some kind of a military man.

Well, we all had to go, of course. I sat at the table with the others from the branch, Miss Church, and Helm, and Snelling, and Snelling's wife, and Sheila. I made it a point not to sit with Sheila. I was afraid to. So after the banquet, when the dancing started, I went over to shake hands with the Old Man. He always treated me fine, just like he treats everybody. He's got that natural courtesy that no little guy ever quite seems capable of. He asked how I was, and then: "How much longer do you think you'll be out there in Glendale? Are you nearly done?"

An icy feeling began to go over me. If he yanked me now, and returned me to the home office, there went all chance of covering that shortage, and God only knew what they would find out, if it was half covered and half not.

"Why, I tell you, Mr. Ferguson, if you can possibly arrange it, I'd like to stay out there till after the first of the month."

". . . So long?"

"Well, I've found some things out there that are well worth making a thorough study of, it seems to me. Fact of the matter, I had thought of writing an article about them in addition to my report. I thought I'd send it to the American Banker, and if I could have a little more time—"

"In that case, take all the time you want."

"I thought it wouldn't hurt us any."

"I only wish more of our officials would write."

"Gives us a little prestige."

"—and makes them *think*!"

My mouth did it all. I was standing behind it, not knowing what was coming out from one minute to the next. I hadn't thought of any article, up to that very second, and I give you one guess how I felt. I felt like a heel, and all the worse on account of the fine way he treated me. We stood there a few minutes, he telling me how he was leaving for Honolulu the next day, but he'd be back within the month, and looked forward to reading what I had to say as soon as he came back. Then he motioned in the direction of the dance floor. "Who's the girl in blue?"

"Mrs. Brent."

"Oh yes, I want to speak to her."

We did some broken-floor dodging, and got over to where Sheila was dancing with Helm. They stopped, and I introduced the Old Man, and he asked how Brent was coming along after the operation, and then cut in on Helm, and danced Sheila off. I wasn't in much of a humor when I met her outside later, and took her home. "What's the matter, Dave?"

"Couldn't quite look the Old Man in the eye, that's all."

"Have you got cold feet?"

"Just feeling the strain."

"If you have got cold feet, and want to quit, there's nothing I can say. Nothing at all."

"All I got to say is I'll be glad when we're clear of that heel, and can kick him out of the bank and out of our lives."

"In two weeks it'll be done."

"How is he?"

"He's leaving the hospital Saturday."

"That's nice."

"He's not coming home yet. The doctor insists that he go up to Arrowhead to get his strength back. He'll be there three or four weeks. He has friends there."

"What have you told him, by the way?"

"Nothing."

"Just nothing?"

"Not one word."

"He had an ulcer, is that what you said?"

"Yes."

"I was reading in a medical magazine the other day what causes it. Do you know what it is?"

"No."

"Worry."

"So?"

"It might help the recuperating process if he knew it was O.K. about the shortage. Lying in a hospital, with a thing like that staring you in the face, that may not be so good. For his health anyway."

"What am I to tell him?"

"Why, I don't know. That you've fixed it up."

"If I tell him I've fixed it up, so nobody is going to know it, he knows I've got some kind of assistance in the bank. That'll terrify him, and I don't know what he's likely to do about it. He may speak to somebody, and the whole thing will come out. And who am I going to say has let me have the money, so I can put it back? You?"

"Do you have to say?"

"No. I don't have to say anything at all, and I'm not going to. The less you're involved in this the better. If he worries, he ought to be used to it by now. It won't hurt that young man to do quite a little suffering over what he's done to me—and to you."

"It's up to you."

"He knows something's cooking, all right, but he doesn't know what. I look forward to seeing his face when I tell him I'm off to—where did you say?"

". . . I said Reno."

"Do you still say Reno?"

"I don't generally change my mind, once it's made up."

"You can, if you want to."

"Shut up."

"I don't want you to."

"Neither do I."

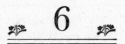

6

WE KEPT putting the money back, and I kept getting jitterier every day. I kept worrying that something would happen, that maybe the Old Man hadn't left a memo about me, before he went away, and that I'd get a call to report to the home office; that maybe Sheila would get sick and somebody else would have to do her work; that some depositor might think it was funny, the slip he had got to bring his book in, and begin asking about it somewhere.

One day she asked me to drive her home from the bank. By that time I was so nervous I never went anywhere with her in the daytime, and even at night I never met her anywhere that somebody might see us. But she said one of the children was sick, and she wanted a ride in case she had to get stuff from the drugstore that the doctor had ordered, and that anyway nobody was there but the maid and she didn't matter. By that time Brent had gone to the lake, to get his strength back, and she had the house to herself.

So I went. It was the first time I'd ever been in her home, and it was fixed up nice, and smelled like her, and the kids were the sweetest little pair you ever saw. The oldest was named Anna, and the younger was named Charlotte. She was the one that was sick. She was in bed with a cold, and took it like a little soldier. Another time, it would have tickled me to death to sit and watch her boss Sheila around, and watch Sheila wait on her, and take the bossing just like that was how it ought to be. But now I couldn't even keep still that long. When I found out I wasn't needed I ducked, and went home and filled up some more paper with the phoney article I had to have ready for the Old Man when he got back. It was called, "Building a Strong Savings Department."

We got to the last day before the monthly check on cash. Six hundred dollars had to go into her box that day, over and above the regular day's receipts. It was a lot, but it was a Wednesday, the day the factories all around us paid off, and deposits were sure to be heavy, so it looked like we could get away with it. We had all the passbooks in. It had taken some strong-arm work to get the last three we needed, and what she had done was go to those people the night before, like Brent had always done, and ask where they'd been, and why they hadn't put anything on savings. By sitting around a few minutes she managed to get their books, and then I drove her over to my place and we checked it all up. Then

I gave her the cash she needed, and it looked like she was set.

But I kept wanting to know how she stood, whether it had all gone through like we hoped. I couldn't catch her eye and I couldn't get a word with her. They were lined up at her window four and five deep all day long, and she didn't go out to lunch. She had sandwiches and milk sent in. On Wednesday they send out two extra tellers from the home office, to help handle the extra business, and every time one of them would go to her for help on something, and she'd have to leave her window for a minute, I'd feel the sweat on the palms of my hands, and lose track of what I was doing. I'm telling you it was a long day.

Along about two-thirty, though, it slacked off, and by five minutes to three there was nobody in there, and at three sharp Adler, the guard, locked the door. We went on finishing up. The home office tellers got through first, because all they had to do was balance one day's deposits, and around three-thirty they turned in their sheets, asked me to give them a count, and left. I sat at my desk, staring at papers, doing anything to keep from marching around and tip it that I had something on my mind.

About quarter to four there came a tap on the glass, and I didn't look up. There's always that late depositor trying to get in, and if he catches your eye you're sunk. I went right on staring at my papers, but I heard Adler open and then who should be there but Brent, with a grin on his face, a satchel in one hand, and a heavy coat of sunburn all over him. There was a chorus of "Hey's," and they all went out to shake hands, all except Sheila, and ask him how he was, and when he was coming back to work. He said he'd got home last night, and would be back any time now. There didn't seem to be much I could do but shake hands too, so I gritted my teeth, and did it, but I didn't ask him when he was coming back to work.

Then he said he'd come in for some of his stuff, and on his way back to the lockers he spoke to Sheila, and she spoke, without looking up. Then the rest of them went back to work. "Gee, he sure looks good, don't he?"

"Different from when he left."

"He must have put on twenty pounds."

"They fixed him up all right."

Pretty soon he came out again, closing his grip, and there was some more talk, and he went. They all counted their cash, turned in their sheets, and put their cash boxes into the vault. Helm wheeled the trucks in, with the records on them, and then he went. Snelling went back to set the time lock.

That was when Church started some more of her apple-polishing. She was about as unappetizing a girl as I ever saw. She was thick, and dumpy, with a delivery like she was making a speech all the time. She sounded like a dietician demonstrating a range in a department store basement, and she started in on a wonderful new adding machine that had just come on the market, and didn't I think we ought to have one. I said it sounded good, but I wanted to think it over. So then she said it all over again, and just about when she got going good she gave a little squeal and began pointing at the floor.

Down there was about the evilest-looking thing you ever saw in your life. It was one of these ground spiders you see out here in California, about the size of a tarantula and just about as dangerous. It was about three inches long, I would say, and was walking toward me with a clumsy gait but getting there all the time. I raised my foot to step on it, and she gave another squeal and said if I squashed it she'd die. By that time they were all standing around—Snelling, Sheila and Adler. Snelling said get a piece of paper and throw it out the door, and Sheila said yes, for heaven's sake do something about it quick. Adler took a piece of paper off my desk, and rolled it into a funnel, and then took a pen and pushed the thing into the paper. Then he folded the funnel shut and we all went out and watched him dump the spider into the gutter. Then a cop came along and borrowed the funnel and caught it again and said he was going to take it home to his wife, so they could take pictures of it with their home movie camera.

We went back in the bank, and Snelling and I closed the vault, and he went. Church went. Adler went back for his last tour around before closing. That left me alone with Sheila. I stepped back to where she was by the lockers, looking in the mirror while she put on her hat. "Well?"

"It's all done."

"You put back the cash?"

"To the last cent."

"The cards are all in?"

"It all checks to the last decimal point."

That was what I'd been praying for, for the last month, and yet as soon as I had it, it took me about one fifth of a second to get sore, about Brent.

"Is he driving you home?"

"If so, he didn't mention it."

"Suppose you wait in my car. There's a couple of things I want to talk to you about. It's just across the street."

She went, and Adler changed into his street clothes, and he and I locked up, and I bounced over to the car. I didn't head for her house, I headed for mine, but I didn't wait till we got there before I opened up.

"Why didn't you tell me he was back?"

"Were you interested?"

"Yeah, plenty."

"Well, since you ask me, I didn't know he was back—when I left you last night. He was there waiting for me when I got in. Today, I haven't had one minute to talk to you, or anybody."

"I thought he was due to spend a month up there."

"So did I."

"Then what's he doing back?"

"I haven't the faintest idea. Trying to find out what's going to happen to him, perhaps. Tomorrow, you may recall, you'll check my cash, and he knows it. That may account for why he cut his recuperation short."

"Are you sure he didn't have a date with you, now he's feeling better? To be waiting for you after you said good-night to me?"

"I stayed with the children, if that's what you mean."

I don't know if I believed any of that or not. I think I told you I was nuts about her, and all the money she'd cost me, and all the trouble she'd brought, only seemed to make it worse. The idea that she'd spent a night in the same house with him, and hadn't said anything to me about it, left me with a prickly feeling all over. Since I'd been going around with her, it was the first time that part of it had come up. He'd been in the hospital, and from there he'd gone right up to the lake, so in a way up to then he hadn't seemed real. But he seemed real now, all right, and I was still as sore as a bear when we got to my house, and went in. Sam lit the fire, and she sat down, but I didn't. I kept marching around the room, and she smoked, and watched me.

"All right, this guy's got to be told."

"He will be."

"He's got to be told *everything*."

"Dave, he'll be told, he'll be told everything, and a little more even than you know he's going to be told—when I'm ready to tell him."

"What's the matter with now?"

"I'm not equal to it."

"What's that—a stall?"

"Will you sit down for a moment?"

"All right, I'm sitting."

"Here—beside me."

I moved over beside her, and she took my hand and looked me in the eyes. "Dave, have you forgotten something?"

"Not that I know of."

"I think you have. . . . I think you've forgotten that today we finished what we started to do. That, thanks to you, I don't have to lie awake every night staring at the ceiling, wondering whether my father is going to be ruined, my children are going to be ruined—to say nothing of myself. That you've done something for me that was so dangerous to you I hate to think what would have happened if something had gone wrong. It would have wrecked your career, and it's such a nice, promising career. But it wasn't wrong, Dave. It was wonderfully right. It was decenter than any man I know of would have done, would even have thought of doing. And now it's done. There's not one card, one comma, one missing penny to show—and I can sleep, Dave. That's all that matters to me today."

"O.K.—then you're leaving him."

"Of course I am, but—"

"You're leaving him tonight. You're coming in here, with your two kids, and if that bothers you, then I'll move out. We're going over there now, and—"

"We're doing nothing of the kind."

"I'm telling you—"

"And I'm telling *you*! Do you think I'm going over there now, and starting a quarrel that's going to last until three o'clock in the morning and maybe until dawn? That's going to wander all over the earth, from how horribly he says I've treated him to who's going to have the children—the way I feel now? I certainly shall not. When I'm ready, when I know exactly what I'm going to say, when I've got the children safely over to my father's, when it's all planned and I can do it in one terrible half hour—then I'll do it. In the meantime, if he's biting his finger nails, if he's frightened to death over what's going to happen to him—that's perfectly all right with me. A little of that won't hurt him. When it's all done, then I go at once to Reno, if you still want me to, and then my life can go on. . . . Don't you know what I'm trying to tell you, Dave? What you're worried about just couldn't happen. Why—he hasn't even looked at me that way in over a year. Dave, tonight I want to be happy. With you. That's all."

I felt ashamed of myself at that, and took her in my arms, and that catch came in my throat again when she sighed, like some child and relaxed, and closed her eyes.

"Sheila?"

"Yes?"

"We'll celebrate."

"All right."

So we celebrated. She phoned her maid, and said she'd be late, and we went to dinner at a downtown restaurant, and then we drove to a night club on Sunset Boulevard. We didn't talk about Brent, or the shortage, or anything but ourselves, and what we were going to do with our lives together. We stayed till about one o'clock. I didn't think of Brent again till we pulled up near her house, and then this same prickly feeling began to come over me. If she noticed anything she didn't say so. She kissed me good-night, and I started home.

❧ **7** ❧

I TURNED in the drive, put the car away, closed the garage, and walked around to go in the front way. When I started for the door I heard my name called. Somebody got up from a bench under the trees and walked over. It was Helm. "Sorry to be bothering you this hour of night, Mr. Bennett, but I've got to talk to you."

"Well, come in."

He seemed nervous as I took him inside. I offered him a drink, but he said he didn't want anything. He sat down and lit a cigarette, and acted like he didn't know how to begin. Then: "Have you seen Sheila?"

". . . Why?"

"I saw you drive off with her."

"Yes—I had some business with her. We had dinner together. I—just left her a little while ago."

"Did you see Brent?"

"No. It was late. I didn't go in."

"She say anything about him?"

"I guess so. Now and then. . . . What's this about?"

"Did you see him leave the bank? Today?"

"He left before you did."

"Did you see him leave the second time?"

". . . He only came in once."

He kept looking at me, smoking and looking at me. He was a young fellow, twenty-four or five, I would say, and had only been with us a couple of years. Little by little he was losing his nervousness at talking with me.

". . . He went in there twice."

"He came in once. He rapped on the door, Adler let him in, he stood there talking a few minutes, then he went back to get some stuff out of his locker. Then he left. You were there. Except for the extra tellers, nobody had finished up yet. He must have left fifteen minutes before you did."

"That's right. Then I left. I finished up, put my cash box away, and left. I went over to the drugstore to get myself a malted milk, and was sitting there drinking it when he went in."

"He couldn't have. We were locked, and—"

"He used a key."

". . . When was this?"

"A little after four. Couple of minutes before you all come out with that spider, and dumped it in the gutter."

"So?"

"I didn't see him come out."

"Why didn't you tell me?"

"I haven't seen you. I've been looking for you."

"You saw me drive off with Sheila."

"Yeah, but it hadn't occurred to me, at the time. That cop, after he caught the spider, came in the drugstore to buy some film for his camera. I helped him put the spider in an ice cream container, and punch holes in the top, and I wasn't watching the bank all that time. Later, it just happened to run through my head that I'd seen all the rest of you leave the bank, but I hadn't seen Brent. I kept telling myself to forget it, that I'd got a case of nerves from being around money too much, but then—"

"Yeah? What else?"

"I went to a picture tonight with the Snellings."

"Didn't Snelling see him leave?"

"I didn't say anything to Snelling. I don't know what he saw. But the picture had some Mexican stuff in it, and later, when we went to the Snellings' apartment, I started a bum argument, and got Snelling to call Charlie to settle it. Brent spent some time in Mexico once. That was about twelve o'clock."

"And?"

"The maid answered. Charlie wasn't there."

We looked at each other, and both knew that twelve o'clock was too late for a guy to be out that had just had a bad operation.

"Come on."

"You calling Sheila?"

"We're going to the bank."

The protection service watchman was due on the hour, and we caught him on his two-o'clock round. He took it as a personal insult that we would think anybody could be in the bank without him knowing it, but I made him take us in there just the same, and we went through every part of it. We went upstairs, where the old records were stored, and I looked behind every pile. We went down in the basement and I looked behind every gas furnace. We went all around back of the windows and I looked under every counter. I even looked behind my desk, and under it. That seemed to be all. The watchman went up and punched his clock and we went out on the street again. Helm kind of fingered his chin.

"Well, I guess it was a false alarm."

"Looks like it."

"Sorry."

"It's all right. Report everything."

"Guess there's no use calling Sheila."

"Pretty late, I'm afraid."

What he meant was, we ought to call Sheila, but he wanted me to do it. He was just as suspicious as he ever was, I could tell that from the way he was acting. Only the watchman was sure we were a couple of nuts. We got in the car, and I took him home, and once more he mumbled something about Sheila, but I decided not to hear him. When I let him out I started for home, but as soon as I was out of sight I cut around the block and headed for Mountain Drive.

A light was on, and the screen door opened as soon as I set my foot on the porch. She was still dressed, and it was almost as though she had been expecting me. I followed her in the living room, and spoke low so nobody in the house could hear us, but I didn't waste any time on love and kisses.

"Where's Brent?"

". . . He's in the vault."

She spoke in a whisper, and sank into a chair without looking at me, but every doubt I'd had about her in the beginning, I mean, every hunch that she'd been playing me for a sucker, swept back over me so even looking at her made me tremble. I had to lick my lips a couple of times before I could even talk. "Funny you didn't tell me."

"I didn't know it."

"What do you mean you didn't know it? If you know it now, why didn't you know it then? You trying to tell me he stepped out of there for a couple of minutes, borrowed my telephone, and called you up? He might as well be in a tomb as be in that place, till it opens at eight-thirty this morning."

"Are you done?"

"I'm still asking you why you didn't tell me."

"When I got in, and found he wasn't home, I went out looking for him. Or at any rate, for the car. I went to where he generally parks it—when he's out. It wasn't there. Coming home I had to go by the bank. As I went by, the red light winked, just once."

I don't know if you know how a vault works. There's two switches inside. One lights the overhead stuff that you turn on when somebody wants to get into his safe deposit box, the other works the red light that's always on over the door in the daytime. That's the danger signal, and any employee of the bank always looks to see that it's on whenever he goes inside. When the vault is closed the light's turned off, and I had turned it off myself that afternoon, when I locked the vault with Snelling. At night, all curtains are raised in the bank, so cops, watchman, and any passer-by can see inside. If the red light went on, it would show, but I didn't believe she'd seen it. I didn't believe she'd even been by the bank. "So the red light winked, hey? Funny it wasn't winking when I left there not ten minutes ago."

"I said it winked once. I don't think it was a signal. I think he bumped his shoulder against it, by accident. If he were signaling, he'd keep on winking it, wouldn't he?"

"How'd he get in there?"

"I don't know."

"I think you do know."

"I don't know, but the only way I can think of is that he slipped in there while we were all gathered around, looking at that spider."

"That you conveniently on purpose brought in there."

"Or that he did."

"What's he doing in there?"

"I don't know."

"Come on, come on, quit stalling me!"

She got up and began walking around. "Dave, it's easy to see you think I know all about this. That I know more than I'm telling. That Charles and I are in some kind of plot. I don't know anything I can say. I know a lot I could say if I wasn't—"

She stopped, came to life like some kind of a tiger, and began hammering her fists against the wall.

"—Bought! That was what was wrong! I ought to have cut my heart out, suffered anything rather than let you give me that money! Why did I ever take it? Why didn't I tell you to—"

"Why didn't you do what I begged you to do? Come over here today and let him have it between the eyes—tell him the truth, that you were through, and this was the end of it?"

"Because, God help me, I wanted to be happy!"

"No! . . . Because, God help you, you knew he wasn't over here! Because you knew he was in that vault, and you were afraid I'd find it out!"

"It isn't true! How can you say that?"

"Do you know what I think? I think you took that money off me, day by day, and that not one penny of it ever found its way into your cash box. And then I think you and he decided on a little phoney hold-up, to cover that shortage, and that that's what he's doing in the vault. And if Helm hadn't got into it, and noticed that Brent didn't come out of the bank the second time he went in, I don't see anything that was to stop you from getting away with it. You knew I didn't dare open my trap about the dough *I* had put up. And if he came out of there masked, and made a quick getaway, I don't know who was going to swear it was him, if it hadn't been for Helm. Now it's in the soup. All right, Mrs. Brent, that vault that don't take any messages till eight thirty, that works both ways. If he can't get any word to you, you can't get any word to him. Just let him start that little game that looked so good yesterday afternoon, and he's going to get the surprise of his life, and so are you. There'll be a reception committee waiting for him when he comes out of there, and maybe they'll include you in it too."

She looked straight at me the whole time I was talking, and the lamplight caught her eyes, so they shot fire. There was something catlike about her shape anyway, and with her eyes blazing like that, she looked like something out of the jungle. But all of a sudden that woman was gone, and she was crumpled up in front of me, on the sofa, crying in a queer, jerky way. Then I hated myself for what I had said, and had to dig in with my finger nails to keep from crying too.

After a while the phone rang. From what she said, I could tell it was her father, and that he'd been trying to reach her all afternoon and all night. She listened a long time, and when she hung up she lay back and closed her eyes. "He's in there to put the money back."

". . . Where'd he get it?"

"He got it this morning. Yesterday morning. From my father."

"Your father had that much—*ready*?"

"He got it after I talked to him that night. Then when I told him I wouldn't need it, he kept it, in his safe deposit box—just in case. Charles went over there yesterday and said he had to have it—against the check-up on my cash. Papa went down to the Westwood bank with him, and got it out, and gave it to him. He was afraid to call me at the bank. He kept trying to reach me here. The maid left me a note, but it was so late when I got in I didn't call. . . . So, now I pay a price for not telling him. Charles, I mean. For letting him worry."

"I was for telling him, you may remember."

"Yes, I remember."

It was quite a while after that before either of us said anything. All that time my mind was going around like a squirrel cage, trying to reconstruct for myself what was going on in that vault. She must have been doing the same thing, because pretty soon she said, "Dave?"

"Yes?"

"Suppose he *does* put the money back?"

"Then—we're sunk."

"What, actually, will happen?"

"If I find him in there, the least I can do is hold him till I've checked every cent in that vault. I find nine thousand more cash than the books show. All right. What then?"

"You mean the whole thing comes out?"

"On what we've been doing, you can get away with it as long as nobody's got the least suspicion of it. Let a thing like this happen, let them really begin to check, and it'll come out so fast it'll make your head swim."

"And there goes your job?"

"Suppose you were the home office, how would you like it?"

". . . I've brought you nothing but misery, Dave."

"I—asked for it."

"I can understand why you feel bitter."

"I said some things I didn't mean."

"Dave."

"Yes?"

"There's one chance, if you'll take it."

"What's that?"

"Charles."

"I don't get it."

"It may be a blessing, after all, that I told him nothing. He can't be sure what I've done while he's been away—whether I carried his false entries right along, whether I corrected them, and left the cash short—and it does look as though he'd check, before he did anything. He's a wizard at books, you know. And every record he needs is in there. Do you know what I'm getting at, Dave?"

"Not quite."

"You'll have to play dummy's hand, and let him lead."

"I don't want anything to do with him."

"I'd like to wring his neck. But if you just don't force things, if you just act natural, and let me have a few seconds with him, so we'll know just what he *has* done, then—maybe it'll all come out all right. He certainly would be a boob to put the money back when he finds out it's already been put back."

"*Has* it been?"

"Don't you know?"

I took her in my arms then, and for that long was able to forget what was staring us in the face, and I still felt close to her when I left.

8

FOR THE second time that night I went home, and this time I turned out all lights, and went upstairs, and took off my clothes, and went to bed. I tried to sleep, and couldn't. It was all running through my mind, and especially what I was going to do when I opened that vault at eight-thirty. How could I act natural about it? If I could guess he was in the vault, Helm must have guessed it. He'd be watching me, waiting for every move, and he'd be doing that even if he didn't have any suspicion of me, which by now he must have, on account of being out that late with Sheila. All that ran through my mind, and after a while I'd figured a way to cover it, by openly saying something to him, and telling him I was going to go along with it, just wait and see what Brent had to say for himself, in case he was really in there. Then I tried once more to go to sleep. But this time it wasn't the play at the vault that was bothering me, it was Sheila. I kept going over and over it, what was said between us, the dirty cracks I had made, how she had taken them, and all the rest of it. Just as day began to break I found myself sitting up in bed. How I knew it I don't know, what I had to go on I haven't any idea, but I knew perfectly well that she was holding out on me, that there was something back of it all that she wasn't telling.

I unhooked the phone and dialed. You don't stay around a bank very long before you know the number of your chief guard. I was calling Dyer, and in a minute or two he answered, pretty sour. "Hello?"

"Dyer?"

"Yeah, who is it?"

"Sorry to wake you up. This is Dave Bennett."

"What do you want?"

"I want some help."

"Well, what the hell is it?"

"I got reason to think there's a man in our vault. Out in the Anita Avenue Branch in Glendale. What he's up to I don't know, but I want you out there when I open up. And I'd like you to bring a couple of men with you."

Up to then he'd been just a sleepy guy that used to be a city detective. Now he snapped out of it like something had hit him. "What do you mean you got reason to think? Who is this guy?"

"I'll give you that part when I see you. Can you meet me by seven o'clock? Is that too early?"

"Whenever you say, Mr. Bennett."

"Then be at my house at seven, and bring your men with you. I'll give you the dope, and I'll tell you how I want you to do it."

He took the address, and I went back to bed.

I went to bed, and lay there trying to figure out what it was I wanted him to do anyway. After a while I had it straightened out. I wanted him close enough to protect the bank, and myself as well, in case Sheila was lying to me, and I wanted him far enough away for her to have those few seconds with Brent, in case she wasn't. I mean, if Brent was really up to something, I wanted him covered every way there was, and by guys that would shoot. But if he came out with a foolish look on his face, and pretended he'd been locked in by mistake, and she found out we could still cover up that book-doctoring, I wanted to leave that open too. I figured on it, and after a while I thought I had it doped out so it would work.

Around six o'clock I got up, bathed, shaved, and dressed. I routed out Sam and had him make me some coffee, and fix up some bacon and eggs. I told him to stand by in case the men that were coming hadn't had any breakfast. Then I went in the living room and began to march around. It was cold. I lit the fire. My head kept spinning around.

Right on the tick of seven the doorbell rang and there they were, Dyer and his two muggs. Dyer's a tall, thin man with a bony face and eyes like gimlets. I'd say he was around fifty. The other two were around my own age, somewhere over thirty, with big shoulders, thick necks, and red faces. They looked exactly like what they were: ex-cops that had got jobs as guards in a bank. One was named Halligan, the other Lewis. They all said yes on breakfast, so we went in the dining-room and Sam made it pretty quick with the service.

I gave it to Dyer, as quick as I could, about Brent being off for a couple of months, with his operation, and how he'd come in yesterday to get his stuff, and Helm had seen him go in the bank a second time, and not come out, and how Sheila had gone out looking for him late at night, and thought she saw the red light flash. I had to tell him that much, to protect myself afterward, because God only knew what was going to come out, and I didn't even feel I was safe on Sheila's end of it. I didn't say anything about the shortage, or Sheila's father, or any of that part. I told what I had to tell, and made it short.

"Now what I figure is, Brent got in there somehow just before we closed it up, maybe just looking around, and that he got locked in there by accident. However, I can't be sure. Maybe—it doesn't seem very likely—he's up to something. So what I'd like you guys to do is be outside, just be where you can see what's going on. If it's all quiet, I'll give you the word, and you can go on home. If anything happens, you're there. Of course, a man spends a night in a vault, he may not feel so good by morning. We may need an ambulance. If so, I'll let you know."

I breathed a little easier. It had sounded all right, and Dyer kept on wolfing down his toast and eggs. When they were gone he put sugar and cream in his coffee, stirred it around, and lit a cigarette. "Well—that's how you got it figured out."

"I imagine I'm not far off."

"All I got to say, you got a trusting disposition."

"What do you make of it?"

"This guy's a regular employee, you say?"

"He's been head teller."

"Then he *couldn't* get locked in by mistake. He couldn't no more do that than a doctor could sew himself up in a man's belly by mistake. Furthermore, you couldn't lock him in by mistake. You take all the usual care, don't you, when you lock a vault?"

"I think so."

"And you done it regular, yesterday?"

"As well as I can recall."

"You looked around in there?"

"Yes, of course."

"And you didn't see nothing?"

"No, certainly not."

"Then he's in there on purpose."

The other two nodded, and looked at me like I must not be very bright.

Dyer went on: "It's possible for a man to hide hisself in a vault. I've thought of it, many a time, how it could be done. You think of a lot of things in my business. Once them trucks are wheeled in, with the records on them, if he once got in without being seen, he could stoop down behind them, and keep quiet, and when you come to close up you wouldn't see him. But not by accident. Never."

I was feeling funny in the stomach. I had to take a tack I didn't like.

"Of course, there's a human element in it. There's nothing in this man's record that gives any ground whatever for thinking he'd pull anything. Fact of the matter, that's what I'm doing in the branch. I was sent out there to study his methods in the savings department. I've been so much impressed by his work that I'm going to write an article about it."

"When did he get in there, do you think?"

"Well, we found a spider. A big one."

"One of them bad dreams with fur all over them?"

"That's it. And we were all gathered around looking at it. And arguing about how to get it out of there. I imagine he was standing there looking at it too. We all went out to throw it in the street, and he must have gone in the vault. Perhaps just looking around. Perhaps to open his box, I don't know. And—was in there when I closed it up."

"That don't hit you funny?"

"Not particularly."

"If you wanted to get everybody in one place in that bank, and everybody looking in one direction, so you could slip in the vault, you couldn't think of nothing better than one of them spiders, could you? Unless it was a rattlesnake."

"That strikes me as a little far-fetched."

"Not if he's just back from the mountains. From Lake Arrowhead, I think you said. That's where they have them spiders. I never seen one around Glendale. If he happened to turn that spider loose the first time he come in, all he had to do was wait till you found it, and he could easy slip in."

"He'd be running an awful risk."

"No risk. Suppose you seen him? He was looking at the spider too, wasn't he? He come in with his key to see what all the fuss was about. Thought maybe there was trouble. . . . Mr. Bennett, I'm telling you, he's not locked in by accident. It couldn't happen."

". . . What would you suggest?"

"I'd suggest that me, and Halligan, and Lewis, are covering that vault with guns when you open the door, and that we take him right in custody and get it out of him what he was doing in there. If he's got dough on him, then we'll know. I'd treat him just like anybody else that hid hisself in a vault. I wouldn't take no chances whatever."

"I can't stand for that."

"Why not?"

For just a split second I didn't know why not. All I knew was that if he was searched, even if he hadn't put his father-in-law's money back in the cash box, they'd find it on him, and a man with nine thousand dollars on him, unaccounted for, stepping out of a bank vault, was going to mean an investigation that was going to ruin me. But if you've got to think fast, you can do it. I acted like he ought to know why not. "Why—morale."

"What do you mean, morale?"

"I can't have those people out there, those other employees, I mean, see that at the first crack out of the box, for no reason whatever, I treat the senior member of the staff like some kind of a bandit. It just wouldn't do."

"I don't agree on that at all."

"Well, put yourself in their place."

"They work for a bank, don't they?"

"They're not criminals."

"Every person that works for a bank is automatically under suspicion from the minute he goes in until he comes out. Ain't nothing personal about it. They're just people that are entrusted with other people's money, and not nothing at all is taken for granted. That's why they're under bond. That's why they're checked all the time—they know it, they want it that way. And if he's got any sense, even when he sees our guns, supposing he is on the up-and-up, and he's in there by mistake, *he* knows it. But he's not on the up-and-up, and you owe it to them other people in there to give them the protection they're entitled to."

"I don't see it that way."

"It's up to you. But I want to be on record, in the presence of Halligan and Lewis, that I warned you. You hear what I say, Mr. Bennett?"

". . . I hear what you say."

My stomach was feeling still worse, but I gave them their orders. They were to take positions outside. They weren't to come in unless they were needed. They were to wait him out.

I led, driving over to the bank, and they followed, in Dyer's car. When I went past the bank I touched the horn and Dyer waved at me, so I could catch him in the mirror. They had wanted me to show them the bank, because they were all from the home office and had never been there. A couple of blocks up Anita Avenue I turned the corner and stopped. They pulled in ahead of me and parked. Dyer looked out. "All right. I got it."

I drove on, turned another corner, kept on around the block and parked where I could see the bank. In a minute or two along came Helm, unlocked the door and went in. He's first in, every morning. In about five minutes Snelling drove up, and parked in front of the drugstore. Then Sheila came walking down the street, stopped at Snelling's car, and stood there talking to him.

The curtains on the bank door came down. This was all part of opening the bank, you understand, and didn't have anything to do with the vault. The first man in goes all through the bank. That's in case somebody got in there during the night. They've been known to chop holes in the roof even, to be there waiting with a gun when the vault is opened.

He goes all through the bank, then if everything's O.K. he goes to the front door and lowers the curtains. That's a signal to the man across the street, who's always there by that time. But even that's not all. The man across the street doesn't go in till the first man comes out of the bank, crosses over, and gives the word. That's also in case there's somebody in there with a gun. Maybe he knows all about those curtains. Maybe he tells the first man to go lower the curtains, and be quick about it. But if the first man doesn't come out, as soon as he lowers the curtains, the man across the street knows there's something wrong, and puts in a call, quick.

The curtains were lowered, and Helm came out, and Snelling got out of his car. I climbed out and crossed over. Snelling and Helm went in, and Sheila dropped back with me.

"What are you going to do, Dave?"

"Give him his chance."

"If only he hasn't done something dumb."

"Get to him. Get to him and find out what's what. I'm going to take it as easy as I can. I'm going to stall, listen to what he has to say, tell him I'll have to ask him to stick around till we check— and then you get at it. Find out. And let me know."

"Do the others know?"

"No, but Helm's guessed it."

"Do you ever pray?"

"I prayed all I know."

Adler came up then and we went in. I looked at the clock. It was twenty after eight. Helm and Snelling had their dust cloths, polishing up their counters. Sheila went back and started to polish hers. Adler went back to the lockers to put on his uniform. I sat down at my desk, opened it, and took out some papers. They were the same papers I'd been stalling with the afternoon before. It seemed a long time ago, but I began stalling with them again. Don't ask me what they were. I don't know yet.

My phone rang. It was Church. She said she wasn't feeling well, and would it be all right if she didn't come in today? I said yeah, perfectly all right. She said she hated to miss a day, but she was afraid if she didn't take care of herself she'd really get sick. I said certainly, she ought to take care of herself. She said she certainly hoped I hadn't forgotten about the adding machine, that it was a wonderful value for the money, and would probably pay for itself in a year by what it would save. I said I hadn't forgotten it. She said it all over again about how bad she felt, and I said get well, that was the main thing. She hung up. I looked at the clock. It was twenty-five after eight.

Helm stepped over, and gave my desk a wipe with his cloth. As he leaned down he said: "There's a guy in front of the drugstore I don't like the looks of, and two more down the street."

I looked over. Dyer was there, reading a paper.

"Yeah, I know. I sent for them."

"O.K."

"Have you said anything, Helm? To the others?"

"No sir, I haven't."

"I'd rather you didn't."

"No use starting anything, just on a hunch."

"That's it. I'll help you open the vault."

"Yes, sir."

"See the front door is open."

"I'll open it now."

At last the clock said eight-thirty, and the time lock clicked off. Adler came in from the lockers, strapping his belt on over his uniform. Snelling spoke to Helm, and went over to the vault. It takes two men to open a vault, even after the time lock goes off, one to each combination. I opened the second drawer of my desk, took out the automatic that was in there, threw off the catch, slipped it in my coat pocket, and went back there.

"I'll do that, Snelling."

"Oh, that's all right, Mr. Bennett. Helm and I have it down to a fine art. We've got so we can even do it to music."

"I'll try it, just once."

"O.K.—you spin and I'll whistle."

He grinned at Sheila, and began to whistle. He was hoping I'd forgotten the combination, and would have to ask help, and then he'd have a laugh on the boss. Helm looked at me, and I nodded. He spun his dial, I spun mine. I swung the door open.

At first, for one wild second, I thought there was nobody in there at all. I snapped on the switch, and couldn't see anything. By then my eye caught bright marks on the steel panels of the compartments that hold the safe deposit boxes. Then I saw the trucks had all been switched. They're steel frames, about four feet high, that hold the records. They run on rubber wheels, and when they're loaded they're plenty heavy. When they were put in there, they were all crosswise of the door. Now they were end to it, one jammed up against the other, and not three feet away from me. I dropped my hand in my gun pocket, and opened my mouth to call, and right that second the near truck hit me.

It hit me in the pit of the stomach. He must have been crouched behind it, like a runner, braced against the rear shelves and watching the time lock for the exact second we'd be in there. I went over backwards, still trying to get out the gun. The truck was right over me, like it had been shot out of a cannon. A roller went over my leg, and then I could see it crashing down on top of me.

I must have gone out for a split second when it hit my head, because the next thing I knew screams were ringing in my ears, and then I could see Adler and Snelling, against the wall, their hands over their heads.

But that wasn't the main thing I saw. It was this madman, this maniac, in front of the vault, waving an automatic, yelling that it was a stick-up, to put them up and keep them up, that whoever moved was going to be killed. If he had hoped to get away with it without being recognized, I can't say he didn't have a chance. He was dressed different from the way he was the day before. He must have brought the stuff in the grip. He had on a sweat shirt that made him look three times as big as he really was, a pair of rough pants and rough shoes, a black silk handkerchief over the lower part of his face, a felt hat pulled down over his eyes—and this horrible voice.

He was yelling, and the screaming was coming from Sheila. She seemed to be behind me, and was telling him to cut it out. I couldn't see Helm. The truck was on top of me, and I couldn't see anything clear, on account of the wallop on my head. Brent was standing right over me.

Then, right back of his head, a chip fell out of the wall. I didn't hear any shot at all, but he must have, because Dyer fired, from the street, right through the glass window. Brent turned, toward the street, and I saw Adler grab at his holster. I doubled up my legs and drove against the truck, straight at Brent. It missed him, and crashed against the wall, right beside Adler. Brent wheeled and fired. Adler fired. I fired. Brent fired again. Then he made one leap, and heaved the grip, that he had in his other hand, straight through the glass at the rear of the bank. You understand: the bank is on a corner, and on two sides there's glass. There's glass on half the third side too, at the rear, facing the parking lot. It was through that window that he heaved the grip. The glass broke with a crash, and left a hole the size of a door. He went right through it.

I jumped up, and dived after him, through the hole. I could hear Dyer and his two men coming up the street behind me, shooting as they came. They hadn't come in the bank at all. At the first yelp that Sheila let out they began shooting through the glass.

He was just grabbing up the grip as I got there and leveled his gun right at me. I dropped to the ground and shot. He shot. There was a volley of shots from Dyer and Halligan and Lewis. He ran about five steps, and jumped into a car. It was a blue sedan, the door was open and it was already moving when he landed on it. It shot ahead, straight across the parking lot and over to Grove Street. I raised my gun to shoot at the tires. Two kids came around the corner carrying school books. They stopped and blinked. I didn't fire. The car was gone.

I turned around and stepped back through the hole in the glass. The place was full of smoke, from the shooting. Sheila, Helm, and Snelling were stooped down, around Adler. He was lying a little to one side of the vault, and a drop of blood was trickling down back of his ear. It was the look on their faces that told me. Adler was dead.

9

I STARTED for the telephone. It was on my desk, at the front of the bank, and my legs felt queer as I walked along toward it, back of the windows. Dyer was there ahead of me. He came through the brass gate, from the other side and reached for it.

"I'm using that for a second, Dyer."

He didn't answer, and didn't look at me, just picked up the phone and started to dial. So far as he was concerned, I was the heel that was responsible for it all, by not doing what he said, and he was letting me know it. I felt that way about it too, but I wasn't taking anything off him. I grabbed him by the neck of his coat and jerked him back on his heels.

"Didn't you hear what I said?"

His face got white, and he stood there beside me, his nostrils fanning and his little gray eyes drawn down to points. I broke his connection and dialed the home office. When they came in I asked for Lou Frazier. His title is vice president, same as mine, but he's special assistant to the Old Man, and with the Old Man in Honolulu, he was in charge. His secretary said he wasn't there, but then she said wait a minute, he's just come in. She put him on.

"Lou?"

"Yeah?"

"Dave Bennett, in Glendale."

"What is it, Dave?"

"We've had some trouble. You better get out. And bring some money. There'll be a run."

"What kind of trouble?"

"Stick-up. Guard killed. I think we're cleaned."

"O.K.—how much do you need?"

"Twenty thousand, to start. If we need more, you can send for it later. And step on it."

"On my way."

While I was talking, the sirens were screeching, and now the place was full of cops. Outside, an ambulance was pulling in, and about five hundred people standing around, with more coming by the second. When I hung up, a drop of blood ran off the end of my nose on the blotter, and then it began to patter down in a stream. I put my hand to my head. My hair was all sticky and wet, and when I looked, my fingers were full of blood. I tried to think what caused it, then remembered the truck falling on me.

"Dyer?"

". . . Yes sir."

"Mr. Frazier is on his way out. He's bringing money to meet all demands. You're to stay here with Halligan and Lewis, and keep order, and hold yourself ready for anything he tells you. Let the police take care of Adler."

"They're taking him out now."

I looked, and two of them, with the ambulance crew, were carrying him out. They were going the front way. Halligan had opened the door. Lewis and five or six cops were already outside, keeping the people back. They put him in the ambulance. Helm started out there, but I called him.

"Get in the vault, check it up."

"We've been in. Snelling and I."

"What did he get?"

"He got it all. Forty-four thousand, cash. And that's not all. He got in the boxes. He left the little boxes alone. He went in the others with a chisel, the ones that had big valuables and securities in them, and he took it all from them, too. He knew which ones."

"Mr. Frazier is on his way out with cash for the depositors. As soon as that's under way, make a list of all the rifled boxes, get the box holders on the phone if you can, send them wires otherwise, and get them in here."

"I'll start on it now."

The ambulance crew came in, and started over toward me. I waved them away, and they went off with Adler. Sheila came over to me.

"Mr. Kaiser wants to speak to you."

He was right behind her, Bunny Kaiser, the guy she had brought in for the $100,000 loan the afternoon I had found the shortage. I was just opening my mouth to tell him that all demands would be met, that he could take his turn with the other depositors as soon as we opened, when he motioned to the windows. Every window on one side was full of breaks and bullet holes, and the back window had the big hole in it where Brent had thrown his grip through it.

"Mr. Bennett, I just wanted to say, I've got my glaziers at work now, they're just starting on the plate glass windows for my building, they've got plenty of stock, and if you want, I'll send them over and they can get you fixed up here. Them breaks don't look so good."

"That would help, Mr. Kaiser."

"Right away."

"And—thanks."

I stuck out my left hand, the one that wasn't covered with blood, and he took it. I must have been pretty rung up. For just that long it seemed to me I loved him more than anybody on earth. At a time like that, what it means to you, one kind word.

The glaziers were already ripping out the broken glass when Lou Frazier got there. He had a box of cash, four extra tellers, and one uniformed guard, all he could get into his car. He came over, and I gave it to him quick, what he needed to know. He stepped out on the sidewalk with his cash box, held it up, and made a speech:

"All demands will be met. In five minutes the windows will open, all depositors kindly fall in line, the tellers will identify you, and positively nobody but depositors will be admitted!"

He had Snelling with him, and Snelling began to pick depositors out of the crowd, and the cops and the new guard formed them in line, out on the sidewalk. He came in the bank again, and his tellers set the upset truck on its wheels again, and rolled the others out, and they and Helm started to get things ready to pay. Dyer was inside by now. Lou went over to him, and jerked his thumb toward me.

"Get him out of here."

It was the first it had dawned on me that I must be an awful-looking thing, sitting there at my desk in the front of the bank, with blood all over me. Dyer came over and called another ambulance. Sheila took her handkerchief and started to wipe off my face. It was full of blood in a second. She took my own handkerchief out of my pocket, and did the best she could with it. From the way Lou looked away every time his eye fell on me, I figured she only made it worse.

Lou opened the doors, and forty or fifty depositors filed in. "Savings depositors on this side, please have your passbooks ready."

He split them up to four windows. There was a little wait, and then those at the head of the line began to get their money. Four or five went out, counting bills. Two or three that had been in line saw we were paying, and dropped out. A guy counting bills stopped, then fell in at the end of the line, to put his money back in.

The run was over.

My head began to go around, and I felt sick to my stomach. Next thing I knew, there was an ambulance siren, and then a doctor in a white coat was standing in front of me, with two orderlies beside him. "Think you can go, or you going to need a little help?"

"Oh, I can go."

"Better lean on me."

I leaned on him, and I must have looked pretty terrible, because Sheila turned away from me, and started to cry. It was the first she had broken down since it happened, and she couldn't fight it back. Her shoulders kept jerking and the doctor motioned to one of the orderlies.

"Guess we better take her along too."

"Guess we better."

They rode us in together, she on one stretcher, me on the other, the doctor riding backwards, between us. As we went he worked on my cut. He kept swabbing at it, and I could feel the sting of the antiseptic. But I wasn't thinking about that. Once out of the bank, Sheila broke down completely, and it was terrible to hear the sound in her voice, as the sobs came out of her. The doctors talked to her a little, but kept on working on me. It was a swell ride.

10

IT WAS the same old hospital again, and they lifted her out, and wheeled her away somewhere, and then they took me out. They wheeled me in an elevator, and we went up, and they wheeled me out of the elevator to a room, and then two more doctors came and looked at me. One of them was an older man, and he didn't seem to be an interne. "Well, Mr. Bennett, you've got a bad head."

"Sew it up, it'll be all right."

"I'm putting you under an anaesthetic, for that."

"No anaesthetic, I've got things to do."

"Do you want to bear that scar the rest of your life?"

"What are you talking about, scar?"

"I'm telling you, you've got a bad head. Now if—"

"O.K.—but get at it."

He went, and an orderly came in and started to undress me, but I stopped him and made him call my house. When he had Sam on the line I talked, and told him to drop everything and get in there with another suit of clothes, a clean shirt, fresh necktie, and everything else clean. Then I slipped out of the rest of my clothes, and they put a hospital shirt on me, and a nurse came in and jabbed me with a hypodermic, and they took me up to the operating room. A doctor put a mask over my face and told me to breathe in a natural manner, and that was the last I knew for a while.

When I came out of it I was back in the room again, and the nurse was sitting there, and my head was all wrapped in bandages. They hadn't used ether, they had used some other stuff, so in about five minutes I was myself again, though I felt pretty sick. I asked for a paper. She had one on her lap, reading it, and handed it over. It was an early edition, and the robbery was smeared all over the front page, with Brent's picture, and Adler's picture, and my picture, one of my old football pictures. There was no trace of Brent yet, it said, but the preliminary estimate of what he got was put at $90,000. That included $44,000 from the bank, and around $46,000 taken from the private safe deposit boxes. The story made me the hero. I knew he was in the vault, it said, and although I brought guards with me, I insisted on being the first man in the vault, and suffered a serious head injury as a result. Adler got killed on the first exchange of shots, after I opened fire. He left a wife and one child, and the funeral would probably be held tomorrow.

There was a description of Brent's sedan, and the license number. Dyer had got that, as the car drove off, and it checked with the plates issued in Brent's name. There was quite a lot about the fact that the car was moving when he jumped aboard, and how that proved he had accomplices. There was nothing about Sheila, except that she had been taken to the hospital for nervous collapse, and nothing about the shortage at all. The nurse got up and came over to feed me some ice. "Well, how does it feel to be a hero?"

"Feels great."

"You had quite a time out there."

"Yeah, quite a time."

Pretty soon Sam got there with my clothes, and I told him to stand by. Then two detectives came in and began asking questions. I told them as little as I could, but I had to tell them about Helm, and Sheila seeing the red light, and how I'd gone against Dyer's advice, and what happened at the bank. They dug in pretty hard, but I stalled as well as I could, and after a while they went.

Sam went out and got a later edition of the afternoon paper. They had a bigger layout now on the pictures. Brent's picture was still three columns, but my picture and Adler's picture were smaller, and in an inset there was a picture of Sheila. It said police had a talk with her, at the hospital, and that she was unable to give any clue as to why Brent had committed the crime, or as to his whereabouts. Then, at the end, it said: "It was intimated, however, that Mrs. Brent will be questioned further."

At that I hopped out of bed. The nurse jumped up and tried to stop me, but I knew I had to get away from where cops could get at me, anyway until the thing broke enough that I knew what I was going to do.

"What are you doing, Mr. Bennett?"

"I'm going home."

"But you can't! You're to stay until—"

"I said I'm going home. Now if you want to stick around and watch me dress, that's O.K. by me, but if you're a nice girl, now is the time to beat it out in the hall."

While I was dressing they all tried to stop me, the nurse and the interne, and the head nurse, but I had Sam pitch the bloody clothes into the suitcase he had brought, and in about five minutes we were off. At the desk downstairs I wrote a check for my bill, and asked the woman how was Mrs. Brent.

"Oh, she'll be all right, but of course it was a terrible shock to her."

"She still here?"

"Well, they're questioning her, you know."

"Who?"

"The police. . . . If you ask me, she'll be held."

"You mean—arrested?"

"Apparently she knows something."

"Oh, I see."

"Don't say I told you."

"I won't, of course."

Sam had a taxi by then, and we got in. I had the driver go out to Glendale, and pull up beside my car, where I had left it on Anita Avenue. I had Sam take the wheel, and told him to drive around and keep on driving. He took Foothill, and went on up past San Fernando somewhere, I didn't pay any attention where.

Going past the bank, I saw the glass was all in place, and a gold-leafer was inside, putting on the lettering. I couldn't see who was in there. Late in the afternoon we came back through Los Angeles, and I bought a paper. My picture was gone now, and so was Adler's, and Brent's was smaller. Sheila's was four columns wide, and in an inset was a picture of her father, Dr. Henry W. Rollinson, of U.C.L.A. The headline stretched clear across the page, and called it a "cover-up robbery." I didn't bother to read any more. If Dr. Rollinson had told his story, the whole thing was in the soup.

Sam drove me home then, and fixed me something to eat. I went in the living room and lay down, expecting cops, and wondered what I was going to tell them.

Around eight o'clock the doorbell rang, and I answered myself. But it wasn't cops, it was Lou Frazier. He came in and I had Sam fix him a drink. He seemed to need it. I lay down on the sofa again, and held on to my head. It didn't ache, and I felt all right, but I was getting ready. I wanted an excuse not to talk any more than I had to. After he got part of his drink down he started in.

"You seen the afternoon papers?"

"Just the headlines."

"The guy was short in his accounts."

"Looks like it."

"She was in on it."

"Who?"

"The wife. That sexy-looking thing known as Sheila. She doctored the books for him. We just locked up a half hour ago. I've just come from there. Well boy, it's a crime what that dame got away with. That system in the savings department, all that stuff you went out there to make a report on—that was nothing but a cover. The laugh's on you, Bennett. Now you got a real article for the American Banker."

"I doubt if she was in on it."

"I know she was in on it."

"If she was, why did she let him go to her father for the dough to cover up the shortage? Looks to me like that was putting it on a little too thick."

"O.K.—it's taken me all afternoon to figure that one out, and I had to question the father pretty sharp. He's plenty bitter against Brent. All right, take it from their point of view, hers and Brent's. They were short on the accounts, and they figured on a phoney hold-up that would cover their deficit, so nobody would even know there *had* been a shortage. The first thing to do was get the books in shape, and I'm telling you she made a slick job of that. She didn't leave a trace, and if it wasn't for her father, we'd never have known how much they were short. All right, she's got to get those books in shape, and do it before your next check on her cash. That was the tough part, they were up against time, but she was equal to it, I'll say that for her. All right, now she brings a spider in, and he slips in the vault and hides there. But they couldn't be sure what was going to happen next morning, could they? He might get away with it clean, with that handkerchief over his face nobody could identify him, and then later she could call the old man up and say please don't say anything, she'll explain to him later, that Charles is horribly upset, and when the cops go to his house, sure enough he is. He's in bed, still recovering from his operation, and all this and that—but no money anywhere around, and nothing to connect him with it.

"But look: they figure maybe he don't get away with it. Maybe he gets caught, and then what? All the money's there, isn't it? He's got five doctors to swear he's off his nut anyway, on account of illness—and he gets off light. With luck, he even gets a suspended sentence, and the only one that's out is her old man. She shuts him up, and they're not much worse off than they were before. Well, thanks to a guy named Helm it all went sour. None of it broke like they expected—he got away, but everybody knew who he was, and Adler got killed. So now he's wanted for murder —*and* robbery, and she's held for the same."

"Is she held?"

"You bet your sweet life she's held. She doesn't know it yet— she's down at that hospital, with a little dope in her arm to quiet her after the awful experience she had, but there's a cop outside the door right now, and tomorrow when she wakes up maybe she won't look quite so sexy."

I lay there with my eyes shut, wondering what I was going to do, but by that time my head was numb, so I didn't feel anything any more. After a while I heard myself speak to him. "Lou?"

"Yeah?"

"I knew about that shortage."

". . . You mean you suspected it?"

"I knew—"

"You mean you suspected it!"

He fairly screamed it at me. When I opened my eyes he was standing in front of me, his eyes almost popping out of their sockets, his face all twisted and white. Lou is a pretty good-looking guy, big and thickset, with brown eyes and a golf tan all over him, but now he looked like some kind of a wild man.

"If you knew about it, and didn't report it, *there goes our bond! Don't you get it, Bennett? There goes our bond!*"

It was the first I had even thought of the bond. I could see it, though, the second he began to scream, that little line in fine type on the bond. We don't make our people give individual bond. We carry a group bond on them, ourselves, and that line reads: ". . . The assured shall report to the Corporation any shortage, embezzlement, defalcation, or theft on the part of any of their employees, within twenty-four hours of the time such shortage, embezzlement, defalcation, or theft shall be known to them, or to their officers, and failure to report such shortage, embezzlement, defalcation, or theft shall be deemed ground for the cancellation of this bond, and the release of the Corporation from liability for such shortage, embezzlement, defalcation, or shortage." I felt my lips go cold, and the sweat stand out on the palms of my hands, but I went on:

"You're accusing a woman of crimes I know damned well she didn't commit, and bond or no bond, I'm telling you—"

"You're not telling me anything, get that right now!"

He grabbed his hat and ran for the door. "And listen: If you know what's good for you, you're not telling anybody else either! If that comes out, there goes our fidelity bond and our burglary bond—we won't get a cent from the bonding company, we're hooked for the whole ninety thousand bucks, and—God, ninety thousand bucks! Ninety thousand bucks!"

He went, and I looked at my watch. It was nine o'clock. I called up a florist, and had them send flowers to Adler's funeral. Then I went upstairs and went to bed, and stared at the ceiling trying to get through my head what I had to face in the morning.

11

DON'T ASK me about the next three days. They were the worst I ever spent in my life. First I went in to the Hall of Justice and talked to Mr. Gaudenzi, the assistant district attorney that was on the case. He listened to me, and took notes, and then things began to hit me.

First I was summoned to appear before the Grand Jury, to tell what I had to say there. I had to waive immunity for that, and boy, if you think it's fun to have those babies tearing at your throat, you try it once. There's no judge to help you, no lawyer to object to questions that make you look like a fool, nothing but you, the district attorney, the stenographer, and them. They kept me in there two hours. I squirmed and sweated and tried to get out of admitting why I put up the money for Sheila, but after a while they had it. I admitted I had asked her to divorce Brent and marry me, and that was all they wanted to know. I was hardly home before a long wire from Lou Frazier was delivered, telling me the bonding company had filed notice they denied liability for the money that was gone, and relieving me of duty until further notice. He would have fired me, if he could, but that had to wait till the Old Man got back from Honolulu, as I was an officer of the company, and couldn't be fired until the Old Man laid it before the directors.

But the worst was the newspapers. The story had been doing pretty well until I got in it, I mean it was on the front page, with pictures and all kinds of stuff about clues to Brent's whereabouts, one hot tip putting him in Mexico, another in Phoenix, and still another in Del Monte, where an auto court man said he'd registered the night of the robbery. But when they had my stuff, they went hog wild with it. That gave it a love interest, and what they did to me was just plain murder. They called it the Loot Triangle, and went over to old Dr. Rollinson's, where Sheila's children were staying, and got pictures of them, and of him, and stole at least a dozen of her, and they ran every picture of me they could dig out of their files, and I cursed the day I ever posed in a bathing suit while I was in college, with a co-ed skinning the cat on each arm, in an "Adonis" picture for some football publicity.

And what I got for all that hell was that the day before I appeared before them, the Grand Jury indicted Sheila for alteration of a corporation's records, for embezzlement, and for accessory to robbery with a deadly weapon. The only thing they didn't indict her for was murder, and why they hadn't done that I couldn't understand. So it all went for nothing. I'd nailed myself to the cross, brought all my federal mortgage notes to prove I'd put up the money, and that she couldn't have had anything to do with it, and she got indicted just the same. I got so I didn't have the heart to put my face outside the house, except when a newspaper man showed up, and then I'd go out to take a poke at him, if I could. I sat home and listened to the short wave radio, tuned to the police broadcasts, wondering if I could pick up something that would mean they were closing in on Brent. That, and the news broadcasts. On of them said Sheila's bail had been set at $7,500, and that her father had put it up, and that she'd been released. It wouldn't have done any good for me to have gone down to put up bail. I'd given her all I had, already.

That day I got in the car and took a ride, just to keep from going nuts. Coming back I drove by the bank and peeped in. Snelling was at my desk. Church was at Sheila's window. Helm was at Snelling's place, and there were two tellers I'd never seen before.

When I tuned in on the news, after supper that night, for the first time there was some sign the story was slackening off. The guy said Brent hadn't been caught yet, but there was no more stuff about me, or about Sheila. I relaxed a little, but then after a while something else began to bore into me. Where was Brent? If she was out on bail, was she meeting him? I'd done all I could to clear her, but that didn't mean I was sure she was innocent, or felt any different about her than I had before. The idea that she might be meeting him somewhere, that she had played me for a sucker that way, right from the start, set me to tramping around that living room once more, and I tried to tell myself to forget it, to forget her, to wipe the whole thing off the slate and be done with it, and I couldn't. Around eight-thirty I did something I guess I'm not proud of. I got in the car, drove over there, and parked down the street about half a block, to see what I could see.

There was a light on, and I sat there a long time. You'd be surprised what went on, the newspaper reporters that rang the bell, and got kicked out, the cars that drove by, and slowed down so fat women could rubber in there, the peeping that was going on from upstairs windows of houses. After a while the light went off. The door opened, and Sheila came out. She started down the street, toward me. I felt if she saw me there I'd die of shame. I dropped down behind the wheel, and bent over on one side so I couldn't be seen from the pavement, and held my breath. I could hear her footsteps coming on, quick, like she was in a hurry to get somewhere. They went right on by the car, without stopping, but through the window, almost in a whisper, I heard her say: "You're being watched."

I knew in a flash then, why she hadn't been indicted for murder. If they'd done that, she wouldn't have been entitled to bail. They indicted her, but they left it so she could get out, and then they began doing the same thing I'd been doing: watching her, to see if she'd make some break that would lead them to Brent.

Next day I made up my mind I had to see her. But how to see

her was tough. If they were watching her that close, they'd probably tapped in on her phone, and any wire I sent her would be read before she got it, that was a cinch. I figured on it a while, and then I went down in the kitchen to see Sam. "You got a basket here?"

"Yes sir, a big market basket."

"O.K., I tell you what you do. Put a couple of loaves of bread in it, put on your white coat, and get on over to this address on Mountain Drive. Go in the back way, knock, ask for Mrs. Brent. Make sure you're talking to her, and that nobody else is around. Tell her I want to see her, and will she meet me tonight at seven o'clock, at the same place she used to meet me downtown, after she came from the hospital. Tell her I'll be waiting in the car."

"Yes sir, seven o'clock."

"You got that all straight?"

"I have, sir."

"There's cops all around the house. If you're stopped, tell them nothing, and if possible, don't let them know who you are."

"Just leave it to me."

I took an hour that night shaking anybody that might be following me. I drove up to Saugus, and coming in to San Fernando I shoved up to ninety, and I knew nobody was back of me, because I could see everything behind. At San Fernando I cut over to Van Nuys, and drove in to the hospital from there. It was one minute after seven when I pulled in to the curb, but I hadn't even stopped rolling before the door opened and she jumped in. I kept right on.

"You're being followed."

"I think not. I shook them."

"I couldn't. I think my taxi driver had his instructions before he came to the house. They're about two hundred yards behind."

"I don't see anything."

"They're there."

We drove on, me trying to think what I wanted to say. But it was she that started it.

"Dave?"

"Yes?"

"We may never see each other again, after tonight. I think I'd better begin. You've—been on my mind, quite a lot. Among other things."

"All right, begin."

"I've done you a great wrong."

"I didn't say so."

"You didn't have to. I felt everything you were thinking in that terrible ride that morning in the ambulance. I've done you a great wrong, and I've done myself a great wrong. I forgot one thing a woman can never forget. I didn't forget it. But I—closed my eyes to it."

"Yeah, and what was that?"

"That a woman must come to a man, as they say in court, with clean hands. In some countries, she has to bring more than that. Something in her hand, something on her back, something on the ox cart—a dowry. In this country we waive that, but we don't waive the clean hands. I couldn't give you them. If I was going to come to you, I had to come with encumbrances, terrible encumbrances. I had to be bought."

"I suggested that."

"Dave, it can't be done. I've asked you to pay a price for me that no man can pay. I've cost you a shocking amount of money, I've cost you your career, I've cost you your good name. On account of me you've been pilloried in the newspapers, you've endured torture. You've stood by me beautifully, you did everything you could for me, before that awful morning and since—but I'm not worth it. No woman can be, and no woman has a right to think she is. Very well, then, you don't have to stand by me any longer. You can consider yourself released, and if it lies in my power, I'll make up to you what I've cost you. The career, the notoriety, I can't do any-thing about. The money, God willing, some day I shall repay you. I guess that's what I wanted to say. I guess that's all I wanted to say. That—and goodbye."

I thought that over for five or ten miles. It was no time for lolly-gagging. She had said what she meant and I had to say what I meant. And I wasn't kidding myself that a lot of it wasn't true. The whole mess, from the time we had started doctoring those books, and putting the money back, I had just hated, and they weren't love scenes, those nights when we were getting ready for the next day's skulduggery. They were nervous sessions, and she never looked quite so pretty going home as she had coming over. But it still wasn't what was on my mind. If I could be sure she was on the up-and-up with me, I'd still feel she was worth it, and I'd still stand by her, if she needed me and wanted me. I made up my mind I was going to hit it on the nose. "Sheila?"

"Yes, Dave."

"I did feel that way in the ambulance."

"There's no need to tell me."

"Partly on account of what you've been talking about, maybe. There's no use kidding ourselves. It was one awful morning, and we've both had awful mornings since. But that wasn't the main thing."

". . . What was the main thing?"

"I wasn't sure, I haven't been sure from the beginning, and I'm not sure now, that you haven't been two-timing me."

"What are you talking about? Two-timing you with whom?"

"Brent."

"With *Charles?* Are you crazy?"

"No, I'm not crazy. All right, now you get it. I've known from the beginning, and I'm perfectly sure of it now, that you know more about this than you've been telling, that you've held out on me, that you've held out on the cops. All right, now you can put it on the line.

Were you in on this thing with Brent or not?"

"Dave, how can you ask such a thing?"

"Do you know where he is?"

". . . Yes."

"That's all I want to know."

I said it mechanically, because to tell you the truth I'd about decided she was on the up-and-up all the way down the line, and when she said that it hit me between the eyes like a fist. I could feel my breath trembling as we drove along, and I could feel her looking at me too. Then she began to speak in a hard, strained voice, like she was forcing herself to talk, and measuring everything she said.

"I know where he is, and I've known a lot more about him than I ever told you. Before that morning, I didn't tell you because I didn't want to wash a lot of dirty linen, even before you. Since that morning I haven't told anybody because—*I want him to escape!*"

"Oh, you do!"

"I pulled you into it, when I discovered that shortage, for the reason I told you. So my children wouldn't grow up knowing their father was in prison. I'm shielding Charles now, I'm holding out on you, as you put it, because if I don't, they're going to grow up knowing their father was executed for murder. I won't have it! I don't care if the bank loses ninety thousand dollars, or a million dollars, I don't care if your career is ruined—I might as well tell you the truth, Dave—*if there's any way I can prevent it my children are not going to have their lives blighted by that horrible disgrace.*"

That cleared it up at last. And then something came over me. I knew we were going through the same old thing again, that I'd be helping her cover up something, that I wasn't going to have any more of that. If she and I were to go on, it had to be a clean slate between us, and I felt myself tighten. "So far as I'm concerned, I won't have that."

"I'm not asking you to."

"And not because of what you said about me. I'm not asking you to put me ahead of your children, or anything ahead of your children."

"I couldn't, even if you did ask me."

"It's because the game is up, and you may as well learn that your children aren't any better than anybody else."

"I'm sorry. To me they are."

"They'll learn, before they die, that they've got to play the cards God dealt them, and you'll learn it too, if I know anything about it. What you're doing, you're ruining other lives, to say nothing of your own life, and doing wrong, too—to save them. O.K., play it your own way. But that lets me out."

"Then it's good-bye?"

"I guess it is."

"It's what I've been trying to tell you."

She was crying now, and she took my hand and gave it a little jerky shake. I loved her more than I'd ever loved her, and I wanted to stop, and put my arms around her, and start all over again, but I didn't. I knew it wouldn't get us anywhere at all, and I kept right on driving. We'd got to the beach by then, by way of Pico Boulevard, and I ran up through Santa Monica to Wilshire, then turned back to take her home. We were done, and I could feel it that she had called the turn. We'd never see each other again.

How far we'd got I don't know, but we were somewhere coming in toward Westwood. She had quieted down, and was leaning against the window with her eyes closed, when all of a sudden she sat up and turned up the radio. I had got so I kept it in short wave all the time now, and it was turned low, so you could hardly hear it, but it was on. A cop's voice was just finishing an order, and then it was repeated: "Car No. forty-two, Car No. forty-two . . . Proceed to No. six eight two five Sanborn Avenue, Westwood, at once

. . . Two children missing from home of Dr. Henry W. Rollin
son . . ."

I stepped on it hard, but she grabbed me.

"Stop!"

"I'm taking you there!"

"Stop! I said stop—will you please stop!"

I couldn't make any sense out of it, but I pulled over and we
skidded to a stop. She jumped out. I jumped out. "Will you kindly
tell me what we're stopping here for? They're your kids, don't you
get it—?"

But she was on the curb, waving back the way we had come. Just
then a pair of headlights snapped on. I hadn't seen any car, but it
dawned on me this must be that car that had been following us.
She kept on waving, then started to run toward it. At that, the car
came up. A couple of detectives were inside. She didn't even wait
till she stopped before she screamed: "Did you get that call?"

"What call?"

"The Westwood call, about the children?"

"Baby, that was for car forty-two."

"Will you wipe that grin off your face and listen to me? Those
are my children. They've been taken by my husband, and it means
he's getting ready to skip, to wherever he's going—"

She never even finished. Those cops hopped out and she gave it
to them as fast as she could. She said he'd be sure to stop at his
hideout before he blew, that they were to follow us there, that we'd
lead the way if they'd only stop talking and hurry. But the cops
had a different idea. They knew by now it was a question of time,
so they split the cars up. One of them went ahead in the police car,
after she gave him the address, the other took the wheel of my car,
and we jumped in on the back seat. Boy, if you think you can drive,
you ought to try it once with a pair of cops. We went through
Westwood with everything wide open, it wasn't five minutes

before we were in Hollywood, and we just kept on going. We didn't stop for any kind of a light, and I don't think we were under eighty the whole trip.

All the time she kept holding onto my hand and praying: "Oh God, if we're only in time! If we're only in time!"

12

WE PULLED up in front of a little white apartment house in Glendale. Sheila jumped out, and the cops and myself were right beside her. She whispered for us to keep quiet. Then she stepped on the grass, went around to the side of the house and looked up. A light was on in one window. Then she went back to the garage. It was open, and she peeped in. Then she came back to the front and went inside, still motioning to us to keep quiet. We followed her, and she went up to the second floor. She tiptoed to the third door on the right, stood there a minute, and listened. She tiptoed back to where we were. The cops had their guns out by now. Then she marched right up to the door, her heels clicking on the floor, and rapped. It opened right away, and a woman was standing there. She had a cigarette in one hand and her hat and coat on, like she was getting ready to go out. I had to look twice to make sure I wasn't seeing things. It was Church.

"Where are my children?"

"Well, Sheila, how should I know—?"

Sheila grabbed her and jerked her out into the hall. "Where are my children, I said?"

"They're all right. He just wanted to see them a minute before he—"

She stopped when one of the cops walked up behind her, stepped

through the open door with his gun ready, and went inside. The
other cop stayed in the hall, right beside Sheila and Church, his
gun in his hand, listening. After a minute or two the cop that went
in came to the door and motioned us inside. Sheila and Church
went in, then I went in, then the other cop stepped inside, but stood
where he could cover the hall. It was a one-room furnished apartment, with a dining alcove to one side, and a bathroom. All doors
were open, even the closet door, where the cop had opened them,
ready to shoot if he had to. In the middle of the floor were a couple
of suitcases strapped up tight. The cop that went in first walked
over to Church.

"All right, Fats, spit it out."

"I don't even know what you're talking about."

"Where are those kids?"

"How should I know—?"

"You want that puss mashed in?"

". . . He's bringing them here."

"When?"

"Now. He ought to be here by now."

"What for?"

"To take with us. We were going to blow."

"He using a car?"

"He's using his car."

"O.K.—open them suitcases."

"I have no key. He—"

"I said open them."

She stooped down and began to unstrap the suitcases. The cop
poked her behind with the gun.

"Come on, step on it, step on it!"

When she had them unstrapped, she took keys from her handbag
and unlocked them. The cop kicked them open. Then he whistled.
From the larger of the two suitcases money began tumbling out on
the floor, some of it in bundles, with rubber bands around it, some

of it with the paper wrappers still on, showing the amounts. That was the new money we had had in the vault, stuff that had never even been touched. Church began to curse at Sheila.

"It's all there, and now you've got what you want, haven't you? You think I didn't know what you were doing? You think I didn't see you fixing those cards up so you could send him up when they found that shortage? All right, he beat you to it, and he took your old man for a ride too—that sanctimonious old fool! But you haven't got him yet, and you haven't got those brats! I'll—"

She made a dive for the door, but the cop was standing there and threw her back. Then he spoke to the other one, the one that was stooped down, fingering the money. "Jake!"

"Yeah?"

"He'll be here for that dough. You better put in a call. No use taking chances. We need more men."

"God, I never seen that much dough."

He stepped over to the phone and lifted the receiver to dial. Just then, from outside, I heard a car horn give a kind of a rattle, like they give when they're tapped three or four times quick. Church heard it too, and opened her mouth to scream. That scream never came out. Sheila leaped at her, caught her throat with one hand and covered her mouth with the other. She turned her head around to the cops.

"Go on, hurry up, he's out there."

The cops dived out and piled down the stairs, and I was right after them. They no sooner reached the door than there was a shot, from a car parked out front, right behind my car. One cop ducked behind a big urn beside the door, the other ran behind a tree. But I didn't duck behind any urn and I didn't run behind any tree. The car was moving now, and I meant to get that guy if it was the last thing I did on earth. I ran off to the right, across the apartment house lawn and the lawn next to it and the lawn next to that, as hard as I could. There was no way he could turn. If he was going to get away, he had to pass me. I got to a car that was parked about fifty feet up the street, and crouched down in front of it, right on the front bumper, so that the car was between him and me. He was in second now, and giving her the gun, but I jumped and caught the door handle.

What happened in the next ten seconds I'm not sure I know myself. The speed of the car threw me back, so I lost my grip on the door handle, and I hit my head on the fender. I was still wearing a bandage, from the other cut, so that wasn't so good. But I caught the rear door handle, and hung on. All that happened quicker than I can tell it, but being thrown back that way, I guess that's what saved me. He must have thought I was still up front, because inside the car he began to shoot, and I saw holes appear in the front door, one by one. I had some crazy idea I had to count them, so I'd know when he'd shot his shells out. I saw three holes, one right after the other. But then I woke up that there were more shots than holes, that some of those shots were coming from behind. That meant the cops had got in it again. I was right in the line of fire, and I wanted to drop off and lay in the street, but I held on. Then these screams began coming from the back seat, and I remembered the kids. I yelled at the cops that the children were back there, but just then the car slacked and gave a yaw to the left, and we went crashing into the curb and stopped.

I got up, opened the front door, and jumped aside, quick. There was no need to jump. He was lying curled up on the front seat, with his head hanging down, and all over the upholstery was blood. But what I saw, when one of the cops ran up and opened the rear door was just pitiful. The oldest of the kids, Anna, was down on the floor moaning, and her sister, the little three-year-old, Charlotte, was up on the seat, screaming to her father to look at Anna, that Anna was hurt.

Her father wasn't saying anything.

It seemed funny that the cop, the one that had treated Church so rough, could be so swell when it came to a couple of children. He kept calling them Sissy, and got the little one calmed down in just about a minute, and the other one too, the one that was shot. The other cop ran back to the apartment house, to phone for help, and to collar Church before she could run off with that dough, and he caught her just as she was beating it out the door. This one stayed right with the car, and he no sooner got the children quiet than he had Sheila on his hands, and about five hundred people that began collecting from every place there was.

Sheila was like a wild woman, but she didn't have a chance with that cop. He wouldn't let her touch Anna, and he wouldn't let Anna be moved till the doctors moved her. There on the floor of the car was where she was going to stay, he said, and nothing that Sheila said could change him. I figured he was right, and put my arms around her, and tried to get her quiet, and in a minute or two I felt her stiffen and knew she was going to do everything she could to keep herself under control.

The ambulances got there at last, and they put Brent in one, and the little girl in the other, and Sheila rode in with her. I took little Charlotte in my car. As she left me Sheila touched my arm.

"More hospitals."

"You've had a dose."

"But this—Dave!"

It was one in the morning before they got through in the operating room, and long before that the nurses put little Charlotte to bed. From what she said to me on the way in, and what the cops and I were able to piece together, it wasn't one of the cop's shots that had hit Anna at all.

What happened was that the kids were asleep on the back seat, both of them, when Brent pulled up in front of the apartment house, and didn't know a thing till he started to shoot through the door at me. Then the oldest one jumped up and spoke to her father. When he didn't answer she stood up and tried to talk to him on his left side, back of where he was trying to shoot and drive at the same time. That must have been when he turned and let the cops have it over his shoulder. Except that instead of getting the cops, he got his own child.

When it was all over I took Sheila home. I didn't take her to Glendale. I took her to her father's house in Westwood. She had phoned him what had happened and they were waiting for her. She looked like a ghost of herself, and leaned against the window with her eyes closed. "Did they tell you about Brent?"

She opened her eyes.

". . . No. How is he?"

"He won't be executed for **murder.**"

"You mean—?"

"He died. On the table."

She closed her eyes again, and didn't speak for a while, and when she did it was in a dull, lifeless way.

"Charles was all right, a fine man—until he met Church. I don't know what effect she had on him. He went completely insane about her, and then he began to go bad. What he did, I mean at the bank that morning, wasn't his think-up, it was hers."

"But *why,* will you tell me that?"

"To get back at me. At my father. At the world. At everything. You noticed what she said to me? With her that meant an obsession that I was set to ruin Charles, and if I was, then they would strike first, that's all. Charles was completely under her, and she's bad. Really, I'm not sure she's quite sane."

"What a looking thing to call a sweetie."

"I think that was part of the hold she had on him. He wasn't a very masculine man. With me, I think he felt on the defensive, though certainly I never gave him any reason to. But with her, with that colorless, dietician nature that she had—I think he felt like a man. I mean, she excited him. Because she is such a frump, she gave him something I could never give him."

"I begin to get it now."

"Isn't that funny? He was my husband, and I don't care whether he's alive or dead—I simply don't care. All I can think of is that little thing down there—"

"What do the doctors say?"

"They don't know. It's entirely her constitution and how it develops. It was through her abdomen, and there were eleven perforations, and there'll be peritonitis, and maybe other complications—and they can't even know what's going to happen for two or three days yet. And the loss of blood was frightful."

"They'll give her transfusions."

"She had one, while they were operating. That was what they were waiting for. They didn't dare start till the donor arrived."

"If blood's what it takes, I've got plenty."

She started to cry, and caught my arm. "Even blood, Dave? Is there anything you haven't given me?"

"Forget it."

"Dave?"

"Yes?"

"If I'd played the cards that God dealt me, it wouldn't have happened. That's the awful part. If I'm to be punished—all right, it's what I deserve. But if only the punishment—*doesn't fall on her!*"

13

THE NEWSPAPERS gave Sheila a break, I'll say that for them, once the cops exonerated her. They played the story up big, but they made her the heroine of it, and I can't complain of what they said about me, except I'd rather they hadn't said anything. Church took a plea and got sent over to Tehachapi for a while. She even admitted she was the one that brought in the spider. All the money was there, so Dr. Rollinson got his stake back, and the bonding company had nothing to pay, which kind of eased off what had been keeping me awake nights.

But that wasn't what Sheila and I had to worry about. It was that poor kid down there in the hospital, and that was just awful. The doctors knew what was coming, all right. For two or three days she went along and you'd have thought she was doing fine, except that her temperature kept rising a little bit at a time, and her eyes kept getting brighter and her cheeks redder. Then the peritonitis broke, and broke plenty. For two weeks her temperature stayed up around a hundred and four, and then when it seemed she had that licked, pneumonia set in. She was in oxygen three days, and when she came out of it she was so weak you couldn't believe she could live at all. Then, at last, she began to get better.

All that time I took Sheila in there twice a day, and we'd sit and watch the chart, and in between we'd talk about what we were going to do with our lives. I had no idea. The mess over the bond was all cleared up, but I hadn't been told to come back to work, and I didn't expect to be. And after the way my name had been plastered on the front pages all over the country I didn't know where I could get a job, or whether I could get a job. I knew a little about banking, but in banking the first thing you've got to have is a good name.

Then one night we were sitting there, Sheila and myself, with the two kids on the bed, looking at a picture book, when the door opened, and the Old Man walked in. It was the first time we had seen him since the night he danced with Sheila, just before he sailed for Honolulu. He had a box of flowers, and handed them to Sheila with a bow. "Just dropped in to see how the little girl is getting along."

Sheila took the flowers and turned away quickly to hide how she felt, then rang for the nurse and sent them out to be put in water. Then she introduced him to the children, and he sat on the bed and kidded along with them, and they let him look at the pictures in the picture book. The flowers came back, and Sheila caught her breath, and they were jumbo chrysanthemums all right. She thanked him for them, and he said they came from his own garden in Beverly. The nurse went and the kids kind of quieted down again, and Sheila went over to him, and sat down beside him on the bed, and took his hand. "You think this is a surprise, don't you?"

"Well, I can do better."

He dug in his pocket and fished up a couple of little dolls. The kids went nuts over them, and that was the end of talk for about five minutes. But Sheila was still hanging onto the Old Man's hand, and went on: "It's no surprise at all. I've been expecting you."

"Oh, you have."

"I saw you were back."

"I got back yesterday."

"I knew you'd come."

The Old Man looked at me and grinned. "I must have done pretty well in that dance. I must have uncorked a pretty good rhumba."

"I'd say you did all right."

Sheila laughed, and kissed his hand, and got up and moved into a chair. He moved into a chair too, and looked at his chrysanthemums and said, "Well, when you like somebody you have to bring her flowers."

"And when you like somebody, you know they'll do it."

He sat there a minute, and then he said, "I think you two are about the silliest pair of fools I ever knew. Just about the silliest."

"We think so too."

"But not a pair of crooks . . . I read a little about it, in Honolulu, and when I got back I went into it from beginning to end, thoroughly. If I'd been here, I'd have let you have it right in the neck, just exactly where Lou Frazier let you have it, and I haven't one word of criticism to offer for what he did. But I wasn't here. I was away, I'm glad to say. Now that I'm back I can't find it in me to hold it against you. It was against all rules, all prudence, but it wasn't morally wrong. And—it was silly. But all of us, I suppose, are silly now and then. Even I feel the impulse—especially when dancing the rhumba."

He stopped, and let his fingertips touch in front of his eyes, and stared through them for a minute or so. Then he went on:

"But—the official family is the official family, and while Frazier isn't quite as sore as he was, he's not exactly friendly, even yet. I don't think there's anything for you in the home office for some little time yet, Bennett—at any rate, until this blows over a little. However, I've about decided to open a branch in Honolulu. How would you like to take charge of *that*?"

Brother, does a cat like liver?

So Honolulu's where we are now, all five of us, Sheila, and myself, and Anna, and Charlotte, and Arthur, a little number you haven't heard about yet, that arrived about a year after we got here, and that was named after the Old Man. They're out there on the beach now, and I can see them from where I'm writing on the veranda, and my wife looks kind of pretty in a bathing suit, if anybody happens to ask you. The Old Man was on a few weeks ago, and told us that Frazier's been moved east, and any time I want to go back, it's all clear, and he'll find a spot for me. But I don't know. I like it here, and Sheila likes it here, and the kids like it here, and the branch is doing fine. And another thing: I'm not so sure I want to make it too handy for Sheila and the Old Man to dance the rhumba.

DOUBLE

INDEMNITY

DOUBLE INDEMNITY

1

I DROVE out to Glendale to put three new truck drivers on a
brewery company bond, and then I remembered this renewal over
in Hollywoodland. I decided to run over there. That was how I
came to this House of Death, that you've been reading about in the
papers. It didn't look like a House of Death when I saw it. It was
just a Spanish house, like all the rest of them in California, with
white walls, red tile roof, and a patio out to one side. It was built
cock-eyed. The garage was under the house, the first floor was over
that, and the rest of it was spilled up the hill any way they could
get it in. You climbed some stone steps to the front door, so I
parked the car and went up there. A servant poked her head out. "Is
Mr. Nirdlinger in?"

"I don't know, sir. Who wants to see him?"

"Mr. Huff."

"And what's the business?"

"Personal."

Getting in is the tough part of my job, and you don't tip what you came for till you get where it counts. "I'm sorry, sir, but they won't let me ask anybody in unless they say what they want."

It was one of those spots you get in. If I said some more about "personal" I would be making a mystery of it, and that's bad. If I said what I really wanted, I would be laying myself open for what every insurance agent dreads, that she would come back and say, "Not in." If I said I'd wait, I would be making myself look small, and that never helped a sale yet. To move this stuff, you've got to get in. Once you're in, they've got to listen to you, and you can pretty near rate an agent by how quick he gets to the family sofa, with his hat on one side of him and his dope sheets on the other.

"I see. I told Mr. Nirdlinger I would drop in, but—never mind. I'll see if I can make it some other time."

It was true, in a way. On this automobile stuff, you always make it a point that you'll give a reminder on renewal, but I hadn't seen him for a year. I made it sound like an old friend, though, and an old friend that wasn't any too pleased at the welcome he got. It worked. She got a worried look on her face. "Well—come in, please."

If I had used that juice trying to keep out, that might have got me somewhere.

I pitched my hat on the sofa. They've made a lot of that living room, especially those "blood-red drapes." All I saw was a living room like every other living room in California, maybe a little more expensive than some, but nothing that any department store wouldn't deliver on one truck, lay out in the morning, and have the credit O. K. ready the same afternoon. The furniture was Spanish, the kind that looks pretty and sits stiff. The rug was one of those 12 x 15's that would have been Mexican except it was made in Oakland, California. The blood-red drapes were there, but they didn't mean anything. All these Spanish houses have red velvet

drapes that run on iron spears, and generally some red velvet wall
tapestries to go with them. This was right out of the same can, with
a coat-of-arms tapestry over the fireplace and a castle tapestry over
the sofa. The other two sides of the room were windows and the
entrance to the hall.

"Yes?"

A woman was standing there. I had never seen her before. She
was maybe thirty-one or two, with a sweet face, light blue eyes, and
dusty blonde hair. She was small, and had on a suit of blue house
pajamas. She had a washed-out look.

"I wanted to see Mr. Nirdlinger."

"Mr. Nirdlinger isn't in just now, but I am Mrs. Nirdlinger. Is
there something I could do?"

There was nothing to do but spill it. "Why no, I think not, Mrs.
Nirdlinger, thanks just the same. Huff is my name, Walter Huff,
of the General Fidelity of California. Mr. Nirdlinger's automobile
coverage runs out in a week or two, and I promised to give him a
reminder on it, so I thought I'd drop by. But I certainly didn't
mean to bother you about it."

"Coverage?"

"Insurance. I just took a chance, coming up here in the daytime,
but I happened to be in the neighborhood, so I thought it wouldn't
hurt. When do you think would be a good time to see Mr. Nirdlinger? Could he give me a few minutes right after dinner, do you
think, so I wouldn't cut into his evening?"

"What kind of insurance has he been carrying? I ought to know,
but I don't keep track."

"I guess none of us keep track until something happens. Just the
usual line. Collision, fire, and theft, and public liability."

"Oh yes, of course."

"It's only a routine matter, but he ought to attend to it in time,
so he'll be protected."

"It really isn't up to me, but I know he's been thinking about the

Automobile Club. Their insurance, I mean."

"Is he a member?"

"No, he's not. He's always intended to join, but somehow he's never got around to it. But the club representative was here, and he mentioned insurance."

"You can't do better than the Automobile Club. They're prompt, liberal in their view of claims, and courteous straight down the line. I've not got a word to say against them."

That's one thing you learn. Never knock the other guy's stuff.

"And then it's cheaper."

"For members."

"I thought only members could get it."

"What I mean is this. If a man's going to join the Automobile Club anyway, for service in time of trouble, taking care of tickets, things like that, then if he takes their insurance too, he gets it cheaper. He certainly does. But if he's going to join the club just to get the insurance, by the time he adds that $16 membership fee to the premium rate, he's paying more. Figure that in, I can still save Mr. Nirdlinger quite a little money."

She talked along, and there was nothing I could do but go along with it. But you sell as many people as I do, you don't go by what they say. You feel it, how the deal is going. And after a while I knew this woman didn't care anything about the Automobile Club. Maybe the husband did, but she didn't. There was something else, and this was nothing but a stall. I figured it would be some kind of a proposition to split the commission, maybe so she could get a ten-spot out of it without the husband knowing. There's plenty of that going on. And I was just wondering what I would say to her. A reputable agent don't get mixed up in stuff like that, but she was walking around the room, and I saw something I hadn't noticed before. Under those blue pajamas was a shape to set a man nuts, and how good I was going to sound when I started explaining the high ethics of the insurance business I didn't exactly know.

But all of a sudden she looked at me, and I felt a chill creep straight up my back and into the roots of my hair. "Do you handle accident insurance?"

Maybe that don't mean to you what it meant to me. Well, in the first place, accident insurance is sold, not bought. You get calls for other kinds, for fire, for burglary, even for life, but never for accident. That stuff moves when agents move it, and it sounds funny to be asked about it. In the second place, when there's dirty work going on, accident is the first thing they think of. Dollar for dollar paid down, there's a bigger face coverage on accident than any other kind. And it's the one kind of insurance that can be taken out without the insured knowing a thing about it. No physical examination for accident. On that, all they want is the money, and there's many a man walking around today that's worth more to his loved ones dead than alive, only he don't know it yet.

"We handle all kinds of insurance."

She switched back to the Automobile Club, and I tried to keep my eyes off her, and couldn't. Then she sat down. "Would you like me to talk to Mr. Nirdlinger about this, Mr. Huff?"

Why would she talk to him about his insurance, instead of letting me do it? "That would be fine, Mrs. Nirdlinger."

"It would save time."

"Time's important. He ought to attend to this at once."

But then she crossed me up. "After he and I have talked it over, then you can see him. Could you make it tomorrow night? Say seven-thirty? We'll be through dinner by then."

"Tomorrow night will be fine."

"I'll expect you."

I got in the car bawling myself out for being a fool just because a woman had given me one sidelong look. When I got back to the office I found Keyes had been looking for me. Keyes is head of the Claim Department, and the most tiresome man to do business with in the whole world. You can't even say today is Tuesday without

he has to look on the calendar, and then check if it's this year's calendar or last year's calendar, and then find out what company
printed the calendar, and then find out if their calendar checks
with the World Almanac calendar. That amount of useless work
you'd think would keep down his weight, but it don't. He gets
fatter every year, and more peevish, and he's always in some kind
of a feud with other departments of the company, and does nothing
but sit with his collar open, and sweat, and quarrel, and argue, until
your head begins spinning around just to be in the same room with
him. But he's a wolf on a phoney claim.

When I got in there he got up and began to roar. It was a truck
policy I had written about six months before, and the fellow had
burned his truck up and tried to collect. I cut in on him pretty quick.

"What are you beefing to me for? I remember that case. And I
distinctly remember that I clipped a memo to that application when
I sent it through that I thought that fellow ought to be thoroughly
investigated before we accepted the risk. I didn't like his looks, and
I won't—"

"Walter, I'm not beefing to you. I know you said he ought to be
investigated. I've got your memo right here on my desk. That's
what I wanted to tell you. If other departments in this company
would show half the sense that you show—"

"Oh."

That would be like Keyes, that even when he wanted to say
something nice to you, he had to make you sore first.

"And get this, Walter. Even after they issued the policy, in plain
disregard of the warning on your memo, and even with that warning still looking them in the face, day before yesterday when the
truck burned—they'd have paid that claim if I hadn't sent a tow-
car up there this afternoon, pulled the truck out, and found a pile
of shavings under the engine, that proved it up on him that he
started the fire himself."

"Have you got him?"

"Oh, he confessed. He's taking a plea tomorrow morning, and that ends it. But my point is, that if you, just by looking at that man, could have your suspicions, why couldn't they—! Oh well, what's the use? I just wanted you to know it. I'm sending a memo to Norton about it. I think the whole thing is something the president of this company might very well look into. Though if you ask me, if the president of this company had more . . ."

He stopped and I didn't jog him. Keyes was one of the holdovers from the time of Old Man Norton, the founder of the company, and he didn't think much of young Norton, that took over the job when his father died. The way he told it, young Norton never did anything right, and the whole place was always worried for fear he'd pull them in on the feud. If young Norton was the man we had to do business with, then he was the man we had to do business with, and there was no sense letting Keyes get us in dutch with him. I gave Keyes' crack a dead pan. I didn't even know what he was talking about.

When I got back to my office, Nettie, my secretary, was just leaving. "Good night, Mr. Huff."

"Good night, Nettie."

"Oh—I put a memo on your desk, about a Mrs. Nirdlinger. She called, about ten minutes ago, and said it would be inconvenient for you to call tomorrow night about that renewal. She said she'd let you know when to come."

"Oh, thanks."

She went, and I stood there, looking down at the memo. It crossed my mind what kind of warning I was going to clip to *that* application, if, as, and when I got it.

If any.

2

THREE DAYS later she she called and left word I was to come at
three-thirty. She let me in herself. She didn't have on the blue
pajamas this time. She had on a white sailor suit, with a blouse
that pulled tight over her hips, and white shoes and stockings. I
wasn't the only one that knew about that shape. She knew about
it herself, plenty. We went in the living room, and a tray was on the
table. "Belle is off today, and I'm making myself some tea. Will
you join me?"

"Thank you, no, Mrs. Nirdlinger. I'll only be a minute. That is,
if Mr. Nirdlinger has decided to renew. I supposed he had, when
you sent for me." Because it came over me that I wasn't surprised
that Belle was off, and that she was just making herself some tea.
And I meant to get out of there, whether I took the renewals with
me or not.

"Oh, have some tea. I like tea. It makes a break in the afternoon."

"You must be English."

"No, native Californian."

"You don't see many of them."

"Most Californians were born in Iowa."

"I was myself."

"Think of that."

The white sailor suit did it. I sat down. "Lemon?"

"No thanks."

"Two?"

"No sugar, just straight."

"No sweet tooth?"

She smiled at me and I could see her teeth. They were big and
white and maybe a little bit buck.

"I do a lot of business with the Chinese. They've got me out of the American way of drinking tea."

"I love the Chinese. Whenever I make chow mein I buy all the stuff at the same place near the park. Mr. Ling. Do you know him?"

"Known him for years."

"Oh, you *have*!"

Her brow wrinkled up, and I saw there was nothing washed-out about her. What gave her that look was a spray of freckles across her forehead. She saw me looking at them. "I believe you're looking at my freckles."

"Yes, I was. I like them."

"I don't."

"I do."

"I always used to wear a turban around my forehead when I went out in the sun, but so many people began stopping by, asking to have their fortunes told, that I had to stop it."

"You don't tell fortunes?"

"No, it's one California accomplishment I never learned."

"Anyway I like the freckles."

She sat down beside me and we talked about Mr. Ling. Now Mr. Ling wasn't anybody but a Chinese grocery dealer that had a City Hall job on the side, and every year we had to bond him for $2,500, but you'd be surprised what a swell guy he turned out to be when we talked about him. After a while, though, I switched to insurance. "Well, how about those policies?"

"He's still talking about the Automobile Club, but I think he's going to renew with you."

"I'm glad of that."

She sat there a minute, making little pleats with the edge of her blouse and rubbing them out. "I didn't say anything to him about the accident insurance."

"No?"

"I hate to talk to him about it."

"I can understand that."

"It seems an awful thing to tell him you think he ought to have
an accident policy. And yet—you see, my husband is the Los
Angeles representative of the Western Pipe and Supply Company."

"He's in the Petroleum Building, isn't he?"

"That's where he has his office. But most of the time he's in the
oil fields."

"Plenty dangerous, knocking around there."

"It makes me positively ill to think about it."

"Does his company carry anything on him?"

"Not that I know of."

"Man in a business like that, he ought not to take chances."

And then I made up my mind that even if I did like her freckles,
I was going to find out where I was at. "I tell you, how would you
like it if I talked with Mr. Nirdlinger about this? You know, not say
anything about where I got the idea, but just bring it up when I
see him."

"I just *hate* to talk to him about it."

"I'm telling you. *I'll* talk."

"But then he'll ask me what I think, and—I won't know what to
say. It's got me worried sick."

She made another bunch of pleats. Then, after a long time, here
it came. "Mr. Huff, would it be possible for me to take out a policy
for him, without bothering him about it at all? I have a little
allowance of my own. I could pay you for it, and he wouldn't know,
but just the same all this worry would be over."

I couldn't be mistaken about what she meant, not after fifteen
years in the insurance business. I mashed out my cigarette, so I
could get up and go. I was going to get out of there, and drop those
renewals and everything else about her like a red-hot poker. But I
didn't do it. She looked at me, a little surprised, and her face was
about six inches away. What I did do was put my arm around her,
pull her face up against mine, and kiss her on the mouth, hard. I

was trembling like a leaf. She gave it a cold stare, and then she closed her eyes, pulled me to her, and kissed back.

"I liked you all the time."

"I don't believe it."

"Didn't I ask you to tea? Didn't I have you come here when Belle was off? I liked you the very first minute. I loved it, the solemn way you kept talking about your company, and all this and that. That was why I kept teasing you about the Automobile Club."

"Oh, it was."

"Now you know."

I rumpled her hair, and then we both made some pleats in the blouse. "You don't make them even, Mr. Huff."

"Isn't that even?"

"The bottom ones are bigger than the top. You've got to take just so much material every time, then turn it, then crease it, and then they make nice pleats. See?"

"I'll try to get the hang of it."

"Not now. You've got to go."

"I'm seeing you soon?"

"Maybe."

"Well listen, I *am*."

"Belle isn't off every day. I'll let you know."

"Well—*will* you?"

"But don't *you* call *me* up. I'll let you know. I promise."

"All right then. Kiss me good-bye."

"Good-bye."

I live in a bungalow in the Los Feliz hills. Daytime, I keep a Filipino house boy, but he don't sleep there. It was raining that night, so I didn't go out. I lit a fire and sat there, trying to figure out where I was at. I knew where I was at, of course. I was standing right on the deep end, looking over the edge, and I kept telling myself to get out of there, and get quick, and never come back. But that was what I kept telling myself. What I was doing was peeping over that edge, and all the time I was trying to pull away from it, there was something in me that kept edging a little closer, trying to get a better look.

A little before nine the bell rang. I knew who it was as soon as I heard it. She was standing there in a raincoat and a little rubber swimming cap, with the raindrops shining over her freckles. When I got her peeled off she was in sweater and slacks, just a dumb Hollywood outfit, but it looked different on her. I brought her to the fire and she sat down. I sat down beside her.

"How did you get my address?" It jumped out at me, even then, that I didn't want her calling my office asking questions about me.

"Phone book."

"Oh."

"Surprised?"

"No."

"Well I like that. I never heard such conceit."

"Your husband out?"

"Long Beach. They're putting down a new well. Three shifts. He had to go down. So I hopped on a bus. I think you might say you're glad to see me."

"Great place, Long Beach."

"I told Lola I was going to a picture show."

"Who's Lola?"

"My stepdaughter."

"Young?"

"Nineteen. Well, *are* you glad to see me?"

"Yeah, sure. Why—wasn't I expecting you?"

We talked about how wet it was out, and how we hoped it didn't turn into a flood, like it did the night before New Year's, 1934, and how I would run her back in the car. Then she looked in the fire a while. "I lost my head this afternoon."

"Not much."

"A little."

"You sorry?"

"—A little. I've never done that before. Since I've been married. That's why I came down."

"You act like something really happened."

"Something did. I lost my head. Isn't that something?"

"Well—so what?"

"I just wanted to say—"

"You didn't mean it."

"No. I did mean it. If I hadn't meant it I wouldn't have had to come down. But I do want to say that I won't ever mean it again."

"You sure?"

"Quite sure."

"We ought to try and see."

"No—please. . . . You see, I love my husband. More, here lately, than ever."

I looked into the fire a while then. I ought to quit, while the quitting was good, I knew that. But that thing was in me, pushing me still closer to the edge. And then I could feel it again, that she wasn't saying what she meant. It was the same as it was that first afternoon I met her, that there was something else, besides what she was telling me. And I couldn't shake it off, that I had to call it on her.

"Why 'here lately'?"

"Oh—worry."

"You mean that down in the oil fields, some rainy night, a crown block is going to fall on him?"

"Please don't talk like that."

"But that's the idea."

"Yes."

"I can understand that. Especially with this set-up."

". . . I don't quite know what you mean. What set-up?"

"Why—a crown block will."

"Will what?"

"Fall on him."

"Please, Mr. Huff, I asked you not to talk like that. It's not a laughing matter. It's got me worried sick. . . . What makes you say that?"

"*You're* going to drop a crown block *on* him."

"I—*what!*"

"Well, you know, maybe not a crown block. But something. Something that's accidentally-on-purpose going to fall on him, and then he'll be dead."

It nailed her between the eyes and they flickered. It was a minute before she said anything. She had to put on an act, and she was caught by surprise, and she didn't know how to do it.

"Are you—joking?"

"No."

"You must be. Or you must be crazy. Why—I never heard of such a thing in my life."

"I'm not crazy, and I'm not joking, and you've heard of such a thing in your life, because it's all you've thought of since you met me, and it's what you came down here for tonight."

"I'll not stay here and listen to such things."

"O. K."

"I'm going."

"O. K."

"I'm going this minute."

"O. K."

So I ran away from the edge, didn't I, and socked it into her so she knew what I meant, and left it so we could never go back to it again? I did not. That was what I tried to do. I never even got up when she left, I didn't help her on with her things, I didn't drive her back, I treated her like I would treat an alley cat. But all the time I knew it would be still raining the next night, that they would still be drilling at Long Beach, that I would light the fire and sit by it, that a little before nine the doorbell would ring. She didn't even speak to me when she came in. We sat by the fire at least five minutes before either one of us said anything. Then she started it. "How could you say such things as you said to me last night?"

"Because they're true. That's what you're going to do."

"*Now?* After what you've said?"

"Yes, after what I've said."

"But—Walter, that's what I've come for, again, tonight. I've thought it over. I realize that there have been one or two things I've said that could give you a completely wrong impression. In a way, I'm glad you warned me about them, because I might have said them to somebody else without knowing the—construction that could be put upon them. But now that I do know, you must surely see that—anything of that sort must be out of my mind. Forever."

That meant she had spent the whole day sweating blood for fear I would warn the husband, or start something, somehow. I kept on with it. "You called me Walter. What's your name?"

"Phyllis."

"Phyllis, you seem to think that because I can call it on you, you're not going to do it. You *are* going to do it, and I'm going to help you."

"*You!*"

"I."

I caught her by surprise again, but she didn't even try to put on an act this time. "Why—I couldn't have anybody help me! It would be—impossible."

"You couldn't have anybody help you? Well let me tell you something. You had better have somebody help you. It would be nice to pull it off yourself, all alone, so nobody knew anything about it, it sure would. The only trouble with that is, you can't. Not if you're going up against an insurance company, you can't.

You've got to have help. And it had better be help that knows its stuff."

"What would you do this for?"

"You, for one thing."

"What else?"

"Money."

"You mean you would—betray your company, and help me do this, for me, and the money we could get out of it?"

"I mean just that. And you better say what you mean, because when I start, I'm going to put it through, straight down the line, and there won't be any slips. But I've got to know. Where I stand. You can't fool—with this."

She closed her eyes, and after a while she began to cry. I put my arm around her and patted her. It seemed funny, after what we had been talking about, that I was treating her like some child that had lost a penny.

"Please, Walter, don't let me do this. We can't. It's simply—insane."

"Yes, it's insane."

"We're going to do it. I can feel it."

"I too."

"I haven't any reason. He treats me as well as a man can treat a woman. I don't love him, but he's never done anything to me."

"But you're going to do it."

"Yes, God help me, I'm going to do it."

She stopped crying, and lay in my arms for a while without saying anything. Then she began to talk almost in a whisper.

"He's not happy. He'll be better off—dead."

"Yeah?"

"That's not true, is it?"

"Not from where he sits, I don't think."

"I know it's not true. I tell myself it's not true. But there's something in me, I don't know what. Maybe I'm crazy. But there's something in me that loves Death. I think of myself as Death, sometimes. In a scarlet shroud, floating through the night. I'm *so* beautiful, then. And sad. And hungry to make the whole world happy, by taking them out where I am, into the night, away from all trouble, all unhappiness. . . . Walter, this is the awful part. I know this is terrible. I tell myself it's terrible. But to me, it doesn't *seem* terrible. It seems as though I'm doing something—that's really best for him, if he only knew it. Do you understand me, Walter?"

"No."

"Nobody could."

"But we're going to do it."

"Yes, we're going to do it."

"Straight down the line."

"Straight down the line."

A night or two later, we talked about it just as casually as if it was a little trip to the mountains. I had to find out what she had been figuring on, and whether she had gummed it up with some bad move of her own. "Have you said anything to him about this, Phyllis? About this policy?"

"No."

"Absolutely nothing?"

"Not a thing."

"All right, how are you going to do it?"

"I was going to take out the policy first—"

"Without him knowing?"

"Yes."

"Holy smoke, they'd have crucified you. It's the first thing they look for. Well—anyway that's out. What else?"

"He's going to build a swimming pool. In the spring. Out in the patio."

"And?"

"I thought it could be made to look as though he hit his head diving or something."

"That's out. That's still worse."

"Why? People do, don't they?"

"It's no good. In the first place, some fool in the insurance business, five or six years ago, put out a newspaper story that most accidents happen in people's own bathtubs, and since then bathtubs, swimming pools, and fishponds are the first thing they think of. When they're trying to pull something, I mean. There's two cases like that out here in California right now. Neither one of them are on the up-and-up, and if there'd been an insurance angle those people would wind up on the gallows. Then it's a daytime job, and you never can tell who's peeping at you from the next hill. Then a swimming pool is like a tennis court, you no sooner have one than it's a community affair, and you don't know who might come popping in on you at any minute. And then it's one of those things where you've got to watch for your chance, and you can't plan it in advance, and know where you're going to come out to the last decimal point. Get this, Phyllis. There's three essential elements to a successful murder."

That word was out before I knew it. I looked at her quick. I thought she'd wince under it. She didn't. She leaned forward. The firelight was reflected in her eyes like she was some kind of leopard. "Go on. I'm listening."

"The first is, help. One person can't get away with it, that is unless they're going to admit it and plead the unwritten law or something. It takes more than one. The second is, the time, the place, the way, all known in advance—to us, but not to him. The third is, audacity. That's the one that all amateur murderers forget. They know the first two, sometimes. But that third, only a professional knows. There comes a time in any murder when the only thing that can see you through is audacity, and I can't tell

you why. You know the perfect murder? You think it's this swimming pool job, and you're going to do it so slick nobody would
ever guess it. They'd guess it in two seconds, flat. In three seconds,
flat, they'd prove it, and in four seconds, flat, you'd confess it.
No, that's not it. The perfect murder is the gangster that goes on
the spot. You know what they do? First they get a finger on
him. They get that girl that he lives with. Along about six o'clock
they get a phone call from her. She goes out to a drugstore to buy
some lipstick, and she calls. They're going to see a picture tonight,
he and she, and it's at such and such a theatre. They'll get there
around nine o'clock. All right, there's the first two elements. They
got help, and they fixed the time and the place in advance. All
right, now watch the third. They go there in a car. They park
across the street. They keep the motor running. They put a sentry
out. He loafs up an alley, and pretty soon he drops a handkerchief
and picks it up. That means he's coming. They get out of the car.
They drift up to the theatre. They close in on him. And right
there, in the glare of the lights, with a couple hundred people
looking on, they let him have it. He hasn't got a chance. Twenty
bullets hit him, from four or five automatics. He falls, they scram
for the car, they drive off—and then you try to convict them. You
just try to convict them. They've got their alibis ready in advance,
all airtight, they were only seen for a second, by people who were
so scared they didn't know what they were looking at—and there
isn't a chance to convict them. The police know who they are, of
course. They round them up, give them the water cure—and then
they're habeas corpused into court and turned loose. Those guys
don't get convicted. They get put on the spot by other gangsters.
Oh yeah, they know their stuff, all right. And if we want to get
away with it, we've got to do it the way they do it, and not the way
some punk up near San Francisco does it, that's had two trials
already, and still he's not free."

"Be bold?"

"Be bold. It's the only way."

"If we shoot him it wouldn't be accident."

"That's right. We don't shoot him, but I want you to get the principle through your head. Be bold. It's the only chance to get away with it."

"Then how—?"

"I'm coming to that. Another trouble with your swimming pool idea is that there's no money in it."

"They'd have to pay—"

"They'd have to pay, but this is a question of how much they'd have to pay. All the big money on an accident policy comes from railroad accidents. They found out pretty quick, when they began to write accident insurance, that the apparent danger spots, the spots that people think are danger spots, aren't danger spots at all. I mean, people always think a railroad train is a pretty dangerous place to be, or they did, anyway, before the novelty wore off, but the figures show not many people get killed, or even hurt, on railroad trains. So on accident policies, they put in a feature that sounds pretty good to the man that buys it, because *he's* a little worried about train trips, but it doesn't cost the company much, because it knows he's pretty sure to get there safely. They pay double indemnity for railroad accidents. That's just where we cash in. You've been thinking about some piker job, maybe, and a fat chance I'd be taking a chance like this for that. When we get done, we cash a $50,000 bet, and if we do it right, we're going to cash it, don't make any mistake about that."

"Fifty thousand dollars?"

"Nice?"

"My!"

"Say, this is a beauty, if I do say it myself. I didn't spend all this time in this business for nothing, did I? Listen, he knows all about this policy, and yet he don't know a thing about it. He applies for it, in writing, and yet he don't apply for it. He pays me for it with his own check, and yet he don't pay me. He has an accident happen to him and yet he don't have an accident happen to him. He gets on the train, and yet he don't get on it."

"What *are* you talking about?"

"You'll find out. The first thing is, we've got to fix him up with that policy. I sell it to him, do you get that?—except that I don't sell him. Not quite. I give him the works, the same as I give any other prospect. And I've got to have witnesses. Get that. There's got to be somebody that heard me go right after him. I show him that he's covered on everything that might hurt the automobile, but hasn't got a thing that covers personal injury to himself. I put it up to him whether a man isn't worth more than his car. I—"

"Suppose he buys?"

"Well—suppose he does? He won't. I can bring him within one inch of the line and hold him there, don't you think I can't. I'm a salesman, if I'm nothing else. But—I've got to have witnesses. Anyway, one witness."

"I'll have somebody."

"Maybe you better oppose it."

"All right."

"You're all for the automobile stuff, when I start in on that, but this accident thing gives you the shivers."

"I'll remember."

"You better make a date pretty quick. Give me a ring."

"Tomorrow?"

"Confirm by phone. Remember, you need a witness."

"I'll have one."

"Tomorrow, then. Subject to call."

"Walter—I'm so excited. It does terrible things to me."

"I too."

"Kiss me."

You think I'm nuts? All right, maybe I am. But you spend fifteen years in the business I'm in, maybe you'll go nuts yourself. You think it's a business, don't you, just like your business, and maybe a little better than that, because it's the friend of the widow, the orphan, and the needy in time of trouble? It's not. It's the biggest gambling wheel in the world. It don't look like it, but it is, from the way they figure the percentage on the oo to the look on their face when they cash your chips. You bet that your house will burn down, they bet it won't, that's all. What fools you is that you didn't *want* your house to burn down when you made the bet, and so you forget it's a bet. That don't fool them. To them a bet is a bet, and a hedge bet don't look any different than any other bet. But there comes a time, maybe, when you *do* want your house to burn down, when the money is worth more than the house. And right there is where the trouble starts. They know there's just so many people out there that are out to crook that wheel, and that's when they get tough. They've got their spotters out there, they know every crooked trick there is, and if you want to beat them you had better be good. So long as you're honest, they'll pay you with a smile, and you may even go home thinking it was all in a spirit of good clean fun. But you start something, and then you'll find out.

All right, I'm an agent. I'm a croupier in that game. I know all their tricks, I lie awake nights thinking up tricks, so I'll be ready for them when they come at me. And then one night I think up a trick, and get to thinking I could crook the wheel myself if I could only put a plant out there to put down my bet. That's all. When I met Phyllis I met my plant. If that seems funny to you, that I would kill a man just to pick up a stack of chips, it might not seem so funny if you were back of that wheel, instead of out front. I had seen so many houses burned down, so many cars wrecked, so many corpses with blue holes in their temples, so many awful things that people had pulled to crook the wheel, that

that stuff didn't seem real to me any more. If you don't understand that, go to Monte Carlo or some other place where there's a big casino, sit at a table, and watch the face of the man that spins the little ivory ball. After you've watched it a while, ask yourself how much he would care if you went out and plugged yourself in the head. His eyes might drop when he heard the shot, but it wouldn't be from worry whether you lived or died. It would be to make sure you didn't leave a bet on the table, that he would have to cash for your estate. No, he wouldn't care. Not that baby.

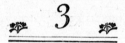

3

"*THEN ANOTHER* thing I call your attention to, Mr. Nirdlinger, a feature we've added in the last year, at no extra cost, is our guarantee of bail bond. We furnish you a card, and all you have to do, in case of accident where you're held responsible, or in any traffic case where the police put you under arrest, is to produce that card and if it's a bailable offense, it automatically procures your release. The police take up the card, that puts us on your bond, and you're free until your case comes up for trial. Since that's one of the things the Automobile Club does for members, and you're thinking about the Automobile Club—"

"I've pretty well given that idea up."

"Well then, why don't we fix this thing up right now? I've pretty well outlined what we do for you—"

"I guess we might as well."

"Then if you'll sign these applications, you'll be protected until the new policies are issued, which will be in about a week, but there's no use your paying for a whole week's extra insurance. There's for the collision, fire, and theft, there's for the public liability—and if you don't mind sticking your name on these two, they're the agent's copies, and I keep them for my files."

"Here?"

"Right on the dotted line."

He was a big, blocky man, about my size, with glasses, and I played him exactly the way I figured to. As soon as I had the applications, I switched to accident insurance. He didn't seem much interested, so I made it pretty stiff. Phyllis cut in that the very idea of accident insurance made her shiver, and I kept on going. I didn't quit till I had hammered in every reason for taking out accident insurance that any agent ever thought of, and maybe a couple of reasons that no agent ever had thought of. He sat there drumming with his fingers on the arms of his chair, wishing I would go.

But what bothered me wasn't that. It was the witness that Phyllis brought out. I thought she would have some friend of the family in to dinner, maybe a woman, and just let her stay with us, there in the sitting room, after I showed up around seven-thirty. She didn't. She brought the stepdaughter in, a pretty girl, named Lola. Lola wanted to go, but Phyllis said she had to get the wool wound for a sweater she was knitting, and kept her there, winding it. I had to tie her in, with a gag now and then, to make sure she would remember what we were talking about, but the more I looked at her the less I liked it. Having to sit with her there, knowing all the time what we were going to do to her father, was one of the things I hadn't bargained for.

And next thing I knew, when I got up to go, I had let myself in for hauling her down to the boulevard, so she could go to a picture show. Her father had to go out again that night, and he was using the car, and that meant that unless I hauled her she would have to go down by bus. I didn't want to haul her. I didn't want to have anything to do with her. But when he kind of turned to me there was nothing I could do but offer, and she ran and got her hat and coat, and in a minute or two there we were, rolling down the hill.

"Mr. Huff?"

"Yes?"

"I'm not going to a picture show."

"No?"

"I'm meeting somebody. At the drugstore."

"Oh."

"Would you haul us both down?"

"Oh—sure."

"You won't mind?"

"No, not a bit."

"And you won't tell on me? There are reasons why I don't want them to know. At home."

"No, of course not."

We stopped at the drugstore, and she jumped out and in a minute came back with a young guy, with an Italian-looking face, pretty good-looking, that had been standing around outside. "Mr. Huff, this is Mr. Sachetti."

"How are you, Mr. Sachetti. Get in."

They got in, and kind of grinned at each other, and we rolled down Beachwood to the boulevard. "Where do you want me to set you down?"

"Oh, anywhere."

"Hollywood and Vine all right?"

"Swell."

I set them down there, and after she got out, she reached out her hand, and took mine, and thanked me, her eyes shining like stars. "It was darling of you to take us. Lean close, I'll tell you a secret."

"Yes?"

"If you hadn't taken us we'd have had to walk."

"How are you going to get back?"

"Walk."

"You want some money?"

"No, my father would kill me. I spent all my week's money. No, but thanks. And remember—don't tell on me."

"I won't."

"Hurry, you'll miss your light."

I drove home. Phyllis got there in about a half hour. She was humming a song out of a Nelson Eddy picture. "Did you like my sweater?"

"Yeah, sure."

"Isn't it a lovely color? I never wore old rose before. I think it's going to be really becoming to me."

"It's going to look all right."

"Where did you leave Lola?"

"On the boulevard."

"Where did she go?"

"I didn't notice."

"Was there somebody waiting for her?"

"Not that I saw. Why?"

"I was just wondering. She's been going around with a boy named Sachetti. A perfectly terrible person. She's been forbidden to see him."

"He wasn't on deck tonight. Anyway, I didn't see him. Why didn't you tell me about her?"

"Well? You said have a witness."

"Yeah, but I didn't mean her."

"Isn't she as good a witness as any other?"

"Yeah, but holy smoke there's a limit. A man's own daughter, and we're even using her—for what we're using her for."

An awful look came over her face, and her voice got hard as glass. "What's the matter? Are you getting ready to back out?"

"No, but you could have got somebody else. Me, driving her

down to the boulevard, and all the time I had this in my pocket."
I took out the applications, and showed them to her. One of those
"agent's copies" was an undated application for a $25,000 personal
accident policy, with double indemnity straight down the line for
any disability or death incurred on a railroad train.

It was part of the play that I had to make two or three calls on
Nirdlinger in his office. The first time, I gave him the bail-bond
guarantee, stuck around about five minutes, told him to put it in
his car, and left. The next time I gave him a little leather memo
book, with his name stamped on it in gilt, just a little promotion
feature we have for policy holders. The third time I delivered the
automobile policies, and took his check, $79.52. When I got back
to the office that day, Nettie told me there was somebody waiting
for me in my private office. "Who?"

"A Miss Lola Nirdlinger and a Mr. Sachetti, I think she said.
I didn't get his first name."

I went in there and she laughed. She liked me, I could see that.
"You surprised to see us again?"

"Oh, not much. What can I do for you?"

"We've come in to ask a favor. But it's your own fault."

"Yeah? How's that?"

"What you said the other night to Father about being able to
get money on his car, if he needed it. We've come in to take you
up on it. Or anyway, Nino has."

That was something I had to do something about, the competi-
tion I was getting from the Automobile Club on an automobile
loan. They lend money on a member's car, and I got to the point
where I had to, too, if I was going to get any business. So I organ-
ized a little finance company of my own, had myself made a direc-
tor, and spent about one day a week there. It didn't have anything to do with the insurance company, but it was one way I
could meet that question that I ran into all the time: "Do you

lend money on a car?" I had mentioned it to Nirdlinger, just as part of the sales talk, but I didn't know she was paying attention. I looked at Sachetti. "You want to borrow money on your car?"

"Yes sir."

"What kind of car is it?"

He told me. It was a cheap make.

"Sedan?"

"Coupe."

"It's in your name? And paid for?"

"Yes sir."

They must have seen a look cross my face, because she giggled. "He couldn't use it the other night. He didn't have any gas."

"Oh."

I didn't want to lend him money on his car, or anything else. I didn't want to have anything to do with him, or her, in any way, shape, or form. I lit a cigarette, and sat there a minute. "You sure you want to borrow money on this car? Because if you're not working now, what I mean if you don't absolutely see your way clear to pay it back, it's a sure way to lose it. The whole second-hand car business depends on people that thought they could pay a small loan back, and couldn't."

She looked at me very solemnly. "It's different with Nino. He isn't working, but he doesn't want this loan just to have money to spend. You see, he's done all his work for his Sc. D., and—"

"Where?"

"U. S. C."

"What in?"

"Chemistry. If he can only get his degree, he's sure of work, he's been promised that, and it seems such a pity to miss a chance for a really good position just because he hasn't taken his degree. But to take it, he has to have his dissertation published, and pay this and that, for his diploma for instance, and that's what he wants this money for. He won't spend it on his living. He has friends that will take care of that."

I had to come through. I knew that. I wouldn't have, if it didn't make me so nervous to be around her, but all I could think of now was to say yes and get them out of there. "How much do you want?"

"He thought if he could get $250, that would be enough."

"I see. I see."

I figured it up. With charges, it would amount to around $285, and it was an awfully big loan on the car he was going to put up. "Well—give me a day or two on it. I think we can manage it."

They went out, and then she ducked back. "You're awfully nice to me. I don't know why I keep bothering you about things."

"That's all right, Miss Nirdlinger, I'm glad—"

"You can call me Lola, if you want to."

"Thanks, I'll be glad to help any time I can."

"This is secret, too."

"Yes, I know."

"I'm terribly grateful, Mr. Huff."

"Thanks—Lola."

The accident policy came through a couple of days later. That meant I had to get his check for it, and get it right away, so the dates would correspond. You understand, I wasn't going to deliver the accident policy, to him. That would go to Phyllis, and she would find it later, in his safe deposit box. And I wasn't going to tell him anything about it. Just the same, I had to get his check, in the exact amount of the policy, so later on, when they checked up his stubs and his cancelled checks, they would find he had paid for it himself. That would check with the application in our files, and it would also check with those trips I had made to his office, if they put me on the spot.

I went in on him pretty worried, and shut the door on his secretary, and got down to brass tacks right away. "Mr. Nirdlinger, I'm in a hole, and I'm wondering if you'll help me out."

"Well I don't know. I don't know. What is it?"

He was expecting a touch, and I wanted him to be expecting a touch. "It's pretty bad."

"Suppose you tell me."

"I've charged you too much for your insurance. For that automobile stuff."

He burst out laughing. "Is that all? I thought you wanted to borrow money."

"Oh. No. Nothing like that. It's worse—from my point of view."

"Do I get a refund?"

"Why sure."

"Then it's better—from my point of view."

"It isn't as simple as that. This is the trouble, Mr. Nirdlinger. There's a board, in our business, that was formed to stop cutthroating on rates, and see to it that every company charges a rate sufficient to protect the policy holder, and that's the board I'm in dutch with. Because here recently, they've made it a rule that *every* case, every case, mind you, where there's an alleged mischarge by an agent, is to be investigated by them, and you can see where that puts me. And you too, in a way. Because they'll have me up for fifteen different hearings, and come around pestering you till you don't know what your name is—and all because I looked up the wrong rate in the book when I was out to your house that night, and never found it out till this morning when I checked over my month's accounts."

"And what do you want me to do?"

"There's one way I can fix it. Your check, of course, was deposited, and there's nothing to do about that. But if you'll let me give you cash for the check you gave me—$79.52—I've got it right here with me—and give me a new check for the correct amount—

$58.60—then that'll balance it, and they'll have nothing to investigate."

"How do you mean, balance it?"

"Well, you see, in multiple-card bookkeeping—oh well, it's so complicated I don't even know if I understand it myself. Anyway, that's what our cashier tells me. It's the way they make their entries."

"I see."

He looked out the window and I saw a funny look come in his eye. "Well—all right. I don't know why not."

I gave him the cash and took his check. It was all hooey. We've got a board, but it doesn't bother with agents' mistakes. It governs rates. I don't even know if there's such a thing as multiple-card bookkeeping, and I never talked with our cashier. I just figured that when you offer a man about twenty bucks more than he thought he had when you came in, he wouldn't ask too many questions about why you offer it to him. I went to the bank. I deposited the check. I even knew what he wrote on his stub. It just said "Insurance." I had what I wanted.

It was the day after that that Lola and Sachetti came in for their loan. When I handed them the check she did a little dance in the middle of the floor. "You want a copy of Nino's dissertation?"

"Why—I'd love it."

"It's called 'The Problem of Colloids in the Reduction of Low-Grade Gold Ores'."

"I'll look forward to it."

"Liar—you won't even read it."

"I'll read as much as I can understand."

"Anyway, you'll get a signed copy."

"Thanks."

"Good-bye. Maybe you're rid of us for a while."

"Maybe."

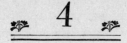

4

ALL THIS, what I've been telling you, happened in late winter, along the middle of February. Of course, in California February looks like any other month, but anyway it would have been winter anywhere else. From then on, all through the spring, believe me I didn't get much sleep. You start on something like this, and if you don't wake up plenty of times in the middle of the night, dreaming they got you for something you forgot, you've got better nerves than I've got. Then there were things we couldn't figure out, like how to get him on a train. That was tough, and if we didn't have a piece of luck, maybe we never would have put it over. There's plenty of people out here that have never been inside a train, let alone taken a ride on one. They go everywhere by car. That was how he travelled, when he travelled, and how to make him use a train just once, that was something that gave us a headache for quite some time. We got a break on one thing though that I had sweated over plenty. That was the funny look that came over his face when I got that check. There was something back of it, I knew that, and if it was something his secretary was in on, and especially if he went out after I left and made some crack to the secretary about getting $20 he didn't expect, it would look plenty bad later, no matter what kind of story I made up. But that wasn't it. Phyllis got the low-down on it, and it startled me, how pretty it broke for us. He charged his car insurance to his company, under expenses, and his secretary had already entered it when I came along with my proposition. She had not only entered it, but if he went through with what I wanted, he still had his cancelled check to show for it, the first one, I mean. All he had to do was keep his mouth shut to the secretary and he could put his

$20 profit in his pocket, and nobody would be the wiser. He kept his mouth shut. He didn't even tell Lola. But he had to brag to somebody how smart he was, so he told Phyllis.

Another thing that worried me was myself. I was afraid my work would fall off, and they'd begin talking about me in the office, wondering why I'd begun to slip. That wouldn't do me any good, later I mean, when they began to think about it. I had to sell insurance while this thing was cooking, if I never sold it before. I worked like a wild man. I saw every prospect there was the least chance of selling, and how I high-pressured them was a shame. Believe it or not, my business showed a 12% increase in March, it jumped 2% over that in April, and in May, when there's a lot of activity in cars, it went to 7% over that. I even made a hook-up with a big syndicate of second-hand dealers for my finance company, and that helped. The books didn't know anything to tell on me. I was the candy kid in both offices that spring. They were all taking off their hats to me.

"He's going to his class reunion. At Palo Alto."
"When?"
"June. In about six weeks."
"That's it. That's what we've been waiting for."
"But he wants to drive. He wants to take the car, and he wants me to go with him. He'll raise an awful fuss if I don't go."
"Yeah? Listen, don't give yourself airs. I don't care if it's a class reunion or just down to the drugstore, a man would rather go alone than with a wife. He's just being polite. You talk like you're not interested in his class reunion, and he'll be persuaded. He'll be persuaded so easy you'll be surprised."
"Well I like that."
"You're not supposed to like it. But you'll find out."
That was how it turned out, but she worked on him a whole week and she couldn't change him on the car. "He says he'll have

to have it, and there'll be a lot of things he'll want to go to, picnics and things like that, and if he doesn't have it he'll have to hire one. Besides, he hates trains. He gets trainsick."

"Can't you put on an act?"

"I did. I put on all the act I dare put, and still he won't budge. I put on such an act that Lola is hardly speaking to me any more. She thinks it's selfish of me. I can try again, but—"

"Holy smoke no."

"I could do this. The day before he's to start, I could bang the car up. Mess up the ignition or something. So it had to go in the shop. Then he'd *have* to go by train."

"Nothing like it. Nothing even a little bit like it. In the first place, if you've already put on an act, they'll smell something, and believe me Lola will be hard to talk down, later. In the second place, we need the car."

"*We* need it?"

"It's essential."

"I still don't know—what we're going to do."

"You'll know. You'll know in plenty of time. But we've got to have the car. We've got to have two cars, yours and mine. Whatever you do, don't pull any monkey business with the car. That car's got to run. It's got to be in perfect shape."

"Hadn't we better give up the train idea?"

"Listen, it's the train or we don't do it."

"Well my goodness, you don't have to snap at me."

"Just pulling off some piker job, that don't interest me. But this, hitting it for the limit, that's what I go for. It's all I go for."

"I was just wondering."

"Quit wondering."

Two or three days later was when we had our piece of luck. She called me at the office around four in the afternoon. "Walter?"

"Yes."

"Are you alone?"

"Is it important?"

"Yes, terribly. Something has happened."

"I'll go home. Call me there in a half hour."

I was alone, but I don't take chances on a phone that runs through a switchboard. I went home, and the phone rang a couple of minutes after I got there. "The Palo Alto trip is off. He's broken his leg."

"What!"

"I don't even know how he did it, yet. He was holding a dog or something, a neighbor's dog that was chasing a rabbit, and slipped and fell down. He's in the hospital now. Lola's with him. They'll be bringing him home in a few minutes."

"I guess that knocks it in the head."

"I'm afraid so."

I was at dinner before it came to me that instead of knocking it in the head, maybe this fixed it up perfect. I walked three miles, around the living room, wondering if she'd come that night, before I heard the bell ring.

"I've only got a few minutes. I'm supposed to be on the boulevard, buying him something to read. I could cry. Whoever heard of such a thing?"

"Listen, Phyllis, never mind that. What kind of break has he got? I mean, is it bad?"

"It's down near the ankle. No, it's not bad."

"Is it in pulleys?"

"No. There's a weight on it, that comes off in about a week. But he won't be able to walk. He'll have to wear a cast. A long time."

"He'll be able to walk."

"You think so?"

"If you get him up."

"What do you mean, Walter?"

"On crutches, he can get up, if you get him up. Because with his foot in a cast, *he won't be able to drive.* He'll have to go by train. Phyllis, this is what we've been hoping for."

"You think so?"

"And then another thing. I told you, he gets on that train but he don't get on it. All right, then. We've got a question of identification there, haven't we? Those crutches, that foot in a cast—there's the most perfect identification a man ever had. Oh yeah, I'm telling you. If you can get him off that bed, and make him think he ought to take the trip anyway, just as a vacation from all he's been through—we're in. I can feel it. We're in."

"It's dangerous, though."

"What's dangerous about it?"

"I mean, getting a broken leg case out of bed too soon. I used to be a nurse, and I know. It's almost certain to affect the length. Make one leg shorter than the other, I mean."

"Is that all that's bothering you?"

It was a minute before she got it. Whether one leg was going to be shorter than the other, that was one thing he didn't have to worry about.

Decoration Day they don't have mail delivery, but the day watchman sends over to the General Fidelity box and gets it. There was a big envelope for me, marked personal. I opened it and found a booklet. It was called "Colloids in Gold Mining. An examination of methods in dealing with the problem." Inside, it was inscribed, "To Mr. Walter Huff, in appreciation of past favors, Bernanino Sachetti."

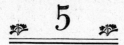

5

HIS TRAIN was to leave at 9:45 at night. Around four o'clock, I drove down to San Pedro Street and talked employers' liability to the manager of a wine company. There wasn't a chance of landing him until August, when the grapes came in and his plant opened up, but I had a reason. He explained why he wasn't ready to do business yet, but I put on an act and went back to the office. I told Nettie I thought I had a real prospect, and to make out a card for him. The card automatically gave the date of the first call, and that was what I wanted. I signed a couple of letters, and around five-thirty I left.

I got home around six, and the Filipino was all ready to serve dinner. I had seen to that. This was June 3, and I should have paid him on the first, but I had pretended I had forgotten to go to the bank, and put him off. Today, though, I had stopped at the house for lunch, and paid him. That meant that when night came he could hardly wait to go out and spend it. I said O.K., he could serve dinner, and he had the soup on the table before I even got washed up. I ate, as well as I could. He gave me steak, mashed potatoes, peas, and carrots, with fruit cup for dessert. I was so nervous I could hardly chew, but I got it all down somehow. I had hardly finished my coffee when he had everything washed up, and had changed to cream-colored pants, white shoes and stockings, a brown coat, and white shirt open at the neck, ready to go out with the girl. It used to be that what a Hollywood actor wore on Monday a Filipino house boy wore on Tuesday, but now, if you ask me, it's the other way around, and the boy from Manila beats Clark Gable to it.

He left around a quarter to seven. When he came up to ask if there was anything else for him to do, I was taking off my clothes getting ready to go to bed. I told him I was going to lie there and do a little work. I got some paper and pencils and made a lot of notes, like I was figuring up the public liability stuff for the man I talked to in the afternoon. It was the kind of stuff you would naturally save and put in the prospect's folder. I took care there was a couple of notes on the date.

Then I went down and called the office. Joe Pete, the night watchman, answered. "Joe Pete, this is Walter Huff. Do me a favor, will you? Go up to my office, and right on top of the desk you'll find my rate book. It's a looseleaf book, with a soft leather back, and my name stamped in gold on the front, and under that the word 'rates.' I forgot to bring it home, and I need it. Will you get it and send it up to me by messenger, right away?"

"O. K., Mr. Huff. Right away."

Fifteen minutes later he rang back and said he couldn't find it. "I looked all over the desk, Mr. Huff, and through the office besides, and there's no such book there."

"Nettie must have locked it up."

"I can call her if you want, and ask where she put it."

"No, I don't need it that bad."

"I'm sorry, Mr. Huff."

"I'll have to get along without it."

I had put that rate book in a place where he'd never find it. But it was one person that had called me at home that night, and I was there, working hard. There'd be others. No need to say anything to him that would make him remember the date. He had to keep a log, and enter everything he did, not only by date, but also by time. I looked at my watch. It was 7:38.

A quarter to eight the phone rang again. It was Phyllis. "The blue."

"Blue it is."

That was a check on what suit he would wear. We were pretty sure it would be the blue, but I had to be sure, so she was to duck down to the drugstore to buy him an extra tooth brush, and call. No danger of its being traced, there's no record on dial calls. Soon as she hung up I dressed. I put on a blue suit too. But before that I wrapped up my foot. I put a thick bandage of gauze on it, and over that adhesive tape. It looked like the tape was wrapped on the ankle, like a cast for a broken leg, but it wasn't. I could cut it off in ten seconds when I was ready to. I put the shoe on. I could barely lace it, but that was how I wanted it. I checked on a pair of horn-rim glasses, like he wore. They were in my pocket. So was 58 inches of light cotton rope, rolled small. So was a handle I had made, like stores hook on packages, but heavier, from an iron rod. My coat bulged, but I didn't care.

Twenty minutes to nine I called Nettie. "Did you see my rate book before I left?"

"Indeed I didn't, Mr. Huff."

"I need it, and I don't know what I did with it."

"You mean you lost it?"

"I don't know. I phoned Joe Pete, and he can't find it, and I can't imagine what I did with it."

"I can run in, if you want, and see if I can—"

"No, it's not that important."

"I didn't see it, Mr. Huff."

Nettie lives in Burbank, and it's a toll call. The record would show I called from the house at 8:40. As soon as I got rid of her I opened the bell box and tilted half a visiting card against the clapper, so if the phone rang it would fall down. Then I did the same for the doorbell clapper, in the kitchen. I would be out of the house an hour and a half, and I had to know if the doorbell rang or the phone rang. If they did, that would be while I was in the bathroom taking a bath, with the door shut and the water running, so I didn't hear. But I had to know.

Soon as I had the cards fixed I got in my car and drove over to Hollywoodland. It's just a few minutes from my house. I parked on the main street, a couple of minutes' walk from the house. I had to be where a car wouldn't attract any attention, but at the same time I couldn't be so far off that I had to do much walking. Not with that foot.

Around the bend from the house is a big tree. There's no house in sight of it. I slipped behind it and waited. I waited exactly two minutes, but it seemed like an hour. Then I saw the flash of headlights. The car came around the bend. She was at the wheel, and he was beside her with his crutches under his elbow on the door side. When the car got to the tree it stopped. That was exactly according to the play. Next came the ticklish part. It was how to get him out of the car for a minute, with the bags in back and everything all set, so I could get in. If he had been all right on his two feet there would have been nothing to it, but getting a cripple out of a car once he gets set, and especially with a well person sitting right beside him, is like getting a hippopotamus out of a car.

She opened up just like I had coached her. "I haven't got my pocketbook."

"Didn't you take it?"

"I thought so. Look on the back seat."

"No, nothing back there but my stuff."

"I can't think what I've done with it."

"Well come on, we'll be late. Here, here's a dollar. That'll be enough till you get back."

"I must have left it on the sofa. In the living room."

"Well all right, all right, you left it on the sofa in the living room. Now get going."

She was coming to the part I had taken her over forty times. She was all for *asking* him to step out and get it. I finally beat it into her head that if she did that, she was just setting herself up to him to ask her why *she* didn't step out and get it, so he wouldn't have to unlimber the crutches. I showed her that her only chance was to talk dumb, not start the car, and wait him out, until he would get so sore, and so worried over the time, that he would make a martyr out of himself and get it himself. She kept at it, just like she was coached.

"But I want my pocketbook."

"What for? Isn't a buck enough?"

"But it's got my lipstick in it."

"Listen, can't you get it through your head we're trying to catch a train? This isn't an automobile trip, where we start when we get ready. It's a railroad train, and it goes at nine-forty-five, and when it goes it goes. Come on. Start up."

"Well if you're going to talk that way."

"What way?"

"All I said was that I wanted my—"

He ripped out a flock of cusswords, and at last I heard the crutches rattling against the side of the car. As soon as he was around the bend, hobbling back to the house, I dove in. I had to dive in the front door and climb over the seat into the back, so he wouldn't hear the back door close. That's a sound that always catches your ear, a car door closing. I crouched down there in the dark. He had his bag and his briefcase on the seat.

"Did I do it all right, Walter?"

"O. K. so far. How did you get rid of Lola?"

"I didn't have to. She was invited to something over at U.C.L.A. and I took her to the bus at seven."

"O. K. Back up, now, so he won't have so far to walk. Try and smooth him down."

"All right."

She backed up to the door and he got in again. She started off. Believe me it's an awful thing to kibitz on a man and his wife, and hear what they really talk about. Soon as she got him a little smoothed down, he began to beef about Belle, the way she passed things at dinner. She panned Belle for the way she broke so many dishes. Then they got switched off to somebody named Hobey, and a woman named Ethel, that seemed to be Hobey's wife. He said he was through with Hobey and Hobey might as well know it. She said she used to like Ethel but the high-hat way she's been acting lately was too much. They figured it out whether they owed Hobey and Ethel a dinner or the other way around, so they found out they were one down, and decided that after they knocked that one off that was going to be the end of it. When they got that all settled, they decided he was to take a taxi wherever he went, up in Palo Alto, even if it did cost a little money. Because if he had to slog along on crutches everywhere he went, he wouldn't have a good time, and besides he might strain his leg. Phyllis talked just like he was going to Palo Alto, and she didn't have a thing on her mind. A woman is a funny animal.

Back where I was, I couldn't see where we were. I was even afraid to breathe, for fear he'd hear me. She was to drive so she didn't make any sudden stops, or get herself tangled in traffic, or do anything that would make him turn his head around to see what was back of us. He didn't. He had a cigar in his mouth, and lay back in the seat, smoking it. After a while she gave two sharp raps on the horn. That was our signal that we had come to a dark street we had picked out, about a half mile from the station.

I raised up, put my hand over his mouth, and pulled his head back. He grabbed my hand in both of his. The cigar was still in his fingers. I took it with my free hand and handed it to her. She took it. I took one of the crutches and hooked it under his chin. I won't tell you what I did then. But in two seconds he was curled down on the seat with a broken neck, and not a mark on him except a crease right over his nose, from the crosspiece of the crutch.

6

WE WERE right up with it, the moment of audacity that has to be part of any successful murder. For the next twenty minutes we were in the jaws of death, not for what would happen now, but for how it would go together later. She started to throw the cigar out, but I stopped her. He had lit that cigar in the house, and I had to have it. She held it for me, and wiped the end of it as well as she could, while I went to work with the rope. I ran it across his shoulders, just below the neck, under his arms, and across his back. I tied it hard, and hooked the handle on, so it caught both sections of the rope, and drew them tight. A dead man is about the hardest thing to handle there is, but I figured with this harness we could do it, and do it quick.

"We're there, Walter. Shall I park now or drive around the block?"

"Park now. We're ready."

She stopped. It was on a side street, about a block from the station. That stumped us for a while, where to park. If we went on the regular station parking lot, it was a 10 to 1 shot that a red-cap would jerk the door open to get the bags, and we'd be sunk. But parking here, we would be all right. If we got a chance, we were to have an argument about it in front of somebody, with me complaining about how far she made me walk, to cover up on something that might look a little funny, later.

She got out and took the bag and briefcase. He was one of the kind who puts his toilet articles in a briefcase, for use on the train, and that was a break for me, later. I wound up all windows, took the crutches, and got out. She locked the car. We left him right where he was, curled down on the seat, with the harness on him.

She went ahead with the bag and briefcase, and I came along behind, with the bandaged leg half lifted up, walking on the crutches. That looked like a woman making it easy for a cripple. Really, it was a way to keep the red-cap from getting a good look at me when he took the bags. Soon as we got around the corner, in sight of the station, here came one, running. He did just what we figured on. He took the bags from her, and never waited for me at all.

"The nine forty-five for San Francisco, Section 8, Car C."

"Eight in Car C, yas'm. Meet you on the train."

We went in the station. I made her drop back on me, so if anything came up I could mumble to her. I had the glasses on, and my hat pulled down, but not too much. I kept my eyes down, like I was watching where I put the crutches. I kept the cigar in my mouth, partly so it covered some of my face, partly so I could screw my face out of shape a little, like I was trying to keep the smoke out of my eyes.

The train was on a siding, out back of the station. I made a quick count of the cars. "Holy smoke, it's the third one." It was the one that both conductors were standing in front of, and not only them, but the porter, and the red-cap, waiting for his tip. Unless we did something quick, it would be four people that had a good look at me before I went in the car, and it might hang us. She ran on ahead. I saw her tip the red-cap, and he went off, all bows. He didn't pass near me. He headed for the far end of the station, where the parking lot was. Then the porter saw me, and started for me. She took him by the arm. "He doesn't like to be helped."

The porter didn't get it. The Pullman conductor did.

"Hey!"

The porter stopped. Then he got it. They all turned their backs and started to talk. I stumped up the car steps. I got to the top. That was her cue. She was still down on the ground, with the conductors. "Dear."

I stopped and half turned. "Come back to the observation platform. I'll say good-bye to you there, and then I won't have to worry about getting off the train. You still have a few minutes. Maybe we can talk."

"Fine."

I started back, through the car. She started back, on the ground, outside.

All three cars were full of people getting ready to go to bed, with most of the berths made up and bags all out in the aisle. The porters weren't there. They were at their boxes, outside. I kept my eyes down, clinched the cigar in my teeth, and kept my face screwed up. Nobody really saw me, and yet everybody saw me, because the minute they saw those crutches they began snatching bags out of the way and making room. I just nodded and mumbled "thanks."

When I saw her face I knew something was wrong. Outside on the observation platform, I saw what it was. A man was there, tucked back in a corner in the dark, having a smoke. I sat down on the opposite side. She reached her hand over. I took it. She kept looking at me for a cue. I kept making my lips say, "Parking . . . parking . . . parking." After a second or two she got it.

"Dear."

"Yes?"

"You're not mad at me any more? For where I parked?"

"Forget it."

"I thought I was headed for the station parking lot, honestly. But I get all mixed up in this part of town. I hadn't any idea I was going to make you walk so far."

"I told you, forget it."

"I'm terribly sorry."

"Kiss me."

I looked at my watch, held it up to her. It was still seven minutes before the train would leave. She needed a six-minute start for what she had to do. "Listen, Phyllis, there's no use of you waiting around here. Why don't you blow?"

"Well—you don't mind?"

"Not a bit. No sense dragging it out."

"Good-bye, then."

"Good-bye."

"Have a good time. Three cheers for Leland Stanford."

"I'll do my best."

"Kiss me again."

"Good-bye."

For what I had to do, I had to get rid of this guy, and get rid of him quick. I hadn't expected anybody out there. There seldom is when a train pulls out. I sat there, trying to think of something. I thought he might leave when he finished his cigarette, but he didn't. He threw it over the side and began to talk.

"Women are funny."

"Funny and then some."

"I couldn't help hearing that little conversation you had with your wife just now. About where she parked, I mean. Reminds me of an experience I had with my wife, coming home from San Diego."

He told the experience he had with his wife. I looked him over. I couldn't see his face. I figured he couldn't see mine. He stopped talking. I had to say something.

"Yeah, women are funny all right. Specially when you get them behind the wheel of a car."

"They're all of that."

The train began to roll. It crawled through the outskirts of Los

Angeles, and he kept on talking. Then an idea came to me. I remembered I was supposed to be a cripple, and began feeling through my pockets.

"You lose something?"

"My ticket. I can't find it."

"Say, I wonder if I've got my ticket. Yeah, here it is."

"You know what I bet she did? Put that ticket in my briefcase, right where I told her not to. She was to put it here in the pocket of this suit, and now—"

"Oh, it'll turn up."

"Don't that beat all? Here I've got to go and hobble all through those cars, just because—"

"Don't be silly. Stay where you are."

"No, I couldn't let you—"

"Be a pleasure old man. Stay right where you are and I'll get it for you. What's your space?"

"Would you? Section 8, Car C."

"I'll be right back with it."

We were picking up speed a little now. My mark was a dairy sign, about a quarter of a mile from the track. We came in sight of it and I lit the cigar. I put the crutches under one arm, threw my leg over the rail, and let myself down. One of the crutches hit the ties and spun me so I almost fell. I hung on. When we came square abreast of the sign I dropped off.

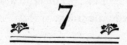

7

THERE'S NOTHING so dark as a railroad track in the middle of the night. The train shot ahead, and I crouched there, waiting for the tingle to leave my feet. I had dropped off the left side of

the train, into the footpath between the tracks, so there wouldn't
be any chance I could be seen from the highway. It was about two
hundred feet away. I stayed there, on my hands and knees, strain-
ing to see something on the other side of the tracks. There was
a dirt road there, that gave entry to a couple of small factories,
further on back. All around it were vacant lots, and it wasn't lit.
She ought to be there by now. She had a seven-minute start, the
train took six minutes to that point, and it was an eleven-minute
drive from the station to this dirt road. I had checked it twenty
times. I held still and stared, trying to spot the car. I couldn't see it.

I don't know how long I crouched there. It came to me that
maybe she had bumped somebody's fender, or been stopped by a
cop, or something. I seemed to turn to water. Then I heard something. I heard a panting. Then with it I heard footsteps. They
would go fast for a second or two, and then stop. It was like being
in a nightmare, with something queer coming after me, and I
didn't know what it was, but it was horrible. Then I saw it. It was
her. That man must have weighed 200 pounds, but she had him
on her back, holding him by the handle, and staggering along
with him, over the tracks. His head was hanging down beside her
head. They looked like something in a horror picture.

I ran over and grabbed his legs, to take some of the weight off
her. We ran him a few steps. She started to throw him down. "Not
that track! The other one!"

We got him over to the track the train went out on, and dropped
him. I cut the harness off and slipped it in my pocket. I put the
lighted cigar within a foot or two of him. I threw one crutch over
him and the other beside the track.

"Where's the car?"

"There. Couldn't you see it?"

I looked, and there it was, right where it was supposed to be, on
the dirt road.

"We're done. Let's go."

We ran over and climbed in and she started the motor, threw in the gear. "Oh my—his hat!"

I took the hat and sailed it out the window, on the tracks. "It's O. K., a hat can roll,—*get going*!"

She started up. We passed the factories. We came to a street.

On Sunset she went through a light. "Watch that stuff, can't you, Phyllis? If you're stopped now, with me in the car, we're sunk."

"Can I drive with that thing going on?"

She meant the car radio. I had it turned on. It was to be part of my alibi, for the time I was out of the house, that I knocked off work for a while and listened to the radio. I had to know what was coming in that night. I had to know more than I could find out by reading the programs in the papers. "I've got to have it, you know that—"

"Let me alone, let me drive!"

She hit a zone, and must have been doing seventy. I clenched my teeth, and kept quiet. When we came to a vacant lot I threw out the rope. About a mile further on I threw out the handle. Going by a curb drain I shot the glasses into it. Then I happened to look down and saw her shoes. They were scarred from the track ballast.

"What did you carry him for? Why didn't you let me—"

"Where were you? *Where were you?*"

"I was there. I was waiting—"

"Did I know that? Could I just sit there, with *that* in the car?"

"I was trying to see where you were. I couldn't see—"

"Let me alone, *let me drive*!"

"Your shoes—"

I choked it back. In a second or two, she started up again. She raved like a lunatic. She raved and she kept on raving, about him, about me, about anything that came in her head. Every now and then I'd snap. There we were, after what we had done, snarling at each other like a couple of animals, and neither one of us could stop. It was like somebody had shot us full of some kind of dope. "Phyllis, cut this out. We've got to talk, and it may be our last chance."

"Talk then! Who's stopping you?"

"First then: You don't know anything about this insurance policy. You—"

"How many times do you have to say that?"

"I'm only telling you—"

"You've already told me till I'm sick of hearing you."

"Next, the inquest. You bring—"

"I bring a minister, I know that, I bring a minister to take charge of the body, how many times have I got to listen to that— *are you going to let me drive?*"

"O. K., then. Drive."

"Is Belle home?"

"How do I know? No!"

"And Lola's out?"

"Didn't I tell you?"

"Then you'll have to stop at the drugstore. To get a pint of ice cream or something. To have witnesses you drove straight home from the station. You got to say something to fix the time and the date. You—"

"Get out! Get out! I'll go insane!"

"I can't get out. I've got to get to my car! Do you know what that means, if I take time to walk? I can't complete my alibi! I—"

"I said get out!"

"Drive on, or I'll sock you."

When she got to my car she stopped and I got out. We didn't kiss. We didn't even say good-bye. I got out of her car, got in mine, started, and drove home.

When I got home I looked at the clock. It was 10:25. I opened the bell box of the telephone. The card was still there. I closed the box and dropped the card in my pocket. I went in the kitchen and looked at the doorbell. That card was still there. I dropped it in my pocket. I went upstairs, ripped off my clothes, and got into pajamas and slippers. I cut the bandage off my foot. I went down, shoved the bandage and cards into the fireplace, with a newspaper, and lit it. I watched it burn. Then I went to the telephone and started to dial. I still had one call-back to get, to round out the late part of my alibi. I felt something like a drawstring pull in my throat, and a sob popped out of me. I clapped the phone down. It was getting me. I knew I had to get myself under some kind of control. I swallowed a couple of times. I wanted to make sure of my voice, that it would sound O. K. A dumb idea came to me that maybe if I would sing something, that would make me snap out of it. I started to sing the Isle of Capri. I sang about two notes, and it swallowed into a kind of a wail.

I went in the dining room and took a drink. I took another drink. I started mumbling to myself, trying to get so I could talk. I had to have something to mumble. I thought of the Lord's Prayer. I mumbled that, a couple of times. I tried to mumble it another time, and couldn't remember how it went.

When I thought I could talk, I dialed again. It was 10:48. I dialed Ike Schwartz, that's another salesman with General.

"Ike, do me a favor, will you? I'm trying to figure out a proposition on a public liability bond for a wine company to have it ready for them tomorrow morning, and I'm going nuts. I came off without my rate book. Joe Pete can't find it, and I'm wondering if you'll look up what I want in yours. You got it with you?"

"Sure, I'll be glad to."

I gave him the dope. He said give him fifteen minutes and he'd call back.

I walked around, digging my fingernails into my hands, trying to hold on to myself. The drawstring began to jerk on my throat again. I began mumbling again, saying over and over what I had just said to Ike. The phone rang. I answered. He had it figured for me, he said, and began to give it to me. He gave it to me three different ways, so I'd have it all. It took him twenty minutes. I took it down, what he said. I could feel the sweat squeezing out on my forehead and running down off my nose. After a while he was done.

"O. K., Ike, that's just what I wanted to know. That's just how I wanted it. Thanks a thousand times."

Soon as he hung up everything cracked. I dived for the bathroom. I was sicker than I had ever been in my life. After that passed I fell into bed. It was a long time before I could turn out the light. Then I lay there staring into the dark. Every now and then I would have a chill or something and start to tremble. Then that passed and I lay there, like a dope. Then I started to think. I tried not to, but it would creep up on me. I knew then what I had done. I had killed a man. I had killed a man to get a woman. I had put myself in her power, so there was one person in the world that could point a finger at me, and I would have to die. I had done all that for her, and I never wanted to see her again as long as I lived.

That's all it takes, one drop of fear, to curdle love into hate.

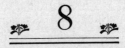

8

I GULPED down some orange juice and coffee, and then went up in the bedroom with the paper. I was afraid to open it in front of the Filipino. Sure enough, there it was, on Page 1:

OIL MAN, ON WAY TO JUNE RALLY, DIES IN TRAIN FALL

H. S. Nirdlinger, Petroleum Pioneer, Killed In Plunge from Express En Route to Reunion At Leland Stanford.

With injuries about the head and neck, the body of H. S. Nirdlinger, Los Angeles representative of the Western Pipe & Supply Company and for a number of years prominently identified with the oil industry here, was found on the railroad tracks about two miles north of this city shortly before midnight last night. Mr. Nirdlinger had departed on a northbound train earlier in the evening to attend his class reunion at Leland Stanford University, and it is believed he fell from the train. Police point out he had fractured his leg some weeks ago, and believe his unfamiliarity with crutches may have caused him to lose his balance on the observation platform, where he was last seen alive.

Mr. Nirdlinger was 44 years old. Born in Fresno, he attended Leland Stanford, and on graduation, entered the oil business, becoming one of the pioneers in the opening of the field at Long Beach. Later he was active at Signal Hill. For the last three years he had been in charge of the local office of the Western Pipe & Supply Company.

Surviving are a widow, formerly Miss Phyllis Belden of Mannerheim, and a daughter, Miss Lola Nirdlinger. Mrs. Nirdlinger, before her marriage, was head nurse of the Verdugo Health Institute here.

Twenty minutes to nine, Nettie called. She said Mr. Norton wanted to see me, as soon as I could possibly get down. That meant they already had it, and I wouldn't have to put on any act, going in there with my paper and saying this is the guy I sold an accident policy to last winter. I said I knew what it was, and I was right on my way.

I got through the day somehow. I think I told you about Norton
and Keyes. Norton is president of the company. He's a short, stocky
man about 35, that got the job when his father died and he's so
busy trying to act like his father he doesn't seem to have time for
much else. Keyes is head of the Claim Department, a holdover
from the old regime, and the way he tells it young Norton never
does anything right. He's big and fat and peevish, and on top of
that he's a theorist, and it makes your head ache to be around him,
but he's the best claim man on the Coast, and he was the one I was
afraid of.

First I had to face Norton, and tell him what I knew, or anyway
what I was supposed to know. I told him how I propositioned Nirdlinger about the accident policy, and how his wife and daughter
opposed it, and how I dropped it that night but went over to his
office a couple of days later to give him another whirl. That would
check with what the secretary saw. I told him how I sold him, then,
but only after I promised not to say anything to the wife and
daughter about it. I told how I took his application, then when the
policy came through, delivered it, and got his check. Then we went
down in Keyes' office and we went all over it again. It took all
morning, you understand. All while we were talking phone calls
and telegrams kept coming in, from San Francisco, where Keyes
had our investigators interviewing people that were on the train,
from the police, from the secretary, from Lola, after they got her
on the phone to find out what she knew. They tried to get Phyllis,
but she had strict instruction from me not to come to the phone, so
she didn't. They got hold of the coroner, and arranged for an
autopsy. There's generally a hook-up between insurance companies
and coroners, so they can get an autopsy if they want it. They
could demand it, under a clause in their policy, but that would
mean going to court for an order, and would tip it that the deceased
was insured, and that's bad all the way round. They get it on the
quiet, and in this case they had to have it. Because if Nirdlinger

died of apoplexy, or heart failure, and fell off the train, then it wouldn't any longer be accident, but death from natural causes, and they wouldn't be liable. About the middle of the afternoon they got the medical report. Death was from a broken neck. When they heard that they got the inquest postponed two days.

By four o'clock, the memos and telegrams were piled on Keyes' desk so he had to put a weight on top of them to keep them from falling over, and he was mopping his brow and so peevish nobody could talk to him. But Norton was getting more cheerful by the minute. He took a San Francisco call from somebody named Jackson, and I could tell from what he said that it was this guy I had got rid of on the observation platform before I dropped off. When he hung up he put one more memo on top of the others and turned to Keyes. "Clear case of suicide."

If it was suicide, you see, the company wouldn't be liable either. This policy only covered accident.

"Yeah?"

"All right, watch me while I check it over. First, he took out this policy. He took it out in secret. He didn't tell his wife, he didn't tell his daughter, he didn't tell his secretary, he didn't tell anybody. If Huff here, had been on the job, he might have known—"

"Known what?"

"No need to get sore, Huff. But you've got to admit it looked funny."

"It didn't look funny at all. It happens every day. Now if *they* had tried to insure *him*, without *him* knowing, *that* would have looked funny."

"That's right. Leave Huff out of it."

"All I'm saying, Keyes, is that—"

"Huff's record shows that if there had been anything funny, he'd have noted it and we'd have known it. You better find out something about your own agents."

"All right, skip it. He takes out this policy in absolute secrecy.

Why? Because he knew that if his family knew what he had done, they would know what he was up to. They knew what was on his mind, we can depend on that, and when we go into his books and his history, we'll find out what the trouble was. All right, next point, he fractured his leg, but he didn't put a claim in. Why? That looks funny, don't it, that a man had an accident policy, and didn't put a claim in for a broken leg? *Because he knew he was going to do this, and he was afraid if he put a claim in the family would find out about this policy and block him off.*"

"How?"

"If they called us up, we'd cancel on him wouldn't we? You bet we would. We'd return his unused premium so fast you couldn't see our dust, and he knew it. Oh no, he wasn't taking a chance on our doctor going out there to look at his leg and tipping things off. That's a big point."

"Go on."

"All right, he figures an excuse to take a train. He takes his wife with him to the station, he gets on the train, he gets rid of her. She goes. He's ready to do it. But he runs into trouble. There's a guy out there, on the observation platform, and for this he don't want any company. You bet he doesn't. So what does he do? He gets rid of him, by putting up some kind of a story about not having his ticket, and leaving it in his briefcase, and as soon as this guy goes, he takes his dive. That was the guy I just talked to, a man by the name of Jackson that went up to Frisco on a business trip and is coming back tomorrow. He says there's no question about it, he had the feeling even when he offered to get Nirdlinger's briefcase for him that he was trying to get rid of him, but he didn't quite have the heart to say no to a cripple. In my mind, that clinches it. It's a clear case of suicide. You can't take any other view of it."

"So what?"

"Our next step is the inquest. We can't appear there, of course, because if a jury finds out a dead man is insured they'll murder us. We can send an investigator or two, perhaps, to sit in there, but nothing more than that. But Jackson says he'll be glad to appear and tell what he knows, and there's a chance, just a chance, but still a chance, that we may get a suicide verdict anyway. If we do, we're in. If we don't, then we've got to consider what we do. However, one thing at a time. The inquest first, and you can't tell what the police may find out; we may win right in the first round."

Keyes mopped his head some more. He was so fat he really suffered in the heat. He lit a cigarette. He drooped down and looked away from Norton like it was some schoolboy and he didn't want to show his disgust. Then he spoke. "It was not suicide."

"What are you talking about? It's a clear case."

"It was not suicide."

He opened his bookcase and began throwing thick books on the table. "Mr. Norton, here's what the actuaries have to say about suicide. You study them, you might find out something about the insurance business."

"I was raised in the insurance business, Keyes."

"You were raised in private schools, Groton, and Harvard. While you were learning how to pull bow oars there, I was studying these tables. Take a look at them. Here's suicide by race, by color, by occupation, by sex, by locality, by seasons of the year, by time of day when committed. Here's suicide by method of accomplishment. Here's method of accomplishment subdivided by poisons, by fire-arms, by gas, by drowning, by leaps. Here's suicide by poisons sub-divided by sex, by race, by age, by time of day. Here's suicide by poisons subdivided by cyanide, by mercury, by strychnine, by thirty-eight other poisons, sixteen of them no longer procurable at pre-scription pharmacies. And here—here, Mr. Norton—are leaps sub-divided by leaps from high places, under wheels of moving trains, under wheels of trucks, under the feet of horses, from steamboats.

But there's not one case here out of all these millions of cases of a leap from the rear end of a moving train. That's just one way they don't do it."

"They could."

"Could they? That train, at the point where the body was found, moves at a maximum of fifteen miles an hour. Could any man jump off it there with any real expectation of killing himself?"

"He might dive off. This man had a broken neck."

"Don't trifle with me. He wasn't an acrobat."

"Then what are you trying to tell me? That it was on the up-and-up?"

"Listen, Mr. Norton. When a man takes out an insurance policy, an insurance policy that's worth $50,000 if he's killed in a railroad accident, and then three months later he *is* killed in a railroad accident, it's not on the up-and-up. It can't be. If the train got wrecked it might be, but even then it would be a mighty suspicious coincidence. A *mighty* suspicious coincidence. No, it's not on the up-and-up. But it's not suicide."

"Then what do you mean?"

"You know what I mean."

". . . Murder?"

"I mean murder."

"Well wait a minute, Keyes, wait a minute. Wait till I catch up with you. What have you got to go on?"

"Nothing."

"You must have *something*."

"I said nothing. Whoever did this did a perfect job. There's nothing to go on. Just the same, it's murder."

"Do you suspect anybody?"

"The beneficiary of such a policy, so far as I am concerned, is automatically under suspicion."

"You mean the wife?"

"I mean the wife."

"She wasn't even on the train."

"Then somebody else was."

"Have you any idea who?"

"None at all."

"And this is all you have to go on?"

"I told you, I have nothing to go on. Nothing but those tables and my own hunch, instinct, and experience. It's a slick job, but it's no accident, and it's no suicide."

"Then what are we going to do?"

"I don't know. Give me a minute to think."

He took a half hour to think. Norton and I, we sat there and smoked. After a while, Keyes began to bump the desk with the palm of his hand. He knew what he meant, you could see that.

"Mr. Norton."

"Yes, Keyes."

"There's only one thing for you to do. It's against practice, and in some other case I'd oppose it. But not in this. There's a couple of things about this that make me think that practice is one of the things they're going to count on, and take advantage of. Practice in a case like this is to wait, and make them come to you, isn't it? I advise against that. I advise jumping in there at once, tonight if possible, and if not tonight, then certainly on the day of that inquest, and filing a complaint against that woman. I advise filing an information of suspected murder against her, and smashing at her as hard and as quick as we can. I advise that we demand her arrest, and her detention too, for the full forty-eight hours incommunicado that the law allows in a case of this kind. I advise sweating her with everything the police have got. I particularly advise separating her from this accomplice, whoever he is, or she is, so we get the full value of surprise, and prevent their conferring on future plans. Do that, and mark **my words you're going to find out** things that'll amaze you."

"But—*on what?*"

"On nothing."

"But Keyes, we can't do a thing like that. Suppose we don't find out anything. Suppose we sweat her and get nothing. Suppose it *is* on the up-and-up. Look where that puts us. Holy smoke, she could murder us in a civil suit, and a jury would give her every nickel she asks for. I'm not sure they couldn't get us for *criminal* libel. And then look at the other side of it. We've got an advertising budget of $100,000 a year. We describe ourselves as the friend of the widow and orphan. We spend all that for goodwill, and then what? We lay ourselves open to the charge that we'd accuse a woman of *murder* even, rather than pay a just claim."

"It's not a just claim."

"It will be, unless we prove different."

"All right. What you say is true. I told you it's against practice. But let me tell you this, Mr. Norton, and tell you right now: Whoever pulled this was no punk. He, or she, or maybe the both of them, or the three of them or however many it took—knew what they were doing. They're not going to be caught just by your sitting around hoping for clues. They thought of clues. There aren't any. The only way you're going to catch them is to move against *them*. I don't care if it's a battle or a murder case, or whatever it is, surprise is a weapon that *can* work. I don't say it will work. But I say it can work. And I say nothing else is going to work."

"But Keyes, we can't do things like that."

"Why not?"

"Keyes, we've been over that a million times, every insurance company has been over it a million times. We have our practice, and you can't beat it. These things are a matter for the police. We can help the police, if we've got something to help with. If we discover information, we can turn it over to them. If we have our suspicions, we can communicate them to them. We can take any lawful, legitimate step—but as for this—"

He stopped. Keyes waited, and he didn't finish.

"What's unlawful about this, Mr. Norton?"

"Nothing. It's lawful enough—but it's wrong. It puts us out in the open. It leaves us with *no* defenses—in case we miss on it. I never heard of a thing like that. It's—tactically wrong, that's what I'm trying to say."

"But strategically right."

"We've got our strategy. We've got our ancient strategy, and you can't beat it. Listen, it *can* be suicide. We can affirm our belief that it's suicide, at the proper time, and we're safe. The burden of proof is on her. That's what I'm trying to say. Believe me, on a keg of dynamite like this, I don't want to get myself in the position where the burden of proof is on us."

"You're not going to move against her?"

"Not yet, Keyes, not yet. Maybe later, I don't know. But so long as we can do the conservative, safe thing, I don't get mixed up with the other kind."

"Your father—"

"Would have done the same thing. I'm thinking of him."

"He would not. Old Man Norton could take a chance."

"Well I'm not my father!"

"It's your responsibility."

I didn't go to the inquest, Norton didn't, and Keyes didn't. No insurance company can afford to let a jury know, whether it's a coroner's jury or any other kind of jury, that a dead man is insured. It just gets murdered if that comes out. Two investigators were sent over, guys that look like everybody else and sit with the newspaper men. We got what happened from them. They all identified the body and told their story, Phyllis, the two conductors, the red-cap, the porter, a couple of passengers, the police, and especially this guy Jackson, that pounded it in that I tried to get rid of him. The jury brought in a verdict "that the said Herbert S. Nirdlinger came to his death by a broken neck received in a fall from a railroad train at or about ten o'clock on the night of June 3 in a manner unknown to this jury." It took Norton by surprise. He really hoped for a suicide verdict. It didn't me. The most important person at that inquest never said a word, and I had beat it into Phyllis' head long before that he had to be there, because I had figured on this suicide stuff, and we had to be ready for it. That was the minister that she asked to come with her, to confer with the undertaker on arrangements for the funeral. Once a coroner's jury sees that it's a question of burial in consecrated ground, the guy could take poison, cut his throat, and jump off the end of a dock, and they would still give a verdict, "in a manner unknown to this jury."

After the investigators told their story, we sat around again, Norton, Keyes, and myself, in Norton's office this time. It was about five o'clock in the afternoon. Keyes was sore. Norton was disappointed, but still trying to make it look like he had done the right thing. "Well, Keyes, we're no worse off."

"You're no better off."

"Anyway, we haven't done anything foolish."

"What now?"

"Now? I follow practice. I wait her out. I deny liability, on the ground that accident is not proved, and I make her sue. When she sues, then we'll see what we see."

"You're sunk."

"I know I'm sunk, but that's what I'm going to do."

"What do you mean you know you're sunk?"

"Well, I've been talking to the police about this. I told them we suspect murder. They said they did too, at first, but they've given up that idea. They've gone into it. They've got their books too, Keyes. They know how people commit murder, and how they don't. They say they never heard of a case where murder was committed, or even attempted, by pushing a man off the rear end of a slow-moving train. They say the same thing about it you say. How could a murderer, assuming there was one, be sure the man would die? Suppose he only got hurt? Then where would they be? No, they assure me it's on the up-and-up. It's just one of those freak things, that's all."

"Did they cover everybody that was on that train? Did they find out whether there was a single one of them that was acquainted with this wife? Holy smoke, Mr. Norton, don't tell me they gave up without going into that part. *I tell you, there was somebody else on that train!*"

"They did better than that. They covered the observation car steward. He took a seat right by the door, to mark up his slips for the beginning of the trip, and he's certain nobody was out there with Nirdlinger, because if anybody had passed him he would have had to move. He remembers Jackson going out there, about ten minutes before the train pulled out. He remembers the cripple going by. He remembers Jackson coming back. He remembers Jackson going out there again with the briefcase, and Jackson coming back, the second time. Jackson didn't report the disappearance right away. He just figured Nirdlinger went in a washroom or something, and as a matter of fact it wasn't till midnight, when he wanted to go to bed and he still had the briefcase that he supposed had Nirdlinger's ticket in it, that he said anything to the conductor about it. Five minutes after that, at Santa Barbara, was where the Los Angeles yardmaster caught the conductor with a wire and he impounded Nirdlinger's baggage and began taking names. There was nobody out there. This guy fell off, that's all. We're sunk. It's on the up-and-up."

"If it's on the up-and-up, why don't you pay her?"

"Well wait a minute. That's what I think. That's what the police think. But there's still considerable evidence of suicide—"

"Not a scrap."

"Enough, Keyes, that I owe it to my stockholders to throw the thing into court, and let a jury decide. I may be wrong. The police may be wrong. Before that suit comes to trial, we may be able to turn up plenty. That's all I'm going to do. Let a jury decide, and if it decides we're liable, then I pay her, and do it cheerfully. But I can't just make her a present of the money."

"That's what you'll be doing, if you allege suicide."

"We'll see."

"Yeah, we'll see."

I walked back with Keyes to his office. He snapped on the lights. "He'll see. I've handled too many cases, Huff. When you've handled a million of them, you know, and you don't even know how you know. This is murder. . . . So they covered the porter, did they. Nobody went out there. How do they know somebody didn't swing aboard from the outside? How do they know—"

He stopped, looked at me, and then he began to curse and rave like a maniac. "Didn't I tell him? Didn't I tell him to drive at her right from the start? Didn't I tell him to have her put under arrest, without waiting for this inquest? Didn't I tell him—"

"What do you mean, Keyes?" My heart was pounding, plenty.

"He was never on the train!"

He was yelling now, and pounding the desk. "He was never on the train at all! Somebody took his crutches and went on the train for him! Of course that guy had to get rid of Jackson! He couldn't be seen alive beyond the point where that body was to be put! And now we've got all those sworn identifications against us—"

"Those what?" I knew what he meant. Those identifications at the inquest were something I had figured on from the start, and that was why I took such care that nobody on that train got a good look at me. I figured the crutches, the foot, the glasses, the cigar, and imagination would be enough.

"At the inquest! How well did any of those witnesses see this man? Just a few seconds, in the dark, three or four days ago. Then the coroner lifts a sheet on a dead man, the widow says yes, that's him, and of course they all say the same thing. And now look at us! If Norton had thrown the gaff into her, all those identifications and everything else about it could have been challenged, the police would have waked up, and we might be somewhere. But now—! So he's going to let her sue! And just let him try, now, to break down those identifications. It'll be impossible. Any lawyer can crucify those witnesses if they change their story now. So that's being conservative! That's playing it safe! That's doing what the old man would have done! Why, Huff, Old Man Norton would have had a confession out of that woman by now. He'd have had a plea of guilty out of her, and already on her way to do a life stretch in Folsom. And now look at us. Just look at us. The very crux of the thing is over already, and we've lost it. We've lost it. . . . Let me tell you something. If that guy keeps on trying to run this company, the company's sunk. You can't take many body blows like this and last. Holy smoke. Fifty thousand bucks, and all from dumbness. Just sheer, willful stupidity!"

The lights began to look funny in front of my eyes. He started up again, checking over how Nirdlinger got knocked off. He said this guy, whoever he was, had left his car at Burbank, and dropped off the train there. He said she met him there, and they drove down in separate cars, with the corpse in one of them, to the place where they put the body on the track. He figured it up that she would have time to get to Burbank, and then get back in time to buy a pint of ice cream at the drugstore at 10:20, when she showed up there. He even had that. He was all wrong on how it was done, but he was so near right it made my lips turn numb just to listen to him.

"Well, Keyes, what are you going to do?"

". . . All right, he wants to wait her out, make her sue,—that suits me. He's going to cover the dead man, find out what he can about why he maybe committed suicide. That suits me. I'm going to cover *her*. Every move she makes, everything she does, I'm going to know about it. Sooner or later, Huff, that guy's got to show. They'll have to see each other. And as soon as I know who he is, then watch me. Sure, let her sue. And when she goes on the witness stand, believe me, Huff, Norton's going to eat it. He's going to eat every word he's said, and the police may do some eating too. Oh no. I'm not through yet."

He had me, and I knew it. If she sued, and lost her head on the witness stand, God knows what might happen. If she didn't sue, that would be still worse. Her not trying to collect on that policy, that would look so bad it might even pull the police in. I didn't dare call her up, because for all I knew even now her wires might be tapped. I did that night what I had done the other two nights, while I was waiting on the inquest. I got stinko, or tried to. I knocked off a quart of cognac, but it didn't have any effect. My legs felt funny, and my ears rang, but my eyes kept staring at the dark, and my mind kept pounding on it, what I was going to do. I didn't know. I couldn't sleep, I couldn't eat, I couldn't even get drunk.

It was the next night before Phyllis called. It was a little while after dinner, and the Filipino had just gone. I was even afraid to answer, but I knew I had to. "Walter?"

"Yes. First, where are you? Home?"

"I'm in a drugstore."

"Oh. O. K., then, go on."

"Lola's acting so funny I don't even want to use my own phone any more. I drove down to the boulevard."

"What's the matter with Lola?"

"Oh, just hysteria, I guess. It's been too much for her."

"Nothing else?"

"I don't think so."

"All right, shoot, and shoot quick. What's happened?"

"An awful lot. I've been afraid to call. I had to stay home until the funeral, and—"

"The funeral was today?"

"Yes. After the inquest."

"Go on."

"The next thing, tomorrow they open my husband's safe deposit box. The state has something to do with that. On account of the inheritance tax."

"That's right. The policy's in there?"

"Yes. I put it in there about a week ago."

"All right then, this is what you do. It'll be at your lawyer's office, is that it?"

"Yes."

"Then you go there. The state tax man will be there, under the law he has to be present. They'll find the policy, and you hand it to your lawyer. Instruct him to put your claim in. Everything waits until you do that."

"Put the claim in."

"That's right. Now wait a minute, Phyllis. Here's something you mustn't tell that lawyer—yet. They're not going to pay that claim."

"What!"

"They're not going to pay it."

"Don't they have to pay it?"

"They think it's—suicide—and they're going to make you sue, and put it in the hands of a jury, before they pay. Don't tell your lawyer that now, he'll find it out for himself later. He'll want to sue, and you let him. We'll have to pay him, but it's our only chance. Now Phyllis, one other thing."

"Yes."

"I can't see you."

"But I want to see you."

"We don't dare see each other. Suicide is what they hope for, but they're mighty suspicious all the way around. If you and I began seeing each other, they might tumble to the truth so fast it would make your blood run cold. They'll be on your trail, for what they can find out, and you simply must not communicate with me at all, unless it's imperative, and even then you must call me at home, and from a drugstore, never the same drugstore twice in succession. Do you get me?"

"My you sound scared."

"I am scared. Plenty. They know more than you'd think."

"Then it's really serious?"

"Maybe not, but we've got to be careful."

"Then maybe I'd better not sue."

"You've *got* to sue. If you don't sue, then we *are* sunk."

"Oh. Oh. Yes, I can see that."

"You sue. But be careful what you tell that lawyer."

"All right. Do you still love me?"

"You know I do."

"Do you think of me? All the time?"

"All the time."

"Is there anything else?"

"Not that I know of. Is that all with you?"

"I think so."

"You better hang up. Somebody might come in on me."

"You sound as though you want to get rid of me."

"Just common sense."

"All right. How long is this all going to take?"

"I don't know. Maybe quite some time."

"I'm dying to see you."

"Me too. But we've got to be careful."

"Well then—good-bye."

"Good-bye."

I hung up. I loved her like a rabbit loves a rattlesnake. That night I did something I hadn't done in years. I prayed.

9

IT WAS about a week after that that Nettie came into my private office quick and shut the door. "That Miss Nirdlinger to see you again Mr. Huff."

"Hold her a minute. I've got to make a call."

She went out. I made a call. I had to do something to get myself in hand. I called home, and asked the Filipino if there had been any calls. He said no. Then I buzzed Nettie to send her in.

She looked different from the last time I had seen her. Then, she looked like a kid. Now, she looked like a woman. Part of that may have been that she was in black, but anybody could see she had been through plenty. I felt like a heel, and yet it did something to me that this girl liked me. I shook hands with her, and sat her down, and asked her how her stepmother was, and she said she was all right, considering everything, and I said it was a terrible thing, and that it shocked me to hear of it. "And Mr. Sachetti?"

"I'd rather not talk about Mr. Sachetti."

"I thought you were friends."

"I'd rather not talk about him."

"I'm sorry."

She got up, looked out the window, then sat down again. "Mr. Huff, you did something for me once, or anyhow I felt it was for me—"

"It was."

"And since then I've always thought of you as a friend. That's why I've come to you. I want to talk to you—as a friend."

"Certainly."

"But only as a friend, Mr. Huff. Not as somebody—in the insurance business. Until I feel I know my own mind, it has to be in the strictest confidence. Is that understood, Mr. Huff?"

"It is."

"I'm forgetting something. I was to call you Walter."

"And I was to call you Lola."

"It's funny how easy I feel with you."

"Go ahead."

"It's about my father."

"Yes?"

"My father's death. I can't help feeling there was something back of it."

"I don't quite understand you, Lola. How do you mean, back of it?"

"I don't know what I mean."

"You were at the inquest?"

"Yes."

"One or two witnesses there, and several people later, to us, intimated that your father might have—killed himself. Is that what you mean?"

"No, Walter, it isn't."

"Then what?"

"I can't say. I can't make myself say it. And it's so awful. Because this isn't the first time I've had such thoughts. This isn't the first time I've been through this agony of suspicion that there might be something more than—what everybody else thinks."

"I still don't follow you."

"My mother."

"Yes."

"When she died. That's how I felt."

I waited. She swallowed two or three times, looked like she had decided not to say anything at all, then changed her mind again and started to talk.

"Walter, my mother had lung trouble. It was on account of that

that we kept a little shack up at Lake Arrowhead. One week-end, in the middle of winter, my mother went up to that shack with her dearest friend. It was right in the middle of the winter sports, when everything was lively up there, and then she wired my father that she and this other woman had decided to stay on for a week. He didn't think anything of it, wired her a little money, and told her to stay as long as she wanted; he thought it would do her good. Wednesday of that week my mother caught pneumonia. Friday her condition became critical. Her friend walked twelve miles through snowdrifts, through the woods, to get a doctor—the shack isn't near the hotels. It's on the other side of the lake, a long way around. She got into the main hotel there so exhausted she had to be sent to a hospital. The doctor started out, and when he got there my mother was dying. She lived a half hour."

"Yes?"

"Do you know who that best friend was?"

I knew. I knew by the same old prickle that was going up my back and into my hair. "No."

"Phyllis."

". . . Well?"

"What were those two women doing in that shack, all that time, in the dead of winter? Why didn't they go to the hotel, like everybody else? Why didn't my mother telephone, instead of wiring?"

"You mean it wasn't she that wired?"

"I don't know what I mean, except that it looked mighty funny. Why did Phyllis tramp all that distance to get a doctor? Why didn't she stop some place, and telephone? Or why didn't she put on her skates, and go across the lake, which she could have done in a half hour? She's a fine skater. Why did she take that three-hour trip? *Why didn't she go for a doctor sooner?*"

"But wait a minute. What did your mother say to the doctor when he—"

"Nothing. She was in high delirium, and besides he had her in oxygen five minutes after he got there."

"But wait a minute, Lola. After all, a doctor is a doctor, and if she *had* penumonia—"

"A doctor is a doctor, but you don't know Phyllis. There's some things I could tell. In the first place, she's a nurse. She's one of the best nurses in the city of Los Angeles—that's how she met my mother, when my mother was having such a terrible fight to live. She's a nurse, and she specialized in pulmonary diseases. She would know the time of crisis, almost to a minute, as well as any doctor would. And she would know how to bring on pneumonia, too."

"What do you mean by that?"

"You think Phyllis wouldn't be capable of putting my mother out in the night, in that cold, and keeping her locked out until she was half frozen to death—you think Phyllis wouldn't do that? You think she's just the dear, sweet, gentle thing that she looks like? That's what my father thought. He thought it was wonderful, the way she trudged all that distance to save a life, and less than a year after that he married her. But I don't think so. You see—I know her. That's what I thought, the minute I heard it. And now—this."

"What do you want me to do?"

"Nothing—yet. Except listen to me."

"It's pretty serious, what you're saying. Or at any rate intimating. I suppose I know what you mean."

"That's what I mean. That's exactly what I mean."

"However, as I understand it, your mother wasn't *with* your father at the time—"

"She wasn't with my mother either. At the time. But she had been."

"Will you let me think this over?"

"Please do."

"You're a little wrought up today."

"And I haven't told you all."

"What else?"

". . . I can't tell you. That, I can't make myself believe. And yet—never mind. Forgive me, Walter, for coming in here like this. But I'm so unhappy."

"Have you said anything to anybody about this?"

"No, nothing."

"I mean—about your mother? Before this last?"

"Not a word, ever, to anybody."

"I wouldn't if I were you. And especially not to—your step-mother."

"I'm not even living home now."

"No?"

"I've taken a little apartment. Down in Hollywood. I have a little income. From my mother's estate. Just a little. I moved out. I couldn't live with Phyllis any more."

"Oh."

"Can I come in again?"

"I'll let you know when to come. Give me your number."

I spent half the afternoon trying to make up my mind whether to tell Keyes. I knew I ought to tell him, for my own protection. It was nothing that would be worth a nickel as evidence in court, and for that matter it was nothing that any court would admit as evidence, because that's one break they give people, that they have to be tried for one thing at a time, and not for something somebody thinks they did two or three years before this happened. But it was something that would look mighty bad, if Keyes found out I knew it, and hadn't told him. I couldn't make myself do it. And I didn't have any better reason than that this girl had asked me not to tell anybody, and I had promised.

About four o'clock Keyes came in my office and shut the door.

"Well, Huff, he's showed."

"Who?"

"The guy in the Nirdlinger case."

"*What?*"

"He's a steady caller now. Five nights in one week."

". . . Who is he?"

"Never mind. But he's the one. Now watch me." ⸱

That night I came back in the office to work. As soon as Joe Pete made his eight o'clock round on my floor I went to Keyes's office. I tried his desk. It was locked. I tried his steel filing cabinets. They were locked. I tried all my keys. They didn't work. I was about to give it up when I noticed the dictation machine. He uses one of them. I took the cover off it. A record was still on. It was about three quarters filled. I made sure Joe Pete was downstairs, then came back, slipped the ear pieces on and started the record. First a lot of dumb stuff came out, letters to claimants, instructions to investigators on an arson case, notification of a clerk that he was fired. Then, all of a sudden, came this:

Memo. to Mr. Norton
Re. Agent Walter Huff
Confidential—file Nirdlinger

With regard to your proposal to put Agent Huff under surveillance for his connection with the Nirdlinger case, I disagree absolutely. Naturally, in this case as in all cases of its kind, the agent is automatically under suspicion, and I have not neglected to take necessary steps with regard to Huff. All his statements check closely with the facts and with our records, as well as with the dead man's records. I have even checked, without his knowledge, his whereabouts the night of the crime, and find he was at home all night. This in my opinion lets him out. A man of his experience can hardly fail to know it if we attempt to watch his movements, and we should thus lose the chance of his cheerful cooperation on this case, which so far has been valuable, and may become imperative. I point out to you further, his record which has been exceptional in cases of fraud. I strongly recommend that this whole idea be dropped.

Respectfully

I lifted the needle and ran it over again. It did things to me. I don't only mean it was a relief. It made my heart feel funny.

But then, after some more routine stuff, came this:

Confidential—file Nirdlinger

SUMMARY—investigators' verbal reports for week ending June 17th:

Daughter Lola Nirdlinger moved out of home June 8, took up residence in two-room apartment, the Lycee Arms, Yucca Street. No surveillance deemed necessary.

Widow remained at home until June 8, when she took automobile ride, stopped at drug store, made phone call, took ride two succeeding days, stopped markets and store selling women's gowns.

Night of June 11, man caller arrived at house 8:35, left 11:48. Description:—Tall, dark—age twenty six or seven. Calls repeated June 12, 13, 14, 16. Man followed night of first visit, identity ascertained as Beniamino Sachetti, Lilac Court Apartments, North La Brea Avenue.

I was afraid to have Lola come down to the office any more. But finding out they had no men assigned to her meant that I could take her out somewhere. I called her up and asked her if she would go with me to dinner. She said she would like it more than anything she could think of. I took her down to the Miramar at Santa Monica. I said it would be nice to eat where we could see the ocean, but the real reason was I didn't want to take her to any place downtown, where I might run into somebody I knew.

We talked along during dinner about where she went to school, and why she didn't go to college, and a whole lot of stuff. It was kind of feverish, because we were both under a strain, but we got along all right. It was like she said. We both felt easy around each other somehow. I didn't say anything about what she had told me, last time, until we got in the car after dinner and started up the ocean for a ride. Then I brought it up myself.

"I thought over what you told me."

"Can I say something?"

"Go ahead."

"I've had it out with myself about that. I've thought it all over, and come to the conclusion I was wrong. It's very easy when you love somebody terribly, and then suddenly they're gone from you, to think it's somebody's fault. Especially when it's somebody you don't like. I don't like Phyllis. I guess it's partly jealousy. I was devoted to my mother. I was almost as devoted to my father. And then when he married Phyllis—I don't know, it seemed as though something had happened that couldn't happen. And then—these thoughts. What I felt instinctively when my mother died became a dead certainty when my father married Phyllis. I thought that showed why she did it. And it became a double certainty when this happened. But I haven't a thing to go on, have I? It's been terribly hard to make myself realize that, but I have. I've given up the whole idea, and I wish you'd forget that I ever told you."

"I'm glad, in a way."

"I guess you think I'm terrible."

"I thought it over. I thought it over carefully, and all the more carefully because it would be most important for my company if they knew it. But there's nothing to go on. It's only a suspicion. That's all you have to tell."

"I told you. I haven't even got that any more."

"What you would tell the police, if you told them anything, is already a matter of public record. Your mother's death, your father's death—you haven't anything to add to what they already know. Why tell them?"

"Yes, I know."

"If I were you, I would do nothing."

"You agree with me then? That I haven't anything to go on?"

"I do."

That ended that. But I had to find out about this Sachetti, and find out without her knowing I was trying to find out.

"Tell me something. What happened between you and Sachetti?"

"I told you. I don't want to talk about him."

"How did you come to meet him?"

"Through Phyllis."

"Through—?"

"His father was a doctor. I think I told you she used to be a nurse. He called on her, about joining some association that was being formed. But then when he got interested in me, he wouldn't come to the house. And then, when Phyllis found out I was meeting him, she told my father the most awful stories about him. I was supposed not to meet him, but I did. There was something back of it, I knew that. But I never found out what it was, until—"

"Go on. Until what?"

"I don't want to go on. I told you I gave up any idea that there might be something—"

"Until what?"

"Until my father died. And then, quite suddenly, he didn't seem interested in me any more. He—"

"Yes?"

"He's going with Phyllis."

"And—?"

"Can't you see what I thought? Do you have to make me say it? . . . I thought maybe they did it. I thought his going with me was just a blind for—something, I didn't know what. Seeing her, maybe. In case they got caught."

"I thought he was with you—that night."

"He was supposed to be. There was a dance over at the university, and I went over. I was to meet him there. But he got sick, and sent word he couldn't come. I got on a bus and went to a picture show. I never told anybody that."

"What do you mean, sick?"

"He did have a cold, I know that. A dreadful cold. But—please don't make me talk any more about it. I've tried to put it out of my mind. I'm getting so I can believe it isn't true. If he wants to see Phyllis, it's none of my business. I mind. I wouldn't be telling the truth if I said I didn't mind. But—it's his privilege. Just because he does that is no reason for me to—think this of him. That wouldn't be right."

"We won't talk about it any more."

I stared into the darkness some more that night. I had killed a man, for money and a woman. I didn't have the money and I didn't have the woman. The woman was a killer, out-and-out, and she had made a fool of me. She had used me for a cat's paw so she could have another man, and she had enough on me to hang me higher than a kite. If the man was in on it, there were two of them that could hang me. I got to laughing, a hysterical cackle, there in the dark. I thought about Lola, how sweet she was, and the awful thing I had done to her. I began subtracting her age from my age. She was nineteen, I'm thirty-four. That made a difference of fifteen years. Then I got to thinking that if she was nearly twenty, that would make a difference of only fourteen years. All of a sudden I sat up and turned on the light. I knew what that meant.

I was in love with her.

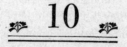

10

RIGHT ON top of that, Phyllis filed her claim. Keyes denied liability, on the ground that accident hadn't been proved. Then she filed suit, through the regular lawyer that had always handled her husband's business. She called me about half a dozen times, always from a drugstore, and I told her what to do. I had got so I felt sick the minute I heard her voice, but I couldn't take any chances. I told her to be ready, that they would try to prove something besides suicide. I didn't give her all of it, what they were thinking and what they were doing, but I let her know that murder was one of the things they would cover anyway, so she had better be ready for it when she went on the stand. It didn't feaze her any. She seemed to have almost forgotten that there was a murder, and acted like the company was playing her some kind of a dirty trick in not paying her right away. That suited me fine. It was a funny sidelight on human nature, and especially on a woman's nature, but it was just exactly the frame of mind I would want her in to face a lot of corporation lawyers. If she stuck to her story, even with all Keyes might have been able to dig up on her, I still didn't see how she could miss.

That all took about a month, and the suit was to come up for trial in the early fall. All during that month, three or four nights a week, I was seeing Lola. I would call for her, at the little apartment house where she was living, and we would go to dinner, and then for a drive. She had got a little car, but we generally went in mine. I had gone completely nuts about her. Having it hanging over me all the time, what I had done to her, and how awful it would be if she ever found out, that had something to do with it, but it wasn't all. There was something so sweet about her, and we got along so nice, I mean we felt so happy when we were together. Anyway I did. She did too, I knew that. But then one night something happened. We were parked on the ocean road, about three miles above Santa Monica. They have places where you can park and sit and look. We were sitting there, watching the moon come up over the ocean. That sounds funny, don't it, that you can watch the moon come up over the Pacific Ocean? You can, just the same. The coast here runs almost due east and west, and when the moon comes up, off to your left, it's pretty as a picture. As soon as it lifted out of the sea, she slipped her hand into mine. I took it, but she took it away, quick.

"I mustn't do that."

"Why not?"

"Lots of reasons. It's not fair to you, for one."

"Did you hear me squawk?"

"You do like me, don't you?"

"I'm crazy about you."

"I'm pretty crazy about you too, Walter. I don't know what I'd have done without you these last few weeks. Only—"

"Only what?"

"Are you sure you want to hear? It may hurt you."

"Better hear it than guess at it."

"It's about Nino."

"Yes?"

"I guess he still means a lot to me."

"Have you seen him?"

"No."

"You'll get over it. Let me be your doctor. I'll guarantee a cure. Just give me a little time, and I'll promise to have you all right."

"You're a nice doctor. Only—"

"Another 'only'?"

"I *did* see him."

"Oh."

"No, I was telling the truth just now. I haven't talked with him. He doesn't know I've seen him. Only—"

"You sure have a lot of 'only's'."

"Walter—"

She was getting more and more excited, and trying not to let me see it.

"—He didn't do it!"

"No?"

"This is going to hurt you terribly, Walter. I can't help it. You may as well know the truth. I followed them last night. Oh, I've followed them a lot of times, I've been insane. Last night, though, was the first time I ever got a chance to hear what they were saying. They went up to the Lookout and parked, and I parked down below, and crept up behind them. Oh, it was horrible enough. He told her he had been in love with her from the first, but felt it was hopeless—until this happened. But that wasn't all. They talked about money. He's spent all of that you let him have, and still he hasn't got his degree. He paid for his dissertation, but the rest he spent on her. And he was talking about where he'd get more. Listen, Walter—"

"Yes?"

"If they had done this together, she'd have to let him have money, wouldn't she?"

"Looks like it."

"They never even mentioned anything about her letting him have money. My heart began to beat when I realized what that meant. And then they talked some more. They were there about an hour. They talked about lots of things, and I could tell, from what they said, that he wasn't in on it, and didn't know anything about it. I could tell! Walter, do you realize what that means? *He didn't do it!*"

She was so excited her fingers felt like steel, where they were clutched around my arm. I couldn't follow her. I could see that she meant something, something a whole lot more important than that Sachetti was innocent.

"I don't quite get it, Lola. I thought you had given up the idea that *anybody* was in on it."

"I'll never give it up! . . . Yes, I did give it up, or try to. But that was only because I thought if there was something like that, *he* must have been in on it, and that would have been too terrible. If he had anything to do with it, I knew it couldn't be that. I *had* to know it, to believe it. But now—oh no, Walter, I haven't given it up. She did it, somehow. I know it. And now, I'll get her. I'll get her for it, if it's the last thing I do."

"How?"

"She's suing your company, isn't she? She even has the nerve to do that. All right. You tell your company not to worry. I'll come and sit right alongside of you, Walter. I'll tell them what to ask her. I'll tell them—"

"Wait a minute, Lola, wait a minute—"

"I'll tell them everything they need to know. I told you there was plenty more, besides what I told you. I'll tell them to ask her about the time I came in on her, in her bedroom, with some kind of foolish red silk thing on her, that looked like a shroud or something, with her face all smeared up with white powder and red lipstick, with a dagger in her hand, making faces at herself in front of a mirror—oh yes, I'll tell them to ask her about that. I'll tell them to ask her why she was down in a boulevard store, a week before my father died, pricing black dresses. That's something she doesn't know I know. I went in there about five minutes after she left. The saleslady was just putting the frocks away. She was telling me what lovely numbers they were, only she couldn't understand why Mrs. Nirdlinger would be considering them, because they were really mourning. That was one reason I wanted my father to take that trip, so I could get him out of the house and find out what she was up to. I'll tell them—"

"But wait a minute, Lola. You can't do that. Why—they can't ask her such things as that—"

"If they can't, I can! I'll stand right up in court and yell them at her. I'll be heard! No judge, no policeman, or *anybody*—can stop me. I'll force it out of her if I have to go up there and choke it out of her. *I'll make her tell! I'll not be stopped!*"

11

I DON'T know when I decided to kill Phyllis. It seemed to me
that ever since that night, somewhere in the back of my head I
had known I would have to kill her, for what she knew about me,
and because the world isn't big enough for two people once they've
got something like that on each other. But I know when I decided
when to kill her, and *where* to kill her and *how* to kill her. It was
right after that night when I was watching the moon come up
over the ocean with Lola. Because the idea that Lola would put
on an act like that in the courtroom, and that then Phyllis would
lash out and tell her the truth, that was too horrible for me to
think about. Maybe I haven't explained it right, yet, how I felt
about this girl Lola. It wasn't anything like what I had felt for
Phyllis. That was some kind of unhealthy excitement that came
over me just at the sight of her. This wasn't anything like that.
It was just a sweet peace that came over me as soon as I was with
her, like when we would drive along for an hour without saying a
word, and then she would look up at me and we still didn't have
to say anything. I hated what I had done, and it kept sweeping
over me that if there was any way I could make sure she would
never find out, why then maybe I could marry her, and forget the
whole thing, and be happy with her the rest of my life. There was
only one way I could be sure, and that was to get rid of anybody
that knew. What she told me about Sachetti showed there was
only one I had to get rid of, and that was Phyllis. And the rest of
what she told me, about what she was going to do, meant I had to
move quick, before that suit came to trial.

I wasn't going to leave it so Sachetti could come back and take
her away from me, though. I was going to do it so he would be

put in a spot. Police are hard to fool, but Lola would never be
quite sure he hadn't done it. And of course if he did one, so far
as she was concerned he probably did the other.

My next day at the finance company, I put through a lot of
routine stuff, sent the file clerk out on an errand, and took out the
folder on Sachetti. I slipped it in my desk. In that folder was a
key to his car. In our finance company, just to avoid trouble in
case of a repossess, we make every borrower deposit the key to his
car along with the other papers on his loan, and of course Sachetti
had had to do the same. That was back in the winter when he took
out the loan on his car. I slipped the key out of its envelope, and
when I went out to lunch I had a duplicate made. When I got
back I sent the file clerk on another errand, put the original key
back in its envelope, and returned the folder to the file. That was
what I wanted. I had the key to his car, and nobody there even
knew I had the folder out of the file.

Next I had to get hold of Phyllis, but I didn't dare ring her. I
had to wait till she called. I sat around the house three nights, and
the fourth night the phone rang.

"Phyllis, I've got to see you."

"It's about time."

"You know the reason I haven't. Now get this. We've got to
meet, to go over things in connection with this suit—and after
that, I don't think we have anything to fear."

"Can we meet? I thought you said—"

"That's right. They've been watching you. But I found out something today. They've cut down the detail assigned to you to one
shift, and he goes off at eleven."

"What's that?"

"They did have three men assigned to you, in shifts, but they
weren't finding out very much, so they thought they'd cut down

the expense, and now they've only got one. He goes on in the afternoon, and goes off at eleven o'clock, unless there's something to hold him. We'll have to meet after that."

"All right. Then come up to the house—"

"Oh no, we can't take a chance like that. But we can meet. Tomorrow night, around midnight, you sneak out. Take the car and sneak out. If anybody drops in in the evening, get rid of them well before eleven o'clock. Get rid of them, turn out all lights, have the place looking like you had gone to bed well before this man goes off. So he'll have no suspicions whatever."

The reason for that was that if Sachetti was going to be with her the next night, I wanted him to be well out of there and home in bed, long before I was to meet her. I had to have his car, and I didn't want the connections to be so close I had to wait. The rest of it was all hooey, about the one shift I mean. I wanted her to think she could meet me safely. As to whether they had one shift on her, or three, or six, I didn't know and I didn't care. If somebody followed her, so much the better, for what I had to do. They'd have to move fast to catch me, and if they saw her deliberately knocked off, why that would be just that much more Mr. Sachetti would have to explain when they caught up with him.

"Lights out by eleven."

"Lights out, the cat out, and the place locked up."

"All right, where do I meet you?"

"Meet me in Griffith Park, a couple of hundred yards up Riverside from Los Feliz. I'll be parked there, and we'll take a ride, and talk it over. Don't park on Los Feliz. Park in among the trees, in the little glade near the bridge. Park where I can see you, and walk over."

"In between the two streets?"

"That's it. Make it twelve-thirty sharp. I'll be a minute or two ahead of time, so you can hop right in and you won't have to wait."

"Twelve-thirty, two hundred yards up Riverside."

"That's right. Close your garage door when you come out, so anybody passing won't notice the car's out."

"I'll be there, Walter."

"Oh, and one other thing. I traded my car in since I saw you. I've got another one." I told her the make. "It's a small dark blue coupe. You can't miss it."

"A blue coupe?"

"Yes."

"That's funny."

I knew why it was funny. She'd been riding around in a blue coupe for the last month, the same one if she only knew it, but I didn't tumble. "Yeah, I guess it's funny at that, me driving around in that oil can, but the big car was costing too much. I had a chance for a deal on this one, so I took it."

"It's the funniest thing I ever heard."

"Why?"

"Oh—nothing. Tomorrow night at twelve thirty."

"Twelve thirty."

"I'm just dying to see you."

"Same here."

"Well—I had something to talk to you about, but I'll let it wait till tomorrow. Good-bye."

"Good-bye."

When she hung up I got the paper and checked the shows in town. There was a downtown theatre that had a midnight show, and the bill was to hold over the whole week. That was what I wanted. I drove down there. It was about ten thirty when I got in, and I sat in the balcony, so I wouldn't be seen by the downstairs ushers. I watched the show close, and paid attention to the gags, because it was to be part of my alibi next night that I had been there. In the last sequence of the feature I saw an actor I knew. He played the part of a waiter, and I had once sold him a hunk of life insurance, $7,000 for an endowment policy, all paid up when he bought it. His name was Jack Christolf. That helped me. I stayed till the show was out, and looked at my watch. It was 12:48.

Next day around lunch time I called up Jack Christolf. They said he was at the studio and I caught him there. "I hear you knocked them for a loop in this new one, 'Gun Play'."

"I didn't do bad. Did you see it?"

"No, I want to catch it. Where's it playing?"

He named five theatres. He knew them all. "I'm going to drop in on it the very first chance I get. Well say old man, how about another little piece of life insurance? Something to do with all this dough you're making."

"I don't know. I don't know. To tell you the truth, I might be interested. Yes, I might."

"When can I see you?"

"Well, I'm busy this week. I don't finish up here till Friday, and I thought I would go away for a rest over the week-end. But next week, any time."

"How about at night?"

"Well, we might do that."

"How about tomorrow night?"

"I tell you. Ring me home tomorrow night, around dinner time, some time around seven o'clock. I'll let you know then. If I can make it, I'll be glad to see you."

That would be why I went to that particular picture tonight, that I had to talk to this actor tomorrow night, and I wanted to see his picture, so I could talk about it and make him feel good.

About four o'clock I drove up through Griffith Park, and checked it over close, what I was going to do. I picked a spot for my car, and a spot for Sachetti's car. They weren't far apart, but the spot for my car was close to one end of the bridle path, where they ride horses in the daytime. It winds all over the hills there, but right above this place it comes out on the automobile road up above. I mean, up high in the hills. This park, they call it a park, but it's really a scenic drive, up high above Hollywood and the San Fernando Valley, for people in cars, and a hilly ride for people on horses. People on foot don't go there much. What I was going to do was let her get in and then start up the hill. When I came to one of those platforms where the road is graded to a little flat place so people can park and look over the valley, I was going to pull in, and say something about parking there, so we could talk. Only I wasn't going to park. The car was accidentally on purpose, going to roll over the edge, and I was going to jump. As soon as I jumped I was going to dive into the bridle path, race on down to my car, and drive home. From where I was going to park Sachetti's car to where I was going to run her over the edge was about two miles, by road. But by bridle path it was only a hundred yards, on account of the road winding all through the hills for an easy grade, and the bridle path being almost straight up and down. Less than a minute after the crash, before even a crowd could get there, I would be away and gone.

I drove up the hill and picked the place. It was one of the little lookouts, with room for just one or two cars, not one of the big ones. The big ones have stone parapets around them. This one didn't have any. I got out and looked down. There was a drop of at least two hundred feet, straight, and probably another hundred feet after that where the car would roll after it struck. I practiced what I was going to do. I ran up to the edge, threw the gear in neutral, and pushed open the door. I made a note I would only half close my door when she got in, so I could open it quick. There was a chance she would grab the emergency as the car went over and save herself, and then have the drop on me. There was a chance I wouldn't jump clear, and that I would go over the edge with her. That was O.K. On this, you have to take a chance.

I ate dinner alone, at a big downtown sea-food house. The waiter knew me. I made a gag with him, to fix it on his mind it was Friday. When I finished I went back to the office and told Joe Pete I had to work. I stayed till ten o'clock. He was down at his desk, reading a detective story magazine when I went out.

"You're working late, Mr. Huff."

"Yeah, and I'm not done yet."

"Working home?"

"No, I got to see a picture. There's a ham by the name of Jack Christolf I've got to talk to tomorrow night, and I've got to see his picture. He might not like it if I didn't. No time for it tomorrow. I've got to catch it tonight."

"They sure do love theirself, them actors."

I parked near the theatre, loafed around, and around eleven o' clock I went in. I bought a downstairs seat this time. I took a program and put it in my pocket. I checked, it had the date on it. I still had to talk with an usher, fix it on her mind what day it was, and pull something so she would remember me. I picked the one on the door, not the one in the aisle inside. I wanted enough light so that she could see me well.

"Is the feature on?"

"No sir, it's just finished. It goes on again at 11:20."

I knew that. That was why I had gone in at 11 o'clock instead of sooner. "Holy smoke, that's a long time to wait. . . . Is Christolf in all of it?"

"I think only in the last part, sir."

"You mean I've got to wait till one o'clock in the morning to see that ham?"

"It'll be on tomorrow night too, sir, if you don't care to wait so long tonight. They'll refund your money at the box office for you."

"Tomorrow night? Let's see, tomorrow's Saturday, isn't it?"

"Yes sir."

"Nope, can't make it. Got to see it tonight."

I had that much of it. Next I had to pull something so she would remember me. It was a hot night, and she had the top button of her uniform unbuttoned. I reached up there, and buttoned it, quick. I took her by surprise.

"You ought to be more careful."

"Listen, big boy, do I have to drip sweat off the end of my nose, just to please you?"

She unbuttoned it again. I figured she would remember it. I went in.

As soon as the aisle usher showed me a seat, I moved once, to the other side of the house. I sat there a minute, and then I slipped out, through a side exit. Later, I would say I stayed for the end of the show. I had my talk with Christolf, for a reason for being there late. I had my talk with Joe Pete, and his log would prove what day it was. I had the usher. I couldn't prove I was there clear to the end, but no alibi ought to be perfect. This was as good a one as most juries hear, and a whole lot better than most. As far as I could go with it, it certainly didn't sound like a man that was up to murder.

I got in the car and drove straight to Griffith Park. That time of night I could make time. When I got there I looked at my watch. It was 11:24. I parked, cut the motor, took the key and turned off the lights. I walked over to Los Feliz, and from there down to Hollywood Boulevard. It's about half a mile. I legged it right along, and got to the boulevard at 11:35. I boarded a street car and took a seat up front. When we got to La Brea it was five minutes to twelve. So far, my timing was perfect.

I got off the car and walked down to the Lilac Court Apartments, where Sachetti lived. It's one of those court places where they have a double row of bungalows off a center lane, one-room shacks mostly that rent for about $3 a week. I went in the front. I didn't want to come up to the park from outside where I would look like a snooper if anybody saw me. I walked right in the front, and down past his bungalow. I knew the number. It was No. 11. There was a light inside. That was O. K. That was just like I wanted it.

I marched straight through, back to the auto court in the rear, where the people that live there keep their cars. Anyway, those of them that have cars. There was a collection of second, third, fourth and ninth-hand wrecks out there, and sure enough right in the middle was his. I got in, shoved the key in the ignition and started it. I cut on the lights and started to back. A car pulled in from the outside. I turned my head so I couldn't be seen in the headlights, and backed on out. I drove up to Hollywood Boulevard. It was exactly twelve o'clock. I checked his gas. He had plenty.

I took it easy, but still it was only 12:18 when I got back to Griffith Park. I drove up into Glendale, because I didn't want to be more than two or three minutes ahead of time. I thought about Sachetti and how he was going to make out with his alibi. He didn't have one, because that's the worst alibi in the world to be home in bed, unless you've got some way to prove it, with phone calls or something. He didn't have any way to prove it. He didn't even have a phone.

Just past the railroad tracks I turned, came on back, went up Riverside a little way, turned facing Los Feliz, and parked. I cut the motor and the lights. It was exactly 12:27. I turned around and looked, and saw my own car, about a hundred yards back of me. I looked into the little glade. No car was parked there. She hadn't come.

I held my watch in my hand. The hand crept around to 12:30. Still she hadn't come. I put my watch back in my pocket. A twig cracked—off in the bushes. I jumped. Then I wound down the window on the right hand side of the car, and sat there looking off in the bushes to see what it was. I must have stared out there at least a minute. Another twig cracked, closer this time. Then there was a flash, and something hit me in the chest like Jack Dempsey had hauled off and given me all he had. There was a shot. I knew then what had happened to me. I wasn't the only one that figured the world wasn't big enough for two people, when they knew that about each other. I had come there to kill her, but she had beaten me to it.

I fell back on the seat, and I heard footsteps running away. There I was, with a bullet through my chest, in a stolen car, and the owner of the car the very man that Keyes had been tailing for the last month and a half. I pulled myself up by the wheel. I reached up for the key, then remembered I had to leave it in there. I opened the door. I could feel the sweat start out on my head from what it took out of me to turn the handle. I got out, somehow. I began staggering up the road to my car. I couldn't walk straight. I wanted to sit down, to ease that awful weight on my chest, but I knew if I did that I'd never get there. I remembered I had to get the car key ready, and took it out of my pocket. I got there and climbed in. I shoved the key in and pulled the starter. That was the last I knew *that* night.

12

I DON'T know if you've ever been under ether. You come out o it a little bit at a time. First a kind of a gray light shines on one par of your mind, just a dim gray light, and then it gets bigger, bu slow. All the time it's getting bigger you're trying to gag the stu out of your lungs. It sounds like an awful groan, like you were i pain or something, but that's not it. You try to gag it out of you lungs, and you make those sounds to try and force it out. But awa inside somewhere your head is working all the time. You knov where you're at, and even if all kind of cock-eyed ideas do swim through that gray light, the main part of you is there, and you can think, maybe not so good, but a little bit.

It seemed to me I had been thinking, even before I began to come to. I knew there must be somebody with me there, but I didn't know who it was. I could hear them talking, but it wouldn't quite reach me what they were saying. Then I could hear it. It was a woman, telling me to open my mouth for a little ice, that would make me feel better. I opened my mouth. I got the ice. I figured the woman must be a nurse. Still I didn't know who else was there. I thought a long time, then figured it out I would open my eyes just a little bit and close them quick, and see who was in the room. I did that. At first I couldn't see anything. It was a hospital room, and there was a table pushed up near the bed, with a lot of stuff on it. It was broad daylight. Over my chest the covers were piled high, so that meant a lot of bandages. I opened my eyes a little bit further and peeped around. The nurse was sitting beside the table watching me. But over back of her was somebody. I had to wait till she moved to see who it was, but I knew anyway even without seeing.

It was Keyes.

It must have been an hour that I lay there after that, and never opened my eyes at all. I was all there in the head by that time. I tried to think. I couldn't. Every time I tried to gag more ether out, there would come this stab of pain in my chest. That was from the bullet. I quit trying to gag out the ether then and the nurse began talking to me. She knew. Pretty soon I had to answer her. Keyes walked over.

"Well, that theatre program saved you."

"Yeah?"

"That double wad of paper wasn't much, but it was enough. You'll bleed a little bit for a while where that bullet grazed your lung, but you're lucky it wasn't your heart. Another eighth of an inch, and it would have been curtains for you."

"They get the bullet?"

"Yeah."

"They get the woman?"

"Yeah."

I didn't say anything. I thought it was curtains for me anyway, but I just lay there. "They got her, and I got plenty to tell you boy. This thing is a honey. But give me a half hour. I got to go out and get some breakfast. Maybe you'll be feeling better then yourself."

He went. He didn't act like I was in any trouble, or he was sore at me, or anything like that. I couldn't figure it out. In a couple of minutes an orderly came in. "You got any papers in this hospital?"

"Yes sir, I think I can get you one."

He came back with a paper and found it for me. He knew what I wanted. It wasn't on Page 1. It was in the second section where they print the local news that's not quite hot enough to go on the front page. This was it:

MYSTERY SHROUDS GRIFFITH PARK SHOOTING

Two Held After Walter Huff, Insurance Man, Is Found Wounded at Wheel of Car on Riverside Drive After Midnight

Police are investigating the circumstances surrounding the shooting of Walter Huff, an insurance man living in the Los Feliz Hills, who was found unconscious at the wheel of his car in Griffith Park shortly after midnight last night, a bullet wound in his chest. Two persons were held pending a report on Huff's condition today. They are:

    Lola Nirdlinger, 19.

    Beniamino Sachetti, 26.

Miss Nirdlinger gave her address as the Lycee Arms Apartments,

Yucca Street, and Sachetti as the Lilac Court Apartments, La Brea Avenue.

Huff apparently was shot as he was driving along Riverside Drive from the direction of Burbank. Police arriving at the scene shortly afterward found Miss Nirdlinger and Sachetti at the car trying to get him out. A short distance away was a pistol with one chamber discharged. Both denied responsibility for the shooting, but refused to make any further statement.

They brought me orange juice and I lay there trying to figure that out. You think I fell for it do you? That I thought Lola had shot me, or Sachetti maybe, out of jealousy, something like that? I did not. I knew who shot me. I knew who I had a date with, who knew I was going to be there, who wanted me out of the way. Nothing could change me on that. But what were these two doing there? I pounded on it a while, and I couldn't make any sense out of it, except a little piece of it. Of course Lola was following Sachetti again that night, or thought she was. That explained what she was doing there. But what was he doing there? None of it made sense. And all the while I kept having this numb feeling that I was sunk, and not only sunk for what I had done, but for what Lola was going to find out. That was the worst.

It was almost noon before Keyes came back. He saw the paper. He pulled up a chair near the bed. "I've been down to the office."

"Yeah?"

"It's been a wild morning. A wild morning on top of a wild night."

"What's going on?"

"Now I'll tell you something you don't know. This Sachetti, Huff, this same Sachetti that plugged you last night, is the same man we've been tailing for what he might know about that other thing. That Nirdlinger case."

"You don't mean it."

"I do mean it. I started to tell you, you remember, but Norton got these ideas about keeping all that stuff confidential from agents, so I didn't. That's it. The same man, Huff. Did I tell you? Did I tell Norton? Did I say there was something funny about that case?"

"What else?"

"Plenty. Your finance company called up."

"Yeah?"

"They popped out with what we'd have known in the first place, I mean me and Norton, if we had taken you into our confidence completely from the beginning. If you had known about this Sachetti, you could have told us what we just found out today, and it's the key to the whole case."

"He got a loan."

"That's right. He got a loan. But that's not it. That's not the important thing. *He was in your office the day you delivered that policy to Nirdlinger.*"

"I couldn't be certain."

"We are. We checked it all up, with Nettie, with the finance company records, with the records in the policy department. He was in there, and the girl was in there, and that's what we've been waiting for. That gives it to us, the hook-up we never had before."

"What do you mean, hook-up?"

"Listen, we know Nirdlinger never told his family about this policy. We know that from a check we've made with the secretary. He never told anybody. Just the same the family *knew* about it, didn't they?"

"Well—I don't know."

"They knew. They didn't put him on the spot for nothing. They knew, and now we know *how* they knew. This ties it up."

"Any court would assume they knew."

"I'm not a court. I'm talking about for my own satisfaction, for my own knowledge that I'm right. Because look, Huff, I migh demand an investigation on the basis of what my instinct tells me. But I don't go into a courtroom and go to bat with it without knowing. And now I know. What's more, this ties the girl in."

"The—who?"

"The girl. The daughter. She was there, too. In your office, I mean. Oh yeah, you may think it funny, that a girl would pull something like that on her own father. But it's happened. It's happened plenty of times. For fifty thousand bucks it's going to happen plenty of times again."

"I—don't believe that."

"You will, before I get done. Now listen Huff. I'm still shy something. I'm shy one link. They put you on the spot for something you could testify to when this suit comes up, I can see that. But what?"

"What do you mean, what?"

"What is it you know about them they would knock you off for? Their being in your office, that's not enough. There must be something else. Now what is it?"

"I—don't know. I can't think of anything."

"There's something. Maybe it's something you've forgotten about, something that doesn't mean anything to you but is important to them. Now what is it?"

"There's nothing. There *can't* be."

"There's something. There must be."

He was walking around now. I could feel the bed shake from his weight. "Keep it on your mind, Huff. We've got a few days. Try to think what it is."

He lit a cigarette, and pounded around some more. "That's the beauty of this, we've got a few days. You can't appear at a hearing until next week at the earliest, and that gives us what we need. A little help from the cops, a few treatments with the rubber hose, something like that, and sooner or later this pair is going to spill it. Especially that girl. She'll crack before long. . . . Believe me this is what we've been waiting for. It's tough on you, but now we've got them where we can really throw the works into them. Oh yeah, this is a real break. We'll clean this case up now. Before night, with luck."

I closed my eyes. I couldn't think of anything but Lola, a lot of cops around her, maybe beating her up, trying to make her spill something that she knew no more about than the man in the moon. Her face jumped in front of me and all of a sudden something hit it in the mouth, and it started to bleed.

"Keyes."

"Yeah?"

"There was something. Now you speak of it."

"I'm listening boy."

"I killed Nirdlinger."

❧ 13 ❧

HE SAT there staring at me. I had told him everything he needed to know, even about Lola. It seemed funny it had only taken about ten minutes. Then he got up. I grabbed him.

"Keyes."

"I've got to go, Huff."

"See that they don't beat her."

"I've got to go now. I'll be back after a while."

"Keyes, if you let them beat her, I'll—kill you. You've got it all now. I've told you, and I've told you for one reason and one reason only. It's so they won't beat her. You've got to promise me that. You owe me that much. Keyes—"

He shook my hand off and left.

While I was telling him I hoped for some kind of peace when I got done. It had been bottled up in me a long time. I had been sleeping with it, dreaming about it, breathing with it. I didn't get any peace. The only thing I could think of was Lola, and how she was going to find out about it at last, and know me for what I was.

About three o'clock the orderly came in with the afternoon papers. They didn't have any of what I had told Keyes. But they had been digging into their files, after the morning story, and they had it about the first Mrs. Nirdlinger's death, and Nirdlinger's death, and now me being shot. A woman feature writer had got in out there and talked with Phyllis. It was she that called it the House of Death, and put in about those blood-red drapes. Once I saw that stuff I knew it wouldn't be long. That meant even a dumb cluck of a woman reporter could see there was something funny out there.

It was half past eight that night before Keyes came back. He shooed out the nurse as soon as he came in the room, and then went out a minute. When he came back he had Norton with him, and a man named Keswick that was a corporation lawyer they called in on big cases, and Shapiro, the regular head of the legal department. They all stood around, and it was Norton that started to speak. "Huff."

"Yes sir."

"Have you told anybody about this?"

"Nobody but Keyes."

"Nobody else?"

"Not a soul. . . . God, no."

"There have been no policemen here?"

"They've been here. I saw them out in the hall. I guess it was me they were whispering about. The nurse wouldn't let them in."

They all looked at each other. "Then I guess we can begin. Keyes, perhaps you had better explain it to him."

Keyes opened his mouth to say something, but Keswick shut him up, and got Norton into a corner. Then they called Keyes over. Then they called Shapiro. I could catch a word, now and then. It was some kind of a proposition they were going to make to me, and it was a question of whether they were all going to be witnesses. Keswick was for the proposition, but he didn't want anybody to be able to say he had been in on it. They finally settled it that Keyes would make it on his own personal responsibility, and the rest of them wouldn't be there. Then they all tip-toed out. They didn't even say good-bye. It was funny. They didn't act like I had played them or the company any particularly dirty trick. They acted like I was some kind of an animal that had an awful sore on his face, and they didn't even want to look at it.

After they left Keyes sat down. "This is an awful thing you've done, Huff."

"I know it."

"I guess there's no need my saying more about that part."

"No, no need."

"I'm sorry. I've—kind of liked you, Huff."

"I know. Same here."

"I don't often like somebody. At my trade, you can't afford to. The whole human race looks—a little bit crooked."

"I know. You trusted me, and I let you down."

"Well—we won't talk about it."

"There's nothing to say. . . . Did you see her?"

"Yes. I saw them all. Him, her, and the wife."

"What did she say?"

"Nothing. . . . I didn't tell her, you see. I let her do the talking. She thinks Sachetti shot you."

"For what?"

"Jealousy."

"Oh."

"She's upset about you. But when she found out you weren't badly hurt, she—. Well, she—"

"—Was glad of it."

"In a way. She tried not to be. But she felt that it proved Sachetti loved her. She couldn't help it."

"I see."

"She was worried about you, though. She likes you."

"Yeah, I know. She . . . likes me."

"She was following you. She thought you were him. That was all there was to that."

"I figured that out."

"I talked to *him*."

"Oh yeah, you told me. What was he doing there?"

He did some more of his pounding around then. The night light over my head was the only light in the room. I could only half see him, but I could feel the bed shake when he marched.

"Huff, there's a story."

"Yeah? How do you mean?"

"You just got yourself tangled up with an Irrawaddy cobra, that's all. That woman—it makes my blood run cold just to think of her. She's a pathological case, that's all. The worst I ever heard of."

"A what?"

"They've got a name for it. You ought to read more of this modern psychology, Huff. I do. I wouldn't tell Norton. He'd think I was going highbrow or something. I find it helpful though. There's plenty of stuff in my field where it's the only thing that explains what they do. It's depressing, but it clears up things."

"I still don't get it."

"You will. . . . Sachetti wasn't in love with her."

"No?"

"He's known her. Five or six years. His father was a doctor. He

had a sanatorium up in the Verdugo Hills about a quarter mile
from this place where she was head nurse."

"Oh yeah. I remember about that."

"Sachetti met her up there. Then one time the old man had
some tough luck. Three children died on him."

The old creepy feeling began to go up my back. He went on.
"They died of—"

"—Pneumonia."

"You heard about it?"

"No. Go on."

"Oh. You heard about the Arrowhead business."

"Yes."

"They died on him, and there was an awful time and the old
man took the rap for it. Not with the police. They didn't find
anything to concern them. But with the Department of Health
and his clientele. It ruined him. He had to sell his place. Not long
after that he died."

"Pneumonia?"

"No. He was quite old. But Sachetti thought there was something funny about it, and he couldn't shake it out of his mind
about this woman. She was over there too much, and she seemed
to take too much interest in the children up there. He had nothing
to go on, except some kind of a hunch. You follow me?"

"Go on."

"He never did anything about it till the first Mrs. Nirdlinger
died. It happened that *one* of those children was related to that Mrs.
Nirdlinger, in such fashion that when that child died, Mrs. Nirdlinger became executrix for quite a lot of property the child was
due to inherit. In fact, as soon as the legal end was cleared up,
Mrs. Nirdlinger came into the property herself. Get that, Huff.
That's the awful part. Just *one* of those children was mixed up
with property."

"How about the other two?"

"Nothing. Those two children died just to cover the trail up a little. Think of that, Huff. This woman would even kill two extra children, just to get the one child that she wanted, and mix things up so it would look like one of those cases of negligence they sometimes have in those hospitals. I tell you, she's a pathological case."

"Go on."

"When the first Mrs. Nirdlinger died, Sachetti elected himself a one-man detective agency to find out what it was all about. He wanted to clear his father for one thing, and the woman had become an obsession with him for another thing. I don't mean he fell for her. I mean he just had to know the truth about her."

"Yeah, I can see that."

"He kept up his work at the university, as well as he could, and then he made a chance to get in there, and talk with her. He already knew her, so when he went up there with some kind of a proposition to join a physicians'-and-nurses' association that was being formed, he figured she wouldn't think anything of it. But then something happened. He met this girl, and it was a case of love at first sight, and then his fine scheme to get at the truth about the wife went on the rocks. He didn't want to make the girl unhappy, and he really had nothing to go on, so he called it off. He didn't want to go to the house after what he suspected about the wife, so he began meeting the girl outside. Just one little thing happened, though, to make him think that maybe he had been right. The wife, as soon as she found out what was going on, began telling Lola cock-eyed stories about him, and got the father to forbid Lola to see him. There was no reason for that, except that maybe this woman didn't want anything named Sachetti within a mile of her, after what happened. Do you follow this?"

"I follow it."

"Then Nirdlinger got it. And suddenly Sachetti knew he had to go after this woman to mean it. He quit seeing Lola. He didn't even tell her why. He went up to this woman and began making love to her, as hard as he knew. That is, almost as hard as he knew. He figured, if it was her he was coming to see, she'd not forbid him to come, not at all. You see, she was Lola's guardian. But if Lola got married, the husband would be the guardian, and that would mix it all up on the property. You see—"

"Lola was next."

"That's it. After she got you out of the way for what you knew about her, Lola was next. Of course at this time Sachetti didn't know anything about you, but he did know about Lola, or was pretty sure he knew."

"Go on."

"That brings us down to last night. Lola followed him. That is, she followed his car when you took it. She was turning into the parking lot when you pulled out."

"I saw the car."

"Sachetti went home early. The wife chased him out. He went to his room and started to go to bed, but he couldn't shake it out of his mind that something was going on that night. For one thing, being chased out looked funny. For another thing, the wife had asked him earlier in the day a couple of things about Griffith Park, when they closed the roads down there for the night, and which roads they closed—things that could only mean she had something cooking in that park late at night sometime, he didn't know when. So instead of going to bed, he decided to go up to her house and keep an eye on her. He went out to get his car. When he found it gone, he almost fainted, because Lola had a key to it. Don't forget, he knew Lola was next."

"Go on."

"He grabbed a cab and went down to Griffith Park. He began walking around blind—he didn't have any idea what was up, or even when to look. He started at the wrong place—at the far end of the little glade. Then he heard the shot. He ran over, and he and Lola got to you about the same time. He thought Lola was shot. She thought he was shot. When Lola saw who it was, she thought Sachetti shot him, and she was putting on an act about it when the police got there."

"I get it now."

"That woman, that wife, is an out-and-out lunatic. Sachetti told me he found five cases, all before the three little children, where patients died under her while she was a nurse, two of them where she got property out of it."

"All of pneumonia?"

"Three. The other two were operative cases."

"How did she do it?"

"Sachetti never found out. He thinks she found out some way to do it with the serum, combining with another drug. He wishes he could get it out of her. He thinks it would be important."

"Well?"

"You're sunk, Huff."

"I know it."

"We had it out this afternoon. Down at the company. I had the whip hand. There was no two ways about it. I called it long ago, even when Norton was still talking suicide."

"You did that all right."

"I persuaded them the case ought never to come to trial."

"You can't hush it up."

"We can't hush it up, we know that. But having it come out that an agent of this company committed murder is one thing. Having it plastered all over every paper in the country for the two weeks of a murder trial is something else."

"I see."

"You're to give me a statement. You're to give me a statement setting forth every detail of what you did, and have a notary attest it. You're to mail it to me, registered. You're to do that Thursday of next week, so I get it Friday."

"Next Thursday."

"That's right. In the meantime, we hold everything, about this last shooting, I mean, because you're in no condition to testify at a hearing. Now get this. There'll be a reservation for you, under a name I'll give you, on a steamer leaving San Pedro Thursday night for Balboa and points south. You take that steamer. Friday I get your statement and at once turn it over to the police. That's the first I knew about it. That's why Norton and his friends left just now. There's no witnesses to this. It's a deal between you and me, and if you ever try to call it on me I'll deny it, and I'll prove there was no such deal. I've taken care of that."

"I won't try."

"As soon as we notify the police, we post a reward for your capture. And listen Huff, if you're ever caught, that reward will be paid, and you'll be tried, and if there's any way we can help it along, you're going to be hung. We don't want it brought to trial, but if it is brought to trial, we're going through with it to the hilt. Have you got that?"

"I've got it."

"Before you get on that boat, you'll have to hand to me the registry receipt for that statement. I've got to know I've got it."

"What about her?"

"Who?"

"Phyllis?"

"I've taken care of her."

"There's just one thing, Keyes."

"What is it?"

"I still don't know about that girl, Lola. You say you hold everything. I guess that means you hold her and Sachetti, pending the hearing. The hearing that's not going to be held. Well, listen. I've got to know no harm comes to her. I've got to have your solemn word on that, or you'll get no statement, and the case will come to trial, and all the rest of it. I'll blow the whole ship out of water. Do you get that, Keyes? What about her?"

"We hold Sachetti. He's consented to it."

"Did you hear me? What about her?"

"She's out."

"She's—what?"

"We bailed her out. It's a bailable offense. You didn't die, you see."

"Does she know about me?"

"No. I told you I told her nothing."

He got up, looked at his watch, and tip-toed out in the hall. I closed my eyes. Then I felt somebody near me. I opened my eyes again. It was Lola.

"Walter."

"Yes. Hello, Lola."

"I'm terribly sorry."

"I'm all right."

"I didn't know Nino knew about us. He must have found out. He didn't mean anything. But he's—hot-tempered."

"You love him?"

". . . Yes."

"I just wanted to know."

"I'm sorry that you feel as you do."

"It's all right."

"Can I ask something? That I haven't any right to ask?"

"What is it?"

"That you do not prosecute. That you not appear against him. You don't have to, do you?"

"I won't."

". . . Sometimes I almost love you, Walter."

She sat looking at me, and all of a sudden she leaned over close. I turned my head away, quick. She looked hurt and sat there a long time. I didn't look at her. Some kind of peace came to me then at last. I knew I couldn't have her and never could have had her. I couldn't kiss the girl whose father I killed.

When she was at the door I said good-bye and wished her good luck, and then Keyes came back.

"O. K. on the statement, Keyes."

"It's the best way."

"O. K. on everything. Thanks."

"Don't thank me."

"I feel that way."

"You've got no reason to thank me." A funny look came in his eyes. "I don't think they're going to catch up with you, Huff. I think—well maybe I'm doing you a favor at that. Maybe you'd rather have it that way."

14

WHAT YOU'VE just read, if you've read it, is the statement. It took me five days to write it, but at last, on Thursday afternoon, I got it done. That was yesterday. I sent it out by the orderly to be registered, and around five o'clock Keyes dropped by for the receipt. It'll be more than he bargained for, but I wanted to put it all down. Maybe she'll see it some time, and not think so bad of me after she understands how it all was. Around seven o'clock I put on my clothes. I was weak, but I could walk. After a bite to eat I sent for a taxi and went down to the pier. I went to bed right away, and stayed there till early this afternoon. Then I couldn't stand it any longer, alone there in the stateroom, and went up on deck. I found my chair and sat there looking at the coast of Mexico, where we were going past it. But I had a funny feeling I wasn't going anywhere. I kept thinking about Keyes, and the look he had in his eye that day, and what he meant by what he said. Then, all of a sudden, I found out. I heard a little gasp beside me. Before

I even looked I knew who it was. I turned to the next chair. It was Phyllis.

"You."

"Hello, Phyllis."

"Your man Keyes—he's quite a matchmaker."

"Oh yeah. He's romantic."

I looked her over. Her face was drawn from the last time I had seen her, and there were little puckers around her eyes. She handed me something.

"Did you see it?"

"What is it?"

"The ship's paper."

"No, I didn't. I guess I'm not interested."

"It's in there."

"What's in there?"

"About the wedding. Lola and Nino. It came in by radio a little after noon."

"Oh, they're married?"

"Yes. It was pretty exciting. Mr. Keyes gave her away. They went to San Francisco on their honeymoon. Your company paid Nino a bonus."

"Oh. It must be out then. About us."

"Yes. It all came out. It's a good thing we're under different names here. I saw all the passengers reading about it at lunch. It's a sensation."

"You don't seem worried."

"I've been thinking about something else."

She smiled then, the sweetest, saddest smile you ever saw. I thought of the five patients, the three little children, Mrs. Nirdlinger, Nirdlinger, and myself. It didn't seem possible that anybody that could be as nice as she was when she wanted to be, could have done those things.

"What were you thinking about?"

"We could be married, Walter."

"We could be. And then what?"

I don't know how long we sat looking out to sea after that. She started it again. "There's nothing ahead of us, is there Walter?"

"No. Nothing."

"I don't even know where we're going. Do you?"

"No."

". . . Walter, the time has come."

"What do you mean, Phyllis?"

"For me to meet my bridegroom. The only one I ever loved. One night I'll drop off the stern of the ship. Then, little by little I'll feel his icy fingers creeping into my heart."

". . . I'll give you away."

"What?"

"I mean: I'll go with you."

"It's all that's left, isn't it?"

Keyes was right. I had nothing to thank him for. He just saved the state the expense of getting me.

We walked around the ship. A sailor was swabbing out the gutter outside the rail. He was nervous, and caught me looking at him. "There's a shark. Following the ship."

I tried not to look, but couldn't help it. I saw a flash of dirty white down in the green. We walked back to the deck chairs.

"Walter, we'll have to wait. Till the moon comes up."

"I guess we better have a moon."

"I want to see that fin. That black fin. Cutting the water in the moonlight."

The captain knows us. I could tell by his face when he came out of the radio room a little while ago. It will have to be tonight. He's sure to put a guard on us before he puts into Mazatlan.

The bleeding has started again. The internal bleeding, I mean, from the lung where the bullet grazed it. It's not much but I spit blood. I keep thinking about that shark.

I'm writing this in the stateroom. It's about half past nine. She's in her stateroom getting ready. She's made her face chalk white, with black circles under her eyes and red on her lips and cheeks. She's got that red thing on. It's awful-looking. It's just one big square of red silk that she wraps around her, but it's got no arm-holes, and her hands look like stumps underneath it when she moves them around. She looks like what came aboard the ship to shoot dice for souls in the Rime of the Ancient Mariner.

I didn't hear the stateroom door open, but she's beside me now while I'm writing. I can feel her.

The moon.